3/02

D1083664

TRIAL BY FIRE

BOOKS BY JAMES REASONER

THE LAST GOOD WAR
*Battle Lines**
*Trial by Fire**

Manassas

Shiloh

Antietam

Chancellorsville

Vicksburg

Under Outlaw Flags

The Wilderness Road

The Hunted

*denotes a Forge book

TRIAL BY FIRE

THE LAST GOOD WAR
Book II

JAMES REASONER

A TOM DOHERTY ASSOCIATES BOOK
NEW YORK

TRIAL BY FIRE: THE LAST GOOD WAR, BOOK II

Copyright © 2002 by James Reasoner

Edited by James Frenkel

Maps by Mark Stein

This book is printed on acid-free paper.

A Forge Book
Published by Tom Doherty Associates, LLC
175 Fifth Avenue
New York, NY 10010

www.tor.com

Forge® is a registered trademark of Tom Doherty Associates, LLC.

ISBN: 0-312-87346-8

First Edition: March 2002

Printed in the United States of America

0 9 8 7 6 5 4 3 2 1

For Livia, Shayna, and Joanna

ACKNOWLEDGMENTS

Special thanks to Tom Doherty and James Frenkel; Martin H. Greenberg, John Helfers, and Larry Segriff; Leo Grin, Larry Richter, and Morgan Holmes; Marion Reasoner, Paul Washburn, Sidney Strickland, John Kinchen, and Jack Ballas.

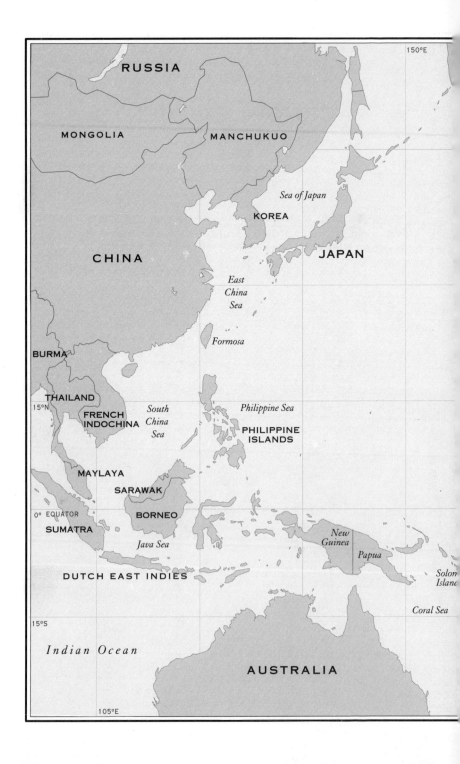

RUSSIA

MONGOLIA

MANCHUKUO

Sea of Japan

KOREA

JAPAN

CHINA

*East
China
Sea*

Formosa

BURMA

THAILAND

15°N

FRENCH
INDOCHINA

*South
China
Sea*

Philippine Sea

PHILIPPINE
ISLANDS

MAYLAYA

SARAWAK

0° EQUATOR

BORNEO

SUMATRA

Java Sea

*New
Guinea*

Papua

*Solon
Island*

DUTCH EAST INDIES

Coral Sea

15°S

Indian Ocean

AUSTRALIA

150°E

105°E

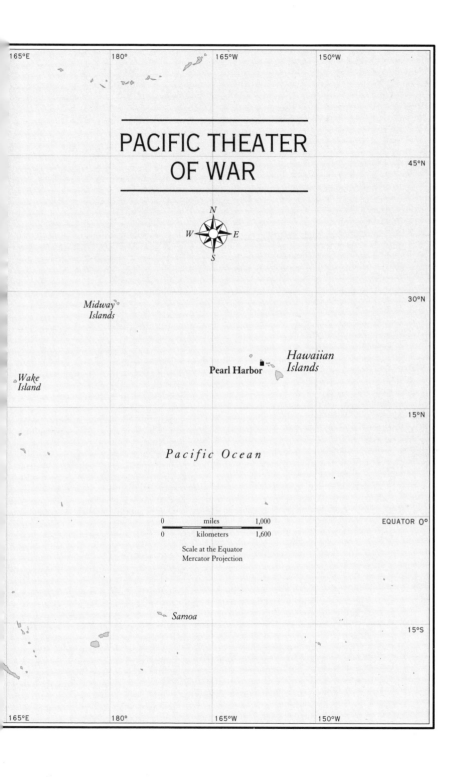

165°E   180°   165°W   150°W

PACIFIC THEATER
OF WAR

45°N

N
W — *E*
S

Midway
Islands

30°N

Hawaiian
Islands
Pearl Harbor

Wake
Island

15°N

Pacific Ocean

0	miles	1,000
0	kilometers	1,600

Scale at the Equator
Mercator Projection

EQUATOR 0°

Samoa

15°S

165°E   180°   165°W   150°W

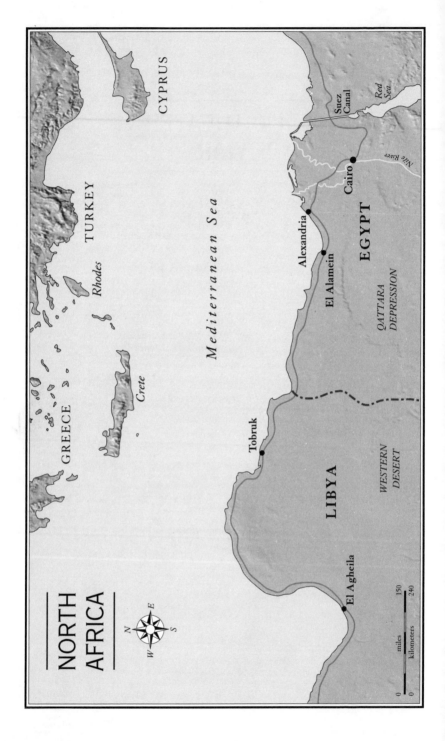

TRIAL BY FIRE

ONE

A tropical paradise, that was what they called these South Pacific islands. But to Adam Bergman, standing at the rail of the U.S.S. *Castor,* Wake looked pretty damned depressing.

"I hear all that lives here is gooney birds and some kind of rat."

Adam looked over at the man who had come up to the rail beside him, a fellow member of the Marine 1st Defense Battalion. Robert Gurnwall was the guy's name. He was called Gurney.

Gurney took a drag on his cigarette and went on. "I don't see Dorothy Lamour in no sarong waitin' on the beach for us, do you?"

Adam shook his head. "No, I don't."

Even if Dorothy Lamour *had* been standing on the beach, Adam wouldn't have cared. The only woman in the world who meant anything to him was his wife Catherine, and she was back at Pearl Harbor, a member of the Navy Nurse Corps serving at the naval hospital there. He had been with her a week and a half earlier, but only for one night as he passed through Pearl on his way to Wake Island. Already it seemed as if they had been separated for months.

"Man, this is the ass-end of nowhere, ain't it?"

Adam nodded this time. "Just about."

The sun was blazingly hot overhead. The temperature got pretty warm sometimes in Chicago, where Adam had lived his whole life before joining the Marines the previous winter, but this was a different sort of heat. It made you want to lie down and just

13

simmer in a puddle of your own sweat. It sucked the air out of your lungs and turned the sky into a blinding silver glare. Adam hated it already.

He had studied the maps of Wake Island, which was really an atoll composed of three separate islands. Wake itself was the largest of the three, shaped like a V pointing southeast. At each end of the legs of the V was a smaller island, Wilkes on the south and Peale on the north. All the islands gave the same impression from the water: long, low mounds of coral, rock, and dirt dotted with thick clumps of thorny scrub brush and occasional clusters of short, ragged-looking trees. At its widest point, Wake wasn't much more than two thousand yards wide.

But that was enough ground for an airstrip, and that was what made the place so important.

Wake Island had belonged to the United States since 1899, but it was off the regular shipping lanes and unimportant until the rise of air travel. When Pan American Airways began flying across the Pacific in the mid-thirties, some bright boy had noticed Wake on a map and decided it was a perfect spot for a refueling stop. Pan Am reached an arrangement with the Navy Department for the use of the island, and an airstrip was built—on Peale Island, actually, not Wake. Also on Peale, Pan Am erected a nice little hotel so the passengers on their Clippers would have a place to stay when the planes remained overnight on the island. But except for employees of the airline, no one came to the atoll with the idea of staying there. They were just passing through.

That had changed back in '38, when the Hepburn Board, a special naval commission headed by Rear Admiral A. J Hepburn and charged with studying the needs for U.S. naval development worldwide, recommended that Wake be given high priority. With tensions in the Pacific region rising and a possible war with Japan looming over the horizon, it was decided that the United States should take advantage of the development already carried out on Wake, Peale, and Wilkes Islands and establish a naval air station there, spending up to seven and a half million dollars if necessary. More runways could be built, more fuel storage and repair facilities, housing for the sailors who would man the station. Improved communications wouldn't be a bad thing, either. At first the jobs had been handled strictly by civilian construction crews, but as the situation worsened, members of the 1st Defense Battalion were sent to Wake, along with some defensive armament, just in case.

Just in case . . .

Now the *Castor* was steaming past Peacock Point, at the southeastern tip of Wake, carrying reinforcements for the 1st Defense Battalion, which still wouldn't bring it up to its normal complement of men.

The ass-end of nowhere, Gurnwall had called Wake Island, and Adam couldn't argue with that. After sailing past two miles of ugly shoreline, the ship came to the channel between Wake Island and Wilkes Island and dropped anchor just outside it. Beyond the narrow passage, which wasn't deep enough for the *Castor,* was the broad lagoon between the islands, dotted with coral heads. In the distance across the lagoon Adam could see Peale Island and the other leg of Wake.

To the right were the tanks of the fuel dump, and past them the tents and temporary buildings of the Marine camp. Adam saw trucks moving along the road that followed the spine of the island.

Adam was in brown wool fatigues, the flat, World War I style helmet cocked to the side of his head, duffel bag and M1 Garand on the deck at his feet. As lighters departed the shore and started out toward the ship, a master sergeant came along and said, "Get your squad together, Corporal."

"Aye, aye," Adam responded. He bent and picked up his bag and rifle, thankful the sergeant hadn't chewed his ass for laying the Garand on the deck. He turned to Gurnwall, who was in his squad. "Come on, Gurney."

The other four members of the squad were standing along the rail, too, looking at the place that would be their new home for God knew how long. Adam gathered them up, feeling a little like a mama hen rounding up a brood of chicks. None of them were any older than twenty, making him the oldest of the bunch at twenty-two. They carried their rifles with a certain self-importance, but Adam knew they would do most, if not all, of their fighting with picks and shovels and axes as they cleared more land for the air station.

By the time an hour had passed, all two hundred of the Marine reinforcements had been taken ashore in the lighters. A slender, dark-haired officer with a narrow mustache and rather prominent ears was waiting for them, accompanied by a master sergeant. A gold oak leaf was pinned to the officer's collar, and his billed cap had the globe-and-anchor insignia of the Marine Corps on it. The new arrivals formed briskly into ranks and saluted the major, who returned the salute and told them to stand at ease.

"I'm Major James Devereux," he said, lifting his voice to be heard over the constant roar of the surf against the coral reef that surrounded the entire atoll, "commander of the Marine First Defense Battalion. Welcome to Wake Island. I'm sure you'll find that it's every bit the tropical paradise it appears to be."

Some of the men smiled at the major's wry comment, but no one laughed. Adam thought it odd that Devereux had used the same turn of phrase as he had thought of earlier. That just showed how ingrained such an attitude was, among people who had never been in the South Pacific.

Devereux grew more serious. "We're doing important work here, and I expect that all of you will do your best. I'll turn you over to Sergeant Chadwick now, and he'll get you settled, but I want to remind you of one thing: We're a long way from any-where out here, and we have to depend on ourselves and each other. Remember that."

The burly master sergeant took over, directing the newcom-ers along a road of crushed and packed coral that led past the round tanks of the fuel dump and the tents and huts of the camp. Gurnwall was behind Adam, and he said quietly, "Hey, Corp, ain't there supposed to be some sort of luxury hotel on this island? Why don't they put us up there instead of in a bunch of fuckin' tents?"

"Because we're Marines," Adam said, "not a bunch of fucking tourists."

* * *

Back in January, when he had walked through the streets of Chicago with a cold wind blowing off the lake and Catherine at his side, Adam had never dreamed he would wind up on this side of the world. He had gone into the Federal Building with his friends, Joe and Dale Parker, knowing that he was going to enlist in the Marines. Joe and Dale were joining the Army because Dale had gotten into some trouble that threatened their whole family and enlisting was the quickest, easiest way out of Chicago. They believed that Adam was going into the Army with them, but he had decided on the Marines instead, because the Marines always wound up where the fighting was the thickest, and in the war that everybody knew was coming Adam had no doubt where that would be.

Europe. War was already raging over there, and Adam wanted his shot at the crazy little Austrian who was trying to wipe out the Jews and take over the world in the process. Yes, sir, Adam Bergman would show Adolf a thing or two, even if it meant giving up law school for a while.

Adam had a habit of giving up things for the greater good. After a sterling career as an outfielder on the University of Chicago baseball team, he could have played for the Cubs. His mother had wanted him to get his law degree, though, so he had forgotten about the offer from the Cubbies. Now he had put aside school as well, until the threat of the Nazis was dealt with.

The only thing he absolutely was not going to give up was Catherine. Her father, a wealthy North Side physician who had immigrated to the United States from Germany in the early twenties, had been opposed to Adam's courtship of his daughter from the start. Adam was convinced that his Jewishness was one reason Dr. Gerald Tancred hated him, but the fact that he came from a poor family was even worse in Tancred's eyes. When they got married, it was in secret, and Catherine's parents hadn't known about it until she had sprung yet another surprise on them, the fact that she had joined the Navy Nurse Corps.

That had come as a surprise to Adam, too. He had expected Catherine to stay safely at home while he was off fighting to rid the world of the Nazi evil. But with her medical background, she was a natural for the NNC, and she had hoped that by enlisting as well, she would be able to stay closer to him.

It had worked out, surprisingly enough. They'd had the all-too-brief reunion at Pearl Harbor, before he went on to Wake Island. And he hoped that maybe, just maybe, he could get back to Hawaii every now and then so that they could be together again.

In the meantime, he wouldn't be fighting Nazis. Far from it. The Marine Corps, in its infinite wisdom, had chosen to send him to the South Pacific instead. And being a good Marine—one of the best in his class of recruits that had gone through Parris Island—he'd said, "Aye, aye," and went where they sent him.

*　　*　　*

It didn't get much cooler when the sun went down. Adam had both flaps in the tent open to catch what little breeze he could as he lay there on his cot in his skivvies.

There were two men in each tent, and Private Gurnwall had latched onto him as his tentmate. As the corporal in charge of the squad, Adam could have picked one of the other men to share the tent with him, but Gurney was okay, even if he got a little annoying from time to time.

Rolofson and Stout were in the next tent, Kennemer and Magruder in the one beyond that. They were all good kids, Adam thought, feeling infinitely older than any of them.

Gurnwall had gone out to take a leak. He came back and stretched out on the other cot. "Hey, Corp," he said. "Whatcha thinkin' about?"

"My wife." As soon as he said it, Adam winced, knowing what was coming.

"Heh, heh. Rememberin' how the two of you played hide the salami, I bet. She's mighty pretty, I bet."

"Beautiful. But she's my *wife,* Gurnwall. Show a little decorum."

"I would if I knew what that was, Corp. I didn't mean no offense."

"None taken, Gurney."

Adam wished it were cooler. He wished he could sleep. He wished he were with Catherine.

"Hey, Corp?"

Adam sighed. "What is it, Gurnwall?"

"You think the Japs are comin' here sometime?"

"I don't know. I'm just a corporal. The brass don't tell me anything."

"But we're out here in the middle of the ocean, kinda right in their way, ain't we?"

"Yes," Adam said, "we are."

He might have put that thought out of his mind, but he knew it was all too true. They were sitting here on Wake Island, smack-dab in the path of Japan's march of empire.

There was no breeze at all now. Adam felt sweat trickle down his back.

TWO

At formation the next morning, the new men were introduced to Nathan D. Teters, the boss of the civilian construction crew. Teters was a broad-shouldered man who looked like he had played football in college. As a matter of fact, he had. He also stood and moved and spoke with an air of authority that came from his service as a sergeant in the Army in the First World War.

Adam liked Teters right away. The construction boss had a gruff, no-nonsense attitude, yet he was still quick to flash a friendly grin.

"My boys and I are primarily responsible for building the roads and the runways and the other construction," Teters explained, "but we'll be calling on you for help from time to time. I've got a good crew. My foremen know what they're doing. If one of them gives you an order, you'll be expected to obey it."

Major Devereux, who was standing beside Teters, nodded to emphasize what the civilian was saying.

Adam had already settled enough into the Marine Corps way of thinking so that the idea of taking orders from a civilian didn't seem right, but if that was what the major wanted, he would go along with it. Besides, it was clear that Teters wasn't an ordinary civilian. The guy was no feather merchant; you could tell that just by looking at him. Adam was willing to bet the other civilian workers weren't, either.

Devereux spoke up. "What you'll be doing for the most part is putting our shore batteries in place and manning the guns once they're mounted. We've been sent enough .50-caliber anti-aircraft machine guns to establish batteries on all the points of the atoll, as well as some extra emplacements around the runways. There are .30-caliber machine guns to set up around the fuel dump, and a dozen 3-inch antiboat guns. Mr. Teters and his crew are relying on us to protect them while they do their work, and that is exactly what we intend to do."

No one had to ask who they would be protecting the civilians *from,* Adam thought. They all knew.

Wearing lace-up boots, khaki trousers and shirts, and the flat helmets, the Marines got to work. Adam's squad was assigned the task of unloading crates full of .50-caliber machine gun ammunition belts that were lightered ashore from the *Castor,* loading the crates onto a three-quarter ton truck, then hauling them all the way around the atoll to a battery on Heel Point, where Wake curved slightly into a fish hook shape.

Adam drove the truck. The crushed coral road was narrow, barely wide enough for the truck, although in places civilian crews were working to widen it. As Adam wrestled the truck around the curves, he thought about Dale Parker, who had been making quite a name for himself as a race car driver back in the Midwest before he'd fouled up and gotten himself in Dutch with a guy who had proven to be dangerous to his health. Dale probably would have sent the truck skidding around the turns with a spray of crushed coral, laughing all the way. Adam took it slow and easy, knowing that the back end was full of ammo.

The road led past the one runway that had been completed and a cross-runway at right angles that was under construction. There were no planes on the runway, since the Marine Fighting Squadron that would be based here had not yet arrived. On the far side of the runways was a scattering of bungalows being framed of raw lumber. No tents down here. When they got to Wake, the Marine aviators would have nicer accommodations than the members of the 1st Defense Battalion. Adam didn't feel particularly jealous, though. He liked having his feet on solid ground and had no desire to go up in an airplane.

When the truck reached Heel Point, Adam brought it to a

stop and saw that a civilian crew was working there, hammering together some sort of framework for a small building. A cement mixer was turning and rumbling and growling nearby. Adam swung down from the truck along with Rolofson, who had ridden up front with him. The other four members of the squad were in the back with the ammo. Adam approached one of the civilians who looked like he might be in charge.

"Got a load of .50-caliber ammunition here," Adam said to the civilian, jerking a thumb over his shoulder toward the truck.

The man was tall and rawboned, with a thatch of red hair under a jammed-down fedora. He grinned at Adam and said, "Good for you. What are you going to do with it?"

"We're supposed to unload it here. Where's the ammunition locker?" For that matter, where was the battery? Adam didn't see any sign of the .50-caliber machine guns.

The redhead gestured toward the framework his men were building. "There's your ammo locker right there, or at least it will be once we finish the forms and pour the concrete and let it set for a day or two."

Adam frowned and asked, "Then where are we supposed to put these crates?"

"Not my problem, ace. I guess you can stack 'em up somewhere, as long as they're not in the way."

Adam felt anger rising inside him. He managed to tamp it down, but he couldn't stop himself from exclaiming, "I can't just leave a bunch of ammunition sitting beside the road!"

"Well, you can't put it in the locker, because we're not finished buildin' it yet."

Gurnwall and the others had climbed out of the back of the truck. Gurney said, "Hey, Corp, this guy's some sort of joker."

"Get back on the truck, Gurnwall. We'll straighten this out." Adam asked the redhead, "Where's your boss?"

"Over there," the civilian said, pointing to a cluster of buildings about a thousand yards farther west, where the road led.

That would be the civilian camp, Adam thought. He saw a water tower rising on spindly legs above the buildings. Beyond the camp was the channel between Wake and Peale. Adam could see Peale Island, where the Pan Am runways and the hotel were located, but he couldn't make out any details at this distance.

"We'll be back," he said as he turned toward the truck.

"We'll be here, ace," the redhead said.

"Wisenheimer," Adam muttered under his breath as he climbed back behind the wheel of the truck. Gurnwall hurried to claim the other side of the seat, relegating Rolofson to the back of the truck with the others. Grinding the gears more than he intended, Adam started toward the civilian camp.

All the buildings except one were located on the left side of the road. To the right was a rambling, one-story clapboard building with a sign over its double-doored entrance that read HOSPI-TAL. As Adam slowed in front of the building, a woman stepped out of the doors, the first woman he had seen so far on Wake Island. She was blond and approaching middle age, but still quite attractive. She was wearing civilian clothes, not a nurse's uniform, and as the truck rumbled past, she smiled and waved.

"Hubba-hubba!" Gurnwall said, turning and sticking his head out the open window so that he could look back at the woman. "Did you see that, Corp? Whatta babe, huh? A little long in the tooth, but not bad."

"She's probably married to one of the construction bosses, Gurney, so watch what you're saying around them."

"Sure, Corp. I know how to be a gentleman."

Adam hadn't seen any signs of that, but he didn't say any-thing. He brought the truck to a halt in front of what looked like an office building. "Stay here," he told Gurnwall, who looked disappointed.

Like nearly all the buildings on Wake, this one was con-structed of raw, unpainted lumber and had an unfinished look to it, both inside and out. That was an indication of how quickly it had been thrown up once the decision to convert Wake into an air station had been made. Just inside the door, Adam found a civilian in shirt sleeves sitting at a desk, a litter of papers spread out in front of him. He was working a slide rule and jotting down figures as he arrived at them.

The civilian glanced up at Adam through thick glasses and asked, "What can I do for you, Corporal?"

"My men and I were supposed to unload some anti-aircraft shells at Heel Point, but there's no place to put them. There's not even a gun there."

"There will be. Some of your men are supposed to start working on the emplacement next week."

"But I was sent up here with the ammunition today."

The civilian shrugged. "What can I tell you, Corporal? I guess you'll just have to take it back."

Adam didn't want to do that, but he didn't see any other solution. He was turning back toward the door when it opened and the blond woman he had seen earlier came into the room.

"Hello, Chip," she said to the man with the slide rule. "Is His Nibs in?"

"In his office, ma'am."

"Thanks." The woman started toward a door on the other side of the room that probably led to an inner office. She stopped and held out her hand to Adam, surprising him. "I'm Mrs. Teters."

Adam hesitated, then took her hand, finding it cooler than it had any right to be in this weather. He sort of hated to let go of it. "Um, Adam Bergman, ma'am. Corporal, U.S. Marine Corps."

"I recognize the two stripes, Corporal," Mrs. Teters said dryly. "I haven't seen you around. You must be one of the men who came in yesterday."

"Yes, ma'am."

"Have you met my husband?"

"Yes, ma'am. Well, not personally, but he spoke to us this morning."

Mrs. Teters chuckled. "I'm sure he did."

The man at the desk said, "The corporal was just leaving, Mrs. Teters. There's nothing we can do for him."

"You have some sort of problem, Corporal?"

Adam didn't hesitate this time. "Yes, ma'am. I have a load of ammunition out there and no place to put it."

"Well, come along with me. I'll introduce you to Dan. I'm sure he can figure out what to do."

Slide Rule didn't look happy about that, but he wasn't going to contradict his boss's wife. Adam followed the blonde over to the office door, which she opened without knocking.

The construction boss got up from behind another desk, leaned over it, and kissed his wife quickly, then looked inquisitively at Adam. Mrs. Teters said, "Dan, this is Corporal Bergman."

Teters gave Adam a handshake that would have been bone-crushing if Adam hadn't met it with equal strength. "Dan Teters. Glad to meet you, Corporal. I saw you in the formation of the new men this morning, didn't I?"

"Yes, sir."

"What are you doing over here? Not that you're not welcome, of course."

Mrs. Teters said, "Corporal Bergman has some ammunition he doesn't know what to do with."

Teters grunted. "Is that so?"

"Yes, sir." Adam filled him in on the problem.

Teters listened, then nodded. "You'll have to take the ammo back to your camp. There are storage sheds there where you can leave them until the ammunition locker on Heel Point is finished. No offense, Corporal, but whoever gave you your orders was putting the cart in front of the horse."

"Yes, sir, it seems so."

"If some leather-lunged non-com starts giving you an earful, just tell him I told you what to do. Unless it's Major Devereux, that'll usually do the trick and get the bogies off your back."

"Yes, sir. Thank you, sir."

Teters grinned. "Don't worry about it. Us old ballplayers have to stick together. What did you play, end or linebacker or both?"

"Outfield, sir."

Teters raised his bushy, reddish-blond eyebrows. "A baseball player? Hell, son, you don't get to hit anything except a ball in that game."

"I don't know, sir," Adam ventured. "I ran over a catcher every now and then on my way in to home plate."

"I'll just bet you did," Teters said with a laugh. "Welcome to Wake Island, Corporal."

THREE

The munitions officer of the 1st Defense Battalion was Marine Gunner John Hamas. Hamas, like many of the first group to come to Wake, was a "regular" Marine, a veteran who knew what he was doing and who was not easily rattled. He could, however, rattle a few windows when he raised his voice, as Adam and the other newcomers to the atoll, mostly recruits who had been through basic training but nothing else, learned over their first few days.

Despite what had been said about the Marines and the civilians working together, that rarely happened. When it did, it was a one-way street, with the Marines pitching in to help out when a construction crew needed more strong backs. The civilians didn't assist in any of the tasks assigned to the Marines.

Their main job, Adam learned, was to build the atoll's defenses. That made sense, considering the name of the battalion. They had to dig out the places where the guns would be located, scraping away the thin layer of sand and then chipping and gouging at the coral until they had a suitable hole. The hole was then floored with cement so that the guns could be bolted down.

Once that was done, barriers made of sandbags were thrown up around the emplacements before the guns were ever hauled out and positioned. Adam found himself working at the battery on Heel Point, which was about as far away from the Marine camp as you could get and still be on Wake Island without venturing into Camp Two, the civilian camp. To get back "home" to Camp One, it would be quicker and shorter to swim straight across the lagoon, rather than following the road all the way back around to the other side of the island.

Of course, Adam knew he wasn't going to swim across the lagoon. The coral was close to the surface in many places, making for dangerous currents and tides. Besides, there might be sharks out there. Some of the men who had been in the first detachment of Marines on Wake Island had told Adam they'd seen dark fins cutting through the water. Adam didn't know whether to believe them or not, but since they'd been on Wake since early August, having arrived as the advance party of the 1st Defense Battalion on the U.S.S. *Regulus,* he gave at least some credence to their warnings.

He and the members of his squad were at the Heel Point battery one day, a week after their arrival, when a jeep went by on the road carrying Dan Teters and his attractive blond wife. Gurnwall paused in stacking sandbags and stared wistfully after the jeep. Adam gave him a couple of seconds, then said, "Get back to work, Gurney, and stop lusting after Mrs. Teters."

Mrs. Teters was the only woman on Wake, and as such, she was the object of much attention from the men, even though she was old enough to have been the mother of many of them.

"I'm not lusting after the lady, Corp. I was just thinking that the brass must consider it pretty safe here, or they wouldn't let her stay."

Adam was holding a shovel he had been using to pat down the concrete they had just poured. Now he leaned on the shovel and frowned in thought. What Gurnwall said made sense. The Navy couldn't very well evacuate the civilian construction crew; they were still working twelve-hour days at a minimum, just like the Marines. But Mrs. Teters fell into the category of non-essential personnel, and if war was imminent, the Navy would surely get her the hell back to Pearl.

"Then I guess as long as she's here, we're all right," Adam said.

"Yeah, that's what I was thinking."

"And since there's no reason for us to be worried, we can get back to work, right?"

Gurnwall grinned. "Right, Corp."

All the men wore their helmets, since officially they were on alert even while digging holes and pouring cement, but in the heat they had stripped off their shirts and worked either in undershirts or bare to the waist. During the first week on the atoll, there had been quite a few cases of sunburn, some of them severe enough to justify a visit to the contractor's hospital at Camp Two. Adam's burn hadn't been that bad, and by now he was peeling and turning brown. He would look like an Indian when he finally got to go home, he thought, and since some people said the Indians were one of the lost tribes of Israel, he supposed that was appropriate.

Late in the afternoon, a Dodge deuce-and-a-half came to pick them up. Its back end was filled with other crews that were on their way back to Camp One. As Adam was climbing in, another civilian jeep went roaring by with crushed coral spraying out from under its wheels. Adam caught a glimpse of fiery red hair and heard someone yell, "Hey, ace!" He recognized the passenger in the jeep as the civilian construction foreman he had encountered on his first day on Wake.

"Who's that, Sarge?" Adam asked the driver of the deuce-and-a-half, a sergeant who had been on the island since August.

"A pain in the ass named Connor. Used to be in the Army, so he doesn't have a very high opinion of Marines."

Adam grunted. He hadn't liked Connor much, either.

By the time they'd gotten back to camp and eaten supper in the mess tent, weariness had overtaken Adam. He had an easier time of it than some of the men because he'd always been athletic and in good shape, but the toll of the long days and the strain of worrying about the Japs was beginning to tell on him. He went back to his tent, tuned out Gurnwall's chatter, and by the light of a small lantern wrote a letter to Catherine.

He knew he hadn't been as good about writing to her as he should have been. He had already received a couple of letters from her, sent with pilots of the PBYs and B-17s that used the completed runway on the southeastern corner of the island for refueling stops on their way to the Philippines, but the letter he was struggling with now would be his first to her.

How could he put what he was feeling into words, he asked himself. He couldn't very well write *Dear Catherine, I'm horny as hell for you.* Even though he was, of course. But there was more to it than that. He missed the cool smoothness of her skin and the hot sweetness of her mouth, but he also missed the sound of her voice and the smell of her perfume and just being around her. He didn't have to be touching her to feel love for her. It was enough that she was just *there*.

He couldn't find a way to say any of that, so he told her about the atoll instead, even though he knew the censors would black out a good deal of what he wrote, and about Gurnwall's antics and the other men in the squad, and about how the weather was, which didn't take long because all he could say was that it was hot.

Then he wrote *I miss you and I hope to see you soon.* Before he could continue, a truck rumbled to a stop outside the tent and a voice yelled, "Flight of seventeens coming in! I need ground crews! Get out here, you feather merchants!"

From the other cot, Gurnwall groaned. "Ah, shit! Not this again!"

The runway was usable, there was fuel in the storage tanks across the road from the camp, but there were no aviation ground crews on Wake. The Marines were pressed into service as needed to handle the refueling when planes flew in. Once before, Adam and his squad had been part of such an impromptu ground crew, and now it appeared they were being "volunteered" for the duty again.

Adam put his letter to Catherine aside and reached for his boots and helmet. "Come on, Gurney," he said. "Time to give the birds a drink."

Parked outside the tents was the island's lone tanker truck, followed by another truck with its bed crammed full of fifty-gallon drums. Adam and his men climbed onto the tanker, Adam riding beside the driver while the other members of the squad rode the running boards or hung onto the back of the tanker.

More men piled onto the other truck; then the two vehicles started down the road toward the air station.

When seagoing tankers full of avgas sailed up to the island, lighters went out to meet them with thick hoses that led back to the storage tanks on shore. The avgas was pumped from the ships into the tanks. The Marines then pumped—manually—the avgas from the storage tanks into fifty-gallon drums which could be taken to other points on the atoll wherever they might be needed. Adam wasn't sure why the fuel dump had been located at the northwestern corner of Wake Island while the runways were at the southeastern corner, but that was the situation.

The tanker and the other truck reached the air station, and the men hopped down from the vehicles. The lieutenant in charge of the detail ordered the drums of fuel unloaded from the truck, and as soon as that was accomplished, it turned around and headed back to the fuel dump for another load. That told Adam a sizable flight was coming in. He glanced up at the night sky with its scattering of stars. He couldn't hear any plane engines, but that came as no surprise. It was difficult to hear much of anything over the pounding of the surf. *The Japs could fly over with their entire air corps,* Adam thought, *and we wouldn't hear them until they were right on top of us.*

A few minutes later, a flight of eight Army Air Corps B-17s—"Flying Fortresses"—came gliding down out of the night and landed one by one on the main runway. Each plane in turn pulled onto the half-completed cross-runway so that it would be out of the landing pattern of the plane behind it. As soon as the first Fortress had come to a stop, the lieutenant had the tanker truck rolling toward it.

He and his men had an easier job than the others, Adam thought as he rode the tanker out to the B-17. The rest of the detail would have to manhandle those fifty-gallon drums over to the next airplane in line and break out the hand pumps to pump the avgas directly from the drums into the Seventeen's fuel tanks. The tanker truck didn't have to be pumped manually.

The crew of the first AAC B-17 in line was already climbing

out of the plane when the tanker truck reached it. Adam sent Gurnwall scrambling up a ladder to open the hatch over the fueling port, while Rolofson and Magruder began unrolling the stiff canvas hose and got ready to pass it up the ladder by way of Kennemer and Stout, who had followed Gurnwall. When Gurnwall had the port open and the end of the hose reached him, he slid it into place and then dogged tight the clamps that held it in position while the three thousand gallons of avgas in the truck's tank spewed into the belly of the B-17. All of this was carried out in semi-darkness, because the only lights were the small ones that marked the edges of the runways.

When Adam was satisfied that the refueling operation was going all right despite the relative inexperience of his men, he turned to find the pilot of the Flying Fortress observing as well. Adam saluted him and said, "Refueling is underway, sir. We'll be done as quickly as possible."

The pilot, a captain who didn't look nearly old enough to be wearing railroad tracks, returned Adam's salute and nodded. "Thank you, Sergeant."

"Begging the captain's pardon, sir, but I'm only a two-striper."

"Really? The light's not very good out here, and you've got those gas monkeys scrambling around like an old hand."

Adam felt a flicker of annoyance at the casually arrogant way the captain referred to his men as gas monkeys, but at the same time he was glad the smoothness of the operation met with the officer's approval. He opted for the surer course of action and said, "Thank you, sir."

"You wouldn't happen to know a Marine corporal named Bergman, would you? Adam Bergman? I've got a back-channel communication for him from a pretty little lady at Pearl."

Adam's eyes widened in surprise. "I'm Corporal Bergman, sir." Another letter from Catherine, he thought. And he hadn't even finished writing his first one to her.

"Really? You're not just saying that so you can get your hands on Bergman's letter and smell the perfume on it, are you?"

"No, sir. I'm really Adam Bergman. I can show you my ID card and have the lieutenant vouch for me."

The pilot shook his head. "No need to bring the lieutenant into this. Like I said, it's back-channel. But I figured one of Bergman's fellow corporals could be trusted." He reached inside his leather flying jacket and brought out an envelope that had been folded in half, then in half again. As he handed it over, he thumbed back the billed cap on his head and grinned. "Enjoy your letter, Bergman."

"Thank you, sir." Adam took the envelope and stowed it away in his pocket.

The captain chuckled. "What, you're not going to try to read it now, even in this bad light?"

"I'll read it later, sir. Right now, we have thirsty birds on the ground." The pump on the tanker truck was chugging away by now, as it filled the tanks of the Flying Fortress.

That brought an outright laugh from the captain. "Like I said, you may be new at this, Corporal, but you act like an old hand."

"Thank you, sir," Adam said, and unaccountably he felt himself flushing with pride at the compliment from a man not much older than he was. He might be on the wrong side of the world, but that was no reason he couldn't do his job as well as he possibly could.

FOUR

Just like pumping gas back home in Tulsa, Robert Gurnwall thought as he undid the clamps and took the hose nozzle out of the port on the B-17. He closed the hatch and fastened it as Corporal Bergman and the other members of the detail rolled the hose back into place on the tanker truck. The trunk would head back to the fuel dump, refill its tank, and return to the airstrip to service one of the other Fortresses. Gurnwall figured it would take a couple of hours to get all the airplanes ready to fly again.

He'd heard that the B-17s were on their way to Clark Field near Manila, in the Philippines. When the Japs attacked—and Gurnwall figured there was no longer a question of *if*—everyone thought that the Philippines would be their first target. The largest concentration of American forces in the Pacific was there.

It was Gurnwall's hope that the Japanese would somehow overlook Wake. After all, the atoll was small, and while he supposed it was strategically important in its way, maybe it wasn't important enough for the Japs to come. Gurnwall went to sleep at night and woke up in the morning with a ball of fear in his gut, fear that the Japs would come.

He didn't want to die. He was twenty years old. He'd dropped out of Tulsa High School after his freshman year when his father died and his drunken bum of a mother had kicked him out of the house because she'd never liked him. But she still expected him to help take care of her and the younger kids, so he'd worked ever since then, even though jobs had been damned hard to come by in the Dust Bowl of Oklahoma in 1934.

Somehow he'd managed, working two and sometimes three jobs at a time. He'd learned to slip the extra money to his little brother Ronnie rather than giving it to the old lady, who would just drink it up. Gurnwall had pumped gas, painted houses, worked in the railroad yards and feed mills. He'd even done a stint in the CCC, cutting fire roads in the Washita Mountains of eastern Oklahoma. That had been the best of the lot. The work was hard but he was outdoors, which he liked, and he got along well with most of the other guys. He clowned around some. They liked that, and liked him.

Then he'd been one of the first ones drafted by the local board, and though he'd hated to say goodbye to his brothers and sisters, he was excited about getting out of Tulsa. The Marines had taken him and sent him to Camp Pendleton, California, for basic training. California had been great, a warm and pretty place unlike anything he had ever seen in Oklahoma. The girls were warm and pretty, too, and especially sympathetic to handsome young Marines who were going overseas and might not be coming back. . . .

Yeah, that was the bad part of it. Being a Marine was okay, but a guy could get killed. And Gurnwall really, really didn't want to die. Hard as his life had been, he still got a kick out of living.

"All buttoned up, Gurney?" Corporal Bergman called up to him.

"All buttoned up, Corp," Gurnwall replied as he started down the ladder. It didn't pay to think too much about anything except the job at hand.

But still, he hoped the Japs wouldn't come here to Wake Island.

*　　*　　*

It was late, after midnight, by the time the Flying Fortresses had thundered off into the sky, heading toward the Philippines. Adam was exhausted when he got back to his tent. He didn't finish the letter to Catherine. He would do it the next day, he told himself.

It was the day after that before he finally finished the letter. Not being an attractive young nurse, he couldn't send it by some sympathetic pilot but had to put it in with the regular mail. It would take two weeks, maybe more, for the letter to reach Pearl Harbor, but that was the best he could do. Besides, he told himself, Catherine knew he wasn't much of a letter writer.

In the meantime, he enjoyed the ones she had written to him, reading them over and over, holding the thin sheets of paper to his nose and breathing in the scent of her until only the faintest hint of it remained. He had hoped that he might be able to get back to Pearl so that he could see her, but that looked pretty damned unlikely. There was still a lot of work to do on the islands before Wake would be able to defend itself in case of an attack.

He and his squad pulled ground crew duty again one day in the middle of November when a PBY landed. As they were pumping avgas into the flying boat, a jeep came down the road from the direction of Camp One. Adam saw the sun reflect on bright hair and knew that Mrs. Teters was in the jeep. As the vehicle came closer, he realized that Dan Teters was at the wheel. The burly construction boss didn't look happy.

Teters brought the jeep to a stop near the PBY and got out. He started taking canvas suitcases from the back of the jeep.

Gurnwall was standing next to Adam. "Uh-oh," he said. "Looks like somebody's going on a trip."

Adam frowned. Mrs. Teters seemed to be crying. But only a little; otherwise she kept her composure as her husband spoke to the pilot of the PBY and then carried the suitcases on board the airplane.

From the corner of his eye, Adam saw Gurnwall moving forward. He hissed, "Gurney!" but Gurnwall ignored him and sidled up to Mrs. Teters, taking off his helmet and smiling politely at her.

"Going somewhere, ma'am?" he asked.

"That's right, Private," she said. "It's been requested that I return to Pearl Harbor."

"All the men will be sorry to see you go, ma'am," Gurnwall said solemnly. "You've been like a ray of sunshine on a cloudy day around here."

That brought a smile to her face. "Why, thank you, Private. I'll miss all of you, too."

Teters came down the steps from the door of the PBY and frowned slightly as he saw Gurnwall talking to his wife. Adam came up beside Gurnwall, put a hand firmly on his arm, and said, "Have a safe journey, ma'am."

"Thank you, Corporal."

Adam nodded to Teters, then steered Gurnwall back toward the tanker truck. "What the hell are you trying to do, Gurney?" he asked under his breath. He glanced over his shoulder and saw Teters and Mrs. Teters embracing. Teters patted his wife on the back, rather awkwardly.

"Aw, Corp, whaddaya expect? She's the only female on the whole damned atoll. Of course we're gonna miss her." Gurnwall paused, then added, "Besides, you know what it means that she's scootin' out of here."

"You heard what she said. She was requested to leave."

"Which is the same thing as bein' ordered to get out while the gettin's good. The brass wouldn't have done that if they didn't know something. We been on alert ever since we got here. If it's about to get worse than that—"

Gurnwall stopped short and Adam glanced over at him. Gurnwall had paled under his sunburn, and he kept swallowing hard.

"You all right, Gurney?"

"Yeah, I just ..." Gurnwall wiped sweat off his face. "It's mighty hot out here, that's all."

"Yeah," Adam said slowly, nodding. "It's mighty hot, all right."

Gurnwall turned away abruptly. "Hey, Corp, whaddaya say we get back to work?"

"I think that's a good idea."

A few minutes later the PBY took off, heading back to Pearl Harbor.

Word got around the island quickly about Mrs. Teters's departure Gurnwall wasn't the only one who understood what her leaving meant. Everyone knew she wouldn't have been allowed to stay on Wake for this long unless the brass considered it safe. Now that she was gone, the threat of the Japanese seemed even more imminent.

Camp One had a small enlisted men's club and an even smaller officers' club. The enlisted men's club was a typical slop chute, a narrow building made of hastily nailed together raw lumber, its insides unfinished, lit by bare bulbs powered by the camp generator. Sometimes the lights grew dim, depending on what else was drawing current from the generator at the moment. The only decorations were a few pinups ripped from magazines and thumbtacked to the unfinished walls. The men who came here didn't care about decorations as long as the beer was cold. The harder stuff was in shorter supply, so it was rationed out, no more than two drinks of whiskey or rum per day per man.

The evening after Mrs. Teters left Wake, Adam sat at one of the tables in the slop chute with his squad, nursing a beer. He had never been a heavy drinker. In his crowd back home, Dale Parker was the one who could really put away the booze, despite being the youngest member of the bunch. Adam had always looked down a little at Dale for drinking so much, and he felt guilty for feeling that way, since Dale was the brother of Adam's best friend. There was no excuse for getting sloppy drunk, though, the way Dale sometimes did.

Gurnwall was telling an extremely lewd and probably untrue story about a couple of girls he had gone to high school with back in Tulsa, twin sisters who had done everything together. "... I mean *everything*," Gurnwall said with a leer, digging his elbow into the ribs of the morose Private Magruder, who sat next to him.

Adam's attention wandered. He was looking at the door when four men came through it. The fact that they wore civilian clothes immediately caught Adam's eye, and so did the fiery red hair under the pushed-back Panama one of the men wore. Conner, Adam recalled. The civilians were out of their bailiwick. Except when they were working, they stayed close to Camp Two.

Gurnwall had his back to the door, so he hadn't seen Conner and the other civilian workers come into the slop chute. He kept telling his story about the Tulsa twins, even as the rest of the conversation in the room died down and finally tapered off entirely. Everyone was looking curiously at the interlopers.

At last, Gurnwall realized he had lost his audience. "Hey, what's the matter?" he demanded, offended by the inattention. "What's wrong with you guys? The story's just gettin' good!"

Adam nudged Gurnwall's foot with his boot and nodded toward the doorway. Gurnwall looked over his shoulder and said, "Oh."

Conner, who carried himself like the leader of the little group, had the fingers of his left hand wrapped around the neck of a bottle. He lifted it and said, "Don't let us spoil your fun, boys. Carry on, Marines."

One of the men at a table near the door said, "That sounds like an order. Marines don't take orders from ex-dogfaces."

That was the truck driver who had told him that Conner had been in the Army, Adam recalled.

Conner swayed a little. The bottle in his hand was less than half-full. He brought it to his mouth, lifted it, and swallowed as the remaining whiskey gurgled in the bottle. Conner lowered the bottle, belched, and wiped the back of his other hand across his mouth.

"Didn't come here to start trouble," he said. "Just thought we'd come help you celebrate."

"Celebrate what?" another Marine asked.

Conner hiccuped. "Bein' abandoned. Bein' left here, staked out like goats for the Japs."

Adam came to his feet, not even thinking about what he was doing. "Shut up that talk," he snapped. "No one is abandoning us." Conner tried, not completely successfully, to focus on Adam. "Why do you think the boss's wife left this afternoon? Th' Japs're on their way. Little yellow bastards'll be all over the island 'fore you know it."

"That's enough." Adam strode across the room toward Conner. He didn't know why he had spoken up or why he was confronting the drunken civilian. There were several non-coms in the room. They outranked him. They should have been the ones to toss Conner and the others out of here. The civilians didn't belong here.

Conner smiled a little as Adam came up to him. "What're you doin', big boy?"

"Telling you to go back to your own camp before there's trouble."

Conner lifted the bottle and drained the rest of the liquid inside it. "Hell, you think I'm scared of a bunch o' Marines? I was a *real* soldier once."

That was the wrong thing to say in these surroundings. Adam reached out to grab Conner's arm, thinking there might still be a chance to hustle the civilians out of the club before all hell broke loose.

But it was too late for that, and as Conner jerked away from Adam's grip, he shouted, "Fuckin' leatherneck!" and swung the empty bottle at Adam's head as hard as he could.

FIVE

Adam ducked instinctively, letting Conner's wild swing go over his head. He bulled forward and wrapped his arms around Conner's waist, lifting the man's feet off the floor. Conner was about the same size as Adam, but he was drunk and Adam had the momentum. Adam was able to rush Conner toward the door. He still harbored a faint hope that he could keep a full-fledged brawl from breaking out.

Hands grabbed him before he could reach the door. Adam heard men shouting angrily as he tried to pull free. At that moment, Conner slammed the bottle into Adam's lower back. Agony shot through Adam's body, and he let go of the civilian.

He might have fallen to his knees if not for the hands holding him up. Hot breath laced with whiskey blew in his face as Conner cursed him. Conner hooked a hard right fist into Adam's midsection. Adam groaned and felt sick.

He shook off the nausea as his mind went back to a snowy day in Chicago when as a kid he had run afoul of three bullying Irish brothers. They had been beating the hell out of him when Joe Parker stepped in to put a stop to it. That had been the beginning of his friendship with Joe, and the beginning, as well, of his awareness that he needed to be able to take care of himself. He would always be Jewish, but he didn't have to be a victim of bigots and thugs.

The muscles in Adam's shoulders bunched. With a shout of anger, he straightened, threw one of the civilians holding his arms away from him, pivoted smoothly, and smashed a right cross to the jaw of the other one. It was just like hitting a baseball, a combination of strength, speed, and timing. The man went flying backward and crashed down on one of the tables, smashing it.

Conner tackled Adam from behind. Both men went down. Conner's right arm went around Adam's throat and locked into place. Conner had caught him in the middle of a breath, and Adam felt a wave of dizziness sweep over him as he struggled unsuccessfully to draw air into his lungs.

Conner's knee dug painfully into Adam's back where he'd hit him with the bottle. Adam gritted his teeth against the pain and the dizziness and heaved himself up off the sawdust-littered floor. He flung himself to the side, rolling over so that his weight came down on Conner. At the same time he drove an elbow back into the redhead's belly. Conner's hold on Adam's throat loosened, and Adam was able to pull free.

Gasping for breath, Adam rolled away. Somebody stepped on him, making him yell. In fact, there were feet all around him. The other two civilians were trying to make a fight of it against the Marines who had swarmed them, but they were outnumbered more than ten to one. Right about now, they were probably regretting getting drunk enough to let Conner convince them to come over here.

Adam had no doubt that Conner had instigated the visit. Conner was the one who ought to be getting the hell beaten out of him, not the other men. Adam grabbed hold of the bar and pulled himself to his feet. He shook the remaining cobwebs out of his brain and looked around for Conner. The redhead was lying on his side a few feet away, retching from Adam's elbow in the guts.

Adam stepped over to him, reached down, and grabbed his shirt. He hauled Conner upright and held him at arm's length with his left hand. Raising his voice, he shouted at the other brawlers, "Stop it! Stop fighting, damn it!" The fact that there were men in the room who outranked him was forgotten at the moment.

He was a little surprised when the fighting actually stopped. Both of the civilians who were still on their feet were backed up against the bar. The Marines who had forced them there looked back over their shoulders at Adam.

"This is between me and this son of a bitch," Adam said as he cocked his right fist. He drove the punch into Conner's jaw.

Conner stumbled backward but somehow caught himself as Adam came after him. Adam was convinced that Conner was only half-conscious, if that, so he was taken by surprise as Conner lifted an uppercut. The blow landed solidly and rocked Adam back. Conner tried to rush in, but he was unsteady on his feet and Adam was able to block his next punch. Adam landed a right to Conner's breastbone that made the redhead turn pale under his deep tan.

Conner didn't go down. He stayed on his feet and slugged, right and left, at Adam. Adam parried both blows, but Conner was too close to him now. The toe of Conner's boot smashed into Adam's shin. Adam's guard dropped as he cried out in pain, and Conner caught him on the chin with a looping left.

Adam twisted around and slapped his hands on the bar to keep from falling. Conner clubbed his fists together, lifted them, and brought them down hard at the back of Adam's neck. Some instinct warned Adam, and he jerked aside at the last instant. Conner hit the bar instead and howled in pain.

Adam caught the back of Conner's neck and drove his face down against the bar. Conner really was almost senseless now. Adam hauled him around and shoved him toward the open door. A lane opened up in the Marines who had been watching the battle. Adam hit Conner with a left that sent him stumbling backward, then moved up fast and threw a right that landed so solidly on Conner's jaw, Adam felt the impact all the way up to his shoulder. Conner was knocked through the door and across the short porch on the front of the slop chute. His feet went out from under him and he sprawled loosely on the sand. He tried to raise his head, then groaned and let it fall back.

Adam stepped onto the porch, fists still clenched, then the roar of engines made him look up. The sound wasn't coming from airplanes, he realized as headlights washed over his face.

Jeeps and trucks were racing into the camp, and as Adam blinked and raised his left hand to shade his eyes from the glare of the lights, he recognized the vehicles as belonging to the civilian construction company. They were covered with workmen, many of them holding shovels.

From behind Adam, Gurnwall said, "*Now* the shit's gonna hit the fan."

The lead jeep in the convoy skidded to a stop in front of the building. The men in it leaped out almost before the jeep stopped moving. Brandishing the shovels, they advanced toward the slop chute.

"Frank!" one of the civilians shouted when he saw the redhead lying senseless on the ground. "The fucking Marines have killed Frank!"

"He's not dead, you idiot," Adam said. "He's just knocked out."

"The Marine ain't livin' what could knock out Frank Conner!"

"That's what you think, you prick!" Gurnwall shouted back. He tried to push past Adam.

Adam put an arm out to block Gurnwall. His chin felt wet, and he realized blood was welling from the corner of his mouth. A couple of teeth were loose, too. And after the shots to the kidneys he had taken, he'd probably be pissing blood for a week. But somehow, he felt better than he had for a long time.

The spokesman for the civilian workers shook the shovel he was holding and said, "We heard some of our boys came down here for a friendly drink with you Marines, and this is what you do to 'em!"

"Friendly drink, my ass!" Gurnwall called past Adam's shoulder. "They insulted the Marine Corps!"

"You fucking leathernecks are gonna get this whole camp pulled down around your ears!"

"Shut up!" Adam's voice roared out with authority, whether he actually had any or not. "What the hell is wrong with you people?"

"You tell 'em, Corp!"

Adam swung around on Gurnwall. "Damn it, pipe down, Gurney! You're as bad as they are." He turned back to the civilians and pointed at Conner. "There's your man. Take him. The other three are inside. Bring 'em out, boys."

The mass of Marines in the doorway behind Adam shifted around, and the three civilians stumbled out, two of them helping the third man, the one Adam had knocked into the table. But they were all conscious, and though bruised and bloody, none of them were hurt too badly.

"Take your friends back to camp and patch them up," Adam told the workers. "And get it through your thick skulls that we don't have the time and energy to waste fighting each other. We've got more important things to worry about."

Conner was being lifted to his feet. The workers' leader said to him, "What about it, Frank? You want us to even the score with these Marines for you?"

Conner shook his head and then groaned. "That big son of a bitch is right, Ralph," he said. "We're all on the same side. I got somethin' to say to him 'fore we go, though." He shook his head again, then said to Adam, "C'mere, you big son of a bitch."

Adam hesitated, then motioned for the other Marines to stay back as he stepped down from the porch and walked ahead to meet Conner. Conner waved his friends back, then stumbled a couple of steps forward. He surprised Adam by extending his hand. "Good fight," he said.

Adam took Conner's hand. "Yeah, I guess."

Conner leaned closer to him and said, in a voice that contained not a hint of drunkenness, "You pack a hell of a wallop, Marine." One eye closed for a second in a wink.

Adam's eyes widened in surprise. Conner let go of his hand and turned away, then, swaying slightly, went to join his friends. He climbed into the back of the lead jeep. Within moments, with much grinding of gears and spraying of sand, the civilian vehicles were turned around and heading back down Wake Island to loop around to Camp Two.

"Well, whaddaya know about that?" Gurnwall said, sounding disgusted.

"Yeah," Adam said, watching the red taillights of the jeeps and trucks dwindle into the distance. "Whaddaya know about that?"

* * *

Major James P. S. Devereux looked up from the chair behind the desk in his office in the battalion command post. The balding officer fixed a cold, intent gaze on Adam, who stood in front of the desk.

"Corporal Bergman, I have been informed that last night you engaged in a brawl with one of the civilian construction workers at the enlisted men's club."

So a squealer had told the major about what had happened in the slop chute. That didn't surprise Adam too much. There was always someone around who tried to curry favor with the officers.

"Considering my current state, sir, I see no point in denying the allegation." Adam's face was bruised and the corner of his mouth was puffy. Anybody could look at him and tell he'd been in a fight.

"Well? What do you have to say for yourself?"

"No excuses, sir." He could explain that he had been trying to head off trouble at first, and after that he had been defending himself. But it didn't really matter. A brawl was still a brawl.

"Who besides the civilian worker was involved in this fight?"

Damn. Did Devereux really expect him to name names? "I couldn't really say, sir. I was occupied at the time."

"You can't identify *any* of the other participants?"

"No, sir."

"Or you *won't* identify any of them?"

"Sir, with all due respect, I did not see anyone else throw a punch except the other person involved in the altercation with me."

That was true enough. Adam was sure a lot of punches had

been thrown, but he hadn't observed any of them, being in the middle of his own battle as he had been.

Those law school classes were finally coming in handy.

Major Devereux must have been thinking the same thing. He said, "I've looked at your records, Bergman, and see that you're going to be an attorney. I suspect you'll be a good one." The major's voice hardened. "But I won't have any guardhouse lawyers in my command. Is that understood, Corporal?"

"Yes, sir."

"You'll be pulling some extra duty for the next few days, and so will the other men in your squad. Be sure and tell them who they have to thank for that."

"Yes, sir," Adam said again, though this time the words came out through clenched teeth.

"That's all," Devereux said. "Dismissed."

Adam saluted, waited until the major returned it, then turned sharply and started to leave the office. Devereux stopped him by saying, "Oh, one last thing, Corporal. I heard that you were giving orders quite freely last night, even to non-coms who outrank you. That's not a wise thing to do."

"No, sir, I suppose not."

"A man who's good at giving orders should consider becoming an officer."

"Sir?"

"Get out of here, Bergman." Devereux picked up a pencil and went back to initialing the never-ending stream of paperwork that came across his desk.

Adam left the reinforced concrete bunker that housed the command post. He had his helmet tucked under his left arm. He put it on, then looked back at the command post and frowned.

What had Major Devereux meant by that last comment about becoming an officer? Surely the major hadn't meant to imply . . .

Or maybe he had. Adam grinned. It was something to think about.

SIX

The fight in the slop chute was the talk of the island for days afterward, especially the slugging match between Adam and Frank Conner. Gurnwall stopped calling Adam "Corp" and called him "Champ" or "Slugger" or "Dempsey" instead, until Adam ordered him to stop it.

Adam didn't see Conner again for over a week. When he did, he was on a truck heading along the road that ran past Camp Two, bound for the narrow bridge that led to Peale Island. The truck was carrying a couple of .50-caliber machine guns that would be positioned on Toki Point at the far end of Peale. Conner was walking alongside the road with a couple of other men, limping slightly and carrying himself as if his muscles were sore. He glanced over at the truck, saw Adam grinning at him, and lifted a hand in a friendly wave which Adam returned. Adam watched him in the truck's side mirror and saw that Conner was making an effort to walk straighter and not limp.

Adam knew how the guy felt. The first morning after the fight, he had barely been able to haul himself out of bed. He hurt all over.

Most of the aches and pains had vanished now. The swelling in his mouth had gone down, and the bruises were fading. The brawl had had some more lasting effects, however. The Marines and the civilian workers were friendlier now, and there was a renewed sense of pulling together against a common enemy. If that had been Conner's intention in provoking the fight, then it had worked.

Or maybe Conner had just been trying to save face and cover up the fact that he'd been a belligerent jerk. Adam didn't know and didn't care.

The .50-caliber machine guns bound for Toki Point would protect the 5-inch seacoast gun that was being set up there to face southwest. A little farther down the island and facing northeast was a 3-inch anti-aircraft gun, augmented by another pair of fifties. Peale Island was well on its way to being as well fortified as Wake Island. Of the three islands that made up the atoll, the one with the fewest defenses was Wilkes. It was also the least developed of the islands in other ways, containing only a rudimentary road, acres of impenetrable thorny brush, and narrow beaches littered with large coral boulders. A 5-inch gun was scheduled to be put in place near its northwestern end, with a few of the .50-caliber machine guns around it.

The most heavily defended part of the atoll was the southeastern corner of Wake Island, where the station's runways were located. Those runways were the reason all of them were here, Adam reflected. In fact, as he looked in that direction while he was working during the afternoon, he saw a PBY come in. He and his squad were busy filling and lugging sandbags, which meant they wouldn't have to act as ground crew today.

The tedious work continued for several days, and the good mood that had followed the brawl in the slop chute gradually evaporated. Every day brought a new alert from Pearl Harbor. It was hard not to think about how all the naval might of the Imperial Japanese Fleet could be lying just over the horizon. The garrison at Wake was scheduled to receive an SCR-270B search radar unit, which would give them some advance warning of the enemy's approach. They were also supposed to get an SCR-268 fire-control radar unit to assist in aiming the guns, but so far neither had arrived. PBYs flew in and out of the air station, but there were no organized reconnaissance patrols.

They were sitting ducks, and the men knew it.

Then, on 29 November 1941, the aircraft tender U.S.S. *Wright* arrived off Wake Island, bringing with it Major Walter

Bayler, a staff officer from Marine Air Group 21. VMF-211, the squadron of F4F-3 Grumman Wildcat fighters that would be stationed on Wake, was part of MAG-21. Bayler had with him 49 more Marines commanded by 2nd Lieutenant Robert J. Conderman, and their job was to prepare the ground facilities for the arrival of VMF-211 a few days later.

Someone else was on the *Wright*—a slender, dark-haired naval officer named Winfield Scott Cunningham. Commander Cunningham was the new Island Commander, supplanting Major Devereux.

Adam and his squad were unloading lumber from one of the lighters that had brought it from the *Wright* when a launch brought Commander Cunningham ashore. Major Devereux was waiting. He saluted crisply as Cunningham stepped off the launch.

Adam tried not to frown as he watched a couple of Marines unloading the naval commander's gear from the launch. Among the commander's belongings was a golf bag with a full set of clubs in it, their heads protected by little felt hoods. Adam had come to like Major Devereux, and he wasn't sure he wanted to see him replaced by some swabbie who brought his golf clubs with him to what was sure to become a combat command.

No one was going to ask his opinion on the matter, though, Adam reminded himself. After all, he was only a lowly corporal.

Gurnwall set down one of the bundles of lumber he had taken from the lighter and jerked a thumb at the newcomer in dress whites. "Who's the fancy pants?"

"The new Island Commander." Adam knew Cunningham's name because he was friends with one of Major Devereux's clerks, who had seen the orders transferring Cunningham to Wake.

"Shit, Corp, you mean we gotta take orders from some seagoin' doorman?"

Gurnwall's voice carried, and Adam saw both Major Devereux and Commander Cunningham glance in their direction. "Get those boards on the truck, damn it," he snapped. "And keep your mouth shut." He lowered his voice to add, "Or that seagoing doorman's liable to make you walk the plank."

*   *   *

Five days later, on 4 December, Adam and many of the other men watched as the Navy PBY that had taken off earlier in the day returned to the island. Flying in formation behind the PBY were the twelve Wildcats of VMF-211. The PBY had led the fighters to Wake from the aircraft carrier U.S.S. *Enterprise,* some two hundred miles northeast of the atoll.

The PBY landed first, then got out of the way as quickly as possible so that the sleek, dangerous-looking Wildcats could swoop down and land. One by one they did so, moving so fast that Adam thought they wouldn't be able to stop before reaching the end of the runway. The Marine aviators were good at their jobs and brought the planes down safely, then taxied onto the cross-runway. Commander Cunningham, who wore khakis and a billed cap now instead of the dress whites he had sported on his arrival, was waiting for the pilots along with Major Devereux. The commander of the squadron climbed down from the cockpit of his F4F-3 and took off his flight helmet as he came over to Cunningham and Devereux. After an exchange of salutes, Cunningham put out his hand and said, "Welcome to Wake Island, Major Putnam."

"Glad to be here, sir," Putnam responded. A round-faced, balding man, he glanced around, and Adam could see the disappointment on his face when he realized the air station consisted of the two narrow runways, a handful of huts that Lieutenant Conderman and his men had thrown up hastily over the past few days as sleeping quarters and a place for the squadron's communications equipment, and a wind sock on a pole. "I understood there were to be revetments for my planes."

"They're on the construction schedule, Major," Cunningham replied.

Putnam grunted, clearly displeased that the Wildcats would have to sit out in the open with no protection when they weren't flying.

Major Bayler emerged from the communications hut to greet Putnam as well. Commander Cunningham said, "When you've had a chance to settle in a bit, Major, why don't you come to the command post, and we'll sit down and discuss the schedule of your patrol flights."

"Yes, sir," Putnam replied, clearly making an effort to conceal his displeasure.

The men Bayler and Conderman had brought with them were now serving as ground crews for the station, so Adam and the other members of the 1st Defense Battalion no longer had to worry about assuming those duties. Adam took a couple of minutes to admire the sleek lines of the Wildcats, then got back to work.

He was in his tent that evening with Gurnwall when the battalion's ordnance officer, Marine Gunner Harold Borth, came around the camp checking on ammunition supplies. Adam and Gurnwall got off their cots and saluted; then Gunner Borth asked, "How many rounds do you have for that M1, Corporal?"

"Fifty-two," Adam replied. He had learned early on at Parris Island that a Marine was expected to be precise about things such as ammunition rounds.

"Then you're in better shape than some of the men," Borth said. "What about you, Private?"

Gurnwall said, "Uh . . ."

Adam tried not to wince.

"About . . . forty?" Gurnwall said uncertainly.

"I suggest you count them so you can be certain," Borth told him in a cold voice. The ordnance officer turned back to Adam and took a holstered pistol from a canvas sack he carried. He held the pistol out toward Adam, who recognized it as a Colt Model 1911A1, .45 ACP caliber, the standard sidearm of the United States military. "We have a few extra of these that we're issuing to some of the men," Borth said. "I know you fired Expert with the M1, Bergman. Doesn't mean you'll be worth a flip with a handgun, but we'll take a chance on you."

Adam took the .45, slid it out of its holster, ejected the clip, and worked the slide to make sure there wasn't a round in the breech. Borth looked satisfied. He took an ammunition box from his bag of goodies and handed it to Adam as well.

"Twenty-five rounds. That's all you get."

"Thank you, Gunner."

"If you have to use it, make them count."

Adam slipped the automatic back into its holster and said, "That's exactly what I intend to do."

When Borth was gone, Gurnwall said, "Hey, Corp, can you shoot that thing?"

Adam nodded. "Didn't they teach you how to handle a sidearm at Pendleton?"

"We shot 'em a couple of times, but hell, everybody knows only officers get sidearms." Gurnwall's face lit up. "Hey, they're gonna promote you, Corp! You're gonna skip sergeant and go right to second looey."

Adam laughed and said, "I don't think so, Gurney."

"Yeah, right. Listen, Corp, when you're an officer, you think you can put in a good word for me?"

"Sure, Gurney. When I make general, I'll see to it that you're promoted to corporal. How about that?"

"Corporal Gurnwall. I like the sound of it."

But it didn't sound as good, Adam had to admit to himself, as Lieutenant Bergman. He knew he was getting ahead of himself, way ahead. Besides, it wasn't like he'd had his heart set on becoming an officer. He'd just wanted to get in on the fighting and do what he could to stop Hitler and the Nazis from taking over the world. That hadn't really worked out so far.

Still, he had a college degree, and the Marines liked that in their officers. Maybe once this business on Wake Island was over, he would think about applying for Officer Candidate School.

Yeah, he thought as he took the automatic out of its holster again and hefted it, all he had to do was survive Wake Island. . . .

SEVEN

Every day, at sunrise and sunset, four of the Grumman Wildcats took off to carry out a patrol flight, flying out at least fifty miles from the atoll and then circling it, while the squadron's other eight planes remained on the ground. While doing this, the pilots also were receiving training in the navigation and instrumentation of their planes, because, simply put, they barely knew how to fly the damned things. The F4F-3 was a new airplane, and the Marine aviators of VMF-211 had very little flight time in them. They had been rushed to Wake Island in the hope that they could learn on the job. The same was true of the mechanics and ground crews who had been charged with keeping the Wildcats flightworthy.

There were problems with the aircraft themselves. The Wildcats were fighters, not patrol planes, and although they flew reconnaissance missions around the atoll, they lacked the range for long-range patrols. Though PBYs flew in and out of Wake, none of the flying boats, which were perfect for patrolling, were assigned there. The F4F-3s also had no armor plating, and in a textbook example of the right hand not knowing what the left hand was doing, the bombs that had been sent to the island would not fit in the bomb racks mounted on the airplanes. Captain Herbert Freuler, VMF-211's ordnance officer, was trying to modify the bomb racks so that they would work, but there was no way to know how long that effort was going to take, or if it would ever be successfully completed.

Those weren't the only shortcomings of the atoll's defenses, and though Adam knew nothing of the problems with the planes, he was all too aware of the other obstacles. On the morning of Saturday, 6 December 1941, Major Devereux held drills for the entire Marine detachment. The call to arms sounded over the loudspeakers in camp, and the men rushed out and scattered over the islands to their assigned positions. As the practice drill continued, something quickly became all too obvious: The 1st Defense Battalion was seriously undermanned, perhaps by as much as two-thirds of what its strength should have been.

All the guns—a full complement of armament for a defense battalion—had been emplaced in batteries scattered around the three islands. Most of the batteries were protected by walls of sandbags, and a few even had camouflage netting rigged over them.

But if it came to a fight, there simply weren't enough Marines to go around, and the guns would be useless if there was no one to fire them.

Other than that, a network of telephone lines connected all the defense positions, but the lines had been run above the ground, where they could be destroyed easily in an attack. There hadn't been enough time to dig trenches and place the lines underground. If the telephone net was broken, the defenders would have to rely on walkie-talkies to communicate with each other.

There was still no sign of the radar units.

Under the circumstances, the drill had run very smoothly, and Major Devereux was satisfied. He issued orders that were welcomed by the men who had been working twelve-hour shifts, seven days a week, for more than a month. Saturday afternoon would be free time, and there would be only light duties on Sunday.

Saturday evening, Adam took his latest letter from Catherine, which had been brought to him by the pilot of a PBY that had arrived from Pearl earlier in the day, to the channel between Wilkes Island and Wake Island and sat down on a rock to read it. The envelope had been taped shut by the censors when they were through with it. Carefully, Adam lifted the flap and slid out the folded sheets of onionskin paper. The scent of Catherine's perfume rose from them and for a moment filled his head with such a dizzying sensation that he had to close his eyes and compose himself before he could start to read.

"Well, what do you know about that?" he muttered as he read that Catherine's younger brother Spencer had shown up at Pearl Harbor in a Navy uniform. Spencer had always been the black sheep of the Tancred family—although Catherine was giving him a run for his money now, what with having married someone who was Jewish *and* joined the Navy herself. Spencer had been booted out of the prestigious prep school back East where he had been sent by his parents. After coming back to Chicago, he had been in trouble almost all the time with his strict, overbearing father. To be honest, Adam thought, the kid *was* a foul-up, but Adam liked him anyway. From the sound of Catherine's letter, Spencer was trying to straighten up and fly right—literally, since he was going to be in training at Pearl Harbor to become a Navy aviator.

"Good for you, kid," Adam said aloud. Maybe eventually Spencer would wind up with the squadron here on Wake Island. Wouldn't that be something, Catherine's brother and husband serving in the same place.

Catherine's letter went on chatting about her roommate, Missy Mitchell, and her other friends in the nurse corps, Alice Sutherland and Bobbie Tabor. Adam remembered them from his stopover at Pearl. Missy had picked him up at the dock and taken him to the bungalow she shared with Catherine, since Catherine had been detained at the hospital. Adam had met Alice and Bobbie there, too, but only briefly because they'd been on their way to a party.

Anyway, he'd had other things on his mind at the time, like making love to his wife. They had gone at it like they were trying to screw themselves to death.

Adam closed his eyes for a moment and told himself not to think about such things. But it was difficult not to when the scent of Catherine's perfume was wafting up at him from the pages he held in his hand.

I think about you every minute of every day, she had written, *and I can't wait until we're together again. You are my heart and my soul and everything that makes me complete. You are my love, Adam, and you always will be.*

He took a deep breath. He told himself that he didn't regret enlisting in the Marines, that it was something he'd had to do. But if he hadn't, he and Catherine could be back home in Chicago right now, together the way they were supposed to be. It wasn't up to him to save the whole damn world.

Then he thought of his grandparents, somewhere in the Ukraine. The Nazis had rolled through there, smashing everything in their path, and Adam's mother had no idea whether her parents were still alive or not. Even if they were, they had probably lost everything. Their lives would have been shattered by the Nazi blitz.

That was why he had signed his name and held up his hand and sworn the oath. To help protect people like his grandparents, who couldn't protect themselves. Sure, he was on the wrong side of the world, facing the wrong enemy, but it was all connected, he told himself. Hitler and the Japanese were allies. *The friend of my enemy is also my enemy.* Adam couldn't recall where he had heard that saying, but it was true.

Besides, when the war started, they would take care of the Japs in a hurry, and then he'd probably be sent to Europe. He could still get in his licks against Hitler.

With all my love, your wife (how I still love writing that!), Catherine.

Adam read the words softly but aloud, relishing the sound of them. Offshore along the coral reef, the surf roared and pounded, drowning out everything else, but Adam heard the words in his heart as the light of day faded.

* * *

Pan American Airways was still using Wake as a stopover on its flights to the Far East, which had been curtailed by the worsening political situation but not suspended entirely. These commercial flights were seaplanes which landed in the lagoon, then taxied onto the concrete ramp near the neat, two-story, frame hotel Pan Am had built on Peale Island. The planes refueled from Pan Am's supply of avgas, then took off again from the lagoon. Flights that arrived late in the day, however, generally stayed there overnight, with the crew and passengers putting up in the hotel.

The Marines had nothing to do with these flights, but they couldn't help but see the large, shiny clippers arrowing down out of the sky as they landed. Late in the afternoon of Sunday, 7 December, Adam was sitting on a folding stool in front of his tent, cleaning the Colt .45, when he saw one of the Pan Am planes dip out of the clouds and land in the lagoon. Its pontoons threw water high in a silvery spray around them as the plane's speed gradually slackened.

The rest of the squad had been playing poker all afternoon. Gurnwall was ahead, naturally. Dressed only in shorts, they were sitting in a circle on a couple of blankets spread out on the ground in front of their tents. Grinning, Gurnwall raked in another pot, and Kennemer said in disgust, "I'm out. You cleaned me, Gurney."

"It was inevitable," Gurnwall said, mangling the word. Adam smiled but didn't bother to correct him. He had learned that Gurnwall had dropped out of high school in order to work and help his family, and he didn't want to embarrass him.

Gurnwall shuffled and said, "Ante up, suckers."

Finished with the .45, Adam put it back in its holster and stretched his legs out in front of him, crossing them at the ankles. After the frantic pace that had ruled their days ever since coming to Wake, it felt good just to relax for a little while. The men needed this breather before they got back to work. Major Devereux had been smart to give them the time off. A good officer had to know when to push his men and when to ease up on them, Adam thought. That was something he needed to remember, if he ever became an officer himself. He had been thinking about that more and more.

The rest of the day passed quietly and peacefully. Some of the Marines held an impromptu luau on the beach, although they had to make do with canned meat instead of roast pig. Gurnwall made himself a grass skirt, rolled up his pants legs, and danced a hula. Everyone watching laughed harder than they had at any time since coming to Wake Island.

It was a well-rested bunch of Marines who rolled out of their cots the next morning when reveille sounded at 0600. Adam and his squad ate breakfast in the mess hall, then returned to their tents to take care of anything that needed to be done before reporting for the day's duties. Adam was standing in front of his tent a short time later as the Pan Am clipper that had landed the previous evening taxied out into the lagoon and took off, rising steadily into the clear blue sky. Adam kept his eye on the plane as it dwindled into the distance, then with a smile turned back toward the tent.

Music had been playing over the camp loudspeakers. It stopped abruptly as Adam pulled back the entrance flap on the tent. He paused, frowning as a few seconds of silence came over the speakers. Then the unmistakable strains of the call to arms rang out.

Gurnwall popped out of the tent, forcing Adam to step back. His eyes were open wide, and he said excitedly, "It's another drill, right, Corp? Just another drill?"

Marines tumbled out of their tents all over Camp One, answering the strident summons playing over the loudspeakers. Adam looked around and said, "I don't think it's a drill, Gurney."

"But it's gotta be! The Japs aren't comin'! They can't be!"

Adam's eyes narrowed as he looked at Gurnwall. The man was almost hysterical. "Get your rifle and fall in," Adam snapped. "Now!"

Gurnwall swallowed, and for a second Adam didn't know if he was going to obey the order or not. Then Gurnwall ducked back into the tent and Adam followed him. Both of them picked up their M1s and stuck boxes of ammunition in their pockets. Adam hesitated, then picked up the holstered Colt .45 automatic and snapped the holster onto his web belt.

The two of them ran outside, where the rest of the squad was forming. The call to arms was still playing, but it was just background noise to Adam. He heard men shouting and truck engines growling, and he wondered what was going on down at the air station. The four-plane dawn patrol had taken off earlier, but the other eight Wildcats were still on the ground. Adam imagined the members of VMF-211 were hustling around preparing to get the birds in the air if necessary.

The uncertainty was the worst, he realized, not knowing what had happened to cause the sounding of the alarm. It was possible the Japanese had attacked somewhere else; rumors had it that the Philippines were the most likely target. But it was also possible that a Japanese task force was steaming up on Wake at this very instant. Their bombers and fighters could be in the air, bound for this little volcanic atoll in the middle of the big ocean.

And all he and the others could do, Adam realized, was to wait for orders.

A jeep containing several officers raced along the road through the camp, then came to a skidding stop near the spot where Adam's squad had formed up. One of the officers shouted to Adam, "Get up on the water tank, Corporal!"

Adam snapped a salute and called back, "Aye, aye, sir!" Carrying his rifle, he turned and ran toward the large, flat-topped water tank that sat atop four fifty-foot legs. A narrow ladder was attached to one of the legs and ran all the way to the top of the tank. That was easily the highest point on the atoll and the only real observation post they had.

Adam became aware that someone was hurrying up alongside him. He glanced over and saw Gurnwall, who was carrying a walkie-talkie. "The brass said to give you this, Corp!" Gurnwall said as he thrust the portable radio toward Adam.

"Hang on to it," Adam told him. "You're going up there with me, Gurney."

"On top of the water tank?" Gurnwall yelped.

Adam reached the ladder and paused at its base long enough to give Gurnwall a grin. "Whatever's coming, we'll see it before anybody else." Then he started to climb.

"Oh, yeah, that makes me feel a whole hell of a lot better, Corp," Gurnwall muttered. He shook his head, reached out to grasp one of the ladder's lower rungs, and started climbing after Adam.

EIGHT

The sun had been up long enough so that the metal skin of the water tank was already hot to the touch. Adam sat cross-legged on the top of the tank and motioned for Gurnwall to do the same. He laid the M1 beside him and started scanning the horizon. The metal helmet didn't shade his eyes, so he lifted a hand to do that.

"What am I doin' up here, Corp?"

"Two sets of eyes are better than one," Adam said. "I'll take the north and east; you take the south and west."

"Okay, but what're we lookin' for?"

"Boats, planes, whatever the Japanese want to throw at us."

"I'd like to throw something at those damned Japs."

"You may get your chance."

"Yeah, that's what I'm worried about."

Even up here, the sound of the pounding surf was loud, but a few minutes later, Adam began to hear what he thought was an airplane engine. Gurnwall cried out, "Somethin' comin', Corp!"

Adam turned and looked to the southwest. Sure enough, there was a shape in the sky that quickly resolved itself into an airplane, but only one. As it came closer, Adam recognized it.

"That's the Pan Am plane that left here earlier," he said to Gurnwall. "Somebody must have called it back."

The clipper dropped down lower and lower and finally landed in the lagoon. It pulled up to the ramp, and Adam saw the figures of its passengers and crew, tiny at this distance, begin disembarking from the airplane.

From up here he could also see the other frenzied preparations that were going on all over the island. Trucks roared along the crushed coral roads, carrying men and equipment and ammunition. As they had discovered during the drill two days earlier, there weren't enough Marines to man all of the guns, but they were being dispersed to as many of the batteries as possible.

Private Rolofson came scrambling up the ladder to the top of the tank, a couple pairs of binoculars slung around his neck. Without actually climbing onto the tank, Rolofson stopped at the top of the ladder and took off the binoculars. "Here you go, Corporal," he said as he handed the binoculars to Adam and Gurnwall. "Compliments of Major Devereux himself. He says to keep a sharp eye out."

"Hey, Rolofson, you want to take my place up here?" Gurnwall asked.

Rolofson grinned. "No, thanks, buddy. If there's gonna be trouble, I'd just as soon have my feet on solid ground."

"Have you heard what happened?" Adam asked.

Rolofson's expression grew more serious. "Just some scuttlebutt. But what it sounds like is that the Japs attacked Pearl Harbor this morning."

Adam had been lifting the binoculars to his eyes as Rolofson spoke. As the words penetrated, he froze, his fingers tightening on the glasses. His head jerked around, and he said in a hoarse voice, "Pearl Harbor?"

"Yeah. From the sound of it, they caught us napping and bombed the hell out of the fleet."

Pearl Harbor. Catherine.

"Fuckin' little yellow bastards," Gurnwall said.

Adam realized he wasn't breathing. He forced himself to take a deep breath and then said, "Let me know if you hear anything else."

"Sure, Corporal." Rolofson went back down the ladder.

"Whattaya think about that? I never thought the Japs'd hit Pearl Harbor . . ." Gurnwall's voice trailed off; then he said, "Oh, shit, your wife's there, ain't she, Corp?"

"Serving in the naval hospital," Adam said. His voice sounded hollow and strange to his ears.

"Oh, well, then, you don't have to worry. Not even the Japs'd bomb a hospital."

Adam wasn't so sure of that. He had heard about the atrocities committed by the Japanese in China and Manchuria over the past few years as they tried to expand their goddamned Greater Southeast Asia Co-Prosperity Sphere. Besides, the Japs wouldn't be able to control exactly where all their bombs fell. He tried to remember the layout of the naval base at Pearl from his brief visit there. The naval hospital was on the point where the channel from the ocean entered the harbor itself. Battleship Row lay along the southeastern shore of Ford Island, in the center of the harbor, and that probably had been the main target of the attack. Still, the hospital was too close for comfort. Way too close.

Adam finally succeeded in lifting the binoculars to his eyes and resumed searching the ocean and the sky for any sign of an enemy force. There was nothing else he could do. Pearl Harbor was two thousand miles away, so far away that it was on the other side of the international date line. It was still 7 December 1941, over there.

The radio transmission had come through from Hickam Field, the Army Air Corps base next to Pearl Harbor, at 0650 that morning. Against regulations, the message was in the clear, rather than encoded, but no one at Hickam was paying too much attention to regulations on this day. The message itself was simple: "Hickam Field has been attacked by Jap dive bombers. This is the real thing."

Captain Henry S. Wilson of the Army Airways Communications Service was the first one to hear the fateful message, as he sat in the AACS radio room near the air station. Captain Wilson and a few other Army communications personnel had been sent to

Wake to help in routing the B-17s to the Philippines. Wilson tore the headphones off his ears, raced out of the hut, leaped into a waiting jeep, and headed for Major Devereux's quarters. He found Devereux shaving and told him what he had just heard from Hickam.

As he wiped shaving soap from his suddenly grim face, Devereux reached for the telephone. Commander Cunningham's headquarters were at Camp Two, the civilian camp on the other side of Wake Island. Devereux rang his number several times, but there was no answer. Grimacing, Devereux called the communications shack at Camp One and was told that a coded priority transmission from Pearl Harbor had just come in and was in the process of being decoded. The simple fact that it was a priority message told Devereux what he needed to know. He was certain it was confirmation of the awful news that had already come from Hickam Field.

Devereux hung up the telephone and turned to his aide, who had hustled in along with Captain Wilson. "Sound the call to arms," Devereux ordered, then as an afterthought added, "and have somebody get up on top of that water tank!"

By a little after 0730, all the scurrying around that Adam and Gurnwall had witnessed from atop the water tank had come to an end. A few vehicles were moving on the roads, but for the most part Wake Island was still. That told Adam that all the defensive positions were manned as well as they could be under the circumstances.

Down at the air station, the four-plane patrol had not returned. In fact, Adam hadn't seen any planes anywhere since the Pan Am clipper had returned to the atoll. The sky overhead was still clear, but clouds were gathering in the distance. Adam hated to see that. If the clouds thickened and moved over the islands, it would be much more difficult to spot any approaching planes.

The loudspeakers had fallen silent a short time earlier, ending the shrill notes of the call to arms. At 0800, the speakers hissed to life once more, and a second later a bugler began to play Morning Colors. Adam looked toward the command post and saw the flag rising on the flagpole. Old Glory flapped and popped in the strong wind.

"Look at that," Gurnwall said in a hushed voice. "Ain't it pretty?"

Adam had trouble talking as he looked at the flag. Emotion clogged his throat. "Yeah," he managed. "Beautiful."

He knew that before the day was over, he would probably be fighting to defend that flag.

An hour later, as the clouds continued boiling closer and closer, the four Wildcats that had been aloft returned to the air station, landing one after another on the narrow runway. Adam put the binoculars on the airstrip and saw the ground crews swarming around the planes while the pilots lifted the Plexiglas covers over the cockpits and climbed out. A short time later, the same four planes took off again, resuming their patrol. The dawn-and-dusk schedule didn't apply today.

The squall line of clouds moved closer. Adam frowned at it, but that didn't make the clouds go away. A few heavy drops of rain fell, making loud pinging noises against the metal skin of the water tank.

"Boy, I wish I was back in Tulsa," Gurnwall said.

Adam kept the binoculars pressed to his eyes and continued to study the horizon and the sky, but he said, "What would you be doing if you were there?" He knew Gurnwall was nervous, and it might help to distract him with a few questions.

"Workin', more than likely." Gurnwall continued looking through his binoculars as well, steadily turning his head from side to side so that he could sweep his searching gaze one hundred and eighty degrees. "Seems like that's all I ever did my whole life."

"What about when you were a kid?"

"I sold newspapers and made deliveries for a drugstore."

"You never played ball, or anything like that?"

"Well, yeah, sometimes," Gurnwall said. "There was this park not far from my folks' house . . . we called it a park, but it was really just a vacant lot. But we played ball there sometimes, come to think of it. You were a ballplayer, weren't you, Corp?"

"University of Chicago, '38 through '40."

Gurnwall let out a low whistle. "Good enough to play in college, huh? We oughta see if we can get up a couple of teams here on the island. I used to be able to throw a pretty good curveball."

Adam lowered the glasses long enough to grin over at his companion. "Bet I could hit it."

"Yeah, well, we ain't gonna find out, 'cause I want to be on your team, Corp. Hell, you're a ringer. We'll lay down a few bets and clean up."

More raindrops fell. Adam heard them hitting his helmet and felt them on his bare forearms where he'd rolled up the sleeves of his shirt. The sun had gone away, obscured now by the dark clouds that were rolling over the island. The wind picked up, and the surf was even louder than usual.

"What the hell?" Gurnwall suddenly exclaimed.

Adam turned quickly, hearing the note of near panic in Gurnwall's voice. He dropped the binoculars and let them dangle from the strap around his neck. He didn't need them to see the V-shaped formation of airplanes coming out of the clouds to the south of the atoll. The planes were dropping at a steep angle, heading straight toward Peacock Point and the air station beyond it.

"Look at that!" Gurnwall said. "The wheels just fell off one of those planes!"

"Those weren't wheels falling, Gurney. Those were bombs!"

The 3-inch gun at Peacock Point suddenly blasted, the sharp roar of its report clearly audible even over the wind and the surf. Dancing sparks that reminded Adam of fireflies were visible in front of the diving airplanes. He knew they were tracers from the planes' machine guns. The .50-caliber guns on the ground began to chatter.

A huge explosion burst out near the edge of one of the runways. Adam felt the ground vibrate through the metal of the water tank. "Shit!" Gurnwall screamed over the tumult. "It's the Japs!"

He was right. The Japanese had finally come to Wake Island.

NINE

Gurnwall picked up his M1, rolled onto his belly, and snugged the butt of the rifle against his shoulder. He started firing at the twin-tailed Japanese dive bombers as they swooped down toward the air station. More bombs exploded around the runways.

Adam reached over and gripped Gurnwall's shoulder hard. "Stop it!" he said. "You're just wasting ammo!" It would be a million-to-one shot if any of Gurnwall's bullets hit one of the Jap planes and actually did any damage.

"Sonsabitches," Gurnwall was saying as he continued to pull the trigger. "Lousy stinkin' sonsabitches."

Adam grabbed the barrel of the M1 and wrenched it upwards. "Gurnwall! Cease fire, damn it!"

Gurnwall's grip on the rifle relaxed, and he blinked rapidly as if just waking up from a sound sleep. He looked up at Adam and said tentatively, "Corp? What do we do now?"

"This is an observation post. We observe."

The water tank shuddered under them again as several bombs detonated at once. Adam understood how Gurnwall was feeling. His every instinct told him to strike back at the attackers, too, but there was really nothing they could do that would accomplish anything. The 3-inch anti-aircraft guns and the .50-caliber machine guns were throwing a curtain of lead into the sky. That was the only real defense Wake Island had.

The Japanese planes were attacking in V-shaped waves. Adam was able to count the third such wave and saw that it had twelve planes in it. That seemed to be the final wave, at least for now, so that meant a total of thirty-six planes were bombing the atoll. As he watched, the first two waves continued across the lagoon toward Camp Two. Adam hoped all the civilians over there were hunting some cover by now. The third wave broke off from the formation and swung around to the west, making a broad circle.

Gurnwall was watching those planes, too. He said, "Holy shit, they're comin' at *us* now!"

It was true. The Japanese planes came out of their circle, zoomed over Kuku Point at the far end of Wilkes Island, and flew southeastward, straight toward Camp One. The .50-caliber batteries on Wilkes were pointed the wrong direction to bring their fire to bear on the planes, and the Japanese weren't even slowed down by the sparse anti-aircraft fire thrown up by the lone 3-inch gun on the island.

"Get down!" Adam shouted at Gurnwall as tracers flickered through the air around them and a line of machine gun bullets stitched across the edge of the water tank a few feet away from them.

Adam stretched out on his belly beside Gurnwall. Both men kept their heads down as the planes strafed the camp. As the low-flying aircraft passed over them, the roar of the engines was so loud that the pounding of the surf on the coral reef was finally drowned out. Rain continued to fall, soaking Adam's uniform. He rolled over, blinked water out of his eyes, and saw that the bombers were past the camp.

"Gurney, you all right? Gurnwall?"

Adam sat up sharply when there was no response from the private. He was afraid Gurnwall had been hit by the machine gun fire from the Jap planes.

Gurnwall still lay on his stomach, his arms crossed over his head. He was shaking violently, so he was still alive. Adam didn't see any blood. He reached over to touch Gurnwall's shoulder. "Gurney?"

Gurnwall jerked and pulled away. "Lemme 'lone!" he shrieked, his face pressed against the water tank. "Lemme 'lone!"

He was too scared to function, Adam realized, but nothing could be done about it now. Adam turned instead toward the air station and picked up the binoculars. He wiped rain off the lenses as best he could and trained the glasses on the runway area. Despite the rain, clouds of black smoke billowed up. From the location, Adam knew that the big avgas tank that had been built by Lieutenant Conderman's men must have been hit by one of the bombs. The tank had been filled only a couple of days earlier with 25,000 gallons of fuel, and now it was all going up in smoke. Small spurts of flame were scattered around the blaze. Those were fifty-gallon drums of avgas exploding from the heat, Adam thought.

He tried to check on the Wildcats through the smoke. During the interval since the first news of the attack on Pearl Harbor had reached Wake, the eight American planes on the ground had been scattered as widely as possible given the limited area that was available for parking them. The idea was not to let one Japanese bomb take out more than one plane. Unfortunately, enough bombs had fallen so that a lot of damage had been done anyway. Adam was no aviation expert, but he could tell that some of the F4F-3s were now nothing but twisted wreckage.

The human toll must have been high, too. The tents and huts where the men of VMF-211 had been housed were either ablaze or totally destroyed. Adam had no idea how many men had been killed over there, but he knew there had to have been casualties.

The sound of engines made him look up. The Japanese bombers were forming into their triple V pattern again and flying south. They must have expended all their bombs and ammunition, Adam thought.

The attack was over. Adam looked at his watch. It was 1210. He wasn't sure when the Japanese planes had first come out of the clouds and dived toward the atoll, but he thought it had been a few minutes before noon. *A quarter of an hour, maybe less.* It seemed a lot longer than that, but at the same time it had been almost the blink of an eye.

"It's over, Gurney. The Japs are leaving."

Gurnwall paid no attention to him but continued trembling.

Adam saw smoke rising from across the lagoon and swung the binoculars in that direction. Fires had broken out in Camp Two, and on Peale Island the Pan American Airways hotel was burning, too. The fact that those were civilian installations hadn't given the Japs a second's pause. They had bombed them anyway.

Adam thought again about the naval hospital at Pearl Harbor. He closed his eyes for a second and prayed that Catherine was all right.

Again, the sound of engines made Adam look up. His heart hammered wildly for a moment as he spotted more planes speeding toward Wake from the north. After a few seconds, however, he realized that there were only four planes, and shortly after that, he recognized them as Wildcats. The patrol that had left earlier was returning.

But they were coming back from the wrong direction. They had been scouting north of the atoll, while the attack had come from the south along with the rain squall. The Japanese had been lucky those clouds had concealed their approach. In fact, they'd had all the luck today. Adam didn't think a single one of the Japanese aircraft had gone down during the raid, or even been hit seriously. He couldn't recall seeing flames or smoke coming from any of them.

"Are . . . are they coming back?"

Adam looked around and saw that Gurnwall had finally lifted his head to stare around wild-eyed. "The Japanese are gone," he said. "Those are our Wildcats coming in. Are you hit, Gurney?"

Gurnwall lifted himself on his left hand and used his right to feel along his torso. "I . . . I don't think so. I don't feel anything."

"They just strafed us with that one burst, and it missed." On hands and knees, Adam crawled over to the edge of the tank where the bullets had struck. The bullets had gone into the top of the tank and punched out through the side, leaving a row of holes out of which water was spurting. That loss would cut down on their supply of drinking water, Adam thought, but there were enough catchment basins and evaporators set up so that nobody was going to die of thirst. In fact, that would probably be one of their lesser worries.

"Can . . . can we get down offa here, Corp?"

"In a minute." Adam sat up and brought the binoculars to his eyes again. The air raid could have been just the first strike, something to soften them up for an invasion. He scanned the horizon, turning slowly through a complete circle, looking for Japanese ships. He didn't see anything but water. The Pacific was living up to its name. It was as peaceful as could be.

"We'll go down and see if we can help," Adam decided. "Maybe one of the other guys can climb up here and keep an eye out."

Gurnwall scuttled over to the ladder, clinging to the tank as if he were afraid that it might leap out from under him. He was still shaking so hard that he had trouble finding the rungs with his feet as he started down. Adam thought he might have to help him, but then Gurnwall's nerves seemed to settle slightly and he was able to begin the descent. Adam climbed down after him and had to admit to himself that he was glad when his feet were back on solid ground.

Gurnwall wiped the back of his hand across his mouth. "Sorry, Corp—" he began.

"Forget it." Adam knew Gurnwall was ashamed that someone had witnessed his fear, but there was no time for worrying about things like that now. He looked around, spotted Magruder, and called out to him to climb onto the water tank. Magruder nodded and took the binoculars that Adam offered him.

"Where are the other guys?" Adam asked as Magruder started up the ladder.

"At our battle station, Corporal," the lean, serious Magruder answered. "I got sent back up here for more ammo."

"I'll see that they get it," Adam said. "Come on, Gurnwall."

As they trotted through Camp One, Adam saw that many of the tents had been shredded by machine gun fire from the Japanese planes. Bomb craters were scattered around the camp. Adam didn't see any bodies, though. When the alarm had been sounded earlier, the Marines of the 1st Defense Battalion had scattered all over the three islands of the atoll, manning the guns they had set up over the past few weeks. The camp had been practically deserted when the attack began, which might have been, at last, a stroke of luck.

It was fortunate, as well, that no bombs had fallen on the ordnance depot. Adam and Gurnwall found it unattended. Each of them slung several belts of .50-caliber rounds over their shoulders and then started down the road toward the air station. The squad's regular defense post was about halfway along the southwestern shore of Wake Island, at one of the machine gun emplacements that was part of Battery E.

Rolofson, Stout, and Kennemer had all come through the attack unharmed, Adam was glad to see when he and Gurnwall reached the gun. They grinned at the newcomers and took the belts of ammunition. "Glad to see you again, Corporal," Rolofson said. "We were afraid you and Gurney were sitting ducks up there on that tank."

"They made one try for us but missed," Adam said. "How did you boys do?"

Stout, from the mountains of Kentucky, said, "We burned a lot of powder but didn't hit anything, far as I could tell."

Adam nodded. "I'm afraid that was the case all over the island. I didn't see any of the Japs go down."

The machine gun was reloaded and its muzzle tilted toward the sky just in case the Japanese came back. The rain had stopped now, the squall moving on at the same speed with which it had come, and the clouds were breaking up overhead. If the Japs returned, they wouldn't be able to hide their approach quite so easily.

And they *would* be back, Adam thought as he looked at the black smoke rising from the air station and, beyond that, from the civilian installations on the other side of Wake Island and on Peale

Island. The Americans had been hit hard today, damned hard, but their flag still flew over the atoll. He had a feeling that the Japanese wouldn't be satisfied until the Rising Sun had been lifted in its place.

TEN

As the tense afternoon went on, the defenders began to realize just how much damage the Japanese had really inflicted. The air station had been hit the hardest. Seven of the eight Wildcats that had been on the ground when the attack began would never fly again. The reserve fuel tank on the remaining F4F-3 had been riddled by machine gun fire, but with time, that could be repaired. Of the four planes that had been in the air, one had seriously damaged its propeller on landing, when its pilot had been unable to avoid some debris thrown onto the strip by the explosions. That left only three of the Wildcats flightworthy, and that was hardly enough to fight off any further air strikes by the Japanese.

In addition, the destruction of the huge avgas tank and its contents was a crippling blow. Fuel supplies for the planes that could still fly would be low, severely restricting their range.

Telephone lines were down all over the island. Major Bayler's communications shack had been hit hard by bomb fragments. For the time being, Wake was effectively cut off from the outside world.

But the worst toll was in human lives. Fully half of VMF-211's personnel had been wiped out and a dozen more men were wounded, giving the unit more than sixty percent casualties. Of the men who were killed, two were pilots, and Lieutenant Conderman was wounded so seriously that he was not expected to survive the night. The squadron's commander, Major Putnam, was wounded but less severely, along with two other pilots in the same condition. Most of the dead were members of the ground crews.

The wounded were taken in jeeps and trucks to the hospital built by the civilian contractors at Camp Two. The hospital's two wards were soon packed and its operating room was in full-time operation, as battalion surgeon Lieutenant (jg) Gustave M. Kahn, USN, and the civilian physician, Dr. Lawton M. Shank, did their best to patch up the flood of patients.

The Pan Am Airways *Philippine Clipper* had been struck quite a few times by Japanese strafing, but none of the bullets had done any major damage. The big airliner was still capable of flight. For a short time, some consideration was given to using it as a patrol plane to search for the Japanese fleet, but that idea soon was abandoned. At least ten of Pan Am's native employees had been killed at the hotel, and the remaining employees were anxious to get off the island, along with the passengers on the ill-fated flight. Commander Cunningham gave his permission for those civilians to be evacuated, and at 1250 the clipper rose once more from the lagoon, carrying its original passengers and all the Pan Am employees who were not so badly wounded that they were unable to travel.

Adam and the rest of his squad, stationed at the .50-caliber machine gun halfway up the island, didn't know the details of everything that was going on, but they heard rumors during the afternoon as men from other squads came by their position on various errands. Around the middle of the afternoon, a truck with the company CO riding in the passenger seat dropped off a large pile of burlap bags and a roll of camouflage netting. "Fill those sandbags and stack them higher around the gun," the CO ordered, "then rig that netting."

"Aye, aye, sir," Adam responded. The CO sketched a salute as the truck roared on down the island.

Adam and his men got to work. A short time later, more clouds gathered overhead, and a chilly breeze began to blow. The men, who had been sweating earlier, now began to shiver as the wind hit uniforms that were still damp from the earlier rain.

Some of the fires had been put out, and the thick, choking pall of smoke that had hung over the atoll earlier had begun to blow away. From his position, Adam could see bulldozers lumbering down the runways at the air station a few hundred yards away. They were trying to clear all the bombing debris off the runways. More bulldozers were gouging out giant furrows in the earth and throwing up walls of dirt to serve as revetments for the remaining airplanes. Ed Collins, Adam's friend from basic training who had been raised on a farm in Iowa, would have called that locking the barn door after the fucking horse was gone, Adam thought wryly. Still, it was a good idea to protect the planes they had as much as possible.

Once the new sandbags had been stacked around the gun emplacement, they formed a three-sided wall that was too high to see over, with the open end pointed inland. Adam had Kennemer, the lightest member of the squad, climb onto the wall of sandbags and stretch out there to keep watch. Rolofson and Stout chopped branches off some of the squat trees nearby and stuck them between the sandbags, then spread the camouflage netting and threw it over the branches so that it formed a roof of sorts over the gun emplacement. The idea was that from the air a Japanese pilot might not notice the gun in time and fly right over it, in which case the .50-caliber rounds would rip out the belly of his plane.

Adam found himself hoping they would get their chance to do just that. Wake's defenders had absorbed a hell of a lot of punishment today. The next time, he hoped grimly, it would be their turn to give some back.

As evening settled down over the island, a cold drizzle began to fall. The camouflage netting provided a little protection, but not much. Adam sat down with his back against one of the walls of sandbags and resigned himself to spending a wet, miserable night in the gun emplacement. No one was going to be relieved tonight; they would be on duty all the way through until morning.

Gurnwall sat down beside him and lit a cigarette. Adam shook his head when Gurnwall offered the pack to him. "Cuts down on the wind," Adam said.

Gurnwall grunted. "I ain't worried about having to run very far. Anywhere you go out here, right there's the fuckin' ocean."

Gurnwall smoked in silence for a moment, then said quietly, "Listen, Corp, about what happened up there on the water tank—"

"Forget about it, Gurney." Adam was in no mood to sit here and listen to Gurnwall's apologies. Even though Kennemer, Rolofson, and Stout weren't paying any attention to what Gurnwall was saying, and even though they probably couldn't have heard the Oklahoman's low-pitched voice anyway over the incessant pounding of the surf, Adam didn't see any reason for them to know about Gurnwall's near panic during the air raid. That could cause dissension within the squad. "Just don't let it happen again."

"I won't, Corp. I'll pull my share of the load. You'll see."

Adam nodded. "I know you will."

Actually, he wasn't sure of that at all. Gurnwall had frozen under pressure once. He might do it again. Adam frowned as he thought about it. Maybe he shouldn't have told Gurnwall to keep quiet. Maybe it would be better if the other guys knew what had happened, so they'd know not to rely too much on Gurnwall. In war, if you put your trust in somebody, he could freeze up at the wrong time and get you killed.

This was the sort of thing that officers had to deal with, Adam thought. Maybe that wasn't so good after all. There was something to be said for being an enlisted man and just following orders. . . .

The engines of the bulldozers, front-loaders, and other heavy equipment growled and stuttered all night as, working in cold, wet darkness, the remaining personnel of VMF-211 and a good number of the civilian construction workers labored to provide shelter for the remaining airplanes. By morning, enough revetments had been erected to house the three undamaged Wildcats, plus the two that had sustained damage but were repairable. After the planes had been rolled into their bunkers, mechanics went to work patching the punctured reserve fuel tank on one and the wrecked propeller on the other. All of the heavy construction equipment that wasn't being used was parked on the runway so that it could not be used in case the Japanese tried to land an airborne invasion.

Telephone service had been restored between most points on the atoll. Most of the trunks were wired in parallel, in hopes that if something happened to one line, the other would remain intact. Some of the lines were being buried underground where they would be safer, but that was slow going.

More digging was going on in other places. Anyone who wasn't already working on some other task, including many of the civilians, grabbed a shovel and started gouging foxholes and crude dugouts into the coral. Most of the tents and lightweight huts that had housed the atoll's inhabitants had been destroyed in the attack, and those that remained offered precious little shelter in the event of another raid. All three islands would soon be honeycombed with holes.

Inevitably, Dr. Kahn and Dr. Shank lost some of their patients. When they did, the bodies were moved to a large refrigerated room in one of the construction company's warehouses. There they joined the rows of canvas-shrouded corpses, men who had been killed outright in the Japanese attack. There was no time for burial details now. The dead would have to wait in this makeshift mortuary.

In the northernmost .50-caliber machine gun installation of Battery E, Adam jerked awake as General Quarters sounded at 0500. Somehow during the attack, the wiring for the loudspeakers scattered around the atoll had remained intact, and they had been working all the time. Adam took off his helmet and scrubbed a hand over his face. He hadn't realized that he'd fallen asleep.

Magruder grinned at him from the opposite wall of sandbags. "Morning, Corporal."

"Damn it, somebody should have woken me."

"We figured you needed your rest," Stout put in. "Besides, if them Japanese'd come back, there'd've been enough commotion to wake you up, I reckon."

Adam had to grin and nod in agreement. "You're probably right," he said. "About the commotion, I mean."

Gurnwall was asleep, too, huddled on his side against the sandbags a few feet away. He was snoring lightly. Rolofson was at the gun, his hands on the trigger grips. Adam looked around and didn't see the other member of the squad.

"Where's Kennemer?"

Magruder jerked a thumb toward the brush outside the gun emplacement. "Went to take a leak."

"Somebody ought to be up there on watch." Adam started to his feet, but before he could get up, Kennemer hurried back into the sandbag bunker, buttoning his trousers.

"Sorry," he muttered. "I'll get back to my post, Corporal."

Adam straightened and put a hand on the smaller man's shoulder to stop him. "Were you up there all night, Kennemer?"

"Well, yeah, I guess so."

"Take a break. I'll watch for a while."

"You sure, Corporal?"

"Yeah, don't worry about it."

Adam climbed awkwardly onto the front wall of sandbags and stretched out on top of it. He was a lot bigger than Kennemer, so it wasn't easy to maneuver his body into a halfway comfortable position. The camouflage netting was only a couple of inches above his head, so he had to hold his neck in such a way that the muscles soon began to ache.

It was still a half hour or more until dawn. The rain had stopped, and the sky had lightened enough in the east so that Adam could tell the clouds had gone away. The waves were pounding as usual at the reef, but beyond that the Pacific was calm and empty. It would be a beautiful morning on Wake Island—if not for all the signs of death and destruction everywhere a person looked.

A truck came to a stop on the road not far from the bunker, and a cheery voice called out, "Room service!"

"Hey!" Stout shouted. "Bring it on in here!"

Adam turned his head and saw a couple of enlisted men come into the bunker carrying a cardboard box and a couple of thermoses. He recognized the men as workers from the mess hall and realized they were bringing breakfast to the Marines manning the defense installations around the island. One of them unscrewed the cap from a thermos, and Adam suddenly smelled hot coffee. The pang of need that went through him when that aroma hit his nostrils was almost painful.

The other man opened the box and started passing around doughnuts. "No powdered eggs and toast this morning, boys," he announced. "Eat hearty, compliments of Uncle Sam and Major Devereux."

Gurnwall was awake now. He looked up, saw Adam on the sandbags, and said, "Hey, Corp, c'mon down and get some of these goodies."

"You go ahead, Gurney," Adam said. "I'll keep my eyes open for visitors."

That cost him quite an effort, especially since the smell of the coffee was so strong and so tantalizing. A few minutes later, Magruder climbed halfway up the wall of sandbags and handed Adam a tin cup. "Careful, it's hot," Magruder warned.

Adam took the cup, propped himself up on his elbows as best he could, and blew on the black liquid in the cup to cool it. When he took a sip a few moments later, it was pure heaven.

"I love the java jive, and it loves me," Gurnwall sang. He seemed to be his usual cocky self again this morning. Adam was glad to see that.

By the time he had slowly drunk the first cup of coffee, Magruder had finished a couple of cups and a pair of doughnuts. He said, "Come on down, Corporal, and I'll take your place. You better get some of those sinkers before Gurney eats them all."

"Hey!" Gurnwall protested. "I'm just eatin' my share."

Adam slid his legs off the sandbags and dropped the rest of the way to the ground inside the bunker. Magruder climbed up and settled down where he had been. Adam picked up one of the thermoses and refilled his cup, then snagged one of the doughnuts from the box. The men from the mess hall had left, continuing on their rounds.

As Adam hunkered on his heels to eat, Stout licked sugar from his fingers and said, "Man, if I'd known all it took to get us some doughnuts was a Japanese air raid, I'd've told 'em to come visitin' earlier."

"Hell, I wonder how bad we'd have to get shot up for them to give us some cake and ice cream," Gurnwall said solemnly.

Adam burst out laughing. He couldn't help it. The others joined in, and as he looked around at them, he couldn't help but see something new on their faces. They were tired, sure, and they were scared, too, and thinking of friends who had been killed in the Japanese attack. But they could still laugh. Even though they'd had only a brief taste of combat, it had hardened them, toughened their spirits so that it took more to get them down than it had even a day earlier. They had come through the fire once and were stronger for it.

Adam's smile faded. Before their time on Wake Island was over, he thought, they would have a lot more chances to grow battle-hardened.

And a lot more chances to die.

ELEVEN

The village was called Bovington and was south of London, not far from the coast. Just outside the village was Bovington Camp, the army base where the British Armour School was located. Joe and Dale Parker were staying there while they instructed their British counterparts in the use and maintenance of the M3 General Grant tanks which the United States had shipped over. As part of a detachment from the United States Army, Joe and Dale had made the dangerous Atlantic crossing with the convoy carrying the tanks and other war supplies bound for England as part of President Franklin D. Roosevelt's Lend-Lease Program. They had stayed to teach the British everything they had learned about the tanks during their own training at Camp Bowie, Brownwood, Texas. Several months had gone by since their arrival, and Joe and Dale and the other American instructors expected to get new orders any day now, telling them to come home to the United States.

In the meantime, during their off-duty hours, the Yanks enjoyed the hospitality of their hosts.

Joe and Dale strolled down the cobblestone street toward their original destination, a pub called the Oaken Barrel. "Uh-oh," Dale said when they were still a block away. "There's Royce. He just went in the Barrel."

"Ignore him," Joe said.

"That's easy for you to say. You don't have him in your face all day acting like he's so damned smart."

Joe didn't say anything, but he had to suppress a grin. His

brother Dale had never been the shy, retiring type, and more often than not, Dale thought he was smarter than anyone else around, especially when it came to engines. Now, in the person of Corporal Jeremy Royce, Dale was getting some of his own back.

"We're not here to get into trouble," Joe reminded Dale. "The sarge will have our heads if we get into a brawl."

"Yeah, yeah, I know." Dale jerked his head toward the warm glow coming through the windows of the Oaken Barrel. "I promise to behave. Come on."

Places like this must smell roughly the same the world over, Joe thought as he and Dale entered the pub. The most prevalent odors were of beer and tobacco smoke, and underlying them was a fainter mixture of disinfectant and perfume. Fainter still, he could smell urine and vomit. No matter how hard people tried, it seemed, nobody could completely rid a tavern or a pub or a beer joint of those smells.

Conversation and laughter came from the tables, the booths along the walls, and the island bar in the center of the room, punctuated by sporadic *thunks* as thrown darts bit into the dartboards hung on the walls. The lights in here were dim and made more so by the thick layer of smoke floating in the air. Joe told himself to be careful and watch out for flying darts.

A glance around revealed to Dale that he and Joe weren't the only American servicemen in the place. He saw several of the instructors who were stationed at the British army base and tank range, as well as a few boys from the U.S. Army Air Corps who were working with the RAF. Mostly, though, the patrons of the Oaken Barrel consisted of British troops and a scattering of civilians. A bald man with a sweeping handlebar mustache wore a white apron and worked behind the bar; half a dozen young Englishwomen carried drinks on trays to the tables and booths. As one of them, an attractive twenty-year-old with auburn hair, passed close by Joe and Dale, she smiled at them and called over the hubbub, "Hello, lads."

"Hi, Audrey," Dale said. He pointed at one of the few vacant tables. "We'll be over there."

"Be right with you," Audrey promised.

As they made their way to the table, Joe noted with satisfaction that it was clear across the room from where Corporal Royce was sitting with some friends. Royce didn't appear to have noticed them.

"See," Joe said when they were sitting down, "you can just pretend that Royce isn't here."

Dale snorted. "Yeah, sure. You know that limey bastard had the balls today to tell me he can strip down an engine faster than I can! Can you imagine?"

Joe leaned forward and said, "What I can't imagine is why you'd talk like that in the middle of an English pub. Keep it down, damn it."

Dale grimaced and muttered something Joe couldn't understand. Just as well, Joe thought. It wasn't anything he wanted to hear, anyway.

Dale seemed to have gotten away with his crack about "limey bastards" without anyone noticing. Joe was grateful for that. A few minutes later, the barmaid called Audrey showed up at their table, her tray held down by her side. She smiled and asked, "What can I get you lads?"

"Stout," Joe said, and Dale nodded.

"Back in a mo'," Audrey said. She turned and headed for the bar, making her way among the tables with smiles and friendly remarks for the customers sitting at them.

Soon after arriving in England, Joe and Dale had learned that it didn't do any good to ask for a cold beer. There didn't seem to be such a thing in this country. Dale had complained on numerous occasions that he would never get used to drinking warm beer, no matter how long he was over here. The stout was pretty potent stuff, especially warm, but Joe didn't mind. That meant he and Dale would nurse each one longer and wind up not drinking too much. With Dale, that was a real concern.

Dale was a grown man, a soldier, Joe reminded himself. He didn't have to play mother hen to his little brother anymore, the way he had done for years back in Chicago.

Of course, maybe if he had kept an even closer eye on him, Dale wouldn't have gotten involved with a married woman—a married woman whose husband was one of the most powerful bankers in the Midwest. The crap had piled up high and in a hurry after that, until it seemed as if the only thing Joe and Dale could do to help their family was to get out of Chicago, as fast and as far away as possible.

Joining the Army had taken care of that problem, and now they were far away, all right. All the way across the Atlantic, in jolly old England, which sometimes didn't seem very jolly anymore after the way the Nazis had pounded it with bombs. At least they didn't have to worry too much about what was going on at home, Joe told himself. His mother's letters had assured her sons that the banker Victor Mason had kept his word. There hadn't been any more trouble.

Dale took a pack of Luckies from his pocket, tapped one out, and lipped it. He dug out his Ronson and spun the wheel, then held the flame to the cigarette. With practiced ease he snapped the lighter closed and blew out a cloud of smoke.

"Where's those drinks?"

"Keep your shirt on," Joe told him. "Audrey'll bring 'em as soon as she can."

To tell the truth, Joe was glad that Audrey was waiting on them tonight. She was sweet and friendly and undeniably pretty. Joe realized he had a bit of a crush on her. Nothing could ever come of it, of course.

Dale's tastes in women ran more toward the tall, blond barmaid named Tess, who was working on the other side of the room. Tess was only as good as she had to be, and Joe had no illusions about what had gone on the times when Dale had walked her back to her flat after she got off work at the Oaken Barrel. Joe was pretty sure no money had changed hands—Tess wasn't a *whore,* after all—but she *was* a tramp.

He had no right to judge her or any of these other people whose country had been under siege by the Germans, Joe reminded himself. Besides, he was just a guy from the South Side of Chicago. He didn't have any business feeling superior to anybody, despite the fact that he'd gone to college and sold some stories to the pulps.

Audrey brought the glasses of stout to the table and set them in front of Joe and Dale. "You'll be runnin' a tab?" she asked.

"Sure," Dale replied before Joe could say anything. Joe had hoped they could have one drink and then head back to the base, but obviously Dale had something else in mind.

"You be sure and let me know if there's anything else I can do for you," Audrey said.

Dale gave her a lecherous grin and wiggled his eyebrows up and down like Groucho Marx. "I can think of a few things."

She threatened to hit him with the tray and said, "Go on with you, you bloody Yank," but she was grinning.

When Audrey was gone, Joe said, "You shouldn't tease her like that."

"Why not? It's all in fun, and she likes it." Dale sucked some of the foam off the top of his glass, then said, "Besides, maybe one of these days she'll give me a chance to show her a good time."

Joe pushed his glass aside with the stout untouched and said, "Don't joke about that."

"Who's jokin'?" Dale did the Groucho eyebrows again. "I'm perfectly serious."

"Well, you can forget about it. Audrey's a nice girl."

"Too nice for a bum like me, but not too nice for you, is that it?"

"I didn't say that," Joe said.

"But that's what you meant. You'd jump into bed with her if you had half a chance, but I'm not supposed to."

"Just forget it." Joe reached for his glass of stout.

"No, I'm not going to forget it," Dale said, angry now. "How come you didn't gripe at me when I made a play for Tess?"

"Tess is different—"

"You mean she's trampy enough for me, but I'm supposed to keep my distance from a *lady* like Audrey. Well, in case you haven't noticed, pal, Audrey's workin' in this place, too."

Joe shook his head. "I don't want to argue with you. Just forget I said anything."

Dale leaned back and crossed his arms. "No, I won't forget it," he said with a glare. "You got the hots for her yourself, so you start makin' noises like some sort of sanctimonious, self-righteous—"

"Where'd you learn a word like sanctimonious?"

Dale's eyes widened. "Now you're callin' me dumb!"

Joe closed his eyes and rubbed his temples. "Just . . . forget . . . it," he said. "I didn't mean anything."

"The hell you didn't." Dale glowered at Joe as he picked up his glass and took a long drink of the stout, making a face at its bitterness. He set the glass down and said, "Maybe what we ought to do is make a little bet on who can get into Audrey's bed first."

"No!" Joe had seen the way Dale operated and knew his brother too well to even consider such a thing, even if it hadn't been so demeaning to Audrey.

"Yeah," Dale went on, "I think that's a damned good idea—"

"Take your hands off me, you bloody git!"

The sharp words, spoken in an angry female voice, cut through the babble in the room and made heads jerk around all over the place. Joe and Dale looked, too, and saw blond Tess trying to pull away from the grip of a British soldier who had stood up from one of the tables and taken hold of her arm. Joe tensed as he saw that the soldier accosting Tess was Jeremy Royce.

"Come on, girl; all I asked you was how much it'd cost me for a tumble. That's your real line o' work, ain't it?"

Across the room, Dale said, "Son of a bitch," and flattened his palms on the table, ready to push himself to his feet.

"No!" Joe said. "Stay out of it, Dale. Tess can take care of herself, and anyway, here comes Harp."

The bald, mustachioed man was coming out from behind the bar. His arms bulged with muscles.

Tess didn't wait for his help, though. She said, "Oh!" and swung her empty tray, smacking it into the side of Jeremy Royce's head.

The blow landed solidly, but Royce just moved one step to the side and then recovered his balance. His left hand still gripped Tess's right arm. He said, "You filthy slut!" and slapped her across the face with his right hand.

That was it, Joe thought. There would be no holding Dale back now.

In fact, Dale was already on his feet, and even though the bartender Harp was closer, Dale got there first, shouting, "Royce!"

Royce turned toward him just in time to catch the punch Dale threw flush on the jaw.

TWELVE

Dale put all his strength into the punch; he was moving forward quickly, which increased his momentum. The perfectly timed blow knocked Royce loose from Tess and sent the British soldier sprawling backward across a table. Beer and ale, whiskey and wine, all flew wildly through the air as glasses overturned and shattered. Tess and several other women screamed, and men shouted angrily.

Joe saw it all unfold, but it was happening too fast for him to do much about it. One of the soldiers with whom Royce had been sitting grabbed Dale's shoulder, hauled him around, and sank a fist in his belly. Dale's eyes bulged, and he doubled over in pain. The Tommie clouted him in the head. Dale fell to the floor.

Audrey was beside Joe, clutching at his arm and saying, "You're not going to let him do that to your brother, are you?"

Under other circumstances, Joe might have felt that Dale had gotten what was coming to him. But Dale had been trying to defend a woman—maybe not a lady, but still a woman—and Joe couldn't fault him for that.

"No," Joe said as he reached up, took off his overseas cap, and tucked it behind his belt. "I'm not."

A second later, as he was about to tackle from behind the British soldier who had knocked Dale down, somebody else in the crowd tackled Joe instead. "Bloody Yank!" the man shouted as he rode Joe to the floor and drove a knee into his back. Joe gasped in pain, then jabbed his right elbow back, driving it into the man's belly. The man grunted, and breath laden with whiskey fumes swirled around Joe's head. He got his knees under him and threw the man off.

The soldier he'd been about to tackle heard the commotion and swung around. The man saw Joe on the floor and said, "Another one, eh?" He drew back his foot for a kick.

Joe threw his hands up and caught the man's boot, then heaved as hard as he could. The soldier let out a surprised yelp as he went over backward and crashed on top of another table, collapsing it in a welter of shattered wood, broken glass, and spilled drink.

"Hey!" an American voice yelled. "Let's help those GIs!"

Joe stumbled to his feet. He had gone his entire life, twenty-two years, without getting into a bar fight, and now this was the second one in less than a year. Back in the spring, while they were in basic training at Camp Bowie, he and Dale had gotten mixed up in a brawl in a tavern in Abilene, Texas. They'd had friends backing them up in that fight, and it was the same here. Most of the American servicemen in the Oaken Barrel were scrambling to help.

But the British soldiers were waiting for them, and in a matter of seconds the formerly sedate pub was filled with chaos and violence. All the resentment the natives felt for their uncouth visitors from across the Atlantic came boiling out, and as for the Americans, they relished the chance to take the stuffed-shirt Brits down a notch or two.

It was one hell of a fight, they all agreed later, sitting around nursing their cuts and bruises.

For now, all Joe wanted to do was find Dale and make sure neither of them was trampled to death. Through the melee, he caught sight of Dale trying to get to his feet and shouldered aside a couple of men who were wrestling with each other. He stumbled over to Dale and caught hold of his brother's arm. Thinking that an enemy had grabbed him, Dale tried to pull free, then looked up and recognized Joe.

"You *had* to throw a punch!" Joe said over the racket of the brawl as he helped Dale to his feet.

A thread of blood ran down Dale's chin from the corner of his mouth. He grinned and said, "Yeah, I did. Did you see what that bastard Royce did to Tess?"

That reminded him of Tess, and he looked around for her. Joe searched for Audrey, since with the way the fight was spreading through the pub, she might be in danger, too. He caught a glimpse of auburn hair and saw Audrey lift her head to peek over the bar. She ducked back down as a beer mug came sailing through the air near her. Joe hoped that Tess and the other barmaids had taken shelter behind the bar as well.

He tugged on Dale's arm and yelled, "Let's get out of here!"

"The hell with that! I want Royce!"

Dale pulled away from Joe. Joe tried to grab him again but failed. He plunged after him as Dale threw himself into the crowd of punching, flailing, staggering men.

The bartender, Harp, stood in the center of the fight, bellowing for everyone to stop, until somebody brought down a chair over his head. That staggered him but didn't make him fall. Roaring in anger, he started flailing around him with his long, powerful arms, striking out at Brits and Americans alike, not caring who he hit.

As struggling men crashed into Joe, he dodged punches, kept his feet somehow, and stayed behind Dale. Dale spotted Royce and called the Englishman's name. As Royce turned toward him, Dale swung an uppercut that missed when Royce jerked his chin back. Off balance, Dale stumbled. Royce hit him.

Joe stepped in from the side, hooking a left into Royce's belly and taking him by surprise. Joe followed with a right jab that rocked Royce's head back. Dale had recovered enough to join in. He yelled and lunged at Royce, getting his hands around the Englishman's neck. Royce swayed back and ran into a table. Dale bent him over it, tightening his grip on Royce's throat. Royce flailed at Dale, but the punches didn't have much power behind them now. Not enough to knock Dale away from him, anyway. Royce's eyes began to bulge as if they were going to crawl right out of their sockets.

The last thing they needed was for Dale to kill the son of a bitch, Joe thought. He got his arms around Dale's waist and locked the fingers of his right hand around his left wrist. He pulled back as hard as he could, tearing Dale away from Royce. "Stop it!" Joe shouted into Dale's ear. "You're going to kill him!"

"Damn right I'm gonna kill him!" Dale howled. "He's got it comin'!"

He swung his arms in Royce's direction but couldn't reach the British soldier because Joe was holding him back. Royce, his face an ugly brick-red, leaned over the table and coughed and hacked. His lips drew back in a snarl and he shot a murderous glance at Dale.

The sudden shrilling of whistles sliced through the chaos in the pub. American MPs, their British counterparts, and even a few local policemen came into the room, quickly putting a stop to the brawl. "Break it up! Break it up, gahddammit!" one of the MPs shouted with a Texas twang in his voice. Gradually, silence fell over the scene of battle, except for some panting and groaning from battered men who were trying to catch their breath.

"All you dogfaces and flyboys get your asses over there next to that wall!" the MP from Texas ordered. "Move, damn it!"

Slowly, grudgingly, the American servicemen sorted themselves out from their opponents and shuffled over to the far wall of the pub. Joe and Dale went along with the others. Joe's back hurt where he had been kneed, and he was afraid he might be pissing blood for a few days. That was his only real injury, though. Dale was going to have a nice shiner around his left eye, which was already swollen halfway shut. His lips were bruised and puffy, too.

Everybody was a little the worse for wear. Even the barmaids were disheveled from scrambling behind the bar when the fight broke out

The Texan MP walked back and forth in front of the soldiers he had lined up against the wall. "You boys like to got yourselves in a world o' trouble," he said. "The brass don't like it when you go to squabblin' with our hosts." The man's lean face grew more grim and solemn as he rubbed at his left eyebrow for a moment.

"You're lucky," he went on, now with a bitter edge to his voice. "The high command's got other things to worry about right now. They ain't got time to fret over a bunch o' kids fightin' in a sandbox, which is just about all that this shit amounts to."

The Texan had a 1st lieutenant's silver bar on his collar. Knowing that it might just get him some more chewing out, Joe asked, "Lieutenant, what's wrong?"

"Wrong?" the Texan repeated. "You wanta know what's wrong, Private?"

"Yes, sir," Joe said, ignoring Dale's warning look.

"Well, then, I'll tell you."

Joe realized at that moment that there were tears in the MP's eyes. The Texan was crying about something, and with a cold feeling in his belly, Joe decided whatever it was, it didn't have anything to do with this bar fight.

"Y'all'll hear about it soon enough, anyway," the Texan went on. "Everybody will. We got word a little while ago that the Japs attacked Pearl Harbor. That's in Hawaii. Bombed the hell out of the place."

There was utter silence in the pub as he stopped talking. Joe stared at the MP lieutenant, sure there must have been some sort of mistake but knowing at the same time that there wasn't.

"Maybe it ain't official yet," the Texan said, "but we're at war, son."

From the other side of the room, one of the British soldiers said, "Welcome to the club, Yank. Now you bloody well know what it feels like."

THIRTEEN

Kenneth Walker sat at the desk, papers littered in front of him. He was a blond young man in his early twenties, handsome as a matinee idol and built like he played halfback on the University of Chicago football team. That was appropriate since this tiny office was one of a rat's warren of chambers buried underneath the grass of Amos Alonzo Stagg Field, on the UC campus.

Kenneth was wearing reading glasses, but they didn't help much. He had been at this work for so long that the numbers stretched across the pages in complicated mathematical formulae were all running together. Kenneth took off the glasses, dropped them on the desk, leaned back against the wooden chair in which he sat, and rubbed his eyes in weariness.

He wondered what time it was. He hoped he hadn't lost an entire day again, misplaced it like some forgotten trinket.

The office door was open a few inches, enough so that Kenneth was able to hear the footsteps coming down the corridor. He straightened in the chair. He had thought that he was alone in the laboratory complex under the football field. Alone, that is, except for the guards who were always on duty, hard-faced men who reminded Kenneth of soldiers except for the fact that they wore plain clothes. Like soldiers, though, they carried guns. More than once, Kenneth had caught a glimpse of Colt .45 automatics in shoulder holsters under their coats.

The person approaching the office had to be either one of the guards or someone the guards had allowed down here. The footsteps paused outside the office, and Kenneth came to his feet.

Despite the fact that he knew there was nothing to worry about, he felt a little nervous.

The sad-faced man who pushed open the door was short and stocky, with close-cropped, receding dark hair. He looked startled when he saw Kenneth standing there behind the desk.

"Ken," he said, "what are you doing here?"

"Hello, Dr. Fermi," Kenneth said. He gestured toward the desk and its confusion of papers. "I was just going over some of these calculations."

"On a Sunday evening?"

Kenneth shrugged. "I knew it would be quiet and I could work." He paused, then added, "Anyway, *you're* here."

Dr. Enrico Fermi smiled, making him look considerably less solemn. "Yes, and I could be home with my wife. She won't soon let me forget that. But something was nagging at my brain concerning that last set of numbers. I suspect the same thing may have been bothering you."

Kenneth felt relieved. For a while there, he had thought he was losing his mind because he was convinced that something was off in the numbers. Now his instinct had been confirmed by the man who was quite possibly the leading atomic physicist in the entire world.

A few months earlier Dr. Fermi, professor of physics at Columbia University in New York, had come to Chicago to work on a special project for the government. That project was being carried out in the labs here under Stagg Field, and Kenneth, a graduate student in physics at UC, had become, through a strange set of circumstances, one of Fermi's assistants. Once he had accidentally discovered the project, Kenneth had had to decide whether to become part of it or sit in some mental hospital for the next few years, imprisoned there as a security risk. That had been an easy choice. Even without the threat of being locked away, Kenneth would have jumped at the chance to work with Fermi.

The physicist came around the desk and waved Kenneth back into the chair. "Sit down; sit down. Show me what you've come up with."

Kenneth's tiredness vanished. He put on his glasses and picked up a pencil. "Here," he said, using the pencil to point at the formula he meant. "I think the exponents are wrong in this equation."

Fermi stood beside the chair and frowned as he studied the numbers Kenneth had written on the paper. After a moment, he said, "You're on the right track, but that's not quite it." He pointed. "Try squaring this one, but raise this one to the fourth power."

Kenneth leaned over the desk and his pencil fairly flew as he rewrote the equation. He stared at it for a long moment, then shook his head. "No, I don't think so." Caught up in the beauty of the math, he forgot for a second who he was talking to. "It'll never work that way."

Fermi shrugged. "Perhaps you're right."

Kenneth caught his breath as an idea came to him. The pencil in his hand began scratching on the paper again. "But if we raise this number to the third power, and take the cube root here on the other side of the equation . . ."

Fermi leaned forward. "That's it!"

Kenneth finished writing the equation, then with a slash of the pencil drew a dark line underneath the formula. "It works!" he said.

"I believe it does." Fermi straightened and patted him on the shoulder. "You should be proud of yourself."

"I can't believe I worked on that for so long. It's so simple!"

"Problems always are, once you've solved them." Fermi walked around to the front of the desk. "Now that you've worked that out, we can both go home. I'm sure you want to be with your family on a day like today."

Kenneth set the pencil on the desk and took off his glasses again. "Excuse me, Doctor? What do you mean, on a day like today?"

"Well, what with the news and all . . ." Fermi stopped when he saw the blank look on Kenneth's face. "You haven't heard?"

"Heard what?"

Fermi frowned. "How long have you been working here, Ken?"

"Today, you mean?"

"That's right."

Kenneth thought about it. "Let's see, I came in about five o'clock . . ."

"This afternoon?"

"No, in the morning."

"My God! You've been here all day? You haven't gone out or talked to anyone?"

Kenneth shook his head. His stomach growled. "I guess it must have been quite a while, all right. I'm starting to get hungry. What time is it?"

"Almost eight o'clock. You've been here fifteen hours."

"It didn't really seem that long." Kenneth came out from behind the desk. "You said something about some news, Dr. Fermi. . . ."

The physicist looked more grim than Kenneth had ever seen him. "The Japanese bombed the naval base at Pearl Harbor this morning. Well, about the middle of the day our time, I should say."

"Bombed?"

Fermi nodded. "That's right. It was a sneak attack, a terrible thing. From what I hear, they destroyed a lot of our Pacific fleet."

Kenneth blinked rapidly and thought about what he had just heard. It seemed impossible. Bombing was what went on in war, and the United States wasn't at war.

And yet, he knew that the work on which he and Dr. Fermi and the other scientists were engaged had something to do with some sort of super-weapon. No country built a super-weapon unless it was threatened with war.

He thought suddenly of his friends Adam Bergman and Catherine Tancred. They had enlisted in the military earlier in the year, Adam in the Marines and Catherine in the Navy Nurse Corps. Kenneth hadn't heard from them directly, but Joe Parker had mentioned them in his letters. Adam and Catherine were somewhere in the Pacific, Kenneth recalled. Catherine might even be stationed at Pearl Harbor; he wasn't sure about that.

"That . . . that's impossible. Why would they do that?"

"It's just been a matter of time, Kenneth. Did you know, when I got the call from Stockholm telling me I'd won the Nobel Prize in physics, it was the day after Kristellnacht? Once the Japanese allied themselves with that madman Hitler . . ." Fermi drew a deep breath. "My wife is Jewish. If we hadn't gotten out of Italy when we did and come to this country, there's no way of knowing what might have happened to us. The Fascists make no secret of how they feel about the Jews."

"I'm sorry, sir."

"Don't be," Fermi said, his voice brisk again. "We're doing important work here, vital work. Especially with a war coming on. And right now I'd say we're in one."

That was true. The United States wouldn't stand for being attacked like that. All the rumors and rumblings of the past couple of years were now coming true. America was going to war.

Kenneth turned toward the desk. His fingers fumbled for the pencil. "I think I'll work a while longer," he said. "There are a few other spots where I think the theoretical reaction could be a little smoother—"

The pencil snapped as his fingers clenched on it.

He stared down at the broken pencil for a second; then his fingers opened and the two pieces dropped onto the floor. Fermi came a step closer and put a hand on Kenneth's arm.

"You're upset, of course. That's natural enough. The whole country is upset. But on a night like this, you don't need to be stuck in a little cave of an office like this. You need to be with people. Go home to your family. Or come with me. My wife can put on a pot of coffee, and we'll talk about the project or anything else you'd like."

"Thank you, sir, but I'll be all right." Kenneth took a deep breath, then bent over and picked up the broken pencil. He tossed the pieces on the desk. "Don't worry about me. I'm fine."

"You're sure?"

Kenneth nodded. "Positive."

Fermi looked at him for a moment, then tilted his head to the side. "If you're sure. Come on; I'll walk out with you."

"You go ahead," Kenneth said quickly. He waved a hand toward the desk. "I want to clean up this mess. Besides, those calculations need to be locked up in the files."

"That's true. All right, then. Good night, Kenneth. And good work on that formula."

"Thank you, sir."

Fermi paused at the door. "You're sure?" he asked again.

"Of course."

Fermi nodded and went out. Kenneth sank into the chair and listened to the physicist's footsteps as they receded down the hallway.

Then Kenneth propped his elbows on the desk and rested his face in his hands. He was dry-eyed. The news had shocked him, but it wasn't as if war had been totally unexpected.

War. And Joe and Dale, Adam and Catherine, were all out there somewhere, in the faraway places of the world, facing it head-on.

While he sat here, cowering underground like a rabbit.

FOURTEEN

Mike Chastain liked to sleep late on Sunday. Hell, come right down to it, he slept late just about every day, because his work was done at night, in places like the Dells, the Empire Room, the Atlas Club, and the other gambling joints and roadhouses he frequented. So on this day it wasn't unusual that it was well after noon before he stretched and sat up and yawned. He'd been in a hot poker game the night before, and he hadn't gotten to bed until after dawn.

And then, since he'd been too jazzed up from the game to fall asleep right away, there had been Karen. . . .

He liked the starched crispness of the sheets in the hotel suite's bedroom. Some guys might go for silk, but not him. When he was growing up, his ma had always starched the sheets. That was about the only thing from his childhood he'd hung onto. The rest of it had been crap, and he was glad to forget about it.

He swung his legs out of bed and stood up, then padded barefoot over to the dressing table. His dark hair, which was normally oiled down, was now mussed up from sleep. He ran his fingers through it, looked in the mirror, and saw that he hadn't helped it much. Hell with it.

He wore the bottom half of a pair of pajamas, that was all. The room was warm from the radiator in the corner. He turned back toward the bed and looked at the shape under the covers. Karen wore the pajama top and nothing else, which meant that under those covers the shirt had probably hiked up so that she was naked from the waist down. The thought aroused Mike, and he walked over to stand beside the bed and look at her.

The mass of thick red curls was spread out in disarray around her head. She lay on her side, the left half of her face pressed against the pillow. Mike studied the curve of her right cheek. Without makeup, her skin was fair, with just the faintest scattering of freckles. Her lips were naturally red. Her mouth was open a little, but she wasn't drooling. Even in her sleep she was a classy dame, the classiest Mike had ever known. And what a set of pipes she had! Her singing packed 'em in at the Dells. Beauty, talent, brains—Karen Wells had it all.

So what was a gal like her doing with a bum like him? These days, he made enough money gambling to be able to keep his distance from all the stuff he'd been mixed up with in the past, but Karen knew the truth about him. She knew that not so long ago he'd been nothing more than a common hood, an enforcer for some of the big boys who still ran Chicago even though Capone and the other famous gangsters of the previous decade were long gone.

For some reason, she didn't care what he'd been, what he was only a whisker away from still being. Crazy as it was to think about it, he was convinced she really loved him.

He reached down, stroked her cheek. The dark eyelashes fluttered; then her eyes opened and she turned her head so that she was looking up at him, her green eyes instantly alert even though she had just woken up.

"Good morning," Mike said.

"Is it really still morning?" she asked sleepily.

The curtains were closed over the windows so that no light came into the bedroom, so he glanced at the clock on the dresser. "Nah, it's almost two."

Karen sat up and stretched, making her breasts lift against the fabric of the pajama top. Mike couldn't take his eyes off them. If Karen noticed his interest, though, she gave no sign of it. "I need some coffee and some breakfast," she said.

"Yeah, me, too," Mike said, but what he really wanted to do

was push her back down on the bed and make love to her. Time enough for that later, he told himself.

And there damned well would be, too.

He went over to the phone, picked it up, and called room service. Breakfast and a pot of coffee would be right up, yes, sir, Mr. Chastain, the guy on the other end assured him. While Mike was talking on the phone, Karen pushed back the covers and got out of bed. Yeah, naked from the waist down, just like he had thought. And as she walked toward the bathroom, she peeled the pajama top up and over her head without unbuttoning it.

God, she was beautiful.

The bathroom door closed, shutting off the view. Mike was disappointed, but he could live with it. He hung up the phone, got a gold cigarette case and lighter off the night table beside the bed, and lit a cigarette. It was one of her Players, some sort of fancy English brand, and while Mike would have preferred a Lucky or a Camel or a Chesterfield, Players were a lot classier.

Through the bathroom door, he heard the water running in the tub. He thought about Karen sitting in a tub full of bubble bath. He thought about how she would look rising from those bubbles. He took a deep draw on the cigarette and hoped the damned room service guy would hurry up.

He went into the sitting room to wait. It had a fireplace, and against the wall not far away stood a Philco radio in a big wooden cabinet with a curved top. The cabinet was polished to a high shine, and the hotel maid kept it dusted. Mike reached out and turned the black knob on the left side of the dial. It clicked, and the light came on behind the dial. It took a minute or so for the tubes to warm up.

As they did, a voice began to be heard, rising gradually in volume. Mike had hoped to get some music, but it sounded like they were giving the news instead. He reached for the knob at the other end of the dial, intending to change the station, but paused when he heard the announcer say, ". . . thought likely that a declaration of war will be announced either later today or tomorrow."

More war, was it? Mike wondered what little country Hitler

and the Nazis were trying to gobble up now. He would have thought that by this time, all the countries in Europe had already declared war on somebody.

The announcer went on, "From Pearl Harbor comes word that the U.S.S. *Arizona* has sunk, as feared. Loss of life is expected to be very high."

Pearl Harbor? Mike frowned. That was in Hawaii, wasn't it? That wasn't some little place in Europe that nobody had ever heard of.

That was *us*.

He threw the cigarette into the fireplace and leaned toward the radio. The announcer kept talking, telling about how Japanese bombers had attacked the naval base at Pearl Harbor, the army post at Schofield Barracks, and just about every other military installation on the island of Oahu. Mike's features grew taut as he listened. From what the guy was saying, the attack had taken place this morning, just a couple of hours earlier, in fact. That was why they didn't know too many details yet.

Mike turned away from the radio, leaving it playing, and went into the bedroom. The bathroom door was still closed, but the water wasn't running anymore. That meant Karen was soaking.

He threw the door open and stepped into clouds of steam. He waved an arm through the stuff and said, "Karen."

She was in the tub, all right, mounds of bubbles heaped around her. They covered her almost to her chin. She stared at him in surprise, then said, "Mike, get out of here. You know I need this time to myself—"

"Come on," he said. He yanked a big fluffy towel off a metal rack and held it out. "Wrap this around yourself. You gotta hear this."

"No! You just go on, and I'll be out in a minute."

He ignored her, stepped closer to the tub, and reached down to grab hold of her right arm. She said, "Mike, no!" as he hauled her to her feet. Water and bubbles streamed down her body, and under other circumstances he probably would have thought it was one of the most exciting things he had ever seen. Right now, though, he had other things on his mind.

With a snap of his other wrist, he shook out the towel, then wrapped it around her. "I'll carry you if I have to," he said.

She stepped out of the tub; it was obvious that she wasn't going to be able to argue with him. As she tucked the towel more securely around her, she said, "I don't like this. You could have waited until I was through. I wouldn't have minded waiting until afterward to eat breakfast—"

"This isn't about that, baby." He took hold of her arm again. "Come on."

He led her into the suite's sitting room. Her feet left dainty wet prints on the carpet as she walked. Mike marched her over to the radio, and they stood there while water still dripped from her body.

The announcer was going over all of it again, and as he said something about the Japs bombing Pearl Harbor, Karen gasped. "Pearl Harbor? But that's one of our bases."

"Yeah."

"The Japanese attacked us?"

"That's what he's saying."

Karen stared at the radio as if she could somehow see through it all the way to Pearl Harbor and witness what was going on for herself. Her breasts rose and fell under the towel as her breathing quickened.

"They can't do that!" she exclaimed after a few moments.

"Sounds like they already did."

"The bastards!" Tears began to roll down her cheeks. "All those men. Those poor boys . . ."

She turned toward Mike. He took her into his arms and held her as sobs shook her. He felt a stinging and a smarting in his own eyes, but he hadn't cried since he was a kid and he was damned if he was going to start again now, no matter what the Japs had done.

The towel around her was damp against his bare chest. He patted her back as she hiccuped against his shoulder. After several minutes she stiffened in his arms and lifted her head so that he could see her face. The sorrow that had washed over her was still there, but some of it was turning into anger.

"How dare they? How could they do such a thing?"

He shrugged. "I guess because they think they can get away with it."

"Well, they can't! We won't let them get away with it, will we, Mike?"

"A few minutes ago when I first turned on the radio, the guy was saying something about a declaration of war. We won't let 'em get away with it."

She rested her forehead against his shoulder again, so that her voice was muffled as she said, "I wish there was something we could do. . . ."

He stroked her hair. "Pearl Harbor's halfway across the Pacific Ocean. I don't know of a damned thing us or anybody else can do about it now."

"I guess not. . . ."

A knock on the door made both of them jump a little. "That'll be room service," Mike said. "I forgot about that."

Karen clutched the towel around her and hurried toward the bedroom. "I'll dry off and get dressed." The bedroom door closed with a soft slam behind her.

Mike snapped the radio off and turned toward the sitting room door as a second knock sounded. Not caring that he was half-naked, he opened it and saw a white-jacketed waiter standing there with a wheeled cart covered with a snowy white linen cloth. The cart held several covered trays, cups, plates, glasses, saucers, a pot of coffee, and a pitcher of orange juice. The waiter smiled and said, "Here you go, Mr. Chastain. Just what you wanted."

Not really, Mike thought as the guy wheeled in the cart. So far today, he hadn't gotten anything he wanted. But maybe that would change. He gave the waiter a dollar tip, shooed him off, and poured himself a cup of coffee. War meant a lot of things, and one of them was shortages of all kinds of stuff. Shortages meant

116

high demand, and Mike Chastain was a firm believer in the law of supply and demand.

Yeah, chances were there was money to be made from this. It was just a matter of figuring out the details.

Karen came out of the bedroom wearing a dressing gown. Mike poured her a glass of orange juice and handed it to her, and as he did he fingered the sleeve of her gown. Silk. The Japs were already at war with China, where most silk came from, and it was hard to get now. It sure as hell wouldn't be the only thing hard to get.

Karen said, "This is all so terrible, isn't it?"

"Yeah," Mike said. "Just terrible."

FIFTEEN

Catherine Tancred Bergman knew she probably looked like hell. She had gone almost thirty-six hours with no sleep except for a couple of catnaps snatched sitting up in a chair in the nurses' lounge. Her eyes were gritty, and she felt stale and dirty.

But there was work to do, so she kept going. The naval hospital here at Pearl Harbor had been designed to handle three hundred to four hundred patients. At times during the previous day, 7 December 1941, perhaps twice that many wounded and injured men had been crammed into the place, filling the wards, the clinics, the examining rooms, the halls, and every other bit of open space.

A strange thing had begun to happen today, however. Patients had turned up missing. Doctors and nurses found that beds which had been occupied only a short time earlier were now empty. It had taken a while, but the answer to the riddle had finally been figured out: Patients who were at all ambulatory were getting up out of bed and returning to their ships. If those ships had been sunk by Japanese bombs, the wounded men were volunteering anywhere they could in the ongoing effort to rescue those who had been trapped and clean up the mess that had been left by the air raid.

Catherine understood that attitude. Everyone was pulling together, putting their personal situations aside to work for the common good. In her case, she couldn't let herself think about her brother Spencer, who had been killed in the raid, or her husband Adam, who was stationed with the Marine 1st Defense Battalion on Wake Island. She hadn't heard anything about whether or not the Japanese had also attacked Wake, and for the time being she couldn't allow herself to worry about it.

At least, that was the idea. But Adam and Spencer were never very far from her thoughts. . . .

She was moving through one of the wards, administering injections of morphine to the most severely wounded patients, when quick footsteps sounded behind her. She looked over her shoulder to see Missy Mitchell approaching. Like Catherine and most of the other nurses, Missy had been on her feet for a long time, and she looked tired. But there was something else in her eyes, something that wasn't good.

Catherine's heart suddenly lurched, and her pulse began to race. Missy had heard something. Catherine was sure of it.

"What is it?" she asked as Missy came up to her. "Adam . . . ?"

A strand of curly brunette hair escaped from Missy's cap and fell down over her eyes. She blew it out of the way, then said, "Radio reports have started to come in from Wake. I heard a couple of the doctors talking about them. The Japs hit there yesterday just like they did here."

A sharply indrawn breath hissed between Catherine's teeth. She had to close her eyes for a second as a wave of dizziness hit her. When it passed, she opened them and looked at Missy. "Any word on casualties?"

"A lot of the men from the aviation squadron were killed, and so were some of the civilians. But the Marines came through pretty good, I think."

"You didn't hear any numbers?"

Missy shook her head and tucked the stray hair back under her white cap.

Catherine looked down at the tile floor for a moment, then nodded. "I'm going to assume he's all right, then," she said.

"Of course he's all right. He's gotta be a lucky guy; otherwise he never would have married you, right?" Missy managed to grin.

Catherine couldn't summon up an answering smile. She said,

"Thanks for letting me know, Missy," then turned back to her work. She didn't mean to be rude. She just had to concentrate on the task at hand, or everything would overwhelm her and she would break down. If that happened, she wouldn't be any good to anybody, even herself.

"Okay," Missy said. "I'll come find you if I hear anything else."

Catherine was already giving an injection to a sailor who had been so badly burned that he was bandaged up like a mummy. The painkillers he had been given earlier were starting to wear off, and he made wet little grunting noises from underneath the bandages as fresh jolts of agony wracked him. The morphine took effect quickly, and his shuddering body eased back against the sheets of the hospital bed. A sigh came from him.

Catherine felt her control start to slip as she looked down at the suffering boy. She steeled herself and moved on to the next bed.

Work to do, work to do. The refrain repeated itself endlessly in her head. *Work to do. . . .*

One of the worst things the Japanese bombers had left behind was the uncertainty. The unexpected air raid had been bad enough, but no one knew what was going to happen next. It could be something even worse. The main thing most people feared was the Japanese would invade Hawaii any time now.

After the early morning raid on 7 December, all the rest of that day, throughout the night, and on into the next day, rumors that Japanese troops were landing flew back and forth between Pearl and Honolulu and Hickam Field and Ewa, the Marine air base, and Schofield Barracks, where the Army forces were head-quartered, and every other part of the island of Oahu. The Honolulu radio stations blasted news bulletins and warnings, followed by reassurances that failed to reassure anybody. No one believed that the Japanese would attack the American fleet from the air and not follow up on their advantage with a seaborne invasion.

Nor was it likely that Pearl Harbor was the only target. News stories circulated about a Japanese fleet shelling San Francisco. Variations had the Japs bombing Los Angeles or swarming ashore at San Diego. The entire state of California was about to fall to invaders, according to some people who claimed to have heard it from a reliable source.

Honolulu's radio stations went off the air. Actually, the silence came at the request of the military leaders, who felt that the endless speculation was just fueling the growing panic. The story that Catherine heard, however, was that the radio stations had been seized by Japanese commandos who had parachuted down on them.

Navy ships that hadn't been caught inside the harbor when the bombs started to fall were still at sea, firing at each other and at civilian vessels. More than twenty-four hours after the attack, American airplanes had to dodge anti-aircraft fire from nervous gunners who thought the Jap bombers were coming back. Armed sentries brandished their rifles and screamed demands for passwords from strangers, especially those who appeared even the least bit Oriental. It was not a good time for the native population of Honolulu. One wild story claimed that Japanese fifth columnists had poisoned the city's water supply.

The waters of Pearl Harbor, coated with a film of oil escaping from bombed ships, had burned most of the first day and on into the night, turning what had been a tropical paradise into a vision of hell. Thick black smoke clogged the air, stung the eyes, and choked the throats of the rescue workers as they clambered over the hulls of capsized ships such as the *Utah* and the *Oklahoma,* searching for survivors. The *Arizona* had broken apart in a huge explosion and gone to the bottom of the harbor, and the *California* seemed to be sinking, too.

But when Monday morning came, most of the fires were out, and the smoke was finally beginning to disperse. The *California* was still afloat. The panic which had gripped the entire island began to ease a bit, and as it did it was replaced with a newfound anger and resolve. The enemy had thrown the first punch and the sneak attack had landed hard, but the United States wasn't down. Not by a long shot. The Japanese would pay for what they had done.

The cleanup continued and the wounded were cared for. By evening, doctors and nurses were asleep on their feet and had to be relieved. Catherine was in no mood to return to the bungalow she shared with Missy—for one thing, the bungalow had been where she had shared such a passionate reunion with Adam when he passed through Pearl Harbor, and she didn't need reminders of that—so she stretched out on a sofa in the lounge and was asleep immediately despite the clamor around her.

She woke up during the night, stiff and unable to move because Missy had crowded onto the sofa beside her. Someone had turned the lights down in the lounge until the room was dim. Some of the windows in the room had been shattered by the concussion of nearby explosions, and those panes had been boarded over, blocking any light from outside. The hubbub in the hospital had finally quieted somewhat, so that it sounded more like a hospital again instead of a madhouse.

Catherine lay there, unable to fall asleep again but grateful for the chance to rest. She had been so tired that her sleep had been dreamless, and she was grateful for that. Now, though, there was nothing to distract her, and her thoughts turned to Adam and Spencer.

Adam was all right. Catherine was going to believe that until she had reason to think otherwise. But Spencer was dead, his cocky smile and his carefree laughter snuffed out forever. Catherine felt the heat of tears in her eyes as she thought about him. She wondered if anyone had notified their parents yet. She had tried to call them during one of her few breaks the day before, but she hadn't been able to get a line to the mainland. It was possible that by now a Navy chaplain had visited the big house on the lakefront, bearing the tragic news. Catherine wished she were there, so that she could hold onto her mother and comfort her. Even her father, cool and unemotional though he was most of the time, would surely be hit hard by the news of his only son's death.

Without realizing it, Catherine had begun to shudder as she cried. Her sobs must have woken Missy, because the other young woman rolled over on the sofa and raised herself on an elbow. "Hey!" she whispered. "Hey, kid, you all right?"

"N-no," Catherine choked out.

Missy put an arm around her. "That's all right; neither am I. I don't think anybody is, tonight."

Catherine returned the embrace and buried her face against Missy's shoulder. She cried wordlessly, and after a moment Missy began to sob, too. They held tightly to each other in the darkened lounge as all the terrible strain of the past forty-eight hours caught up to them. All the fear and sorrow came pouring out, although they tried to muffle the sounds so as not to disturb anyone else.

After a while, Catherine wiped her eyes and sniffled, then said, "We ought to go see if we can relieve somebody."

"Yeah, I guess so." Missy swung her legs off the sofa and stood up, swaying a little as she did so. When she had steadied herself, she reached down to give Catherine a hand.

They went out into the hallway, blinking against the brighter lights. One of the doctors was moving along the corridor, studying a medical chart in his hand. He glanced up, saw Catherine and Missy, and stopped.

"Nurse Bergman, your husband's on Wake Island, isn't he?"

Catherine nodded. "That's right." A part of her hated to ask the question, but she went on, "Has there been more news from there?"

With a quick grin, the doctor nodded. "The Marines are holding the island. The Japs aren't going to take it without quite a fight."

"That . . . that's good to know. Thank you, sir."

The doctor nodded and patted her on the shoulder, then moved on.

Missy looked at Catherine's tight-drawn face and said, "The news could be a lot worse, right?"

"Right," Catherine said hollowly. "But if the Marines are still holding the island . . . that means the Japs are still trying to take it."

SIXTEEN

As the sun rose on 9 December 1941, four Wildcat F4F-3s roared one by one along the runway and lifted into the clear blue sky. The punctured reserve fuel tank on one of the planes had been repaired during a long night of hard work. The Wildcat that had damaged its propeller while landing the day before was still being worked on inside one of the revetments that had been built overnight.

The F4F-3s went into formation and climbed to twenty thousand feet, then began their patrol. If they ran into any flights of Japanese bombers, they would immediately radio the news to Major Bayler on Wake Island, then try to delay the Japs.

After two hours of patrolling, however, there was no sign of the enemy, so the Wildcats headed for home. Back on Wake, Major Devereux issued orders relaxing the men of the 1st Battalion to "Defense Condition 2." After the strain of the past twenty-four hours, any easing of tension was more than welcome.

In the .50-caliber anti-aircraft machine gun battery, the breakfast of coffee and doughnuts had made all the members of Adam's squad feel like new men. They were joking and laughing as they emerged from the sandbag-walled bunker. Adam put his fists in the small of his back and stretched, easing stiff muscles. Gurnwall lit a Lucky Strike and said, "You think maybe the Japs're done with us, Corp?"

Adam shook his head and answered honestly. "Not at all. They'll be back. I've studied the maps. Wake has to be important to them. If they let us keep it, we'll have a perfect base for refueling flights of bombers that can reach the Marshalls, the Philippines, hell, even Japan itself."

"Bombin' Japan," Gurnwall mused. "That don't sound half-bad right about now."

That would happen, too, and would be a lot easier if the U.S. could just hang onto Wake, Adam thought.

"You study that sort of stuff, don't you, Corp?" Gurnwall went on.

"You mean military strategy?" Adam shrugged. "Some, I guess. I know I'm just an enlisted man, but I like to have an idea what I'm getting into."

"Yeah, me, too." Gurnwall puffed on the Lucky for a minute, then said, "When do you figure the Japs'll be back?"

Adam frowned in thought for a moment. "If they're flying off of carriers based in the Marshall Islands and took off at dawn, they'd be here about . . . 1130, I'd say."

"So we got a couple of hours."

"That's just a guess, Gurney, nothing more."

"You guess pretty good, Corp. Me, I'm gonna be watchin' the sky pretty close around 1130."

*　　*　　*

1130 came and went with the sky still clear over the atoll. A few white clouds floated high overhead, but they wouldn't provide much cover for any airplanes. The Wildcats were patrolling again, this time to the north.

A telephone line had been run to the top of the water tank, and Gunner Borth had been placed in charge of the observation post there. The veteran Marine had rigged up a piece of tarpaulin to provide some shade for the men assigned to the observation post. He was sitting cross-legged underneath the tarp with a pair of binoculars in his lap when he spotted something in the sky to the south of the atoll. The gunner brought the glasses to his eyes and peered through them, having a pretty good idea already of what he was going to see.

He was right. The Japanese bombers were back, once again in a tightly packed, three-tiered formation.

Borth grabbed the phone and yelled, "Japs!" into it. "Japs coming from the south!"

In a matter of a few heartbeats, the word was passed all over the islands, and Major Bayler was on the radio alerting the Wildcats. Men scrambled back to their guns and fired three-shot bursts, which had been agreed upon as the signal for incoming bombers. There were no air raid sirens on Wake, just as there were no radar units. Somehow, those vital pieces of hardware that had been meant to accompany the 1st Marine Defense Battalion had never been shipped from Pearl Harbor.

Adam was the last man back into the machine gun bunker. He paused long enough to look up into the sky toward the south, where he could see the bombers. They looked to be considerably higher today than they had been the day before. The Japanese hadn't been so lucky today. There was no rain squall for them to hide behind.

The heavy guns on Peacock Point began firing, and a moment later the 3-inch batteries on Peale Island joined in. Anti-aircraft shells burst high in the sky, creating thin black clouds of flak. Adam cursed. The bombers were still at too high an altitude for the machine guns to be effective against them.

The Japanese planes angled down and began dropping their bombs. Suddenly, he saw the Wildcats from VMF-211 on their flank, raking that side of the formation with fire. He could see smoke boiling out of one of the bombers, and flames began to flicker along its fuselage. It listed heavily to one side, then dropped out of the formation and went into a spin.

Adam said, "Yes!" and clenched a fist as he saw the Japanese bomber begin its fatal plunge. The Japs wouldn't get away unscathed today. He said tautly, "Ready on the gun, Rolofson?"

"Ready," the Swede replied.

"Ready with the ammo belts?"

"Ready, Corp," Gurnwall said. He and Stout would feed the

belts into the gun as Rolofson fired. Magruder and Kennemer stood by to help wherever they might be needed.

In the absence of any fire-control radar, elevations had to be calculated manually and passed along over the telephone. Adam had the phone to his ear, waiting for orders and information. Much of the aiming would be strictly a seat-of-the-pants job, however. He hoped Rolofson had a good hand and eye.

As the Jap bombers flew into the wall of anti-aircraft fire, the Wildcats broke off their attack, veering away to the east. They could circle around and hit the Japs again, if necessary.

As the planes dove lower and lower, the order to fire sounded in the phone at Adam's ear. He bellowed, "Fire!" and Rolofson squeezed the triggers of the gun. It began to chatter and shake, and the sound of its shots was like a thousand hammers smacking repeatedly into plywood.

However, the firing was nowhere near loud enough to drown out the sound of bombs detonating nearby. With each blast, the ground shook under Adam's booted feet. The Japs had targeted the planes and the airstrip on their first strike. Today they seemed to be after the defense installations, especially Battery E.

More explosions sounded, but each one was a little farther away, Adam judged. Like the footsteps of a giant, the bomb blasts were walking up the eastern side of Wake Island toward Camp Two. Adam hoped the civilians were taking cover in some of those holes they had spent the night digging.

Rolofson wrestled the fifty through its range of fire as Gurnwall and Stout fed in the ammo belts. The Japanese bombers swooped overhead. Adam saw dark smoke trailing from several of them, and he hoped that some of the damage had come from their machine gun fire, even though he knew it was more likely the bombers had been hit by flak from the anti-aircraft shells thrown up by the 3-inch and 5-inch guns.

The big machine gun fell silent as the bombers began to pass out of sight. One of the trailing planes was smoking, and suddenly it came apart in a huge, mid-air explosion. Adam and his men whooped excitedly as they saw the plane destroyed.

"We got one!" Gurnwall shouted, dancing a little jig. "We got one of the fuckers!"

Adam grinned and didn't correct Gurnwall. After all they had been through, they needed this moment of triumph.

The defenders of Wake Island would need all the victories, big or small, they could get, Adam thought.

The enemy bombers made only the one pass before heading back south. They had paid a price for the destruction they carried out this time. Two of the Japanese planes had been brought down, one by anti-aircraft fire, the other by the F4F-3 fighters. Four more bombers were smoking and wobbling in the sky, but they managed to stay aloft as they limped after their comrades.

The batteries located on Peacock Point, A and E, came through the attack fairly well, considering how the Japanese had concentrated the first salvo of bombs on them. One of the 3-inch guns was damaged, and the range finder on one of the 5-inch guns had been destroyed. Farther up the island, in the vicinity of Camp Two, the defenders hadn't been as fortunate. Many of the buildings were leveled, and some that hadn't been blown down in the explosions had been set afire by them. One of the warehouses and the machine shop were destroyed; so was the garage. The hospital had suffered direct hits and been set ablaze. Dr. Kahn and Dr. Shank managed to get all the patients out safely but were able to save only part of their store of medical supplies before the building burned to the ground.

Over on Peale Island, the seaplane ramp suffered still more damage, and the radio hut was destroyed.

Four Marines were killed in the bombing, and fifty-five more civilians lost their lives. In two days, the Japanese had handed out some severe punishment to Wake Island and the men who now felt trapped there.

At the machine gun emplacement, orders came over the walkie-talkie for Adam and some of the other members of the squad to join the cleanup efforts. Magruder and Kennemer were left on guard duty. Some of the sandbags in the walls around the gun had been pierced by flying debris. Those bags had to be replaced. When Adam saw how the bags were torn and ripped, he realized that the walls had saved his life and the lives of his men. Without the sandbags, those sizzling chunks of metal would have torn the squad apart.

Gurnwall regarded the damage solemnly, then said, "Damn, that was close."

"Close enough," Adam agreed. As far as he had been able to tell at the time, Gurnwall had functioned calmly and efficiently during the air raid, unlike the day before. Being inside the protection of the bunker probably had something to do with that, but Adam sensed that Gurnwall was making an extra effort now to remain cool under fire.

Once they had patched up the wall of sandbags, they helped move Battery E's main 3-inch gun to a new emplacement six hundred yards northeast of its original location. Adam didn't see the point in that unless it was an attempt to confuse the Japs. If they targeted the battery again on their next bombing run, they would find that the 3-incher was in a different place. Maybe that would give the gunners a small advantage. The battery was shored up, too, by some extra guns that were brought down from Wilkes Island, where they had been emplaced earlier but lacked crews to fire them.

Late that afternoon, Adam and the others found themselves carrying crates of ammunition out of the reinforced concrete and steel bunkers where they had been stored. Those two bunkers, which were mostly underground, would replace the destroyed hospital. Patients were carried into them on stretchers and made as comfortable as possible in the primitive surroundings.

Adam watched the burned, shot-up men being carried into the makeshift medical wards and looked around at his squad. None of them had been hurt yet. They had done their jobs splendidly, and they had come through two Japanese air raids unharmed. He was filled with pride and gratitude and relief.

"Hey, Corp," Gurnwall said. "When are we gonna get some more grub?"

SEVENTEEN

"Just put it down over there, Corporal," Major Devereux ordered. It was the morning of 10 December.

Adam lowered the wooden crate to the floor of Devereux's command bunker. The crate was full of papers that had been salvaged from various offices around the island that had been destroyed.

Adam was turning to leave the bunker when Devereux said, "Bergman, isn't it?"

"That's right, sir."

"Where have you been posted, Bergman?"

"My squad is manning the .50-caliber anti-aircraft machine gun down by Battery E, sir."

Devereux nodded. "I've received good reports on your work."

"Thank you, sir. The men deserve the credit."

"Spoken like an officer. We've had this conversation before, haven't we, Bergman?"

Adam hesitated, then shrugged. "One similar to it, sir."

"You were in law school when you enlisted, I believe."

Adam wasn't sure what the major was getting at, but he nodded. "That's right, sir."

Devereux gestured at one of the crates Adam had just set down. "I need someone to work with me and go through all this mess. Want the job, Bergman?"

Adam frowned. Working with Devereux in the command post would mean that he would have to leave the squad. "I'm not sure, sir," he said slowly. "You yourself said that my men and I have been doing good work where we are. . . ."

"Perhaps I should rephrase," Devereux snapped. "I want you for the job, Bergman. You're intelligent, and I can tell that you're trustworthy. There's some sensitive information among those papers. If you're worried about your squad, they can get along without you. I'll promote one of them to corporal to take your place. Surely one of them is fit for command."

"Private First Class Rolofson, sir," Adam said, sensing that Devereux wanted him to supply a name. It was a tough choice between Rolofson and Magruder, but Rolofson was a little older and seemed a little smarter to Adam.

"All right, then. I'll send for Rolofson and take care of that, and you can get started sorting those papers."

Adam's jaw tightened. He had joined the Marines to fight, not to be a pencil-pusher and paper-sorter. But a Marine followed orders, so he nodded and said, "Aye, aye, sir."

He glanced at the clock on Major Devereux's desk. Almost 1000.

It would be time soon for the Japs' daily visit, but today the squad would have to make it through without him.

*　　*　　*

Gurnwall was eating a candy bar when Rolofson came back into the machine gun's sandbag bunker. With his mouth full, he asked, "What'd the brass want, Roley?"

Rolofson pointed to the right sleeve of his shirt, just below the shoulder, where a second stripe had been attached below the one that marked him as a PFC.

"Holy shit!" Gurnwall exclaimed. "You're a corporal now?"

"That's right."

"What happened to the corp?"

"Major Devereux snagged him and put him to work in the CP. I guess I'm in charge here." Rolofson looked around the bunker, clearly a bit uncomfortable with the idea of commanding the squad.

136

Gurnwall came to attention and snapped a salute.

"Stop that. You don't salute corporals."

Magruder slapped Rolofson on the back. "Congratulations, ya big Swede." The other members of the squad gathered around to echo the good wishes.

"Magruder, you take the gun," Rolofson said when the congratulations died down. "Gurnwall, you and Stout are loaders. Kennemer, you're our spotter again."

"Aye, aye, Corp," Gurnwall said as he joined Stout next to the open crate containing the ammo belts. "Damn, that's gonna take some gettin' used to."

"Don't sweat it. We won't be standing on ceremony around here—"

Rolofson stopped short as he heard three shots come from Peacock Point. Everyone in the bunker knew what that signal meant. "Japs!" Rolofson exclaimed. "Everybody, to your battle stations!"

In the close confines of the bunker, they didn't have far to go. In a matter of seconds, everyone was in place. Kennemer, atop the wall of sandbags, used binoculars to scan the ocean and the sky to the south, where the Japanese bombers had come from during the previous two raids.

"I don't see anything," Kennemer said after a few minutes. "Must've been a false alarm."

More shots sounded from the anti-aircraft emplacements on the east side of the island. Kennemer twisted around and trained the binoculars in that direction.

"Crap! They're coming, all right—out of the east this time!"

Magruder rotated the fifty, but it wouldn't turn far enough to give him a shot as the Jap planes came in, bearing straight for Peacock Point. Bombs began to fall, their explosions shaking the ground. Anti-aircraft shells burst high in the sky.

Rolofson shouted, "Kennemer, get down from there!"

Kennemer didn't waste time climbing down the wall of sandbags. He just rolled off the top and dropped to the ground inside the bunker. He landed awkwardly, however, and yelled, "Shit!" He tried to get up and fell as his right leg folded up underneath him. He screamed in pain.

Rolofson dropped to a knee beside him. "What's wrong?"

"I think I broke my fuckin' ankle!"

Rolofson glanced up at the gun. "Magruder, if you get a shot, take it!"

"Aye, aye!"

Rolofson reached for Kennemer's right foot. "Lemme get that boot off and take a look—"

Kennemer screamed again as Rolofson touched the boot. "Don't take it off! It hurts too much!"

Rolofson gritted his teeth. The squad had come through two air raids without a scratch as long as Adam was in charge. Now, before today's fight had hardly gotten started, Rolofson had an injured man on his hands.

He helped Kennemer sit up, propping his back against the sandbags. "Stay there and we'll get you some help once the Japs have left."

Kennemer's face was pale under its permanent tan, washed out from the pain he was suffering. "Okay," he said weakly. "Hey, give 'em hell, all right?"

"Sure," Rolofson told him.

At that moment, the Japanese bombers began roaring over the machine gun emplacement. Magruder opened fire, the heavy gun jumping and chattering under his touch. Gurnwall and Stout expertly fed the ammunition belts through it.

Still kneeling beside Kennemer, Rolofson looked up through the shot-up camouflage netting. Something dropped from the bottom of one of the Jap planes and began spiraling down toward the sandbag bunker. Rolofson's eyes widened in shock. During the previous raids, the Japs must have noticed that there was a machine gun emplacement here, and now one of the bombers had targeted it.

"Bomb!" Rolofson screamed. "Bomb! Get down, damn it! Get—"

The huge blast cut off his warning shouts. The massive explosion was the loudest thing Rolofson had ever heard. It slammed against his ears like a physical blow, and in the same split-second the concussion from the blast threw him into Kennemer. Kennemer cried out sharply, but Rolofson couldn't hear it. The blast had deafened him.

Rolofson was so stunned that several minutes went by before he realized he was still alive. A heavy weight was lying on top of him, pressing down hard and uncomfortably. His mouth was full of sand. He started spitting and trying to wriggle out from under whatever it was on top of him.

"Hey!" a familiar voice said. "What—"

"Gurnwall?" Rolofson spit out more sand. "Gurney, is that you? Get the hell off me!"

Some of the weight went away, and Rolofson was able to push himself up into a sitting position. Sandbags were littered around him. Some of them had burst. That explained the sand. He was practically awash in the stuff. He became aware of choked coughing behind him and looked around to see Kennemer trying to struggle upright. Rolofson caught hold of the smaller man's shoulder and lifted him. Kennemer came free of the sand, spitting and gasping and sputtering as he did so.

Rolofson looked around, trying to take stock of his surroundings and his own situation at the same time. He didn't think he was hurt. His ears were ringing, but he could hear again. His arms and legs seemed to work all right. His eyes burned and smarted from the sand that had gotten in them, but soothing tears filled them as he blinked rapidly.

The western wall of the bunker had been blown down. About ten yards beyond it was a large crater in the coral that made up Wake Island. That was where the bomb had landed, Rolofson realized. If it had landed in a direct hit on the bunker, there wouldn't be anything left of any of them. As it was, Rolofson hoped that luck had been with them. Gurnwall was alive and brushing himself off after having been thrown by the blast across the bunker and on top of Rolofson and Kennemer. Magruder lay beside the machine gun, which was tilted a little on its mounting but otherwise undamaged. Magruder was coughing, so Rolofson knew he was alive. Stout was stretched out behind the gun.

Rolofson looked again at the Kentuckian and said, "Oh, no." Stout lay face down, and the back of his head under the helmet that was still strapped on tightly was a gory, concave mess where something had struck it. Rolofson scrambled over to Stout and rolled him onto his back. Blood had welled from Stout's eyes, nose, mouth, and ears, painting his features a ghastly crimson. Rolofson felt his neck for a pulse but didn't find one.

"Stout?" Gurnwall said when he saw Stout's bloody face. "Stout, you okay, buddy?"

"He's dead," Rolofson said, giving up his futile search for a pulse. "Whatever hit him smashed his skull into a million pieces."

"Goddamnit!" Gurnwall cried. "No!"

Rolofson turned to Magruder, who was still coughing and sputtering. He helped Magruder sit up. "You hit?"

"I . . . I don't think so." Magruder hacked up some more sand and then looked at Stout. "Oh, hell."

"He's gone," Rolofson confirmed. He glanced up at the sky, which was clear now. "So are the Japs, looks like."

He caught hold of the machine gun and used it to steady himself as he pulled himself to his feet. Stumbling out of what was left of the bunker, he looked around. Several more bomb craters were nearby. The Japs had really concentrated on this area today.

Smoke and flame caught his attention, and he looked toward Wilkes Island. The whole place seemed to be on fire, judging by the smoke that was billowing up. Of course, there wasn't much up there to be destroyed. Wilkes was easily the least developed of the three islands in the atoll.

Rolofson turned slowly in a circle. He didn't see any planes anywhere. The air raid was over.

And for the first time the squad had suffered casualties. Rolofson thought about Stout and about Kennemer's broken ankle, and he felt guilt gnawing at his belly. In command for less than an hour, and he had already lost two men. He tried to tell himself that was the nature of the beast, that men died and were injured in war, but he couldn't help but feel that he had let Corporal Bergman down.

With a sigh, he turned back toward the bunker. He, Gurnwall, and Magruder were the only ones left unhurt. He said to them, "Let's get this gun straightened up. No telling when the Japs will be back."

EIGHTEEN

Adam was seated at a small desk in the command post when the three-shot signal warning of an impending air raid sounded outside. Devereux said, "Get your helmet on, Corporal."

"Aye, aye, sir," Adam said as he reached for the flat steel helmet. He put it on and buckled the strap under his chin, then got to his feet.

"Where are you going, Bergman?" Devereux asked.

"My defense station, sir," Adam answered without thinking.

"You're *at* your defense station already, Corporal." Devereux stood up and went over to the telephone switchboard, which was manned by a T-5 communications technician. He took the phone the technician handed him and said briskly into it, "This is Major Devereux. Defense Condition One. All hands on the alert. Batteries commence firing at will."

Adam heard the thump of anti-aircraft guns, the softer reports of the shells bursting, the jackhammer noise of machine guns, the roar of engines, the faint whine of falling bombs, and the earth-shaking explosions as those bombs landed. While sitting at the desk, he had been making a list of the documents from the crates as he sorted them. When he felt a sharp pain in the palm of his hand, he looked down and saw that he had snapped the pencil he was using without even being aware of it. One of the sharp ends of the broken pencil was jabbing into his hand.

Devereux stood tensely beside the switchboard, the phone at his ear, as reports were relayed to him and he issued orders in response.

Adam glanced up nervously at the curving concrete ceiling of the bunker. He wondered if it could withstand a direct hit by a Japanese bomb or would instead come crashing down around their heads. He found that he was more frightened here in the command post than he had been in the sandbag bunker. While he was at his post, even though he was less protected, he was busy with his duties and had had less time to worry. And he had felt like he was actually doing something to strike back against the enemy. . . .

Suddenly, the earth seemed to jump as Wake Island was rocked by the largest explosion yet. Adam was thrown out of his chair and sprawled on the floor. Major Devereux dropped the telephone receiver and staggered several steps, barely catching his balance before he fell. Dust sifted down from the concrete ceiling. Adam looked up at it and wondered if that direct hit he had been thinking about earlier had landed.

The technician at the switchboard had been toppled out of his chair, too. From the floor, he reached over and grabbed the dangling phone, which was swinging back and forth at the end of its cord. "Hold on! Hold on for Major Devereux!" he shouted into the receiver. Then he held out the phone toward the major.

Devereux, looking as shaken as everything else in the CP, took the phone and said, "My God, what was that? Are you sure? Any other damage?"

Adam took hold of the desk and pulled himself to his feet. Devereux laughed hollowly, looked over at him, and said, "One of the Jap bombs landed on that hut up on Wilkes where the construction crew kept its dynamite for the new channel job. All one hundred and twenty-five tons of it!"

"The whole thing went up?" Adam asked.

Devereux nodded. "They felt it all the way over on Peale. The blast blew away most of the brush on the island, and what wasn't blown away is on fire! Thank God we didn't have very many men up there. Only one man was killed, as far as we know now."

The major turned his attention back to the phone as more

information came in. Adam leaned his left hand on the desk and used his right to scrub wearily at his face. He knew that the civilian workers had been blasting and dredging a new channel through the center of Wilkes Island, but with their dynamite gone in one tremendous explosion, that effort would have to be abandoned. It didn't really matter anymore, anyway, Adam thought. Anything that wouldn't help them hold the atoll against the Japanese just wasn't important.

As always, the air raid seemed to go on forever even though it really lasted only about ten minutes. Then the explosions stopped, followed a few moments later by a trailing off of the anti-aircraft fire as the Japanese bombers began to fly out of range.

"Damage reports!" Devereux said into the phone. After several minutes, he said, "I want Battery E relocated north of the airstrip. They're after our anti-aircraft defenses more than anything else now. Yes, begin work on that immediately."

Adam waited anxiously while Devereux continued issuing orders. Even though technically he wasn't in command of the squad anymore, he wanted to see if Gurnwall and the others were all right. They had made it through the first two attacks, but no one expected that sort of luck to continue indefinitely.

Finally, during a lull while Devereux had the phone away from his ear, Adam said, "Sir, request permission to check on the status of Second Squad, Fifth Platoon, Company A."

"Your old squad?" Devereux glared at him. "You have other responsibilities now, Corporal."

"Aye, aye, sir."

After a moment, Devereux sighed. "But I suppose papersorting can wait, under the circumstances, can't it?" He waved his free hand at the door of the command post. "Go on; see about your friends."

"Aye, aye, sir. And thank you."

Adam left the command post hurriedly before Devereux could change his mind. The command post was just south of

Camp One, built into one of the low hills that marked the island. Adam saw several truckloads of Marines heading down the road toward the air station and hopped onto one of the slow-moving vehicles, riding on the running board until he reached a point near the machine gun emplacement. As the truck approached, he saw to his shock that one wall of the sandbag bunker had collapsed. The bomb crater next to it told Adam the cause of the damage.

He dropped off the running board and ran toward the bunker. As he came up to the open end, he saw Gurnwall, Rolofson, and Magruder wrestling with the big .50-caliber machine gun, which had been knocked halfway off its mounts. Kennemer sat propped up against the side wall that was still standing, his legs stretched out in front of him, pain etched on his face. Stout lay motionless on the ground, face covered with blood, obviously dead.

"My God!" Adam said, then asked stupidly, "What happened?"

Gurnwall glanced around at him and exclaimed, "Corp! You're back!"

Rolofson jerked his head toward the crater. "Jap bomb landed right over there. It got Stout."

"I know. I'm sorry." Adam turned to Kennemer. "What happened to you?"

"I fell off the wall and broke my fuckin' ankle before the bomb ever landed. It hurts like blazes, Corporal. Can you do anything to help?"

"We'll have to get you down to those bunkers they're using as a hospital now."

Rolofson said sharply, "We haven't been relieved. Kennemer will have to wait until we are or until somebody comes to get him."

Rolofson sounded angry, and Adam thought he knew why. Rolofson was a conscientious kid. He had been given responsibility for the squad and now they had suffered their first casualties, including one man killed. Rolofson might not be blaming himself for what had occurred, exactly, but he had to hate the fact that it had happened so soon after he assumed command. And having the squad's former leader show up right afterward probably didn't help, either.

Adam stooped and got an arm under Kennemer's right arm and around his shoulders. "Come on," he said as he lifted Kennemer. "I'll give you a hand."

"Be careful, Corporal."

Adam forced a laugh. "What, you don't think a feather merchant like you weighs enough to worry about, do you, Kennemer?"

"I guess not. Thanks, Corporal. Just—ow! Watch it, huh?"

"I'll be careful," Adam promised him. He put his arm around Kennemer's waist and draped the injured Marine's arm over his shoulders. "Looks like you've got everything under control here, Rolofson," he went on. "You don't need me around."

The three of them had gotten the machine gun straightened on its mount. Rolofson nodded curtly to Adam, then said, "Gurnwall, Magruder, we gotta get this wall rebuilt. Come on; let's get to work."

Carefully, Adam walked out of the bunker, supporting Kennemer, who hobbled along beside him. Kennemer winced every time his foot touched the ground. Adam headed for the road, intending to flag down the first jeep or truck to come along.

He didn't have to do that. A Dodge deuce-and-a-half with the cross of the medical corps painted on the canvas covering its bed came to a stop when the driver saw Adam and Kennemer laboriously making their way toward the road. A couple of corpsmen hopped down from the truck and ran over to meet them. They had a stretcher with them, and with practiced efficiency they got Kennemer onto it and carried him back to the truck. The driver leaned over and called through the open window on the passenger side, "You okay, Corporal? Are you hit, too?"

Adam shook his head and waved the truck on. As it rumbled off, he looked back over his shoulder at the machine gun emplacement. As he had said, Rolofson had things under control. He wasn't needed here. Might as well go back to the command post, he decided.

There were papers there that needed pushing.

Major Devereux's idea of having Battery E moved proved to be a good one, because many of the Japanese bombs had fallen where it was before, indicating that the battery had indeed been the enemy's primary target. Quite a bit of damage had been done, especially on Wilkes Island, but none of the big guns on Wake and Peale were knocked out of action.

The Japanese had suffered more losses, too. Two of their bombers were brought down by the heavily outnumbered fighters of VMF-211, and a third one had been damaged by anti-aircraft fire and forced to turn back without releasing its load of bombs. The lost planes had the Japanese at less than full strength now.

Since it had worked once before, Devereux's decision to move Battery E yet again was a logical one. Most of the Jap bombing runs had been along the length of one or the other leg of the atoll, so that they could bomb multiple targets as they flew over. The new location of Battery E placed it in the angle formed by the atoll around the lagoon. If the Japs targeted it, they wouldn't be able to hit anything else in the next raid without flying over and coming back for a second pass. That would give the anti-aircraft guns more time to zero in on them.

By nightfall on 10 December, the worst of the damage had been cleaned up, the wounded had been taken into the hospital bunkers, and the dead joined their fellows in the big refrigerated room in the civilian warehouse. The guns of Battery E were being moved and mounted on their new emplacements. Everything that could be done was being done to meet whatever threat the Japanese came up with for the next day.

As he emerged from the concrete bunker, Adam thought Major Devereux looked more gaunt than ever as he stood just outside the command post that evening and watched the fading light in the sky. He gave the major a salute, which Devereux returned distractedly.

"Beautiful evening, sir," Adam commented. And it really

was. The weather was clear and only slightly chilly. The fan of colors left over in the sky from the sunset was breathtaking, shading from orange to a deep, deep blue and on into black.

"You know, Corporal," Devereux mused, "if I was the sort of man to feel sorry for myself, I might be asking why I was sent out here without the resources to get the job done."

"You've done a good job with what you have, sir."

Devereux looked over at him and chuckled. "From some other non-coms, I'd think that was a bit of apple-polishing, but you don't strike me as that sort, Bergman. You say a thing because you mean it, don't you?"

"I try to be honest, sir. That was the way my mother raised me."

Adam thought about his mother, all those thousands of miles away in Chicago. He wrote to her, almost as much as he wrote to Catherine, but it wasn't like being there with her. It was winter in Chicago now, and he hoped she was well. He hoped she had heard something about the fate of his grandparents. Not all the news had to be bad, did it?

"I meant to ask you . . . how did your former squad fare in the attack?"

"They lost one man," Adam said grimly, "and another was injured, but not too badly. The ones who are left are manning their post tonight, I suppose."

"Sorry to hear about the one that was lost," Devereux said. "Friend of yours?"

"Yes, sir." That was true, Adam thought. He hadn't known Stout for long, but like all the other members of the squad, Adam considered him a friend. War did that, he supposed, made you care deeply about people you might never have even met otherwise.

"I hope we won't have to lose too many more before help gets here."

As the meaning of those words penetrated his brain, Adam felt his pulse quicken. "Help, sir?"

"Keep it under that steel hat of yours, Corporal. Pearl is sending us some relief. Commander Cunningham and I received word late this afternoon."

"That's . . . good to know, sir."

"All we have to do is hold out until they get here." Devereux looked over at Adam. "Think we can do that?"

"Yes, sir. We're Marines, sir."

"You're right about that, Corporal," Devereux said. "I can only pray that you're right about the other, too."

NINETEEN

The weather turned blustery on the evening of 10 December, and even though there was no rain, the wind blew hard and the seas were even higher than usual. The constant roar of the surf against the reef was louder than ever.

As one of Major Devereux's aides, Adam was able to sleep in the command post, stretching out on a cot in one corner of the room. Devereux was asleep, too, as were the two other men on duty in the command post. Exhaustion had claimed them even though they were supposed to be on watch.

The burring of the telephone roused Adam from a dreamless sleep. He sat up sharply, swung his legs off the cot, and got to his feet. The T-5 at the switchboard was fumbling to answer the call. He finally got the receiver to his ear and said, "Command post."

Adam heard excited squawking coming from the phone. The T-5 turned and handed the receiver to Devereux, who had come up behind him and was rubbing his eyes sleepily. The major stifled a yawn, then said into the phone, "Devereux here."

As he listened, Devereux stiffened. The weariness seemed to drop away from him. "Say again," he snapped.

When he had heard the report a second time, he ordered, "Remain on watch," then handed the phone back to the man at the switchboard. Swinging around toward Adam, he said, "That was the OP. They've spotted something moving out on the water, south of the atoll."

Something moving on the water could mean only one thing,

Adam thought. Any relief expedition from Pearl Harbor would be days away, at best. The newcomers had to be Japanese.

Devereux put on his uniform blouse, then shrugged into a raincoat. As he strapped on his helmet, he said, "Let's go down to the beach and take a look, Bergman."

"Aye, aye, sir," Adam said as he reached for his own blouse and helmet. He was fully dressed except for them, just like everyone else in the bunker.

As they left the command post, Adam glanced at his watch. 0300. One of the darkest hours of the night. The lamp in the bunker was put out before the door was opened, just in case someone on the approaching ships was watching for a flash of light. Adam closed the door behind them as he and the major stepped outside. They started toward the beach, less than a hundred yards away.

The wind was still whipping around. Adam bent his head against it as he and Devereux trudged to the edge of the sand. Devereux had brought a pair of night glasses with him. He lifted them to his eyes and studied the ocean. For several long minutes, he watched the sea in silence, and Adam began to hope that the warning from the observation post had been a false alarm. Then Devereux said, "Well, there they are." He turned and extended the night glasses toward Adam. "Take a look."

Adam took the glasses and peered through them in the direction Devereux indicated. At first he saw nothing but a mass of gray, shifting shadows, but then he began to be able to distinguish details. The shadows hardened into the shapes of Japanese ships.

"How many do you see?" Devereux asked.

Adam tried to count, but it was hard to make out that much. "At least a dozen, sir," he said after a moment.

"That was my estimate, too. Come on; let's get back to the command post."

They ran this time, trotting with the wind at their back. Devereux knocked on the door, waited for the all-clear indicating that the lamp was out again, then went inside followed closely by Adam. "Ring Commander Cunningham," Devereux ordered even before the door was closed and the lamp relit.

When he had Cunningham on the horn, he quickly told the Navy man what he and Adam had seen. "They'll hit us first," he said, "but I'm going to try to draw them in."

Cunningham must have agreed, because Devereux rang off with him and then had the switchboard operator call all the defense positions. When all the crews manning the guns had checked in, Devereux ordered, "No matter what happens, no one fires until I give the signal. Repeat, no one fires until my signal. Not a single round."

The next two hours dragged by as the Japanese task force inched closer to the atoll. Adam heard Devereux's end of the reports the major received from the observation post, and he could tell that the heavy seas were slowing the approach of the ships. Finally, as dawn was about to break, Adam heard something that sounded like distant thunder.

The shelling had begun.

Devereux turned to Adam and said, "Take the phone, Bergman. You know my orders." He held out the receiver, and Adam had no choice except to take it. He brought it to his ear while Devereux walked across to the other side of the bunker to pour himself a cup of coffee.

"Battery A reporting that Japanese cruiser eight thousand yards offshore has commenced shelling!" a voice said excitedly over the phone. "Request orders!"

Adam looked at Devereux, who was calmly sipping coffee. "Hold your fire until the major gives the word," Adam said into the phone.

A few moments later, a different voice said, "Battery L reporting! Jap fleet proceeding west and shelling Wilkes Island!"

"Hold your fire," Adam said, trying to sound calmer than he felt.

He glanced at the map on the wall. Battery A was located at Peacock Point, down on the southeastern corner of Wake Island. Battery L was on Kuku Point, at the northern tip of Wilkes.

"Battery L reporting! Jap cruiser and two destroyers are coming about! They're heading back your way, CP!"

"Range?" Adam took it upon himself to ask.

"Six thousand yards!"

Adam covered the mouthpiece and said to Devereux, "A Jap cruiser and two destroyers are making another pass, sir. Range this time six thousand yards."

"Continue to hold fire," Devereux said.

Adam repeated that order into the phone. Suddenly he heard a loud blast somewhere outside and felt the ground shiver under his feet. One of the Japanese shells must have set off something highly explosive. Adam hoped it wasn't anything too important.

Devereux drained the rest of his coffee and said, "Let's go take a look. The sun's up by now, so we don't have to worry about blackout conditions."

Adam didn't know what to do with the phone. He handed it back to the man at the switchboard and followed Devereux to the door of the command post. Devereux opened it and stepped outside into the yellow glow of dawn. Part of the sky held a particularly reddish cast, and when Adam stepped into the doorway he saw the reason why. The explosion a few minutes earlier had been a diesel storage tank blowing up. A few hundred yards away, flames and smoke from the burning tank shot high into the air.

Adam didn't need binoculars to see the Japanese ships this time. They were in plain sight, steaming along parallel to the island as they bombarded it. Most of the Japanese task force was still up toward the northern end of Wilkes, while the cruiser and the destroyers that were still firing had almost reached Peacock Point again.

"Come about," Devereux muttered as he watched the cruiser and the destroyers. "Come about."

From inside the CP, the man at the switchboard called, "They're goin' crazy on those batteries, Major!"

"My orders stand, Corporal," Devereux said to Adam. "Pass that along, will you?"

"Aye, sir." Adam stepped back over to the switchboard, took the phone, and said, "Hold your fire. These orders are direct from Major Devereux."

Adam heard the orders passed along to the gun crews, and in the background an angry voice demanded, "What does the little bastard want us to do? Let 'em run over us without spittin' back?"

He ignored that—there was nothing else he could do—and watched Major Devereux through the open door of the command post. Battery A reported over the phone that the Japanese cruiser and one of the destroyers had come about and were starting yet another pass along the island. "Estimated range four thousand, five hundred yards!"

"Four thousand, five hundred yards, Major!" Adam called to Devereux. The major turned and gave Adam a curt nod.

"Fire," Devereux said in a calm voice.

Adam couldn't keep his own tone as steady. He shouted, "Fire! Fire!" into the phone. The smashing reports of the big guns came clearly through the early morning air as they swung into action.

Adam had to see what was happening. He handed over the phone to the technician and hurried to the doorway in time to see two shots from Battery A slam into the Jap cruiser amidships. Smoke began to rise out of the vessel as its speed slackened. Two more shells from the 5-inch guns crashed into the ship, striking it in about the same place. The smoke grew even thicker. The cruiser began to swing away in an attempt to avoid the firing from onshore.

The destroyer that was close by shot into the gap between the cruiser and the island. The destroyer was trying to protect the cruiser, Adam thought. Its guns fired fiercely, but a moment later a shell struck it in the area of the forecastle, resulting in a violent explosion. The destroyer swung around and put on more steam, trying to get out of the line of fire.

Adam couldn't help himself. He let out a whoop of excitement. "Look at 'em run!"

The cruiser was hit again, perhaps more than once. Its guns had stopped firing, and its crew was concentrating on getting out of there instead of attacking Wake Island.

A tremendous explosion pulled Adam's attention the other

way, toward Wilkes Island and Battery L up on Kuku Point. The range finders had been damaged in the air raids, but even without them, the gun crews had done a spectacular job, sending a volley of shells into one of the Japanese destroyers and blowing it in half. A huge column of smoke rose into the air as the ship finished breaking apart and sank. Another ship had been struck as well and a fire was burning brightly on its deck.

All the vessels in the Japanese fleet were retreating now. A few shots came from some of them, but it was clear they were more interested in getting away while they still could. Several were laying smokescreens deliberately, while others were smoking from the damage that had been inflicted on them. The cruiser that had been hit time and again by Battery A had a definite list to port, Adam noted, as it steamed away from the island.

The coastal batteries fell silent as the ships drew out of range, but planes roared overhead as the four Wildcats from VMF-211 gave chase to the fleeing Japanese fleet. Adam got a pair of binoculars from the command post and watched as the Wildcats dropped bombs from their improvised bomb racks. Far out to sea, another explosion sent smoke and fire into the air as one of the Japanese destroyers was blown apart by a cluster of well-aimed bombs. That made two vessels sunk, Adam thought, and who knew how many others damaged.

The planes swooped around, their work done, and headed back to Wake. Adam watched them come in, and he saw one of them wobbling badly. Smoke trailed from the F4F-3's engine.

"Look at that, Major," Adam said to Devereux. "Looks like one of the birds took a hit."

"I'm sure they all did," Devereux said, "but that one looks bad. Come on."

They piled into a jeep, Adam climbing behind the wheel, and headed for the air station. The damaged Wildcat dropped out of formation, Adam noted as he drove. The plane wasn't going to make it back to the runway.

"He's going down on the beach!" Devereux called, pointing.

Without waiting for orders, Adam turned the jeep and sent it bouncing over the rough coral toward the beach, hoping that it wouldn't do too much damage to the tires. As he brought the jeep to a screeching halt at the edge of the beach, the Wildcat's pilot pancaked the plane onto the tightly packed sand, bouncing it twice before the landing gear snapped off and the plane's nose plowed through the sand. The Wildcat slewed around with a grinding and tearing of metal.

A ground crew from the air station arrived about the same time as Adam and Devereux. All of them raced toward the wrecked plane as it finally came to a shuddering stop. The Plexiglas cover over the cockpit was spiderwebbed with cracks but largely intact. It lifted and the pilot climbed out, seemingly unhurt. As he dropped to the ground, he took off his flying helmet and goggles, and Adam recognized him as Captain Hank Elrod. Elrod looked miserably at Devereux and said, "I'm sorry as hell about the plane, Major."

Devereux just stared at him for a second, then laughed and clapped him on the back. "That was a pretty boring landing, Captain," he said. "Can't you make it a bit more spectacular next time?"

Elrod grinned. "I'll try, sir."

"I take it the Japanese are still running."

"As hard as they can."

"Then the battle is over." Devereux's smile disappeared. "For now."

Adam knew what the major meant. The defenders of Wake Island had given the Japanese a lot hotter welcome than they had been counting on, but the fight wasn't over. The Japs would be back.

And the Marines, Adam thought as he heard faint cheering coming from some of the gun crews, would be waiting.

TWENTY

The defenders of Wake Island did not have long to enjoy their victory over the Japanese invasion fleet. Before the morning of 11 December was over, a flight of bombers appeared from the north-east, closing in quickly on the atoll. They were spotted by the men on the water tank observation post, and the gun crews hustled to get ready for action.

Only two of the Wildcats from VMF-211's original dozen were capable of flying. The plane Captain Elrod had crash-landed on the beach would never fly again, and one of the others that had made it back to the air station had been damaged heavily by anti-aircraft fire from the Japanese ships. The two fighters, with 2nd Lt. Carl Davidson and 2nd Lt. John Kinney at the controls, took to the air and quickly shot down two bombers and forced another to turn back with smoke pouring from its engine. The 3-inch guns of Batteries D and E were also in on the excitement, sending one of the bombers spiraling into the ocean. Three more veered off, too heavily damaged to continue the bombing run. The planes that got through dropped their loads of bombs, but this time the explosions did little damage and inflicted no casualties. The bombers made only one pass, then turned and ran.

It had been quite a day for the Marines. They had sunk at least two Japanese ships, damaged many others, downed three bombers, and killed an unknown number of the enemy. Japanese casualties had to run into the hundreds, maybe more. The defenders' losses in return: four wounded, none seriously.

It was no wonder they felt like celebrating.

*　　*　　*

Adam watched in amazement as the officers held their thumbs over the open necks of beer bottles, shook the bottles, then sprayed each other with the contents. His mother would have said disapprovingly that it smelled like a brewery here in this bunker that served as the Marine Officers' Club. And of course, with all that beer splattered around, it did.

But the officers had a right to let off a little steam, Adam told himself as he sipped on a bottle of warm Coca-Cola. They and the men who served under them had just defeated an enemy force that outnumbered the defenders to the point of ridiculousness.

The officers laughed and whooped in sheer exuberance. The scene reminded Adam of parties he had attended back at the University of Chicago. Men slapped each other on the back in congratulation, and in the corner a group of them put their arms around one another's shoulders and began to sing bawdy songs. Adam smiled.

Major Devereux strolled over to where Adam was sitting on a crate of supplies and used his foot to push another crate into position beside him. As Devereux sat down, he said, "Quite the festive occasion, isn't it, Corporal?"

"Yes, sir," Adam replied, "but I don't think I should be here. You said it yourself—I'm a corporal. I don't belong in the officers' club."

"You're here at my invitation, so I don't think anyone is going to ask you to leave. I have a good reason for wanting you here." Devereux leaned closer and lowered his voice. With all the commotion in the room, no one more than a couple of feet away could hear him as he went on. "You handled yourself quite well this morning, Bergman. You were cool-headed even when the Japanese started shelling us. I've said this before, but I'll say it again: You have the makings of a fine officer."

"Thank you, sir."

"Have you been giving the possibility of officer training some thought?"

"Yes, sir, I have," Adam replied honestly. "But there's one big obstacle."

"What's that?"

"We'd have to get off this island first."

Devereux stared at him for a second, then chuckled. "Quite right. Perhaps when the relief expedition gets here . . ."

"Have you heard from Pearl Harbor, sir? Are they on the way?"

"Pearl Harbor has commended us," Devereux said. "According to the message we received a short time ago, we have carried out our duties in the highest traditions of the Naval Service. And help will soon be on the way. But keep that under your hat, Corporal. I don't want to raise the men's hopes too high just yet. A lot of things can happen."

Adam nodded. "Yes, sir." At the same time, he couldn't help but feel a surge of relief. He and the other men might make it off this damned island alive after all.

The party, such as it was, went on.

*   *   *

At Pearl Harbor, the staff of Admiral Husband E. Kimmel, Commander in Chief, United States Pacific Fleet, was hard at work finalizing the plans for the Wake Island relief effort. Task Force 14 was assembled quickly. Its centerpiece was the aircraft carrier U.S.S. *Saratoga,* with Marine Fighting Squadron VMF-221 on board. The *Saratoga* was to be accompanied by three heavy cruisers—the *Astoria,* the *Minneapolis,* and the *San Francisco*—as well as nine destroyers, a seaplane tender, and a fleet oiler. The seaplane tender, the *Tangier,* would also carry troops from the Fourth Defense Battalion.

Getting more supplies to the defenders on Wake Island was just as crucial. Range finders, fire-control apparatus, cables, and spare parts were all needed for the 3-inch and 5-inch anti-aircraft batteries on the atoll. Ammunition of all sorts, including nine thousand rounds of 5-inch shell and twelve thousand rounds of 3-inch shell; more than enough to replace what had already been used. Literally millions of rounds of .50-caliber and .30-caliber machine gun ammunition. And radar units, an SCR-270 early warning set and an SCR-268 fire-control set, which should have been sent to Wake with the original mission, were now loaded onto the *Tangier.*

The *Saratoga,* with VMF-221 aboard, was still en route to Pearl Harbor from San Diego, but as soon as the carrier arrived, the expedition would set out. All the Marines on Wake Island had to do was hold out until it got there.

The water pressure in the shower was weak, and there wasn't enough hot water. Catherine did the best she could, then stepped out and dried off. She wrapped a towel around her wet hair, tightened the belt of the robe she'd shrugged into, and stepped out of the bungalow onto the tiny porch. She reached into the pocket of the robe, took out a pack of cigarettes and a lighter. She had never smoked in her life until recently, but now she found that it calmed her jangled nerves. Not much, but these days she would take any sort of help she could get.

She lit one of the cigarettes, dropped the pack and the lighter back in her pocket, and inhaled deeply. She blew out the smoke and watched the gray cloud obscure the stars for a second before it dispersed in the night breeze. It was a warm evening, perfect weather for a young woman to go for a stroll on the beach with her husband.

If her husband weren't thousands of miles away, trapped on some stinking little coral atoll surrounded by millions of little Japanese bastards. . . .

Catherine dropped the cigarette on the porch and ground it out with the heel of her slipper. Suddenly it tasted terrible and she didn't want it.

The sound of footsteps made her look up. She saw a figure approaching along the crushed-shell path that led to the nurses' bungalows. The white uniform was easy to spot amidst the shadows cast by the palm trees. Missy came up to the bungalow and stepped onto the porch.

"Hi," she said. "How are you?"

"Fine," Catherine said tightly.

"Seems like a year ago we left here this morning, doesn't it?"

Catherine nodded but didn't say anything. The days at the hospital were long and difficult. Almost a week had passed since the sneak attack on Pearl Harbor. During that time, the hysteria in Honolulu and the alarm around the naval base had faded somewhat. A full-scale invasion by the Japanese seemed a lot less likely now. If they hadn't come in immediately following the bombing raid, they weren't going to, most people believed.

But men who had been wounded in the attack were still dying from their injuries, and even those whose lives weren't really in danger were still suffering. The doctors and the nurses did all they could, working until they were on the verge of dropping in their tracks. They could see some progress, but it was slow, God, so slow.

"Got a cigarette?" Missy asked.

Catherine got out the pack and the lighter again and handed them over to her friend. Missy lit up and then sighed. "You know what I heard?"

"No, what?"

"There was a message from Wake Island. We asked them if there was anything they needed, and they said, 'Send us more Japs.'" Missy laughed hollowly. "Do you believe it?"

What was bad, Catherine did believe it. That sounded just like something Adam would say. The prejudice he had encountered in his life had done more than make him work to be strong enough to take care of himself physically. It had given him an attitude, a way of carrying himself, that was sometimes quick and aggressive. Not arrogant, just a little cocky. Usually, Catherine thought that was a good thing.

But not now. Not with Adam's life on the line.

"I heard the Marines were going to send reinforcements," she said.

"Yeah, that's what I hear, too. A whole task force. You'll see. Adam'll be back here at Pearl before you know it."

"That would be nice." That was a hell of an understatement, Catherine thought. She stretched, trying to ease tired muscles. "I think I'll turn in."

"Yeah, me, too." Missy stifled a yawn. "I'm really tired tonight. I bet I'll sleep like a log."

Catherine wished she could. Her body was weary to the point of exhaustion, but her brain was still racing along a mile a minute. She knew if she went to bed, she would just lie there staring.

Thoughts bounced around crazily inside her head: memories of the wonderful times she'd had with Adam, recollections of her childhood, both good and bad, the clashes with her father, then more recently the pain of her brother's death, and, most horribly of all, the future. In her mind's eye, she saw Adam dying, his body ripped in half by machine gun fire or blown into bloody pieces by an exploding bomb. She saw the grim faces of the officers who would come to tell her that she was a widow. She saw herself dressed in black, a veil over her face, standing next to a marker over an empty grave, empty because Adam's body—or what was left of it—was somewhere far away, lying where he had fallen, lost forever to her. The fear of that future left her cold and sick and shaking inside.

Missy paused at the door. "You coming in?"

"In a little while," Catherine said.

TWENTY-ONE

"Hey, guys, look who's here!" Gurnwall said as Adam ducked into the tent to find the members of his old squad sitting on the ground playing poker. Gurnwall, as usual, had the biggest pile of matchsticks in front of him.

Kennemer and Magruder just grunted their greetings, since they were concentrating on their cards, but Rolofson said, "Hello, Bergman." Even though Adam was longer in grade than him and therefore technically his superior, Rolofson clearly felt they were on equal footing now.

Adam had his right hand behind his back. He brought it around in front of him and the four beer bottles he was holding by their necks clinked together. That got the attention of Kennemer and Magruder. Gurnwall said, "*Hel*-lo! Whatta we got here, Corp?"

"Straight from the officers' club," Adam said. "I'm sorry it's not cold. The icebox isn't working. Something about it being in the middle of a war zone."

He passed around the beers and then squatted on his heels, joining the circle. Kennemer said, "You're not drinkin'?"

"I had some earlier," Adam said, even though he really hadn't.

"What'd you do, swipe these?" Gurnwall asked. He twisted the cap off the bottle and tilted it to his mouth. The beer gurgled as he drank.

"No, Major Devereux had me in there talking to me. He said I could take some beer to my buddies as long as I wasn't too blatant about it."

Magruder said with a grin, "And you, of course, were the soul of discretion."

"Of course."

It felt good to be back here with the guys. To be honest, however, Adam enjoyed being one of Major Devereux's aides. He had been at the nerve center of the atoll's defenses when the Japanese task force showed up, and it had felt good. He'd been able to grasp the big picture that way, instead of only knowing just what was going on right in front of the machine gun his old squad manned. That didn't mean he thought he was better than them, he assured himself.

Rolofson opened his beer, took a swig from the bottle, and said, "Sounds to me like the major's grooming you to be an officer, Bergman."

That was exactly what was going on, Adam thought. But somehow he didn't like the sound of it when it was put into words. "I'm just doing the jobs the Corps asks me to do," he said, his voice a little cooler now.

"Sure you are." Rolofson took another drink. His cards were on the ground in front of him where he had tossed them after he folded.

"Say, we beat the hell outta those Japs today, didn't we?" Gurnwall said. "I never seen such a pretty sight as that big ol' Jap boat blowin' up."

Dryly, Magruder said, "That didn't stop 'em from bombing us again later."

"We're wearing them down," Adam said. "Sooner or later they're going to realize that they can't get us off of here, and then they'll leave us alone."

Gurnwall nodded. "Yeah, we'll show 'em. You wanta sit in on the next hand, Corp?"

"No thanks, Gurney. You're still too slick for me." Adam put his hands on his knees and pushed himself upright. "I just wanted to stop by and see how you boys were doing and bring you that beer."

"We're obliged," Kennemer said, lifting his bottle in a vague salute.

"Damn right," Magruder added.

Rolofson didn't say anything. Gurnwall drank the rest of his beer, then said, "Hey, are we gonna play cards or sit around here yakkin' the rest of the night?"

Taking that as his cue, Adam turned and left the tent. He had gone only a couple of steps when he heard the canvas flap pushed aside and someone came after him.

"Bergman," Rolofson said.

Adam stopped and swung around. Rolofson stood there tensely in the darkness. The island was under blackout conditions, of course, and the only light came from the stars. Still, the illumination was bright enough for Adam to see the tight-set lines on Rolofson's broad face.

"What is it?"

"It's not that I don't appreciate the beer," Rolofson began. "You don't have any right to come around here, Bergman."

"What are you talking about?" Adam was genuinely puzzled.

"This is *my* squad now. Gurnwall calls you Corp like you're still in charge, but you're not. Your place is up at the command post with Devereux and the rest of his pets."

Adam's hands clenched involuntarily into fists. "What'd you say?"

"You heard me." Rolofson wasn't backing down. "I don't need you coming around here and bringing beer to the guys and undercutting my authority."

"Damn it, that's not what I was doing at all! I just wanted to see if all of you made it through the day all right."

"You mean you came to see who else got killed on my watch. You weren't anywhere around when Stout died, so it wasn't your fault, right? It was mine. That's what you think."

Adam forced himself to control the anger he felt. Rolofson seemed to be blaming himself for Stout's death, and he was turning that guilt into resentment directed toward Adam. Maybe that conclusion was too easy to jump to, the result of a couple of college psychology courses, but Adam thought there was at least a germ of truth to it.

"We're at war," he said. "Men get killed in war. That's just the way it is, Rolofson. Most of the time it's not anybody's fault."

"I don't need your pity, damn it!"

Adam shrugged. "If you don't want me around, I'll stay away."

"You do that. Don't come around reminding the guys how much better they had it when you were in charge."

Adam didn't remember things being that goddamned peachy while he was in command of the squad, but he kept that thought to himself. Instead he said, "All right, Rolofson. I'll see you around." He turned and walked away, and this time no one stopped him.

Adam knew Rolofson was wrong, that the Swede was just bitter and scared like everybody else on the atoll and spewing words just to see where they landed. He also thought that the new job they'd given him was a good job, a necessary job, working with Major Devereux. If that led to something else in the future, like an officer's commission, well, so be it. That was too far away to worry about. Like he'd told the major, they all had to get off this island first.

Adam went back to the command post, knocked, waited for the all-clear, then ducked inside. When the lamp was relit, he saw a technical sergeant at the switchboard and a young lieutenant at the major's desk. The lieutenant had the night duty. He asked, "What are you doing here, Corporal?"

"I thought I'd do some more of that filing, sir," Adam replied as he gestured at the table where he had been sorting documents during his spare time.

"Wouldn't you rather get some sleep, Corporal?"

Adam shook his head. "No, sir. Not right now."

The lieutenant shrugged and said, "Well, go ahead, then." He grinned. "You must be one of those eager beavers who's always bucking for a promotion."

Adam took a deep breath and said, "No, sir." That wasn't what he felt like doing right at this moment, not at all.

But if he *had* been bucking for a promotion, busting a wise-ass lieutenant in the chops sure wouldn't help. And he was still so irritated with Rolofson *that* was what he felt like doing.

Dawn came early on 12 December, and so did the Japanese. A few minutes after sunup, two bombers roared over, dropping their explosives around the runways at the air station. The two Wildcats, already in the air on morning patrol, intercepted the bombers and, with the odds even for a change, had no trouble shooting down one of them. The other Jap hightailed it for home, or whatever passed for home out here in the middle of the Pacific.

While the work of strengthening the defenses and repairing damage from past raids went on during the morning, the defenders kept glancing skyward, expecting more bombers to show up. Noon came and went with no sign of the Japanese. No one was ready yet to breathe a sigh of relief, though.

During the day, Lieutenant Kinney was able to repair the damage that one of the Wildcats had suffered a couple of days earlier, so that evening three of the fighters took off on patrol. One of the planes proved balky, however, and it wasn't able to get off the ground until a quarter of an hour after the other two. Its pilot, 2nd Lt. David Kliewer, was trying to catch up to the others when he spotted a Japanese submarine running on the surface. Unable to resist such a tempting target, Kliewer sent his F4F-3 diving toward it, raking the sub's deck with .50-caliber machine gun fire. He released both of his bombs as he pulled out of the dive. Water geysered high in the air as the bombs bracketed the sub and exploded. Neither had scored a direct hit, but the explosions were close enough to damage the submarine. As Kliewer circled, he saw it dive beneath the surface. A dark oil slick floated on the water where it had been.

Back on Wake Island, as darkness settled in, the atoll's

defenders gathered together for the first time since the siege had begun. Only the observation post and the command post were left manned. Everyone else was carrying out an important duty.

Adam stood with the other Marines along the edge of a long trench that had been scooped out by some of the civilian construction equipment. A bulldozer stood nearby, ready to cover the mass grave. A grim-faced burial detail unloaded the tarpaulin-wrapped corpses from the trucks that had brought them from the refrigerated warehouse at Camp Two which had once been used to store perishables for the luxury hotel.

One by one, the bodies were placed in the trench and lined up carefully side by side. Adam took off his helmet, as did the other Marines. On the other side of the grave, the civilians also uncovered their heads out of respect for the dead.

Adam glanced around but didn't see the members of his old squad. Stout's body was down there in the mass grave, he knew, but of course he wasn't sure which one it was. The canvas shrouds made the dead men anonymous. Adam stayed where he was and didn't seek out his friends.

When all the bodies had been taken from the trucks and placed in the mass grave, a squad of seven riflemen fired three volleys into the air. Major Devereux said a few words, then turned the service over to a lay minister who was one of the civilian construction workers. The man clutched a battered old black leather Bible in his hand as he prayed in a loud voice.

Some of the men who had died were probably Jewish, Adam thought, and it would have been nice if they could have had a proper Jewish burial service performed by a rabbi. Actually, in accordance with their faith, they should have been buried days earlier, as soon as possible after their deaths. Under the circumstances, that hadn't been possible. But there were undoubtedly Catholics in that mass grave, too, and Protestants, and maybe Hindus for all he knew. Surely, despite the lack of familiar rituals, they would all be welcomed into the arms of whatever God they worshipped. Adam wanted very much to believe that was true.

When the prayer was finished, one of the civilians climbed

into the cab of the bulldozer. Its engine rumbled and grumbled and then started with a roar. The 'dozer moved forward, its gears clanking as the blade was lowered. The blade bit into the long mound of dirt and crushed coral heaped beside the grave and shoved it forward. The men began to turn away as the dirt showered down on the canvas-wrapped corpses. Adam had something in his throat, a huge lump that made it difficult to breathe, and he suspected most of the other men, Marines and civilians alike, felt the same way.

Major Devereux and Commander Cunningham were talking in low voices as Adam came up to them. Cunningham said, "I don't think we should do this again, Major. It's too hard on the men, too damaging to morale."

Devereux nodded. "I agree, Commander."

"All right, then. From here on out, when we lose a man, he'll be buried as soon as possible, as close to where he fell as practical."

"Yes, sir."

Cunningham glanced over at Adam, who saluted and said, "Commander."

The naval officer returned the salute. "At ease, Corporal. We're not going to stand on ceremony at a time like this."

"This is Corporal Bergman, Commander," Devereux said. "You remember, I told you about him."

"Yes, of course."

That came as a surprise to Adam. Why in the world would Major Devereux be talking to Cunningham about *him*?

No explanations were forthcoming. Cunningham said good night to Devereux and headed back to Camp Two, where his headquarters were located. Adam returned to the command post along with Devereux, who didn't say anything else about the comment. He would just have to be curious, Adam told himself.

If it was something important, he would find out sooner or later.

TWENTY-TWO

The next day, 13 December, passed with no sign of the Japanese at all for the first time since the attacks had begun. It was a welcome respite. The defenders were able to relax a little. The day wasn't completely good news, however: The fighter patrols went on, and during takeoff that evening one of the Wildcats nearly hit a large crane that unexpectedly flew in front of it. The desperate maneuver undertaken by the pilot to avoid hitting the crane resulted in a loss of control of the aircraft. It crash-landed near the runway, wrecked beyond repair. The only good thing about the fluke accident was that the pilot wasn't hurt.

The Japanese bombers were back early the next morning, striking before dawn but not inflicting much damage. The midday raid that day, 14 December, was a costly one for the defenders. Two Marines were killed in the bombing, and one of the two flightworthy Wildcats took a direct hit near its tail, setting it afire. Three of the men from VMF-211, who had taken cover nearby, were able to run over to the burning plane and, working with remarkably steady nerves, unbolt the engine, drop it from the fuselage, and pull it clear before the flames reached it.

Of the dozen planes that had come to Wake Island with the squadron, now only one of them could still fly.

The Japanese made only one bombing run on 15 December, during the evening, and most of those bombs went harmlessly into the lagoon. One civilian was killed in the raid, however.

Adam was in the command post while the attack was going on. A few minutes after it was over, Major Devereux entered the command post, a grim look on his face. "We've received some new orders from Pearl Harbor," he said. "We're to destroy all of our codes and ciphers."

Adam frowned slightly, unable at first to understand why that seemed to bother the major. Then, suddenly, he realized what the order meant. They were supposed to destroy the codes and ciphers because Pearl Harbor didn't want them falling into enemy hands.

"What about the relief expedition, sir?" Adam asked.

"Nothing was said about that. I assume it is still proceeding according to plan."

Devereux didn't sound completely convinced of that, Adam thought. But there was nothing they could do about it here on Wake. Help either arrived or it didn't. In the meantime, they had to follow orders. Adam began to gather up the paperwork that detailed all the codes and ciphers used by the 1st Defense Battalion.

A short time later, joined by Major Bayler with all of VMF-211's codes, Major Devereux threw the documents into an oil drum, poured gasoline over them, and set them ablaze. Adam stood a few yards away, flinching a little from the heat as flames shot up from the drum, red and gold streaks dancing against the blackness of the night. The codes were completely consumed by the fierce blaze, leaving only a heap of gray ash.

On 16 and 17 December, the Japanese were back in full force, conducting several bombing raids. Life on the atoll fell into a bleak pattern: Scramble to defense positions, fight off the attackers, clean up the mess they left behind, and bury the dead. The weather didn't cooperate, as clouds and drizzle moved in and seemed to be staying around for a while, but the gloom was certainly appropriate to the mood on Wake. The optimism of a few days earlier had seeped away. There was no definite word on when—or if—the relief expedition would arrive.

Working around the clock, the mechanics of VMF-211 managed to repair three of the damaged planes, scavenging parts from the wrecked aircraft and rebuilding what they couldn't replace. Getting the squadron's strength back up to four flyable Wildcats was about the only good news the defenders got, and even that was short-lived because one of the fighters developed engine trouble on takeoff and had to crash-land. Air strength was back to only three planes—but that was still better than just one.

Surprisingly, 18 December was peaceful. The only Japanese plane that flew over the atoll was a high-altitude reconnaissance craft. While the defenders were grateful for another day in which bombs didn't fall, the presence of the Japanese patrol plane didn't bode well. Speculation among the men was that the plane was mapping out a route for another invasion fleet.

The bombers were back the next day, blowing up the mess hall at Camp One but accomplishing little else. And the Japs lost another bomber in the process, shot down by the 3-inch guns of Batteries D and E.

Another weather front moved through on the morning of 20 December, bringing with it hard, driving rain instead of the steady drizzle that had been falling on the atoll. The clouds were thick and low, causing such poor visibility that the Wildcats were grounded. But if the fighters couldn't fly, then neither could the Japanese bombers. At least, that was what Adam thought.

Adam was standing in the open doorway of the command post that afternoon, sipping coffee and watching the rain fall, when he heard something over the steady downpour. He frowned and tilted his head to the side as if that would allow him to hear better. The sound grew louder, and after a moment Adam turned to the desk where Major Devereux was working and said, "I hear a plane, Major!"

Devereux's head snapped up, the reports on his desk instantly forgotten. "Bombers?"

"I don't know," Adam said slowly. "It sounds different somehow. Familiar, though."

The phone rang, and the sergeant on duty at the switchboard snatched it up. After listening intently for a second, he swiveled his chair and said to Devereux, "The boys at the OP say a plane's coming in, sir. They say they think it's one of ours!"

Devereux snatched up his helmet and buckled it on. Adam

followed suit. Both of them shrugged into raincoats. "Let's go, Corporal," Devereux said as he started out of the command post.

Adam drove the jeep through the rain, which pattered loudly on his helmet. As he and the major reached the air station, they saw Major Bayler hurrying out of the radio hut. The roar of airplane engines was loud now. Adam brought the jeep to a stop and looked up at the sky in the direction of the sound.

The thick clouds parted for a second, and the familiar shape of a Navy PBY emerged, angling down toward the lagoon. "Look at that, sir!" Adam exclaimed as he caught sight of the flying boat.

"I see it," Devereux replied.

Bayler came up to the jeep and grinned at him and Devereux. "Looks like the outside world is still there," he said.

Adam knew just what Bayler meant. The atoll had become their entire universe during the past week and a half. Sure, they were in radio contact with Pearl Harbor, but that didn't seem quite real. The disembodied voices might as well have been phantoms from another realm. And as for the Japanese, there was no human connection with them at all. They were just the enemy. That was their only reality.

But now, the PBY touching down on the surface of the lagoon was a physical manifestation of the rest of the world, a world that still cared about the approximately fifteen hundred men stuck on these three little islands in the middle of nowhere. Adam felt his spirits lifting already.

Devereux waited until the flying boat had completed its landing and was taxiing toward the seaplane ramp on Peale Island, then told Adam to take them over there. Major Bayler climbed into the backseat of the jeep and came with them.

In the drenching rain, it took several minutes to drive up the eastern leg of Wake Island and across the bridge onto Peale. By the time the jeep reached the seaplane ramp, the PBY had already tied up there and the two pilots had climbed down from the cockpit. They saluted as Devereux and Bayler got out of the jeep and came over to them.

"Good afternoon, Major," one of the pilots said, raising his voice over the pounding rain. He was a captain and looked barely old enough to be a Boy Scout, let alone the commander of a flying boat. "We bring you greetings from Pearl Harbor."

"The greetings are accepted," Devereux said. "What about the relief expedition?"

"Task Force Fourteen is on its way, sir, led by the *Saratoga* with VMF-two-twenty-one aboard." The young captain reached inside his leather flying jacket and brought out a sheaf of papers wrapped in oilcloth and secured with a string. "Here's a list of the personnel and supplies also being carried by the task force."

That small packet of documents represented salvation for the defenders of Wake, Adam thought as he watched Major Devereux take them.

"I also have detailed orders for you and Commander Cunningham, Major," the Navy captain went on. "Perhaps we could all meet at the Pan American Airways hotel and go over them. I'd like to get out of the rain."

A wry smile tugged at Devereux's mouth. With a thumb, he pointed at a pile of rubble nearby. "*That* is the Pan American hotel, Captain. A small sample of what the Japs have been giving us."

"Oh. Sorry, sir."

Devereux waved off the apology. "Never mind, Captain. We're just glad to see you. Come along, I'll take you to Commander Cunningham's HQ. It's not far."

The jeep was packed with Adam at the wheel, Devereux beside him, and the two pilots in the back along with Major Bayler. The captain had an envelope for Bayler, too. He handed it over, but Bayler didn't open it yet. The rain would have soaked anything inside it.

Devereux, Bayler, and the two pilots went inside the house that served as Cunningham's headquarters. Adam stayed outside on the small porch, letting some of the water drain off him. He took off his helmet so it wouldn't drip down the back of his neck and wondered whether the pilots would be allowed to carry any personal messages with them when the PBY left Wake. That was likely, he decided, so he started thinking about what he would write to Catherine and his mother. The men probably wouldn't be allowed more than a page or two apiece, so whatever he wanted to say, he had to boil it down as much as he could.

Night fell early because of the thick overcast. Adam was still standing on the porch an hour after the meeting began, thinking about Catherine, when an ensign whom he recognized as one of Cunningham's aides stepped out. The ensign wore a raincoat and peaked cap and didn't look happy at the prospect of going out in the downpour.

"What's up, Ensign?" Adam ventured to ask.

"I'm going to pass the word to all personnel that messages are allowed to be sent with the PBY when it takes off tomorrow morning."

"That fast, eh?"

"The pilots' orders say they're to return to Pearl via the Midway route with all possible dispatch."

The ensign was being surprisingly frank, considering that Adam was just a corporal. Adam said, "I hope they're through in there before much longer. I want to get back to the CP and start on a letter to my wife."

"I think you're going to have to wait awhile," the ensign said. "Major Devereux asked me to tell you to step inside."

Adam stiffened. "Excuse me, sir?"

The ensign inclined his head toward the door. "They want you in there, but don't ask me what it's about, Corporal, because I don't know."

Adam had no idea, either. He nodded and said, "Thank you, sir."

The ensign grimaced at the storm and then went out into it. Adam, holding his helmet in his hands, turned toward the door, hesitated for a second, then stepped inside to find out what was going on.

TWENTY-THREE

Commander Cunningham sat behind a metal desk. A photograph of President Roosevelt hung from a nail driven into the raw plywood wall behind him. Major Devereux sat in a straight-backed chair to Cunningham's right. Major Bayler and the two captains who had brought in the PBY were scattered around the office on wooden chairs. One of the pilots had reversed his chair so that he could straddle it.

Adam looked around at the five solemn-faced officers. If he didn't know better, he would have sworn that he had committed some sort of infraction and was facing a court-martial.

Marines didn't salute indoors unless an officer was wearing his cover, and none of these were. Adam stood stiffly, not quite at attention but not at ease, either, and said to Major Devereux, "You wanted to see me, Major?"

"Relax, Corporal," Devereux said. "You're among friends here."

Cunningham waved at the one empty chair in the office. "Have a seat, Bergman."

"Yes, sir." Adam drew the chair up and sat down. He'd left his raincoat hanging on the porch. His uniform was still damp, though, and somewhat uncomfortable.

But not as uncomfortable as sitting here with these officers all around him and not knowing what they wanted.

Thankfully, Devereux came right to the point. "Major Bayler has been ordered to return to Pearl Harbor with these gentlemen when they take off tomorrow. You're going with him, Bergman."

The news was so stunning, so unexpected, that for several seconds Adam's brain was unable to comprehend it. Finally, knowing that he sounded stupid but unable to do anything to avoid it, he said, "To Pearl Harbor, sir?"

"That's right."

Commander Cunningham leaned forward, clasping his hands together on the desk. "Major Devereux says that you can be trusted, Corporal. If he has faith in your discretion, then so do I."

All Adam could think of to say was, "Thank you, sir."

"Major Devereux, Major Putnam, and myself will all be writing reports for CINCPAC concerning the status of our defense of Wake," Cunningham went on. "Major Bayler will deliver those reports. But he'll be carrying something else as well, something that could turn out to be vital to our war effort. You'll be carrying copies of those documents, Corporal."

"What are they, sir?" The words were out of Adam's mouth before he remembered that he was here to receive orders, not to ask questions.

Cunningham's eyes narrowed. "You don't have the need to know that. All that's required of you is to keep safe what you're given and deliver it to Vice Admiral Pye, acting CINCPAC, when you arrive at Pearl Harbor."

"Yes, sir," Adam said crisply. He was getting his wits back about him now, and his brain was beginning to work quickly. He was aware of the concept of redundancy. Major Bayler would be carrying important information, so important that its safe delivery wasn't going to be entrusted to him alone. Adam would have the same information, so that if anything happened to Bayler, the info would still have a chance to reach Pearl Harbor safely.

Of course, if anything happened to the PBY—if it was shot down into the ocean or blown out of the sky by the Japanese—chances were Adam would die right along with Bayler. But if the plane had to ditch for some reason and there were survivors, sending the information with two men doubled the chances of it getting where it was going.

As if he were reading Adam's thoughts, Devereux said,

"You're a smart young man, Corporal. You know what we're asking of you."

"I'll carry out my orders, sir."

Cunningham grunted. "Report to the seaplane ramp tomorrow morning at 0530, Corporal. And if there are any goodbyes you want to say to anyone on the atoll, you'd better say them tonight."

"Yes, sir."

"That's all."

"Yes, sir."

Adam went back out onto the porch to wait for Devereux and Bayler to be finished with the meeting. When they were, he would drive them back to the other side of Wake Island.

In the meantime, his head was spinning. He was leaving Wake. The enormity of that was almost too much for him to grasp. He hadn't expected to be able to go back to Pearl, even when Task Force 14 arrived with the relief expedition. Of course, the long flight might prove to be dangerous, what with all the Jap planes that could be flying around looking for a lone PBY, but once that obstacle was overcome, he would be safe. More than that, he would be where Catherine was.

Catherine. Adam closed his eyes, remembering the smell of her hair, the taste of her mouth, the warmth of her body as he held her in his arms. Catherine. Soon he would be with her again.

And the rest of the men on Wake? They would still be here, thousands of miles away from their wives and sweethearts and families, facing the incredible danger that loomed over them every day.

The thought was like fire in Adam's brain, and guilt hit him like a punch in the gut.

Gurnwall exhaled a cloud of cigarette smoke and squinted through it at the pages of the paperback book in his other hand. The light wasn't very good here in the dugout he shared with

Rolofson. He'd picked up the book at a civilian newsstand in San Diego before boarding the ship that would take him to Pearl Harbor, buying it because it had a little picture of a kangaroo in one corner of the cover and he thought it looked funny. It was called *Lost Horizon* and was by some guy named Hilton. Pretty good story, Gurnwall thought. Not very funny, though. He was almost halfway through the book.

He heard the *scritch-scritch* of Rolofson writing in the journal that he kept. Rolofson scribbled in it every night, writing down everything that happened during the day. Gurnwall wasn't that ambitious. He would rather read something somebody else had written.

From the other side of the blackout curtain hung over the dugout entrance, a voice called, "Put out the light."

Gurnwall sat up on his cot and laid *Lost Horizon* aside. "Corp? That you?" He thought he recognized Adam Bergman's voice.

Rolofson made a little noise of disgust and turned out the lamp. The curtain was pushed aside and Adam stepped into the dugout. A couple of men were with him. When the curtain had been tugged closed again, Rolofson snapped on the lamp. Gurnwall saw that Adam's companions were Kennemer and Magruder.

"What are you doing here, Bergman?" Rolofson asked.

"Take it easy," Adam said. He held out a bottle of whiskey. "Peace offering."

Gurnwall stood up. "I'll take that, Corp," he said with a grin as he reached for the bottle. "I'm in charge of the peace offerings around here."

"You could call it a going-away present, too, I guess."

"Going away?" Rolofson said. "Where are we going?"

"Not you. Me. I'm leaving in the morning on that PBY that came in earlier."

The four remaining members of his old squad stared at him in surprise. Gurnwall said, "You're goin' back to Pearl?"

"That's right, Gurney."

"Running out on us?" Rolofson said.

For a second, Gurnwall thought Adam was going to take a swing at Rolofson. Instead, Adam said tightly, "I have my orders. I intend to follow them like any good Marine, whether I like them or not."

"Oh, you like them, I'll bet."

Gurnwall said, "Shut up, Rolofson."

The Swede's head jerked toward him. "You can't talk to me like that—"

"I don't give a goddamn that you're a corporal and I'm only a private," Gurnwall said. "You got no call to talk to the corp that way. He ran the squad good, and it ain't his fault he ain't here with us no more. Just like it ain't his fault he's bein' sent back to Pearl."

Rolofson was on his feet now, glaring across the close quarters at Gurnwall. Adam said, "Why don't both of you just take it easy? Thanks for the support, Gurney, but Rolofson's right: He's a corporal and entitled to some respect."

"Yeah, yeah," Gurnwall said. He held up the bottle. "Where'd you get this hooch?"

"Scrounged it from the officers' club. They'll never miss it."

Kennemer stepped forward. "Well, we appreciate it. Don't just stand there, Gurney. Open 'er up."

Gurnwall unscrewed the cap from the whiskey and tilted the bottle to his mouth. He took a long swallow, then passed the bottle to Kennemer. The whiskey went around the dugout. Everyone drank. Even Rolofson took a healthy swig, though he was still glaring slightly at Adam and Gurnwall as he lowered the bottle.

They all sat down, Adam and Magruder on the ground. Gurnwall asked, "Why are they sendin' you back to Pearl, Corp?"

"I don't know all the details," Adam said. "I'll be acting as a courier of some sort."

"Don't they usually use officers for that?" Rolofson asked.

Adam shrugged. "All I know is the order came directly from Commander Cunningham and Major Devereux."

Gurnwall had the bottle again. He took a sip, then said, "So you gotta go. You lucky stiff."

Adam smiled. "Don't I know it."

"Yeah, well, when you're back there layin' on the beach with that pretty wife of yours and eatin' roast pig at some luau, you think about us, okay, Corp?"

Adam suddenly looked solemn. "I will, Gurney. You can count on that." He smiled again. "Although I don't know if I'll be going to any luaus."

Rolofson reached over and took the bottle from Gurnwall. He drank again, then said, "Have you heard anything about the relief expedition?"

Adam hesitated. "I can't talk about that."

"Why the hell not? Don't you think we have a right to know?"

"Sure, but that decision isn't up to me. I'm sure Major Devereux will make an announcement about it soon. In the meantime, you boys have tonight to write any letters you want to send back to Pearl with the PBY."

"Damn," Magruder said. "Gimme that bottle. I'll take one more drink; then I got to go write to my gal."

"Me, too," Kennemer added. "Thanks for stopping by our dugout and getting us, Corporal. Good luck on the flight back."

"Thanks. I really will be thinking about you guys."

Rolofson rubbed his jaw. "I suppose I'd better write to my girlfriend, too." The whiskey had mellowed him a little.

"What about you, Gurney?" Adam asked.

"I ain't got no girlfriend, Corp. The girls back in Tulsa weren't exactly linin' up to go steady with a guy like me."

"You must have family . . ."

Gurnwall shrugged. "Yeah, I guess. I'll write 'em a note. Thanks for comin' by and tellin' us about it, Corp."

"My pleasure." Adam put out his hand. "So long, Gurney. Take care of yourself."

Gurnwall hesitated, then took Adam's hand and shook it hard. "Thanks, Corp."

Adam shook hands with the other men, then ducked out of the dugout, leaving the bottle behind. There wasn't much whiskey in it by now. It made one more circuit; then Gurnwall drained the last few drops. Kennemer and Magruder headed back to their own dugout.

"I don't get that guy," Rolofson said as he sat down and picked up his journal and pen.

"What guy?"

"Bergman. He acted like he was really going to miss us. Almost like he didn't really want to leave Wake."

Gurnwall sat down on his cot. "I reckon he wants to leave, all right. A guy'd have to be crazy not to want to get off this stinkin' island."

"That's the truth." Rolofson went back to writing in his journal.

Gurnwall lit another cigarette and stretched out on the cot again, the paperback book propped open on his chest as he smoked for a minute. He thought about Adam. The corp was the only guy in the world who knew how Gurnwall had lost his nerve on top of the water tank during that first Japanese attack. He had never said a word about it to anybody. Gurnwall owed him for that and always would. The corp was just about the best friend Gurnwall had in the world. Come to think of it, he was about as much like family as Gurnwall's real family was. He never would have thought he could feel like that about a Yankee. A Jewish Yankee, at that.

"Good luck, Corp," Gurnwall whispered to himself. *Hope you get back safe to that wife of yours.*

"You say something?" Rolofson asked.

"Nah." Gurnwall puffed on the Lucky, picked up the book, and went back to Shangri-la.

TWENTY-FOUR

The next morning, the weather surprised Adam by cooperating. When he reported as ordered to the seaplane ramp on Peale Island at 0530, the sun was already up and shining through gaps in the clouds. A cool wind was blowing briskly. The PBY wouldn't have to take off through the same sort of downpour in which it had landed the day before.

Adam was wearing his greens again and carrying his duffel bag and rifle. He found Commander Cunningham and Majors Devereux and Bayler waiting for him.

"Corporal Bergman reporting, sir," Adam said to Devereux as he came to attention and snapped a salute.

Devereux returned the salute and said, "At ease, Corporal."

A couple of ensigns from the naval detachment were standing by. Cunningham snapped his fingers at one of them, and the young officer stepped forward and handed him a canvas portfolio which had been folded in half and tied closed. Cunningham held out the portfolio toward Adam.

"This is to be delivered personally to Admiral Pye or his chief of staff," Cunningham said. "The contents are in a waterproof pouch, but I'd appreciate it if you'd do your best to keep them out of the ocean, Corporal."

"Aye, aye, sir. I'll do my best." Adam unbuttoned his blouse and slipped the portfolio into the inner pocket. It made for a rather awkward lump when he fastened the buttons again, but there was nothing he could do about that.

At the ramp, a ground crew from the air station was going

over the flying boat. The two pilots rode up in a jeep, hopped out, and began running through their checklist. A tanker rumbled along a few minutes later, and its hose was stretched out to the fueling port of the PBY. It began pumping avgas into the airplane's tanks.

Quite a few Navy and Marine personnel were around this morning, busy with the usual tasks involved with defending the atoll. The guns of Battery D, on the other side of the island, were fully manned, since the Japanese sometimes liked to come calling early in the day. Adam looked around, thinking that maybe Gurnwall and the other guys from the old squad might show up to bid him farewell, but he didn't see any sign of them. That was all right, he told himself. They were off somewhere else doing their duty, and that was exactly what he would have expected of them had he still been leading them.

Most of the men were wearing grins this morning. Despite the fact that news of the relief expedition was supposed to be a secret, word had gotten around the islands. For days the defenders had been asking themselves why no one came to help them fight off the Japanese. Now it seemed that help was on the way, and morale was high for a change.

It helped, too, that Major Bayler was carrying a thick briefcase full of letters home. All through the night and the early morning, men had come to the atoll's command posts with letters they wanted to send. The letters had been gathered together and delivered to Bayler, who was barely able to close the briefcase once all the messages had been stuffed inside it.

"It'll be a while before the bird takes off," Devereux said to Adam. "You might as well find someplace comfortable to wait."

Comfort was something that had been in short supply on Wake in recent days, but Adam nodded and said, "Yes, sir." He sat down on a stack of planks that had been salvaged from the bombed-out hotel.

Now that he was on the verge of leaving the island, time seemed to drag and the necessary delay as the airplane was refueled and checked out chafed at Adam's nerves. The flight from Wake to Pearl would take at least twenty hours, with another refueling stop at Midway. But with any luck, he would be back with Catherine before another sunrise came and went.

Actually, he would be there in no time at all, considering the international date line, he thought wryly. It was still 19 December on Pearl. If he got there in a day's time or less, it would be 20 December when he arrived, the same date on which he was leaving Wake Island. Adam chuckled and shook his head. That just showed how arbitrary time was. No matter how humans divided it up, the world just kept on turning, the sun rising and setting and rising and setting again and again. . . .

"Time to get aboard, Corporal," Major Bayler called to him.

Adam got to his feet and walked over to the dock that extended into the lagoon next to the seaplane ramp. A glance at his watch told him it was nearly 0700 hours. The breeze was still strong, causing the American flag on a nearby flagpole to flutter and pop. Adam glanced up at it as he walked by, feeling a tightness in his chest that was a mixture of pride, relief, nervousness, and regret.

Devereux, Cunningham, and Bayler were waiting at the door set into the PBY's fuselage. Bayler motioned for Adam to go first. Adam climbed into the plane, stepping into a utilitarian cabin with walls of riveted steel and unpadded metal bench seats. These flying boats weren't built for comfort.

Major Bayler came into the plane behind him. Both of them turned and saluted Devereux, Cunningham, and the flag that flapped on the pole behind them. "Godspeed, Major," Devereux called.

It suddenly occurred to Adam that he hadn't asked anyone what he was supposed to do once he had delivered the documents to CINCPAC, but before he could say anything one of the PBY's crew closed the door and dogged it shut. "Have a seat, sir," he said to Bayler. "You, too, Corporal. Might as well make yourselves as comfortable as you can. We've got a long flight ahead of us."

Adam and Bayler sat down on separate benches across a narrow aisle from each other, placing their gear beside them. Bayler looked over at Adam and asked, "Ever flown before, Corporal?"

"No, sir. All my traveling has been by train or ship."

"Well, then, I hope your first flight is a smooth one."

"Yes, sir, me too."

The engines began to turn over. Adam looked out a port and saw the propellers start to rotate. With a roar, the engines smoothed out and the propellers became nothing but a blur. Adam felt himself pressed back a little against the metal bench as the plane accelerated across the lagoon and then lifted into the air.

This was it, Adam told himself. He was really leaving Wake Island. He closed his eyes and thanked God.

Then he uttered a silent prayer for all the men he was leaving behind.

* * *

In the chaotic days following the Japanese attack on Pearl Harbor, investigations began almost immediately into the question of who was to blame for the Pacific fleet getting caught with its pants down. It was almost inevitable that the Commander in Chief, Pacific Fleet, would shoulder some of the responsibility, whether that conclusion was right or wrong. Accordingly, on 15 December 1941, Admiral Husband E. Kimmel was relieved of command by Secretary of the Navy Frank Knox and replaced by Vice Admiral William Pye. Pye was to serve as CINCPAC only until Rear Admiral Chester W. Nimitz could arrive in the Territory of Hawaii and take command. General Walter Short, commander of the Army detachment at Schofield Barracks, was also relieved and replaced.

The personnel at the naval hospital knew of the situation regarding Admiral Kimmel, of course, but it had little impact on their daily lives, which were consumed with caring for their patients. Whether Kimmel was the incompetent he was portrayed to be in Secretary Knox's report on the attack or simply a convenient scapegoat, it mattered much less to them than did the condition of the men who filled the beds in the hospital's wards.

Catherine was checking on one of those men, who had suffered a broken leg and severe burns on his arms and torso, when Billie Tabor came hurrying up to her. "You've got to go downstairs," Billie said.

Catherine was holding a glass of water so that the injured sailor could drink through a straw. She said, "Why?"

"Don't ask questions," Billie said. "Just do it."

With a frown, Catherine looked over at her redheaded friend. Billie was grinning. "What's going on here?" Catherine asked.

"Just go downstairs," Billie repeated.

The sailor in the bed summoned up a weak smile on his bandaged face. "Better do it, Nurse, before your friend here has a fit."

"All right," Catherine said, "but you'd better not be pulling some sort of prank, Billie."

"Just *go*." Billie reached out and took the glass. "I'll take care of this handsome swabbie."

That made the injured sailor smile even more.

With a shake of her head, Catherine walked down the aisle in the middle of the ward to the exit doors and the stairwell. She paused at the top of the stairs to put her hands in the small of her back and press. She had been on duty for several hours and was already tired.

She went down one flight of stairs to the hospital's ground floor and came out into the lobby. She felt a twinge of sorrow as she recalled coming down those same steps and emerging into this same lobby to find her brother Spencer waiting for her. That had been less than a month earlier, but already it seemed far in the past.

Today Missy Mitchell was waiting for her. The brunette caught hold of Catherine's arm and tugged her toward the lobby entrance. "Outside," she said.

"What? What is this?" Catherine tried to pull away. "Missy, let go!"

"No, ma'am." Missy pushed open the door. "You're coming with me."

Missy was bigger and stronger, and anyway, Catherine was curious now about what was going on, in addition to being a little irritated. She let Missy steer her out the door and onto the hospital's front porch . . .

Where a tall, broad-shouldered man in a Marine uniform smiled at her and said, "Hello, Catherine."

She stopped short, eyes widening in surprise. Her mouth opened and stayed that way for several seconds before she was able to whisper, "Adam . . . ?"

He held out his arms to her, and she couldn't even feel her legs moving as she went forward into his embrace. But she felt it as his arms closed around her and drew her against him. Her arms went around his waist as his head came down and his lips found hers. He kissed her with an intensity that went through her with a shock as if she had just grabbed a live electrical wire.

She barely heard Missy chuckle and say, "Well, my work here is done."

After a minute or more, Adam broke the kiss. They were both short of breath as she pressed her face against his chest, not caring that the uniform blouse was scratchy. His right hand came up and cupped the back of her head. He buried his fingers in her thick blond hair. The white nurse's cap on her head was knocked askew, but neither of them cared.

Finally, she lifted her head and tipped it back so that she could look up into his face. "How . . . how did you get here?" she asked.

"PBY from Wake," he said. "I was ordered back here by my commander."

"You mean the island was evacuated?"

Adam shook his head, and for a second Catherine saw a flash of pain and regret in his eyes. "The other men are still there, holding out against the Japs."

"But why were you sent back?" She laughed, hearing an edge of hysteria in the sound. "Not that I'm complaining."

"It's a long story," Adam said. "All that matters now is that I'm here."

Catherine caught her breath as a thought occurred to her. "Do you have to go back there?"

"No," Adam said, and the simple word sent waves of relief through Catherine. "Not now. Now I'm here with you."

She hugged him again as he stroked her hair and told herself that she would never let him go. It was a lie, of course, but at this moment, she was going to believe it with all her heart.

TWENTY-FIVE

It was a little awkward at first. They wanted each other so badly, but it had been months since they had been together. Adam was afraid that he wouldn't be able to control himself, that it would all be over too soon. Especially when Catherine came into the bedroom from the tiny bathroom with the light behind her, shining through the thin nightgown she wore and letting him see every curve of her supple body. . . .

But it all worked out just fine. They made love with a furious intensity, and although it didn't last long, neither of them minded. The second time, afterward, was the time to linger and luxuriate in each other. The ascent was much slower, but when they finally joined together and reached the crest, the moment of ecstasy was shattering. Adam thought he was going to pass out.

At last, long into the night, when they lay in each other's arms under the sheet, her head resting on his shoulder, they talked in low tones, telling each other everything that had happened. Catherine began to cry as she spoke of her brother's death, and Adam held her tightly until the spasms of grief eased. Then he told her about Wake Island, the things he had endured, the men with whom he had served. Tears came to his eyes, too, and she kissed them away as they rolled onto his cheeks. They held each other, taking comfort in the warmth and intimacy, and comfort turned again into passion.

"What was in those documents you brought back?"

Catherine asked the question as she brought cups of coffee for both of them into the bedroom. Outside, behind the curtains drawn over the window, the sky was beginning to turn gray with the approach of dawn. They had talked and made love all night, but neither of them was tired. That would probably come later, when the euphoria of their reunion wore off, but right now they didn't care.

Adam shook his head. "I'm not sure. I couldn't very well ask Major Bayler, since it was all supposed to be hush-hush. I did some thinking about it, though, during the flight back here. It took a long time, and there wasn't anything else to do."

Catherine sat down beside him. He was propped up on pillows at the head of the bed, still nude. She wore a dressing gown.

"What did you come up with?"

"My best guess is that it had something to do with the Japanese radio transmissions. I know we were monitoring them whenever they were in range. I'll bet the transmissions were in code, though. If we could break the Japs' codes—"

"That would be important."

"Very. Anyway, that's what I think it was all about, some sort of info to help our intelligence boys break those codes." Adam shrugged. "That could be completely off-base, though. Chances are, we'll never know."

Catherine snuggled against his side. "I don't care what it was, as long as it was important enough to get you back here."

"Yeah." Adam sipped his coffee. "I turned all the stuff over to CINCPAC; then Bayler told me I have five days' leave coming."

"What about after that?" Adam heard the worry in Catherine's voice as she asked the question.

"I don't know. I'll have to go over to Ewa and report in. I should get new orders then."

"You . . . you won't have to go back to Wake, will you?"

"They're not going to send another PBY all that way just to ferry me back out there," Adam said, hoping he was right. "And nobody else is headed in that direction except that task force with the relief expedition. I may have to go back eventually, but not any time soon. Chances are, I'll be transferred to some other duty."

"Then there's really no way of knowing where you'll be—"

Adam set his cup on the nightstand and put his arms around her, saying, "Shhh. Don't worry about that now. Don't worry about anything."

She lifted her face to his. "I'm trying not to, but it's hard."

He kissed her forehead and her nose, then said, "I guess I'll have to distract you, then." His hand slipped inside her robe, found her left breast, and cupped it. He stroked her nipple with his thumb. "Feeling distracted yet?"

"Maybe," she said, "but you'd better keep working on it for a while."

"As long as you like." He spread open her robe and leaned down, planting kisses in the valley between her breasts. "You just tell me when to stop."

*   *   *

While the Japanese continued to bombard Wake, Task Force 14 steamed toward the atoll with all possible speed. The relief fleet could travel only as fast as its slowest member, however, and the old oiler *Neches* was notoriously slow. Still, everyone in the task force was anxious to reach Wake and bring some help to the gallant but vastly outnumbered forces holding the atoll against the Japanese.

By 22 December, heavy bombing had knocked out several of Wake's shore batteries. Only two of the fighter planes were airworthy, and in trying to ward off yet another attack, Lieutenant Davidson was shot down by a Japanese Zero, vanishing into the ocean. Captain Freuler, piloting the lone remaining Wildcat, was wounded during the dogfight over Wake Island and was forced to crash-land the badly damaged Wildcat. Freuler survived, but there was no longer any way to patch up the plane. VMF-211 was grounded, this time for good.

With no air power, the defenders of Wake had no choice

except to shore up their ground defenses as best they could. The bombs that had rained down from the dive bombers had caused so much destruction, however, that there was no longer much to work with. During the night of 22 December, the men waited anxiously to see what was going to happen.

Before dawn the next morning, Japanese troop transports barreled ashore at several points on Wake, Wilkes, and Peale Islands. Japanese soldiers swarmed off the barges. The fighting was fierce as the Marines and the civilian volunteers tried to repel the invaders, but the Japanese managed to sever the communications lines among the islands and divide the defenders into pockets of resistance.

When the sun rose, it revealed that the entire atoll was surrounded by Japanese ships. The enemy had expected that the first invasion attempt, a week and a half earlier, would succeed easily, and when it had been turned back, the shame of defeat had stung the Japanese command. Now they would not be denied the prize they sought, no matter how many men, ships, and airplanes it took.

Once the enemy troops were actually on the islands, it was only a matter of time. The only thing that might have saved the defenders was the arrival of the U.S. Navy task force.

But the vessels of Task Force 14 were still more than four hundred miles away, and that same morning Admiral Fletcher, in command of the fleet, received new orders from Pearl Harbor.

The race was lost, CINCPAC had decided. Wake could not be saved. Task Force 14 was ordered to come about and return to base with all due speed.

God would have to help the men on Wake Island, because the Navy couldn't.

Adam had his chair tipped back, his feet crossed at the ankles and resting on the porch railing. He was reading a magazine and waiting for Catherine to return to the bungalow when her shift at the hospital was over. That wouldn't be for another hour yet.

The sound of a vehicle coming to a stop in front of the bungalow made Adam look up from the magazine. He saw Catherine getting out of a jeep that had a sailor behind the wheel. She called her thanks to him as the sailor drove on, then turned toward the bungalow and Adam.

He put a finger in the magazine to mark his place and stood up, a worried frown on his face. "It's not that I'm not glad to see you," he said as Catherine came up the walk, "but what are you doing here? You're not supposed to be off duty yet."

"I know. I got one of the other girls to cover for me for a little while and then begged a ride over here. I'll have to get back pretty quick, though."

Adam forced a grin. "I suppose it's too much to hope you came rushing over here because you couldn't wait until this evening to make love to your handsome husband."

"I wish that was why I was here." Catherine's face was solemn. "We just heard some news at the hospital, Adam."

"What is it?" It couldn't be good, he thought, so it was better to get it over with.

"A Japanese invasion force landed on Wake Island early this morning. They were able to . . . to take the island. The defenders who were left had to surrender."

Adam stared at her. The muscles in his throat stood out as he said, "No!"

"I'm sorry, Adam—"

"What about the task force? What about the goddamned relief expedition?"

Catherine shook her head. "They never got there. They were ordered to turn back."

The magazine slipped unnoticed out of Adam's fingers and fell to the porch. His hands clenched into fists and pressed against his temples. "No! God, no!"

Catherine came closer to him and put a hand on his arm. "Adam, I'm sorry—"

He jerked away from her touch, lowering his arms to stare at her. "I left them there," he said, his voice breaking with pain. "They were my friends, and I left them there."

"You had your orders—"

"I thought they could hold out! Damn it!"

"Adam, listen to me," Catherine said. "You did the only thing you could do. You followed orders. You didn't do anything wrong."

His eyes were dark and bleak. "I left them there."

"And if they're your friends, they don't hold that against you."

He laughed hollowly. "If they're still alive, you mean."

"I don't know that; you don't know that; right now nobody knows who's still alive out there. But the time will come when it's going to be different, when . . . when the Japanese don't just get everything they want."

"When?" Adam's voice was bitter, as caustic as acid. "We lost here at Pearl, we're losing the Philippines, and now we've lost Wake. Every time we turn around, we lose." He turned abruptly and slammed a fist against the wall of the bungalow. "Damn it!"

"I lost my brother, too," Catherine said, her tone a bit harder-edged now. "And a part of me wanted to quit, to just give up and let it all go. But we had work to do at the hospital, and I hung on to that. And I hung on to thoughts of you, too, Adam. I couldn't give up because I knew you wouldn't give up."

For a long moment, Adam stood there in silence. Then he heaved a sigh and said, "I guess you're right. We have to keep fighting." He looked off into the distance, out over the waters of the harbor and the sprawling Marine air base beyond at Ewa. For a second he seemed to see the faces of Gurnwall and Rolofson, Kennemer and Magruder, and even Stout. Stout was dead, but maybe some of the others were still alive. If so, they were prisoners of the Japanese by now, along with Major Devereux and Commander Cunningham and all the other men who had hung onto Wake Island with everything they had. Whatever happened from here on out in this war, Adam owed it to those men to do the best he could, to fight on as long as he had breath in his body.

Catherine hugged him tightly, then said, "I have to get back to the hospital. Are you going to be all right?"

"Yeah. I'm all right."

She came up on her toes and kissed him on the lips. "I love you."

"I love you, too." He summoned up a smile. "Come on. I'll walk you over to the hospital."

"Are you sure?"

"Sure I'm sure." He took her hand, his fingers intertwining with hers. "Let's go."

Together, they stepped down off the porch and went along the walk to the road. They turned toward the hospital.

On the bungalow porch, the pages of the forgotten magazine Adam had dropped turned in the breeze, then, as the wind shifted, blew closed again. It was a pulp magazine with a typically garish cover and the name *THRILLING WESTERN* emblazoned across the top. In the lower left-hand corner, next to the cover illustration of a snarling cowboy firing two six-guns, were the words, *Gun-Thieves of Cougar Basin! A Complete, Fast-Action Novelette by Chance Colt!*

TWENTY-SIX

"Chance Colt!" Joe Parker said. The words were a howl of righteous indignation. "The bastards changed my name to Chance Colt!"

"I think it sounds good," his brother Dale said. "Real westerny."

Joe glared at Dale. For a moment he had been excited to see an American pulp magazine featuring one of his stories in a British newsagent's shop, but that excitement had vanished when he realized that the editor or someone else at the magazine's publishing company had changed the byline on the story.

"I'll bet it was that blasted Margulies," Joe said. "He likes to change titles and names."

"Hey, you got paid, didn't you?" Dale asked with a shrug. Clearly, to him that was the only important consideration.

"Here now, Yank, are you going to buy that magazine or just wave it around and shout like a ruddy madman?" the owner of the shop asked as he came along the row of slanting wooden shelves covered with books and magazines.

Joe dug in the pocket of his brown khaki uniform trousers and found a coin. "I'll buy it," he said as he handed the coin to the proprietor, "but I don't have to like it."

The man rolled his eyes and shook his head as if to say, *Crazy Americans,* but he took the money.

"Come on, Dale; let's get out of here."

"It was your idea to stop in the first place. I just wanted to go down to the pub and have a drink."

They left the shop, stepping out into the intermittent drizzle of a late December evening. Christmas decorations lined the streets but were only dimly visible since blackout curtains were pulled over the windows in all the buildings.

They had been on their way to the Oaken Barrel for the first time in nearly two weeks—since the night of the brawl when they'd learned of the attack on Pearl Harbor, in fact—when Joe had spotted the pulp magazine in the newsagent's shop. Now, to keep the magazine from getting too damp, he rolled it into a tube and stuck it in the inside pocket of his jacket. He would look over his story later, when he and Dale got back to the barracks, and see if any other editorial changes had been made to it. Joe had been a freelancer in the pulp market long enough to know that such changes were common. Usually, they didn't hurt a story too much, but sometimes . . .

Joe sighed. Of course it was nice to see one of his stories in print, but he knew the real reason he was getting so worked up over the pseudonym: He wanted to keep his mind off the fact that Adam Bergman, his best friend, was out there in the Pacific on Wake Island, surrounded by Japanese who wanted to capture the strategically located atoll.

Ever since the attack on Pearl Harbor, the American GIs in England had kept up with the news by reading *Stars & Stripes* and listening to the BBC. Joe had read and heard all about the bombing runs the Japanese were making on Wake and how the Marines were so gallantly defending the island. There had been quite a few American casualties, and Joe had no way of knowing if Adam had been one of them.

Even though Joe had seen Adam play ball and knew that his friend was perfectly capable of taking care of himself, a part of Joe's mind still thought of Adam as the skinny little Jewish kid who'd strayed into the wrong neighborhood over a decade earlier. Adam would've gotten his head handed to him by the three young Irish hooligans who'd jumped him if Joe hadn't pitched in to help him. It had been one of the few fights in Joe's youth, but he recalled it almost fondly. Ever since that day, he and Adam had been friends.

Now Adam was half a world away and in trouble again, and there wasn't a damned thing Joe could do to help him.

"I hope we don't run into Royce in here tonight," Dale said as they reached the pub, breaking into Joe's thoughts.

Joe grunted. "After what happened last time, so do I."

"Hey, Tess was really grateful that I helped her. *Really* grateful, if you know what I mean."

Joe nodded, but not enthusiastically. He didn't want to hear about Dale's amorous adventures. He put his hand on the door latch, ready to open it.

"Joe! Hey, Joe! Dale!"

They turned and saw a man in British uniform hurrying toward them. Joe couldn't see him very well in the shadows, but he recognized the voice as belonging to Bert Crimmens, one of the tankies from the Armour School. Bert was a radioman, like Joe, and they had become friends as Joe had taught Bert how to operate the British Wireless Set No. 19 that was installed in the M3 tank. Even though it was a British radio, the nineteens had been installed in the General Grants on which Joe and Dale had trained in Texas, so Joe knew the unit quite well.

"What's up, Bert?" Dale asked as the British soldier came up to them, puffing slightly from running.

"You'd best get back to camp, lads," Bert said. "In fact, we all have to report in. New orders."

"For you or for us?" Joe asked.

"For all of us." Now that Bert was closer, Joe could see that he was beaming with pleasure. "We're bound for the B.E.F., we are!"

"Wait just a damn minute," Dale said. "You mean *you're* bound for the B.E.F., not Joe and me. We're Americans. We're not part of any British Expeditionary Force."

"You are now. What I hear is that you lads are going along as advisors and instructors."

Joe felt as if the cobblestone street were dropping out from under him. He was so shaken by this news that he put a hand on the door of the pub to steady himself. "Egypt?" he said in disbelief. "We're going to Egypt?"

"That's right. And when we get there, we'll give the bloody Jerries what for, eh?"

Joe and Dale looked at each other. They knew that the United States was officially at war with Germany, had been ever since a few days after the Japs' attack on Pearl Harbor. The U.S. had declared war on Japan, and then Germany and Italy had turned around and declared war on the U.S. Ever since then, the relatively few American troops stationed in England had expected new orders that would reflect the U.S.'s increased level of involvement in the war.

But Joe knew he hadn't expected to be shipped off to Egypt, where the British Expeditionary Force was trying to stop the German Afrika Korps under General Erwin Rommel from rolling unchecked all the way across North Africa.

"This is crazy," Dale said. "We're Americans. It's not right that we have to be part of the British Army."

Bert drew back a little. "Well, you don't have to sound so offended about it."

"I'm sure Dale didn't mean it that way," Joe said. "It's just so sudden, that's all. I suppose the Army can send us anywhere they want, and if that means going to Egypt with you guys . . ." Joe shrugged. "At least we won't be among strangers."

Dale frowned. "Wait a minute. Is Royce going, too?"

"Corporal Royce? Of course he's going. Everyone in our class at the Armour School is."

Dale hit his forehead with the ball of his hand. "Damn! Just my luck. I can't get away from that son of a bitch."

Bert jerked a thumb over his shoulder and said, "Best come along, lads. We're pulling out early in the morning, bound for Portsmouth. Our ship sails tomorrow evening."

"That fast?" Joe said.

"Got to move fast to keep up with the Jerries."

"I guess you're right. Come on, Dale."

Dale gazed at the door of the Oaken Barrel for a long moment, then sighed. "I'm coming," he said. "But I don't have to like it."

That was about the same thing Joe had said about having his byline on the Western story changed to Chance Colt. The way the world was now, Joe thought, there were too many things that had to be accepted, whether people liked them or not. He supposed war had a way of doing that.

★   ★   ★

Master Sergeant Henry Garmon was waiting for them back at the Armour School. The men from the Army Services Force detachment had a barracks of their own, and Master Sergeant Garmon, a stocky, red-faced non-com from Georgia, was standing on the building's steps. He had his arms crossed and a glare on his face.

"About time you two showed up," he said as Joe and Dale walked up to the barracks.

"We got here as soon as we heard about the new orders, Sarge," Dale said. He and Garmon had been sparring with each other for months, ever since Joe and Dale arrived at Camp Bowie.

"Yeah, well, at least I didn't have to send the MPs out after you, like some of the other guys," Garmon admitted grudgingly. "Get inside and get your gear together. We're moving out at 0530 tomorrow morning."

"What about the tanks?" Joe asked. "How are they going to get to Egypt?"

Garmon's eyes narrowed. "You believe in askin' a lot of questions, don't you, Parker? You been promoted, or is that still just one little stripe I see on your arm? You're askin' questions like you're an officer or somethin'."

"I was just curious, Sarge. Sorry."

"Don't apologize, damn it!" Garmon paused, then said, "Not that it's any business of a couple o' lowly dogfaces like you two, but the tanks'll be driven to Portsmouth and loaded on ships there, just like you. We figure to be in Egypt by the new year."

Joe nodded. "Thanks, Sarge. Come on, Dale."

Dale started up the steps after Joe, then stopped and looked at Garmon. "What's our job going to be, Sarge?"

"Same as it is here: teachin' these limeys how to fix tanks, drive tanks, and shoot the guns on tanks."

"You'd better keep Royce away from me. That guy and I don't like each other."

A couple of steps above, Joe muttered, "Uh-oh."

For a second, Garmon didn't say anything. Then he leaned forward, craned his neck so that he could put his face in Dale's face, and said in dangerously low tones, "You think the United States Army gives a rat's ass who you like or don't like, Parker?"

"I'm just sayin'—"

"I know what you're sayin', you fuckin' goldbrick!" Garmon shouted. "If the Army tells you to teach Adolf fuckin' Hitler or Benito fuckin' Mussolini how to fix a tank engine, then by God you'll teach 'em! You got that, Parker?"

All Dale could do was swallow, nod, and say, "Yes, Sergeant."

"Yes, Sergeant, *what?*"

"Yes, I'll teach them," Dale said between gritted teeth.

"Damn right you will." Garmon leveled a finger at the barracks doors. "Now get in there and get your gear together!"

"Yes, Sergeant." Dale went up the steps and joined Joe.

As they went into the building, Joe said, "You know, sometimes I think you're as big an idiot as Sergeant Garmon says you are."

"All I know is, Royce better steer clear of me when we get over there."

"Or you'll do exactly what?"

"I don't know," Dale said, "but he just better steer clear."

*　　*　　*

Two days before Christmas, on the evening of 23 December 1941, the men of the ASF and the British tankies belonging to the 4th

Armoured Brigade of the 7th Armoured Division boarded the troop transport H.M.S. *Leffingford* at Portsmouth. The General Grant tanks, which had been driven to Portsmouth from the Armour School at Bovington, were late in arriving and were still being loaded onto another ship, which would sail later that night. The *Leffingford,* however, pulled out of the Portsmouth docks at 2035 hours, guided by tugs past the Isle of Wight and into the English Channel, where it came about and headed southwest toward the open sea. It was accompanied by several British corvettes, and once the little convoy was out in the Atlantic, making the big loop around France and the Iberian Peninsula to Gibraltar, the RAF would provide some air cover with submarine-hunting planes.

Once again, Joe thought as he stood at the railing of the *Leffingford* that evening, he was setting out across dark waters filled with danger. Like sharks, the Nazi U-boats haunted the waters off the English coast, looking for victims that their torpedoes could send to a watery grave. Once before, Joe and Dale had run that gauntlet and had come through safely, but each time they ventured out to sea, the odds against them rose. The U-boats patrolled all the way into the Mediterranean, so they wouldn't be truly safe until they reached Egypt.

And then, facing them across the vast North African desert would be the onrushing horde of the Deutsche Afrika Korps. The world had become a truly perilous place.

Dale came up beside him. "I just heard a rumor going around," Dale said, and something about the unusual seriousness in his voice made Joe look over at him.

"What's up? Something about where we're going?"

Dale shook his head. "Nah. What I heard is that Wake Island's going to fall any time now. The Marines are going to have to surrender or the Japs'll wipe 'em out."

Joe's hands tightened on the railing. "You're sure about that?"

Dale shrugged and said, "I'm not sure of anything. It's just scuttlebutt. But one of our guys got it from a guy in the ship's radio room." Dale chuckled humorlessly. "I guess he never heard the old saying about how loose lips sink ships. Of course, what's going on halfway around the world doesn't really affect us."

"It affects Adam," Joe snapped.

"Hey, I didn't mean anything. I'm worried about the big lug, too. But what can we do?"

Joe stared out over the dark sea as it rushed past in blackness. "I guess we can pray," he said after a moment.

"Well, if you're going to pray, say one for us, too. It's not going to be a picnic where we're going."

That was true enough, Joe thought. The time of picnics was over.

TWENTY-SEVEN

The film was called *Meet John Doe*. When it began, it seemed rather light, almost the same sort of picture as that bit of fluff about the dog and the missing dinosaur bone that he'd seen a few years earlier. But as it continued, the story became darker and more bleak and quite compelling. This man Capra who directed had a unique vision all his own, but at the same time it was reminiscent of the German masters Lang and von Stroheim. Dr. Gerald Tancred, who considered himself something of a student of the cinema, would not have believed that an American could be capable of such artistic depth.

Ah, but then the climax! Sentimental mush. Cornball, as the young people might call it. How much stronger the picture would have been, Tancred thought as he and his wife left the theater in downtown Chicago, if the character portrayed by Gary Cooper had really committed suicide at the end. He shook his head. Americans and their insistence on a happy ending!

Tancred hailed a cab. "Did you enjoy the picture?" he asked his wife as they waited for the taxi to pull over to the curb.

Elenore had sat quietly through the entire film, not laughing at the amusing parts, unmoved by the drama. Now she said, "It was fine." Her voice was as lifeless as the concrete of the sidewalk under their feet.

"I hoped you might enjoy an evening out," Tancred said.

"Thank you, dear. It was fine."

Tancred's mouth tightened into a grim line. His wife had been like this ever since their son Spencer had died.

It was almost Christmas, and downtown Chicago was awash with brilliance. Decorations and strings of lights hung from the telephone poles along the streets. Every store window sparkled with Christmas scenes. Though the news from Pearl Harbor earlier in the month had dampened spirits throughout the country, people were still trying to capture the joyousness of the season. The sidewalks were crowded with shoppers, and the theater had been almost full as Dr. Tancred and his wife watched the film.

Despite all that, the air had a hushed quality to it. Even the rattle and clatter of the El, so common here in the Loop, seemed subdued, as if the trains were in mourning along with the people who rode them. Children exclaimed over the Christmas displays in the store windows, but their parents stood quietly, thinking their own thoughts. Fathers who might soon be going off to war reached down and clasped the shoulders of their sons, stroked the hair of their daughters. Wives held their husbands' arms more tightly than ever before. And when they looked at each other, their eyes were dark and haunted by what the future might hold for them. . . .

Brakes squealed as the taxi pulled up at the curb. The driver hopped out and came around to the back door. Grains of snow crunched under his shoes. "Where to, buddy?" he asked as he opened the door for the Tancreds.

I am not your "buddy." Tancred swallowed the sharp rebuke before it could escape from his mouth. Despite the fact that he had lived in America for more than fifteen years, he had not completely adjusted to the nation's bumptious egalitarianism. He suspected that he never would. Where he had been raised, people had known their place.

Or at least they had until that scruffy little Austrian had come along. Gerald Tancred had already brought his family to America before Hitler's rise to power, but that didn't mean he wasn't appalled by what he had watched going on in his native land. The World War had devastated Germany and its aristocracy to the point that Tancred had deemed it wise to leave, and then Hitler had turned everything else upside down.

Not that Tancred had any sympathy for the Jews. They were human beings and as such had rights, but they were still a dreadful people, he thought. Hitler and his crowd weren't much better; they certainly weren't fit to run the country.

"Lakeshore Drive," Tancred said as he helped Elenore into the cab.

"Any particular number, or are you and the missus just out for a jaunt?"

In clipped tones, Tancred told the driver the number of the house.

"You got it, ace," the driver said as he started back around the cab, leaving the back door open so that Tancred had to shut it himself after he had gotten in.

Once the cab was moving, Tancred reached over and took hold of his wife's hand. Elenore's skin was cool to the touch. More than that, it was actually cold, almost as lifeless as her voice. Of course, there was quite a chill in the air tonight—Chicago in December, the wind off the lake, and all that—but what afflicted Elenore went beyond that. Tancred had begun worrying about her health. The only time there was any color in her face was when she'd been drinking, which was all too often these days. Other than that, she might as well have been a walking corpse.

From behind the wheel, the driver glanced over his shoulder. "Mind if I turn the radio on, buddy? I don't have to if you'd rather I didn't."

If he refused, Tancred thought, then the driver would most likely attempt to engage him in conversation. That was an unpleasant prospect. "By all means, go right ahead," Tancred told him.

"Thanks. I think Bing Crosby's on right about now. I love Der Bingle, don't you?"

Tancred was saved from having to answer by a burst of static from the cab's radio as the driver turned it on. The cabbie twisted the dial, and a loud voice came from the speaker.

"This is H. V. Kaltenborn, speaking to you from Washington."

The driver reached for the knob and said, "Ah, I hate that guy! Such a know-it-all. Where's Bing?"

"Wait!" Tancred said. "I'd like to listen to the news."

The driver drew his hand back and shrugged. "It's your nickel, buddy. You pay the freight, you call the shots."

Tancred glanced over at his wife as the rich, booming tones of the famous news broadcaster filled the cab. Elenore was staring straight ahead, seeming not to hear. Or if she heard, she paid no attention to what was being said.

Over the past two weeks, Tancred had kept up with the war news more than ever before. He had never believed that the United States had any business involving itself in a European war. But now, since the attack on Pearl Harbor that had cost the life of his son, Tancred hated the Japanese and found himself fascinated by newspaper and radio reports of what was going on in the Pacific. And even though he had strongly opposed his daughter's marriage to that Jew, he wanted to know what was happening at Wake Island, where Adam was stationed. Catherine's letters home in recent days had hinted at how worried she was about him. The newsreel before the film tonight had mentioned that the Japanese were still bombing Wake. For his daughter's sake, Tancred hoped that her husband was all right.

H. V. Kaltenborn was talking about the Congressional hearings going on in Washington which sought to determine exactly who was to blame for what had happened at Pearl Harbor, when Elenore Tancred suddenly turned to her husband and said, "My, it's certainly a beautiful day, isn't it?"

"What?" Tancred said, taken by surprise. He glanced out the window. It wasn't day at all, but rather night, and a particularly dark one at that. The air was cold, and it had snowed a little earlier.

"I thought Reverend Wallace gave a wonderful sermon, didn't you, Gerald?"

"What?" Tancred said again. Reverend Wallace was the pastor of the Lutheran church they attended, but this was Tuesday, not Sunday.

"I believe I'll bake some strudels this afternoon."

Tancred's eyes widened, and he whispered, "Oh, no."

"Would you like some strudels, dear?"

Tancred stared at her and made no reply.

Elenore leaned forward and touched the cab driver on the shoulder. "Spencer, darling, would you like some nice apple strudels?"

The driver twisted his head and looked at her. "You talkin' to me, lady? My name's Frank, not Spencer." He grinned. "Though some folks say I look like Spencer Tracy."

"But if you're not Spencer, then where is he?" Elenore turned to her husband. "Gerald, where are we? This isn't home."

Tancred's jaw clenched, causing a tiny muscle in it to jump for a second. He reached out and took hold of his wife's hand. "We'll be home soon, Elenore. Just rest. Close your eyes—"

"No!" She jerked away from him. "You're lying to me! We're not going home! Where's Spencer? Where is my son?"

Then her eyes grew wide and her mouth opened and she began to scream. The driver cursed, jammed on the brakes, and sent the cab skidding toward the curb. The cab jolted to a stop. The driver twisted around behind the wheel as Elenore continued screaming, loud ragged shrieks that filled the cab and knifed into the ears.

"What's the matter?" the driver shouted over the screams. "What the hell's wrong with her?"

Tancred grabbed Elenore and tried to pull her against him so that he could muffle her screams, but she fought him, punching him in the chest and flailing at his face. He jerked his head from side to side in an attempt to avoid the blows, but some of them landed. He grunted and squinted against the pain and tightened his grip on his wife. "Elenore! Stop it, Elenore!"

"Spencer! I want Spencer!" She started cursing him, words tumbling out of her mouth that were so vile even the cab driver blanched and looked astounded.

"Elenore, you *must* stop this!" Tancred had hold of her shoulders. He shook her, trying to get through to her. "Spencer is dead! Dead, do you hear? Stop asking for him! He is *dead*!"

Without realizing it, he had started screaming himself. Only as Elenore flinched away from him, her eyes full of agony, did he realize that he was shouting in her face. Suddenly, her features seemed to blur and crumple, like spun sugar being washed away in the rain. Only it was tears washing her away, not raindrops.

Tancred gasped in horror at what he had done and clutched her to him. She cried in great wracking sobs that shook her entire body as he pressed her to him.

"Good Lord," the driver said from the front seat. "Who's Spencer?"

Tancred cradled Elenore against him and looked past her shoulder at the man. "Our son," he said, his voice breaking with strain.

"Jeez, I'm sorry, mister. I can't tell you how sorry I am."

"She was like this the day we were notified of his death." Tancred could not have said why he was talking to this man, this American cabbie, but he couldn't seem to stop himself. The words came pouring out. "He was at Pearl Harbor. He was in the Navy, but he was going to fly airplanes. We . . . we didn't even know he was there. There had been trouble in the family and he left. But then an officer from the Navy came the next day with a telegram. . . . My wife had a breakdown then. I am a doctor; I know about these things. I thought she had gotten better, but her mind . . . tonight for some reason it went back to the . . . the day before. When we didn't know yet what had happened . . ."

"It musta been hearin' the war news on the radio that did it. That blasted Kaltenborn!"

Tancred nodded as he stroked his wife's hair. Her hat had fallen off as she flung herself around. "Yes," he said. "Perhaps it was the war news."

"I'm sorry, mister. Gee, if I'd known, I woulda left the radio off—"

"You are not to blame," Tancred told the man. "No one is. If you would just . . . take us home."

"Sure, pal. Sure thing." The cab's engine was still idling. The driver put it in gear, pulled away from the curb, and headed up Lakeshore Drive toward the Tancred house.

Elenore had stopped crying by the time they got there. She lay huddled against Tancred, breathing shallowly. He considered taking her to the hospital, but he decided that she might be better off in familiar surroundings. That had helped before, when she'd collapsed after learning of Spencer's death.

Tancred had been strong then, as he tried to be strong now. Of course he mourned for his lost son, but there was nothing he could do to change things. Life had to go on, after all. As a doctor, he knew the futility of raging against death. His responsibility was to the living.

With the driver's help, he got Elenore out of the cab and into the house. They lowered her onto the sofa in the parlor, and Tancred spread a blanket over her. Later, after Elenore had rested for a while, he would get her upstairs to the bedroom. He believed that the spell would pass and that soon she would be more docile again.

They left her sleeping on the sofa. Tancred followed the driver into the foyer of the mansion and reached for his wallet as the man opened the front door.

"No need for that, buddy," the cab driver said. "The ride's on me."

"Nonsense. You've been a great help—"

"I said to forget it. Listen, doc, I got no kids. Hell, I ain't even got a wife. But you, you've lost your boy, and the lady in there . . ." The man inclined his head toward the parlor and shrugged. "The way I see it, you've paid enough already. I'm too old for the draft, so I get to stay right here in the good ol' U.S. of A. while guys like your boy give everything they got to keep us all safe. So if there's somethin' I can to do lend a hand to folks like you and your missus, I figure it's only right." He put out his hand. "I'm sorry as hell, Doc."

Tancred hesitated, then clasped the man's hand. "Thank you," he said.

The cab driver tugged on the brim of his cap. "Good night."

"Good night." Tancred stood in the doorway and watched the man go down the walk toward the parked cab. Snow was falling again, tiny flakes that swirled down in the glow of the streetlights. A shudder went through Tancred's slender frame, and he put both hands over his face as he began to cry.

He had lied when he said that no one was to blame for Spencer's death. He knew quite well on whose shoulders the responsibility for that tragedy lay.

And he would carry that burden for the rest of his life.

TWENTY-EIGHT

Joe and Dale spent Christmas Day, 1941, at sea. Once through the English Channel, the small convoy had rendezvoused with a pair of Royal Navy destroyers which would also accompany the troop ships and the corvettes. The run south past France, Spain, and Portugal was made as quickly as possible, since the longer the ships were at sea, the more likely the danger they would be stalked by German U-boats or attacked by the Nazis' new Condor bombers. Still, it was a couple of days after Christmas before the convoy swung east and headed for the Strait of Gibraltar and the Mediterranean Sea.

The atmosphere on board the *Leffingford* was somewhat different than it had been on H.M.S. *Starks,* which had brought the American contingent from the States to England back in early summer. During that crossing, tensions had been considerably higher because the U-boats had been sinking British shipping seemingly at will. Indeed, though the *Starks* hadn't suffered any damage, two other ships in the convoy had been sunk, one by torpedoes and the other by aerial bombing. Now, at last, the British seemed to be getting the upper hand in the Battle of the Atlantic. The Anti-Submarine Detection Investigation Commission had developed an echo-sounding apparatus known as asdic equipment to help detect submarines. British radar had improved as well, and back in September the United States had extended the so-called Neutrality Zone and taken on some of the responsibility of patrolling the waters of the North Atlantic. This had freed more British ships to actively hunt down German U-boats.

So British losses had dropped, and the Royal Navy had begun to inflict significant damage on the enemy. In a recent running battle between a British convoy and a group of German submarines, the convoy had made it through with the loss of only four vessels while sinking fully half of the Nazi wolf pack.

Joe and Dale heard all about this from Bert Crimmens and the other tankies of the 4th Armoured Brigade. They were justifiably proud of the job their Navy and the RAF were doing against the Germans.

Joe was still carrying around the manuscript of the story he had started writing during the crossing from the States. He had never finished it, since the days at the Armour School had been so long that he'd been too tired to work on it at night. But now, during the tedious hours aboard ship when there was nothing else to do, he sought out a wardroom with a typewriter he could borrow and started working on the yarn again. It was a pirate story, the sort of thing *Argosy* and *Adventure* ate up. He was no H. Bedford-Jones, but as he read over what he had done so far, he thought it was a pretty good swashbuckler.

Dale sat around the wardroom for a while but got bored in a hurry. He said, "I think I'll go up on deck." Joe nodded and waved, but Dale didn't think his brother had really heard him. With a shake of his head, he left the wardroom and went down the narrow corridor to a series of ladders that ultimately took him out into the open air.

That air was cold. The sky overhead was gray, like the water rushing past the ships of the convoy. Dale pulled his cap down more snugly on his head and turned up the collar of his jacket. Chilly or not, being on deck was still better than being cooped up below.

Quite a few of the *Leffingford*'s passengers seemed to share that opinion. As he strolled toward the railing around the deck, Dale saw Sergeant Garmon and several more men from the ASF detachment, as well as dozens of tankies he recognized from the Armour School.

A burst of laughter came from one of the clusters of British soldiers as Dale walked past them. A loud, familiar voice said, "Here's another one: What's the only thing smaller than an American's willie? Give up? His brain, o' course!"

Dale glanced over and saw Corporal Jeremy Royce laughing at his own joke. Royce's eyes weren't laughing, however. They were cold and hard and fastened on Dale.

So Royce had seen him coming and told that joke on purpose, Dale thought. Dale's jaw tightened, but he told himself to ignore Royce. He wasn't going to act like he was running away, however. He strode on past without paying any more attention to Royce and went up to the rail. The metal was cold, but Dale rested his hands on it anyway.

"And there's one of 'em now," Royce went on. "Livin' proof of what I was sayin', if ever there was such."

Dale peered out over the gray, rolling waves and smiled. Royce could run off at the mouth all he wanted. For a change, Dale wasn't going to rise to the bait.

Joe would be proud of him, he thought.

"Hey, Yank! I'm right, ain't I?"

Royce was speaking directly to him now. Dale's eyes narrowed. So far on this voyage, he had managed to avoid Royce. He wished that had continued.

A hand gripped his shoulder. "I'm talkin' to you, Yank."

Dale turned his head and looked into Royce's belligerent face. The guy wasn't an idiot; he really did know his stuff when it came to engines. But he worked harder at being a bastard than he ever did on his duties at the Armour School.

"I heard you," Dale said.

"Then why didn't you answer my question?"

"Because I didn't think it was worth answering." Dale shrugged his shoulder out of Royce's grip. "Go away, Corporal."

"Here now! You can't talk to me like that, *Private* Parker. I outrank you, remember?"

"All right, then. Request permission to ignore the corporal, Corporal."

Royce squinted at him. "You're a right funny one, ain't you?

All you Yanks think you're bloody hilarious, like you're bloody Bob Hope."

Dale sighed and said, "I'm not trying to be funny. I just don't want to fight with you, Royce."

"You were mighty quick to throw a punch back there in Bovington, when that cow Tess was mouthin' off at me—"

Dale turned away from the railing and faced Royce. "So you're still mad about that brawl."

"You hit me when I wasn't looking!"

Dale looked past Royce and saw that the other British soldiers he'd been joking with had followed him over to the edge of the deck. They formed a half-circle around Royce and Dale. The closest Americans were at least fifty yards away.

Royce smiled and closed his hands into fists. "I think it's time I settled the score with you, Yank, and got a bit of me own back."

So there wasn't going to be any getting out of it, Dale thought. He should have just turned and gone the other way as soon as he spotted Royce. Now it was too late.

Nor was he going to come out on top in this fight. Dale knew he was a pretty good brawler, and if it was just Royce he was facing, he could probably hold his own. But judging from the ugly expressions on the faces of Royce's pals, they were going to close in as soon as the fight started. Some of them would probably grab his arms and hold him while Royce pounded on him. He'd be lucky to come out of it with a pair of black eyes, some missing teeth, and maybe a cracked rib or two.

But knowing all that didn't stop him from smiling at Royce and saying, "If that's the way you want it, come on, you limey bastard."

Royce's face contorted with anger, and his right shoulder went back as he started to throw a punch. Dale struck first, a hard left jab into Royce's solar plexus that caught him by surprise. Royce was knocked back a step, so that the right cross he swung at Dale's jaw missed by six inches or more. While Royce was off balance, Dale clipped him with a left that turned him half-around and sent him stumbling into the men who were crowding up behind him.

"Get him!" one of the tankies yelled. "Get the Yank!"

The crowd of helmeted soldiers surged at Dale. The railing was at his back, so there was no place for him to go. He planted his feet, determined to stay upright for as long as he could, and cocked his fists so that he could deal out some punishment before they beat the hell out of him. He hoped Garmon and some of the other Americans on deck noticed what was going on before the tankies killed him.

Nobody threw a punch, because the wailing sound of a klaxon suddenly rang through the air. One of the ship's officers came running along the deck, yelling over the alarm, "Get below! Everyone below!"

No one obeyed the order. The *Leffingford* changed course so abruptly that several men on the deck were thrown off their feet. Still, the ship's progress seemed maddeningly slow as it swung to port.

"Look there!" a man yelled. *"Torpedo!"*

The dreaded cry sent all the men clamoring to the railing. Dale was already there, so all he had to do was turn around and look out to sea. He wasn't sure what he was looking for at first, but then he saw it, something cutting rapidly through the water and leaving a white, bubbling streak behind it. The torpedo was coming in at an angle, from ahead and to port of the *Leffingford*. By making the sharp turn to port, the skipper of the ship obviously hoped that the ship would swing out of the torpedo's path.

"Bloody hell!" a man said from Dale's left. He looked over and saw that it was Royce. All thoughts of a brawl had been forgotten now. The two men stood side by side, hands gripping the rail, as they waited to see if the torpedo would strike the ship.

Dale thought about Joe, down below in the wardroom pecking away on the typewriter. By now, Joe would know that something was wrong. He would have heard the klaxon and felt the ship turning. Not even Joe got so caught up in what he was writing that he could miss things like that. Joe was a smart guy; he had probably figured out already what was going on.

Dale wished he could be with his brother, but men were packed around him too tightly for him to be able to get away from the rail. If he was about to die, he would do it with the arrogant, troublemaking Royce beside him. Wasn't that a hell of a note? he thought.

"Good luck, Yank," Royce said.

Dale swallowed as he watched the torpedo arrowing toward the ship. "Yeah, good luck to you, too, Royce."

A hundred yards away now. The *Leffingford* was still turning. Fifty. Couldn't the damned boat go any faster? The U-boat commander, somewhere out there in the dark water, had a good eye. The torpedo's aim seemed unerring.

Dale took a deep breath, held it. Twenty yards. It took just a heartbeat for the torpedo to cover that distance. . . .

The torpedo whipped past the prow of the ship and cut through the water alongside the vessel, missing it completely but by no more than ten feet. Dale saw it go by and sagged against the rail, closing his eyes for a second in relief. Explosions in the distance made him open them again. He looked up to see plumes of water flying high in the air in the wake of one of the British destroyers. They were firing depth charges, trying to sink the German U-boat or at least spook it into running.

Royce gripped Dale's left arm. "Do you see any more torpedoes?" he asked.

Dale scanned the surface of the ocean but didn't spot any more of the telltale streaks. He shook his head and said, "I don't see any."

More depth charges went off, the explosions muffled now because the charges were plummeting deeper into the water before going off. Each blast was followed a couple of seconds later by another geyser as its force reached the surface.

"Maybe our lads got him."

"I hope so." Dale looked over at Royce. "Weren't we in the middle of a fight?"

Royce let go of Dale's arm and waved his hand in the air. "Ah, forget about that. I don't feel like it now. I'm too mad at the Jerries for nearly blowin' us out of the water."

"Yeah, me, too."

"But that don't mean we won't finish it another time." Royce thrust his jaw out. "I don't like you, Yank. I don't reckon I'll *ever* like you."

"The feeling is mutual, I'm sure."

Royce grunted, then said to his friends, "Let's go, lads."

The klaxon died away as the troops, British and American both, began making their way belowdecks. After the narrow brush with death, none of them felt like taking the air. The psalm-singers would go read their Bibles and pray, Dale thought. Others would dig out the bottles and flasks they had carefully hidden in their gear. Some would sit down and start writing letters home about how the ship they were on had almost been sunk by a torpedo fired from a Kraut submarine.

He went and found his brother.

Joe was in the compartment where the ASF detachment bunked. As Dale came in, Joe hurried up to him and asked, "Are you all right?"

"Yeah, sure," Dale said. "Why wouldn't I be?"

"What the hell happened? I heard somebody say something about a torpedo, and then I heard explosions."

"Yeah, there was a torpedo, all right," Dale said as he took out a cigarette. "Those explosions were depth charges. Those British destroyers either sunk the sub or ran it off. I hope." Dale lit the cigarette and grinned. "Maybe it's still out there, playing possum and waiting for us to let down our guard."

"Don't even think that!" Joe said. "Damn, I hate submarines. How much did the torpedo miss us by?"

"It wasn't even close," Dale said. "I saw the whole thing, and it must've been eight or ten feet away from the hull when it went past."

Joe just stared at him for a long moment, then repeated in a hollow voice, "Eight or ten feet?"

"Yeah." Dale stretched out on his bunk, blew out some smoke, and added, "At least."

Joe sat down heavily on the bunk across from him and said again, "I hate submarines."

*   *   *

The next day, the *Leffingford* and the rest of the convoy steamed through the Strait of Gibraltar and into the Mediterranean Sea.

Where, according to the best estimates of the Royal Navy, approximately two dozen German U-boats were still lurking and preying on British ships bound, like the *Leffingford,* for Alexandria.

TWENTY-NINE

Located on the western end of the Nile Delta, Alexandria was an ancient city, Joe knew, founded by Alexander the Great while he was staking out his claim to an empire that would span the known world. Now it was Egypt's principal port city, though quite a bit of shipping went in and out of Port Said, at the eastern end of the delta. But Alexandria was where the Royal Navy had placed its main base in Egypt, and it was to Alexandria that the *Leffingford* and the other ships in the convoy were headed.

The trip through the Mediterranean was tense but relatively uneventful. One of the British destroyers reported asdic contact with what was thought to be a German U-boat, but when the depth charges began falling the submarine fled without firing any torpedoes.

It was 29 December 1941 when the convoy steamed into the western harbor at Alexandria. A T-shaped peninsula separated this harbor from the eastern one, where the city's commercial shipping was centered. The docks of the western harbor were lined with military vessels.

From where he stood on the deck of the *Leffingford,* Joe could see the tall sails of the Egyptian dhows that were docked in the eastern harbor. The sight of the exotic craft made a tingle of excitement go through him. The dhows, little changed in the centuries since Cleopatra had ruled this land, plied the waters of the Nile, carrying supplies to the interior of the country, sailing past the great pyramids and the stately Sphinx. Joe had read about such things in books and magazines, and now he was on the verge of seeing them for himself. Even the modern naval base could not disguise the feeling of antiquity that was in the very air.

"You look like a guy who's just been slapped in the mush," Dale said from beside Joe. "Close your mouth; you're gonna catch flies."

"Sorry," Joe muttered. "I just can't hardly believe it. We're in Egypt, Dale. *Egypt.*"

"Yeah, but it's just another dirty little country, and the only reason we're here is because the Nazis want it. If Rommel and the Afrika Korps weren't out there in the desert, we wouldn't give a damn about Egypt."

Politically and militarily, Dale might be right, Joe thought, but he didn't care. He was still excited to be here in a land so filled with history. Thousands upon thousands of years of history....

And he and the others would be adding to that history, he realized suddenly. What was happening here *was* important. If the Nazis seized Egypt, that would give them control of the Suez Canal, and they would be able to choke off the flow of Allied supplies to the rest of the Middle East. It might not sound that vital, but it was one more step in Hitler's plan to take over the entire world.

The *Leffingford* and the other transport ships docked, and the passengers, including the Americans, began to disembark. Carrying their carbines in their right hands, with their duffel bags slung over their left shoulders, Joe and Dale walked down the ramp from the ship to the dock along with the other members of the ASF detachment. Colonel Hoffman, the American officer in charge of the detachment, along with Major Wilton, the liaison from the British Army, saw that they were all loaded onto trucks. As the trucks started down the road from Alexandria to Cairo, Joe felt a twinge of disappointment. He wasn't sure what he had expected—that they would all be riding camels, maybe—but sitting in the back of a Dodge deuce-and-a-half was just like being back in the States.

It was over a hundred miles to Cairo and took most of the

afternoon to get there. Through the open rear of the canvas-covered truck, Joe could see the flat, sometimes swampy farmland of the delta, cut through by the finger-like channels of the Nile. The landscape was boring, and Dale soon dozed off. Joe remained awake, however, hoping to see something interesting.

Later in the day, they came within sight of the pyramids at Giza, across the great river from Cairo. Some of the men rolled up the canvas cover over the back of the truck, and although the air that action allowed to whip through was chilly, Joe didn't mind once he caught a glimpse of the magnificent structures rising abruptly from the ground. Those were pyramids, he told himself, *real* pyramids. He had trouble believing that he was really seeing them, but there they were, undeniable in their ancient majesty.

Joe grinned. This was a hell of an impressive sight for a guy from the South Side of Chicago to be seeing.

The trucks took them to the base on the outskirts of Cairo where the British Eighth Army was headquartered. The Eighth Army had been fighting in Egypt for a little over a year, first against Italian forces, whom they had defeated handily in an offensive into the Western Desert led by General Richard O'Conner, then against General Erwin Rommel's Deutsche Afrika Korps, which had come to the rescue of the hapless Italians.

Rommel had proven to be a much more dangerous foe. In 1940, as commander of the 7th Panzer Division—the so-called "Ghost Division"— he had been responsible for capturing much of northern France for the Nazis. Since being transferred to Tripoli, Libya, his forces had driven relentlessly east throughout 1941, recapturing all of the territory taken by the British with the stubborn exception of the port city of Tobruk.

Rommel's success had led some to start calling him "the Desert Fox"; it had also led Prime Minister Winston Churchill to replace General Sir Archibald Wavell as overall commander of British forces in the Middle East. The new commander was General Sir Claude Auchinleck, known fondly to his men as "the

Great Auk." Auchinleck had revitalized the Eighth Army and counter-attacked Rommel in Operation Crusader, which had forced the Germans back across the desert to the Libyan city of El Agheila. That was how things stood now, in late December 1941.

Joe knew all this from keeping up with the war news in *Stars & Stripes,* from listening to the BBC, and from talks with the British soldiers. The Eighth Army had experienced some success in recent weeks and had an air of optimism again, but Operation Crusader had taken a heavy toll in men and equipment. The men who had come from England on the *Leffingford* and the other troop transports, as well as the tanks that were soon to follow, would be replacements for the losses suffered in the desert.

The Americans piled out of the trucks in front of several long barracks buildings. Sergeant Garmon called them into formation, and the British non-coms were doing the same with their men. When everyone was lined up, a staff car came along the road and braked to a stop nearby. Small yellow pennants were flying from the fenders of the car, but Joe didn't know exactly what they meant. They probably indicated that an officer was inside the car.

That was confirmed a moment later when a dark-haired, middle-aged man with a lot of decorations on his jacket climbed out. Joe had been around the British Army long enough to recognize that the officer wore the insignia of a general. The general put on the cap he was carrying when he got out of the car, tucked a swagger stick under his arm, and walked up and down in front of the troops for a moment before stopping to address them.

"Welcome to Egypt," he said a loud, clear voice. "I am General Auchinleck."

Joe caught his breath. The Great Auk himself had come out to greet them.

"We find ourselves facing a wily foe," Auchinleck went on, "but so far we have prevailed and we will continue to prevail. I have all the confidence in the world in you men, and I know you shall not let me down."

Auchinleck saluted, a salute that all the newcomers returned, American and British alike. He stepped back then and let Colonel Hoffman and Major Wilton come forward to give each group its orders.

Joe and Dale both listened intently, eager to find out where they were going to end up. A few minutes later the officers, reading from documents on clipboards, came to their squad.

"Sixth Squad, ASF, attached to B Squadron, Third Royal Tank Corps, Fourth Armoured Brigade, Seventh Armoured Division, Eighth Army," Colonel Hoffman said. "Report to Barracks A-Seventeen."

Sergeant Garmon saluted. "Yes, sir." When the colonel had returned the salute, Garmon turned to the men and shouted, "Sixth Squad, report to Barracks A-Seventeen! On the double!"

The Americans picked up their duffel bags and trotted toward the barracks, which was about two hundred yards down the road. The air was cool, but the sun, even late in the afternoon like this, was quite warm, and Joe found himself sweating a little by the time they got to the barracks.

They went inside and found most of the barracks already occupied by British soldiers. Unlike at the Armour School, where the American instructors had been housed separately, it appeared that here in Egypt the Americans and the British would bunk together.

Dale stopped short just inside the door and said under his breath, "Oh, shit."

Joe followed his brother's look and understood Dale's reaction. At the other end of the barracks, Corporal Jeremy Royce and several of Royce's cronies were claiming bunks for themselves.

Bert Crimmens was here, too, which was good since both Joe and Dale liked the little tankie. Bert waved at them and called, "Over here, lads. A couple o' empty bunks."

"What do you think?" Joe asked.

Dale shrugged. "Fine with me. We'll be at the other end from Royce, and the farther away from that SOB the better."

Joe tossed his bag on one of the empty bunks Bert had indicated, and Dale followed suit. For the next quarter hour, they unpacked and squared everything away, just as they had been taught in boot camp back in Texas. Bert was babbling about how glad he was to have them in the same unit, but he abruptly fell silent and stiffened, then shouted, "Attention!"

Everyone snapped to as an officer strolled into the barracks. He was a handsome, brown-haired man in his thirties, and when he spoke his accent was subtly different from those of the other Eighth Army officers.

"I'm Captain Neville Sharp of B Squadron, 3R.T.C.," he said. "You gentlemen are now under my command. You'll have two weeks of training in the new General Grant tanks here in Cairo, then move up to the front as replacements for men lost in Operation Crusader. I know you've all been through the Armour School, but you'll find that operating a tank corps in the Western Desert is considerably different than doing so in southern England."

A few men smiled, but no one laughed.

Captain Sharp continued, "A lot of good men have given their lives to push General Rommel and the Afrika Korps back as far as El Agheila. It'll be your job to see that that sacrifice doesn't go for naught." Sharp took off his cap and ran his fingers through his hair, then replaced it and went on, "When we move, we move fast. When we hit the enemy, we hit hard. That's the only way to win a fight in the desert. You men are supposed to be good, and the tanks you're bringing with you are supposed to be the best." Sharp looked around at the men for a moment, then said quietly, "We'll see." With that, he turned and walked out of the barracks.

"Whew," Bert said when the captain was safely gone. "So that was Hell-on-Treads Sharp."

"Who?" Dale asked.

"You haven't heard of him? He's an Aussie, been over here fighting in tanks since last year. They say he's covered more ground and knocked out more Jerry tanks than any other tank company commander in the Eighth Army. Only appropriate, of course."

"What do you mean by that?"

Bert grinned humorlessly at Joe and Dale. "It's appropriate because he's also *lost* more men and tanks than anybody else."

THIRTY

It would be a long time before Honolulu got back to normal after the shocking events of 7 December 1941—if it ever did—but by now, a month after the Japanese sneak attack, the city was at least making an effort. In fact, here in the Palm Tree Room, the elegant lounge and supper club in one of the hotels along Waikiki, it was impossible to tell that the bombs had ever fallen. An orchestra was playing, a young woman with platinum blond hair sang softly into a microphone, and couples held each other close and swayed together on the postage-stamp sized dance floor.

Adam could have danced with Catherine all night. He was in his dress blues, and Catherine wore a tight black dress trimmed with white lace at the throat and sleeves. The feel of her slender body in his arms caused a lump in his throat and a tightness around his chest. After everything he had gone through on Wake Island, it was hard to believe that he was actually here in this fancy Honolulu nightspot, dancing with his wife.

He was the luckiest man in the whole Pacific, he told himself.

He was TDY to the Marine air base at Ewa, the temporary duty consisting of telling everything he could remember about his experiences on Wake to a series of different officers, all of whom he suspected of being connected to G-2, Operations and Planning—Intelligence, in other words. He told them about the defenses on the atoll and every detail he could recall about the Japanese attacks. They were especially interested in times of day and the directions from which the Japanese had attacked.

That tied in with what Adam suspected about the secret documents he had brought back with him from Wake. Intelligence must have intercepted some of the Japanese radio messages and attempted to decode them, and they were checking what they guessed were the translations against the details of the operations the Japs had carried out against Wake. That made sense, Adam decided. He might not have ever thought of such a thing if it had not been for his legal training. His pre-law courses at the university had taught him to think in a logical manner and seek out the most reasonable answers to questions.

But tonight, he didn't want to think about Japanese codes or anything else to do with the Marines. His evenings were free, and whenever Catherine didn't have night duty at the hospital, they made the most of their time together. The first week they had made love with a desperate urgency at every opportunity. Adam wanted to do more than just take Catherine to bed, though. He wanted to do the same sorts of things that other married couples did, live the sort of married life that he and Catherine had been denied because of her father's opposition to their union. They had married in secret, but now they could live in the open as husband and wife. So they went out to eat and went dancing and found themselves in places like the Palm Tree Room.

The number ended to polite applause for the sultry-voiced singer, and the bandleader announced that they would be taking a short break. Along with the other couples, Adam and Catherine went back to their table. The remains of their dinner had been cleared away, but what was left of the bottle of champagne was still there.

Adam took the bottle from its bucket of ice and filled their glasses. He raised his and said, "Here's to the prettiest woman in all of Honolulu."

Catherine glanced around. "Where?" she asked in mock innocence.

"Right here at this table," Adam told her.

She clinked her glass against his. "And she's sitting with the handsomest Marine in the entire Pacific."

"Wow, they must be a hell of a good-looking couple."

"I think so."

They drank and set their glasses down. Catherine put her hand to her mouth as she tried to stifle a yawn. "Goodness, I'm getting sleepy."

"Am I that boring?" Adam asked.

"Of course not! It's just that the food was so good, and I'm not used to drinking champagne, and we've been dancing all evening . . . I'm just tired, that's all."

His face solemn, Adam nodded. "Then I should take you back to the bungalow and put you to bed."

Catherine grinned at him. "Are you going to tuck me in?"

"I just might."

"Don't make promises you can't keep, big boy." Catherine was sitting close to him. She moved her hand under the table, then widened her eyes. "Oh, my. I think maybe you *can* keep that promise after all."

"Catherine, what are you doing?" Adam asked as his wife's hand began to move.

"What do you think?" She giggled. "Have you forgotten already?"

Adam felt his face growing warm with mingled embarrassment and desire. This sure wasn't the right time and place for what Catherine was doing . . .

But it felt so blasted *good*.

"I think you're drunk," he forced himself to say. "We'd better be going."

"I'd rather be coming."

Adam took her hand, holding firmly to it. "Let's go." With his other hand, he dug some money out of his pocket and dropped it on the table. Once they were alone, he would give her whatever she wanted, as often as he possibly could. But for now, he was damned glad the lighting was so dim in the Palm Tree Room. That way everybody couldn't see for themselves the effect she'd had on him.

Their waiter was there before they'd taken half a dozen steps toward the door. "Would you like anything else, Sergeant?"

Adam hesitated, unsure for a second whether or not the man was talking to him. The promotion that had been waiting for him at Ewa was taking some getting used to. He had moved up quickly, considering that he'd been a raw recruit at Parris Island less than a year earlier.

"No thanks," he told the waiter.

"I hope everything was satisfactory."

"Wonderful, just wonderful."

"S'wunnerful," Catherine sang lightly. "S'marvelous."

The waiter smiled. "The lady seems to have enjoyed herself."

Adam didn't know whether to be mad at the guy or not. The smile was almost a smirk. After a second, he decided it wasn't worth it. But he did say, "That's no lady. That's a lieutenant."

"That's right; I outrank you," Catherine said as he linked his arm with hers and walked out of the lounge into the hotel lobby. "I can order you to do *any*thing I want."

"You could do that anyway," Adam told her.

"Yeah, but you wouldn't have to follow orders. Unless you knew what was good for you."

He knew, all right. She was good for him. Always had been, always would be.

He stooped suddenly, put an arm around the backs of her thighs, and scooped her off the tile floor of the lobby. She cried out in surprise and delight as he draped her over his shoulder. "Come on, Lieutenant," he said. "You've got an appointment with a brand-new sergeant."

Both of them were laughing as he carried her out of the hotel, and so were the other people in the lobby.

The next morning, when Adam came into base headquarters at Ewa, the adjutant told him to report to the CO for new orders. Adam stiffened with worry. He had enjoyed the past two weeks, and he didn't want them to end, even though he knew they had to eventually.

"Thank you, Captain," he said to the adjutant. "What about my temporary duties here?"

"I'd say those were over, Sergeant, wouldn't you?"

"Yes, sir, I suppose so."

He was shown into the commanding officer's office, and after he had saluted and been told to stand at ease, the CO handed him a mimeographed sheet of paper. Adam took the flimsy document and looked at it, eyes growing wide with surprise when he saw that he had been reassigned to the 2nd Marine Division, currently in training at Camp Kearney, California, near San Diego.

He was going back to the States.

Adam looked up at the CO. "Sir, is this right? I assumed that given my experience, I would be assigned somewhere in the Pacific."

The CO said, "You can read it for yourself, Sergeant. Do you object to going home?"

Home was Chicago, not southern California, Adam thought, but he didn't voice that. Instead, he said, "No, sir, I'm just surprised, that's all."

Of all the twists of fate! He had joined the Marines thinking that would get him to Europe faster to fight the Nazis. Instead he'd wound up on that speck of coral in the middle of the Pacific. Catherine had enlisted in the nurse corps in order to follow him, and now she would be stuck here in Hawaii while he went back to the States. They were going to be separated again after only a couple of weeks together, and that just wasn't long enough.

No matter how long they were together, it wouldn't be long enough, he realized. He hadn't even shipped out yet, and already he missed her with an ache that was like a knife in the belly.

"Don't count on sitting out the rest of the war," the CO went on. "I don't know what the plans are for the Second Division, but my guess is you'll be back in the middle of this before long."

"I hope so, sir," Adam said. If it meant he would be closer to Catherine, he would go anywhere and do anything the Marines told him to do. Of course, he would do that anyway, he realized.

The CO leaned back in his chair and relaxed a bit. "I'm aware that your wife is a nurse at the naval hospital and that you're staying with her, son. That order tells me to send you back to Dago by the first available transport, priority three A. That's not going to be until day after tomorrow. If your priority was four A, I could get you out of here today, but since I can't, you might as well go back to her quarters."

"Thank you, sir."

"Now if you'll get out of here, I need to call a friend of mine over at the hospital and see if I can get a certain nurse released from her duties for the next couple of days."

Adam's pulse jumped. "Thank you, sir," he said again, more emphatically this time. The CO must have had a good reason for granting him such an unusual favor, he thought.

The CO waved a hand. "No promises, Sergeant. But I'm willing to do what I can for one of the last men off Wake Island."

*　　*　　*

The proper strings had been pulled, and Catherine was waiting for Adam when he got back to the bungalow. She wore a thin nightgown that clung to the lines of her body, and Adam's heart pounded wildly as he swept her into his arms and crushed his lips to hers. He almost popped some buttons on his uniform getting it off.

Afterward, when they lay huddled together in bed, Catherine said, "I'm not complaining, mind you, but what's going on, Adam? Why are we here in the middle of the morning instead of on duty?"

He'd been dreading giving her the news. There was no way to soften the blow. "I've got new orders," he said. "I'm being reassigned to the Second Marine Division in California."

She lifted her head from his shoulder and looked down at him. "They're sending you back to the States?"

He nodded. "I'm sorry."

She stared at him for a couple of seconds, then surprised him by laughing. "My God, why are you sorry? You're going *home*."

"Home is Chicago," he said. He was able to tell her what he'd had to suppress in the CO's office. "And damn it, I don't want to go anywhere without you."

She hugged him tightly. "I don't want us to be apart, either, but this is good news, Adam. You'll be safe."

"What about you?"

"The Japs aren't going to attack Pearl Harbor again. I'll be fine."

"How do you know they won't come back?"

"Well, if they were going to, they would have before now, wouldn't they?"

"You can't know that."

She slid over so that she lay on top of him. She kissed his forehead, his nose, his mouth. Her short blond hair was in disarray around her face from their lovemaking, and he thought she had never looked more beautiful. He slid his hands down her back to the curve of her rump and pressed her against him.

"I'm going to miss you so much," she whispered. "But it'll be worth it to know you're safe."

He didn't tell her what the CO had said about the Second Division getting into the fight in the Pacific. Maybe it wouldn't come to that. Maybe he would stay in California, safe as houses, until she was rotated back stateside and they could be together again. He was going to cling to that hope.

But for now, and for the next couple of days, he was going to cling to her. . . .

THIRTY-ONE

Mike Chastain looked at the cards in his hand, his face carefully expressionless as he did so. He took a bill off the pile in front of him, tossed it into the center of the table, and said, "I'm in." The bill was a twenty.

The game was going on in the sitting room of a fancy hotel suite. The guy staying in the suite was some bigshot manufacturing mogul from the West Coast. He was passing through Chicago on his way to Washington, D.C., for a meeting with a bunch of government officials about converting his plants to wartime production. He was only in town for one night and had put out the word that he wanted to sit in on a good game. Since the stakes were to be high, the game had come to him.

Mike took two cards and improved his hand, but he wasn't sure if it was enough to keep him in. He looked around the table at the other players. The West Coast mogul, whose name was Curtis, was across from him. Jack Kingsley sat to Mike's left, between him and Curtis. To Curtis's right were Roger Hale and Al Bartolo. Mike could get a good read on everybody except Hale; that guy was the great stone face when he had cards in his hand. Curtis was the easiest. The manufacturer was almost chortling with glee every time he glanced at his cards. Mike folded when the betting came around to him.

It came down to Curtis and Roger Hale. Curtis had a good hand, all right, three queens, but Hale beat him with a flush and took the pot. Curtis's round, pudgy face flushed with disappointment. "I thought you were bluffing," he said to Hale.

Hale smiled thinly and shook his head. "I never bluff."

That was a bald-faced lie, Mike thought. He had seen Hale bluff successfully plenty of times. But Curtis swallowed the line, and if the opportunity arose later in the game, Hale would bluff the Californian right out of his socks.

Mike was a couple of hundred bucks ahead. Even though it was early, he started to think about calling it a night. If he packed it in now and headed for the Dells, he could still catch the last half of Karen's show.

But some hunch told him to wait, that there might be a better payoff later on. Bored but willing to give it a little more time, Mike continued playing.

The booze was flowing pretty good, and Curtis was well on his way to being drunk. Once that happened, the game really would be over as far as Mike was concerned. It was easy enough to take Curtis's money when the guy was sober. If he was smashed there wouldn't be any challenge at all. At that point it would cease to be a game and become petty larceny.

By midnight, Curtis was stinking. He'd lost three hands in a row, plunging stupidly on each of them, and he was so shaky he knocked over his drink when he reached for it. Mike started gathering up his winnings and said, "That's it for me."

"What?" Curtis exclaimed. "You can't do that. You can't just quit."

"Watch me," Mike said.

"But you gotta give me a chance to win some back. Come on, Mike." Curtis belched. "You're a good guy."

"Not that good."

Curtis's already red face got redder. "Well, thass just a chickenshit thing to do."

Mike shrugged. "Last I heard it was a free country. You're entitled to your opinion."

"My 'pinion is you're a coward."

Roger Hale touched Curtis's arm and told him, "I wouldn't say that if I were you, Mr. Curtis. This has been a friendly game, and we should keep it that way."

Curtis shook off Hale's hand. "Fuck you."

Hale turned in his seat and hit Curtis very hard in the left side of the belly. Curtis's face turned white and took on the consistency of unbaked dough. He bent forward over the table, gasping and wheezing.

Mike said, "Looks like the game's over."

Hale put his hand on the back of Curtis's head and said, "Friendly game?"

"You . . . bastard!" Curtis rasped out.

Hale bounced Curtis's face off the table. Blood sprayed from the Californian's nose. He screamed and kicked back, toppling his chair and falling onto the floor.

Hale looked around the table. "Sorry, fellas. I seem to have broken up the game."

Mike stood up and looked at Curtis, who had rolled onto his side and drawn his knees up. He held his hands over his face and moaned and whimpered. Mike said, "That's not all you broke."

Hale smiled and reached for his hat. "I can't stand a belligerent drunk."

Everyone gathered up their money and went out, leaving Curtis on the floor. Mike and Hale were the last ones out of the hotel room. As Mike shut the door behind him, Hale said, "Why don't we go downstairs and have a drink?"

"Might be better to go somewhere else," Mike suggested. "Curtis could call the cops."

"Cops don't worry me. But I guess there's no point in asking for trouble, is there?"

They left the hotel and walked four blocks to a watering hole called The Embers Lounge. When they went in, Hale suggested they take a booth rather than sitting at the bar. Mike shrugged his agreement.

The dimly lit lounge wasn't very busy. A jukebox in the corner played an Artie Shaw tune, and a man and a woman stood near the jukebox, holding each other and swaying back and forth. Three men and another woman sat at the bar, while maybe half of the booths and tables were occupied by couples. It was the sort of joint where people came when what they had on their minds wasn't completely on the up and up.

Mike ordered a sidecar from the waiter who came over to the booth. Hale asked for scotch, neat. The waiter said, "Better enjoy 'em while you can, gents. Word is that liquor's going to get scarce while the war's on."

When the waiter was gone, Hale said, "That guy's got a point. The war's going to cause plenty of shortages."

"I've thought the same thing," Mike said.

Hale dropped his hat on the table, leaned back against the upholstered back of the seat, and lit a cigarette. He was about ten years older than Mike, with curly brown hair and a thin mustache.

"I was watching you when Curtis called you a coward. I have a feeling that if I hadn't done what I did, you might have done worse. I figured Curtis would rather have a sore belly and a busted nose than be dead."

"I wouldn't have killed him."

"That's not what your eyes said. And I know a little about you, Mike. People say you're a bad man to cross."

"People say a lot of things. What's really on your mind, Hale?"

Hale exhaled a cloud of smoke, then said, "Hang on. Here's our drinks."

They waited until the waiter had placed the drinks on the table in front of them. Hale gave the man two dollars. When he was gone, Hale went on, "I've been putting together a business deal, Mike, and I think it's something that would interest you. I'd like to have you in on it."

"I'm a gambler, not a businessman."

"You used to do more than gamble."

"Everybody used to do something else, no matter what they're doing now. That doesn't mean I want to go back."

"Hear me out," Hale said. "I've got contacts who tell me that the government's going to start rationing things pretty soon. Basic things like sugar and flour and gasoline and meat."

"I've heard that talk, too. What's it got to do with us?"

"Where the hell were you during Prohibition? When the government says you can't have something, Americans want it that much more. And they're willing to pay for it."

"You're talking about the black market."

"Call it whatever you want," Hale said. "I call it smart business. I've got a refrigerated warehouse where we can store meat, and I know where to get plenty. We freeze it, hang on to it for a while until rationing kicks in, and then we can clean up by selling it."

"Sounds like a good idea. What do you need me for?"

"I don't trust the guys I'm dealing with. I need somebody to watch my back."

"You handled yourself pretty good with Curtis."

Hale waved a hand. "A fat little guy who does nothing but push papers all day. My Aunt Sophie could've decked him, and she's ninety-eight!" He leaned forward. "What do you say, Mike? The money'll be good. You have my word on that."

For a long moment, Mike didn't say anything. Then, "I'll think about it. That's all I can promise right now."

Hale took a card and a fountain pen out of his pocket. He uncapped the pen and wrote on the back of the card. "Eleven o'clock Wednesday night," he said as he slid the card across the table, "that's where I'll be. I hope you decide to show up, Mike."

"We'll see." Mike put the card in his coat pocket, then picked up his drink and downed a healthy swallow. He was tempted to go ahead and tell Hale he would be there. This was just the sort of set-up he had envisioned when the war started, and in the past, he would have jumped at it.

But he was semi-legit now, and Karen liked it that way. What would she say if he told her he was getting back into the business?

He had come along too late for Prohibition, the days when Capone and Nitti and the other bigshots had ruled Chicago. There had been a lot of action during the thirties, but it was never the same after Repeal. Mike had always felt like he'd missed something. The black market wasn't the same thing, but it might be as close as he'd ever come.

"I can tell you're thinking about it," Hale said with a grin.

"I'm thinking," Mike admitted.

"Think hard, Mike. Think really hard." Hale drained his drink. "I know you won't let me down."

★   ★   ★

The wind was cold as hell. Mike tugged down his hat and turned up the collar of his overcoat. He stuffed his hands as deep in his pockets as he could, the right one touching the butt of the .38 revolver. He would have liked to be able to wear gloves, but he'd never been able to shoot very well with gloves on.

Not that he expected any trouble. Roger Hale had assured him that everything was set up. The refrigerated truck full of meat would pull into this alley, the driver would take the money that Hale had for him, and then Hale and Mike would take the truck back to Hale's warehouse. Mike was there in case of an attempted double-cross, which Hale said was highly unlikely. After the meat had been unloaded, the truck would be taken way out on the South Side and left for its owners to pick up.

Karen had been a little P.O.'ed at him for not going to the club with her, but he'd told her not to worry about it, that he had a game somewhere else. He would make it up to her later. He'd waited until she was gone to take the gun out of the closet and put it in his pocket. This was the first time Mike had carried a gun in more than two years. The weight in his pocket felt funny for a minute when he first put it in there, but then it all came back to him and didn't seem odd at all.

Beside him, Hale's teeth were chattering. "We don't really need a freezer tonight, do we?"

"It may be a while before rationing starts."

"I know that. Just making conversation."

That was unusual, Mike thought. Hale seemed a little nervous. Usually Hale was as cool as the wind blowing off the lake.

A rumbling sound came to Mike's ears. Hale stiffened as he heard it, too. "There's the guy now."

A few tense minutes later, headlights washed the alley as a truck turned down it. Hale caught hold of Mike's overcoat sleeve and tugged him back into a small alcove of the building, out of the light. "What's this?" Mike asked. "I thought the guy was expecting us. Why are we hiding?"

"I don't want him to see our faces. That was the deal. He don't know us, and we don't know him. All right?"

"Sure, whatever you say." Mike frowned, though. Something wasn't right.

The truck came to a stop and cut its lights. The engine died. It was parked about twenty feet from the alcove where Mike and Hale waited. The driver got out and slammed the door behind him. He was whistling a tune. Mike recognized it after a second as "Oh, Susanna."

Whistling? A guy comes to sell a truckload of contraband steaks to a couple of black marketeers, and he's whistling "Oh, Susanna"? Mike supposed it was possible, but his instincts were warning him more with each passing second.

"Watch my back," Hale hissed; then he stepped out of the alcove and called, "Hey, buddy!"

The truck driver was heading for a closed door in one of the buildings flanking the alley. He stopped short and turned to face Hale. "What the hell! You gave me quite a start, Mac. What do you want?"

Hale walked closer to the man. "I'm looking for Hannigan's place."

"That dive?" The truck driver snorted. "It's three blocks north of here. Just head up 38th. You can't miss it."

"Thanks," Hale said. The driver turned toward the building again, and Hale brought a gun out of his overcoat pocket and shot him in the back of the head. The slug threw the driver forward so that his face smacked into the door he had been about to open. He hung there for a second, leaning against the door, and then slid down hard onto the pavement. His left leg kicked once, but he didn't move after that.

Mike stood absolutely still in the alcove. He wasn't shocked into immobility. He had figured out what Hale was going to do a couple of seconds before Hale pulled the trigger. Mike stood motionless because Hale still had the gun in his hand. Some guys, after they'd killed somebody, their hearts were pounding so hard and the blood was racing through their veins so fast, they just naturally pulled the trigger again if anything spooked them. Mike didn't think Roger Hale was like that, but he wasn't going to take the chance.

Hale looked down at the gun in his hand. Thick cotton batting had been wrapped around the barrel and taped in place to muffle the sound of the shot. Hale tore off the cotton and stuffed it in his left-hand overcoat pocket. The gun went back in the right.

He stepped over to the dead man and said to Mike, "Give me a hand with him. He fell so that he's in the way of the truck."

"Inconsiderate of him," Mike said as he came out of the alcove and went to join Hale.

"Don't mouth off at me," Hale said. "I don't work with wisenheimers."

"It looks like you didn't need me at all." Mike took the corpse's ankles while Hale took the shoulders. They dragged him over against the wall.

Hale straightened and said, "I didn't know for sure that he was going to be alone. He was supposed to be, but sometimes things don't work out."

"You weren't going to pay him at all, were you? There wasn't any arrangement. This is a straight heist job."

"He was a crook, too. Where do you think he got that load?" Hale jerked a thumb at the truck. "We can sell the meat in there for close to twenty grand if the government starts rationing it. I figure that's worth taking a few chances. If you don't like it, I'll give you a couple of hundred for coming along tonight, and you can take off."

What Hale would give him was a bullet in the back of the head, just like he'd given the truck driver. Mike knew that. He was either in this deal, or he was dead. Or he could try to gun Hale first. . . .

"Is that what you want, Mike? Because if you do, there's no hard feelings."

"You're getting ahead of yourself," Mike said. "Don't worry; I'm in." He glanced at the dead man. "That guy don't mean anything to me. We'd better get moving, though. Somebody might've heard that shot and called the cops."

"There's nothing but warehouses for three blocks. Still, there's no point in standing around in the cold, is there? You want to drive?"

Mike shook his head. "This is your show, Roger. I'm along for the ride, remember."

Hale looked at him and said, "I go pretty fast. You won't want to jump off once I get started."

"Don't worry about that. I'll ride to the end of the line."

THIRTY-TWO

The tank lurched to a halt, throwing Dale forward as he stood in the turret. He caught himself before he could tumble out and turned around to glare down into the smiling face of the driver.

"Can we brew up?"

"What?" Dale asked, shaken by the rough stop. He had called for a halt but hadn't expected it to be that abrupt. He took off the earphones that let him hear not only the radio but also whatever was said on the tank's interphone system.

"I asked if we can brew up," the driver said.

Dale looked out across the desert a few miles west of Cairo and gritted his teeth for a moment. He looked at his watch, swallowed his irritation, and said, "Sure, we'll take a break. It'll take the others a while to catch up to us, anyway."

The other tanks in the training exercise were nowhere in sight. Dale's crew was a good one, and the M3 had been pouring on the speed all morning. It was essential that the British tankies learn to get all the speed they could out of the General Grants, because that was the only advantage they had over the heavier, slower German Mark III and Mark IV Panzers. The Panzer's armor could withstand a direct hit better than the Grant's, and the range of its cannon was greater.

Still, the Grant was an improvement over what the Eighth Army had started out using here in Egypt, the lumbering British tanks called Matildas. Some early model M3s without the British modifications of the Grant had been used in Operation Crusader. The tankies were so pleased with them that instead of using the correct name for the tanks, the General Lee, they had started calling them Honeys. These replacement troops had adopted that nickname for the Grants as well.

Dale used his arms to lever himself out of the turret of the Honey and dropped onto the hull. He clambered down over the tracks and onto the sand. The crew followed him: a driver, a gunner, and an operator who also functioned as a reloader for the gunner as well as handling the wireless set. In theory, in a pinch they could all handle one another's jobs as well as their own. When this tank headed farther west into the desert to join the battle against Rommel, it would carry these three men as its crew, as well as an officer who would command it. The officers were back in Cairo, studying desert battle tactics and strategy in some classroom, while Dale was out here in the hot sun teaching these blokes how to actually run the bloody tank.

He grimaced and rubbed a hand over his face as he realized he was starting to think like the British soldiers, even though he'd been around them for only a month. Next thing you knew, he told himself, he'd be talking like the limeys!

The three crewmen had built a small fire using gasoline—or petrol, as they called it—from a can, and now they had their kettle set up. As always, Dale looked on in wonderment as the tankies went about brewing their tea. They could be in the middle of a battle, he thought, and if the urge struck them they would stop to "brew up."

He had never seen a crazier bunch in all his life.

He became aware that a squawking sound was coming from the earphones he had left on top of the turret. Thinking that it might be important, he sighed and climbed back up there. As he settled the 'phones over his head, he heard his brother Joe's voice coming through them.

"—the hell are you? Blast it, answer me, Dale!"

Dale moved the microphone closer to his mouth and said, "Take it easy, big brother. I'm right here."

"What's your location?" Joe's voice was businesslike now, but Dale thought he heard a hint of relief in it.

"Location? Uh, lemme see. . . ." Dale reached down into the turret and got the map he had stashed there on a small shelf. He unfolded it, studied the markings on it, and thought he had figured out where they were supposed to be, then lifted his head to look around for landmarks to confirm his guess.

Landmarks. In the desert. That was a good one, he thought.

As far as the eye could see, there was nothing but gently rolling hills of sand, dotted here and there by a scrubby clump of stubborn grass. No trees, no rocks, nothing but the desert.

But he knew where the tank had started out that morning, back at the base depot near Cairo, and he knew the compass heading they had followed all day. He knew how fast they'd been going, too, so he muttered, "The hell with it," and went with his calculations. He gave Joe the coordinates.

"How'd you get way out there? You're five miles in front of us." Joe was in one of the other tanks, using a radio that had been giving trouble. He had worked on it, and today's exercise was sort of a test run for it.

Dale grinned and said into the microphone, "Some of us don't sit around twiddling our thumbs all day."

"Twiddling our thumbs, is it?" a new voice said, and Dale tried not to gulp. He recognized the voice of Captain Neville Sharp, the commander of B Squadron. In talking to Joe, Dale had forgotten that what he was saying also went out over the net to the rest of the tanks in the squadron.

"Sorry, sir. I didn't actually mean it like that."

"Well, then, don't say it." Sharp's voice crackled over the earphones. "Stop hanging about, Parker, and get back here. We don't want some lonely Stuka pilot spotting you out there all alone."

Dale hadn't considered the possibility that German planes might be flying around the desert. It seemed unlikely, since Rommel's Afrika Korps had fallen back all the way to El Agheila, on the Libyan coast, but it was better not to take the chance, Dale decided.

"We'll rejoin the squadron as soon as possible, sir," he told Sharp.

"See that you do."

Dale took off the earphones and climbed out of the turret. One of his crew, the driver, looked up at him and asked, "Want a cuppa, Yank?"

Dale shook his head. "Sorry to bust up your tea party, boys, but Captain Sharp says we've got to get back to the rest of the squadron."

"Bloody hell! We just brewed up."

Dale suppressed a grin as he said, "Orders is orders."

With a lot of grumbling, the three tankies put away their kettle and cups, threw sand on the fire, and climbed back into the Honey. The tank reversed, turned, and set off in the direction it had come, rolling over the sand at a little over twenty miles per hour. Dale hoped they wouldn't miss the rest of the squadron. If that happened, they might keep going all the way back to Cairo.

Out here on this flat landscape, it was easy to spot the other tanks. When he did, Dale saw that his tank was on a pretty straight course. He called out a slight correction to the driver, then watched as the Honey drew closer to the squadron, which had drawn up into a formation that the British called a leaguer. It always reminded Dale of the way the wagon trains in Western movies got in a circle when the Indians attacked. He halfway expected John Wayne to peer out from behind one of the tanks, Winchester in hand and ten-gallon hat on his head.

Instead, Neville Sharp walked out from the leaguer to greet the tank and its crew. The captain wore laced-up boots, khaki shorts, and a khaki shirt with his captain's pips sewed to the shoulders. As the Honey came to a stop, Sharp looked up at Dale and said, "I trust you had a merry little jaunt, Parker."

"Sorry, Captain," Dale said as he climbed down from the tank. "I had the boys pour on the speed." He patted one of the treads. "I wanted to see what this baby could do."

"I seem to recall hearing that you drove race cars back in the States. Is that right?"

Dale grinned. "Yeah. I won a lot of races, too."

"This is a tank, not a bloody race car!" Sharp said. "And you're a long way from Indianapolis or wherever the hell it is you Yanks have your races. If you can't obey orders, you can get the blazes out of my squadron!"

Sharp turned on his heel and stalked off, leaving Dale staring openmouthed after him. A moment later, Joe came hurrying up, looking worried.

"Was the captain mad?"

Dale looked at him. "What the hell was that all about? Where does he get off talking to me like I'm under his command? And since when did I disobey orders?"

"Before we left, we were instructed not to disperse more than a mile apart."

"Are you sure? I didn't hear that."

"I'm not surprised. You were barely awake. I had to keep poking you with my elbow so you wouldn't start snoring."

Dale grimaced. "Yeah, well . . . I didn't sleep so good last night. I was tired."

"You were tired because you caught a ride into Cairo and didn't sneak back into camp until after lights-out. You're lucky one of the sentries didn't shoot you."

"Keep it down, willya? I just went to Shepheard's and had a drink in the bar."

Joe shook his head. "You're going to get arrested if you're not careful, Dale."

"Well, it's nice to know you haven't changed. You're as big a damned worrywart over here in Egypt as you were back home."

Joe frowned and looked like he wanted to say something else, but then he just sighed and shook his head. "Come on," he said. "Let's have some tea."

"You know what I'd rather have?" Dale asked as he fell in step beside his brother.

"What's that?"

"A big icy root beer with foam on it about this thick." Dale held his thumb and forefinger an inch and a half apart. "And maybe I could use it to wash down a nice juicy hot dog with onions and sauerkraut and french fried potatoes on the side. And then I'd top it off with a slice of apple pie and a scoop of ice cream."

Joe let out a groan of longing. "Shut up."

Dale slapped him on the shoulder. "Don't worry. I'm sure these Brits will be glad to share their tea and kidney pies."

*   *   *

The squadron stayed in leaguer until after lunch, then moved out and went through a series of maneuvers directed by Captain Sharp. Sharp had his own Honey and a veteran crew which had been through Operation Crusader with him. The tanks dispersed, came together, split up again, and finally concluded with a firing exercise in which the gunners used the tanks' 37-mm cannon to blow up some trucks that were beyond repair.

Joe was pleased with the performance of the radio in his tank. He had never thought of himself as having any sort of aptitude for electronics, but by now he knew the British Wireless Set No. 19 inside and out. He sat with the earphones clamped to his head until all the tanks were back at the depot and parked in their usual spots.

As Joe climbed out of the tank, Captain Sharp was gathering the men of the squadron around him. Joe went over to join them and came up beside Dale, who had taken off the leather helmet that tank commanders wore. Dale's blond hair was matted with sweat.

"Most of you did good work out there today," Sharp said to the group. He repeated, "Most of you."

Joe saw an angry flush creeping into Dale's face. Dale knew he was the target of that barbed comment from the British captain. Joe hoped his brother would have sense enough to keep his mouth shut.

"Nevertheless," Sharp continued, "you could use another

month's practice, the lot of you. Unfortunately, you're not going to get it."

That caused a murmur from the men of the squadron. They fell silent as Sharp glared at them.

"As you may know, General Rommel and the Afrika Korps have left El Agheila and are advancing to the east once again. Today, our forces have pulled back from Benghazi, and the Germans have occupied the city."

Joe wasn't all that familiar with the map of North Africa, but he knew that what Sharp was saying couldn't be good. The British were giving up territory that they had gained during Operation Crusader. Sometimes a retreat could be carried out for strategic reasons, but Joe had the feeling that wasn't the case here.

"Because our lines have been stretched rather thin, all replacements—men and tanks alike—have been ordered to the front by General Auchinleck and General Ritchie. We shall be leaving for Gazala tomorrow morning."

A stirring of both apprehension and excitement went through the men of the squadron. Joe thought excitement won out over apprehension. All of these men knew that their lives would be in considerably more danger once they were at the front facing the German Panzers, but this was what they had trained for these past months, first in England and then here in Egypt: a chance to fight. A chance to strike a blow against the Nazis and perhaps make a difference in the war.

Sharp's voice had less of an edge to it as he went on, "Good luck to all of you. For now, dismissed."

The group broke up, the men heading for their barracks, talking excitedly among themselves. Joe and Dale, along with the other American instructors, started toward the barracks that housed the ASF detachment, but before they could get there Bert Crimmens came trotting up alongside them.

"Hullo, lads," the little Englishman said. "Quite the bit of news the captain delivered, wasn't it?"

Joe and Dale stopped. "It sure was," Joe said.

"I couldn't leave without saying so long to you lads." Bert stuck out his hand. "You've helped me more than I can say. I'd never have learned to drive a tank if it wasn't for you, Dale."

"Ah, hell, I was just doin' my job," Dale said. He took Bert's hand and pumped it. "You're the one who did all the work."

"Well, I appreciate you anyway. And Joe—" They shook hands as well. "You've been a good friend. I hope you keep writing stories." Bert grinned. "And put ol' Bert Crimmons in one of 'em, why don't you?"

"I'll do that," Joe said. "That's a promise."

"Keep your head down, Bert," Dale said.

Bert laughed. "I jolly well intend to, no fear about that."

"Just leave us a few Germans for when we get in on the fighting. It's bound to be just a matter of time."

What Dale said was right, Joe thought. Now that the United States was officially in the war, sooner or later their combat forces would be in action here in North Africa, unless the British and French had already succeeded by then in driving out all the Germans. Joe figured that was pretty unlikely.

This time, the move to the front wouldn't include the handful of American GIs in Cairo. The next time might be completely different.

"Don't worry," Bert said. "There's enough of the bloody Nazis to go around."

THIRTY-THREE

Lieutenant Phillip Lange, USNR, had one hand on the control stick, and his thumb rested on the button that fired the machine gun mounted in front of the SBD Dauntless's cockpit. The airplane, which had been built at the Douglas Aircraft Company's plant in El Segundo, California, in January 1940, was flying at 140 miles per hour, just under its regular cruising speed. Phil was ready to kick the Dauntless up to full power, though, at the first sign of Japs. None of them could be allowed to get away. Captain Sherman had made that clear this morning during the briefing in the ready room back on the *Lexington*.

The *Lady Lex* was steaming through the Southwest Pacific, bound for the vicinity of Rabaul, on the island of New Britain. A month earlier, in late January 1942, the Japanese had captured Rabaul with its excellent harbor and its airfield with long, well-constructed runways. The Japs couldn't have asked for a better advance base as they inched their way closer and closer to Australia. So far, during two and a half months of war, everything had gone their way here in the Pacific. They had no reason to think anything was going to be different now. Their attack on Pearl Harbor had badly crippled the U.S. fleet, and island after island had fallen to their advance.

But the Navy still had four flattops, and one of them was the *Lexington*.

"See anything?" Jerry Bennett asked from the backward-facing rear seat of the Dauntless, where he manned a swivel-mounted machine gun and served as a second observer. The

JAMES REASONER

Dauntless was a dive bomber, but today it was primarily a reconnaissance plane. Several of the SBDs had been sent out from the *Lexington* with orders to shoot down any Japanese patrol planes they encountered. The plans were to surprise the Japanese at Rabaul with a carrier-based attack, and the party would be ruined if the Japs found out they had visitors on the way.

"Nothing," Phil replied over the radio. His blue eyes scanned the ocean all the way to the horizon. "Nothing" was right. Nothing but a lot of water.

As a boy in western New York, growing up in a small town on the shores of Lake Erie, Phil had seen plenty of water. The lake had looked like an ocean to him. But now that he had seen the real thing, he understood the differences. The Pacific just went on and on and on. . . .

It was a lonely thing, flying high like this, nothing else moving except the never-ending waves far below. As far as the eye could see, there was no sign of humanity. He and Jerry might have been the only living beings in a vast world that was nothing but water.

The only air-breathing living beings, that is, he corrected himself. The sea itself was full of life. He knew that from his high school biology classes, the sort of classes that he would be teaching now if he'd been able to go to college and get his degree.

But there hadn't been any money for college, not with seven brothers and sisters back home, so he'd joined the Naval Reserve instead. They had decided to make a pilot out of him—something about the outstanding eye-hand coordination he'd demonstrated when he was taking the battery of examinations that helped determine his assignment—and after flight school he had been commissioned a brand spanking new lieutenant.

Then the war had come, and suddenly there were no more reserves. Everybody was on active duty, probably for the duration. And instead of taking off from and landing on nice, long, comfortable runways, they had him zooming on and off the deck of an aircraft carrier, a space that from the air didn't look a whole hell of a lot bigger than a tabletop.

Phil increased the speed of the Dauntless. Not by much, just enough to show that he was impatient. He and Jerry had taken off before dawn this morning, along with the crews of half dozen more SBDs, and fanned out along the carrier's approach to Rabaul. For several days, the *Lexington* had been making its way south through the Caroline Islands, with every man aboard hoping that they wouldn't be spotted. Now, with the *Lady Lex* almost within striking distance of Rabaul, secrecy was more important than ever.

The plan had been carefully coordinated by Naval Chief of Operations Ernest J. King. Several hundred miles to the east-northeast, in the Marshall Islands, planes from the carrier *Enterprise,* under the command of Vice Admiral William F. Halsey Jr., were raising hell with the Japanese airfields there. South of there, in the Gilberts, Rear Admiral Frank Jack Fletcher had the *Yorktown* poised to cause more trouble for the Japs. With the attention of the Japanese diverted, it was hoped that the *Lexington* could launch a hard strike against Rabaul.

"I don't see a damned thing," Jerry said. Static popped and sparked in Phil's earphones as his companion spoke. "I don't think there's any Japs out here."

"They're here," Phil said. "I can feel 'em."

"All I can feel is a sore butt from sitting so long—wait a second. Damn it!"

Phil tensed. He heard the same orders over the radio that Jerry had just heard.

"We're being called back. Jimmy Thach just shot down a Mavis that stumbled over the *Lex.*"

Phil glanced at his watch and said, "Shit!" The carrier was still too far away from Rabaul to launch its bombers. "Thach got the Mavis, didn't he?"

"Yeah, but you know that don't mean anything, Phil. It don't take but a minute to get on the radio and yell a warning."

Even though Jerry was facing the other way and couldn't see him, Phil nodded. Jimmy Thach was a wizard at the controls of a Grumman F4F-3 Wildcat—he had even invented a new method of aerial combat called the Thach Weave that had proven highly effective in fighting the Japanese Zeros—but not even he could work miracles. By the time Thach and his wingman had taken off from the *Lexington,* the Mavis's pilot would have had plenty of time to radio Rabaul and warn the Japs there that a flattop was on its way.

"Whatta we do now?" Jerry asked as Phil sent the Dauntless into a banking turn that headed it back north.

"Return to the ship as ordered," Phil said. "What did you have in mind?"

"I wouldn't mind getting in one good lick at Rabaul."

"You'd have a long swim back home. You know we don't have enough fuel for that. We'd have to ditch before we ever got back to the *Lexington*."

Jerry sighed. "Yeah, I know. But I'd sure like a shot at those yellow bastards."

Phil understood why Jerry felt like that. Two of Jerry's cousins, twin brothers only nineteen years old, had been killed at Pearl Harbor, going down with the *Arizona*.

But orders, and the reality of a dwindling fuel supply, meant that vengeance would have to wait for another day. Unless, of course, when they got back to the *Lexington* the Japs were attacking it, and Phil wouldn't wish that on anybody, no matter how badly he wanted to get back at the enemy.

Setting a course that ought to take the plane straight back to the carrier, Phil edged the speed up a little more. That used up the gas quicker, but he had plenty to get back.

"You think the captain'll call off the attack?" Jerry asked.

Without the element of surprise, it would be difficult to do much damage to the Japanese at Rabaul, Phil thought. The dive bombers would have a hard time getting through the screen of anti-aircraft fire and fighter planes the Japs would throw up over the city.

"I wouldn't be surprised," he said. "But that'll be up to the captain."

As the scout planes converged on the carrier, gradually they came within sight of each other. By midday they were flying in a loose formation. Phil was keeping an eye out for the carrier and her escort of several battleships when something streaked past the cockpit. "Yow!" Jerry shouted into the radio, hurting Phil's ears. "What was that?"

Phil saw a couple of planes swooping up and away from the flight of SBDs. He recognized them immediately as Wildcats. It had been one of them that had buzzed the Dauntless. And probably, it had been Jimmy Thach at the controls.

Phil switched frequencies on the radio so that he could talk to the Wildcats and then keyed the mike. "This is Sable One," he said. "Sable One. Is that you, Commander?"

"All the way, Sable One," the reply came in Jimmy Thach's familiar voice. "Have already alerted the pretty lady that her wayward children are on their way home."

So Thach had radioed the *Lexington* that the flight of Dauntlesses was on its way back to the carrier. That was good. Nobody wanted to be shot down by his own men, and although all the gunners on the *Lex* were supposed to have been trained to recognize the shapes of all American and Japanese planes, Phil didn't want to count on that.

Phil brought the microphone to his mouth again. "Heard you had a little excitement this morning."

"Just like Christmas, except I didn't get the present I wanted. Somebody else did."

Thach meant the Japanese. The pilot of that lone, doomed Mavis had ruined everything. Now the Americans would just have to wait and see if they could salvage anything out of the operation.

The Wildcats peeled off and the SBDs flew on toward the carrier. The *Lexington* came in sight, and one by one, each Dauntless made its approach and landed. As Phil set his plane down, the flight deck looking like it came to an abrupt end no more than fifty yards in front of him, he felt the same instant of sheer panic that he felt on every landing. He was going to plunge off the flight deck and go crashing into the ocean.

But then the tail hook dropped and caught the arresting cable, and Phil jerked forward against the webbing around him as the Dauntless came to a stop in plenty of time. While Phil and Jerry got ready to climb out of the cockpit, the members of a flight deck crew ran out to take charge of the plane. The airedales, so called because their job was to shepherd the planes around the flight deck, would push the Dauntless over to the elevator, which would drop it down to the hangar deck, where maintenance crews would go over it and fix anything that needed fixing.

Phil took off his goggles and his leather flight helmet. His light brown hair was cut so short that his head almost looked shaved. The regs would have let him have it a little longer, but he liked it this way. He hated the feel of sweat in his hair.

As he had done dozens of times before, he jumped down from the wing of the plane as soon as the wheels were temporarily chocked so that it wouldn't move. This time, however, something was different. His right foot twisted under him when he landed on the flight deck, and he knew immediately that something was wrong. Pain shot through his ankle and up his calf. He gasped as the leg folded up under him and dumped him on the deck.

Jerry was at his side in a second. "Phil! What's wrong? What the hell happened?"

Maybe it was his imagination, but Phil thought that in the split-second when he hopped down from the plane, before his leg had gone out from under him, he had heard a cracking sound. Just like a slender tree branch snapping in two.

"My . . . ankle!" he gasped. He had to grit his teeth against the pain that now consumed his entire right leg. "Something . . . happened . . . to it."

The airedales were standing by, looking confused. Jerry lifted his head and yelled at them, "Don't just stand there, goddamnit! Can't you see the lieutenant's hurt? Go get a corpsman! Get a damned stretcher!" He looked down at Phil again. "It'll be all right, Phil. Help's on the way."

Suddenly, despite the pain, Phil started to laugh. Jerry looked confused and even a little offended.

"What's so funny?"

"They send me up in a plane that flies . . . over two hundred miles an hour . . . and I land it on a flight deck . . . the size of a postage stamp . . . and then I break my ankle getting out of the damn thing!"

For a second, Jerry just stared at him; then he began to laugh, too. The medical corpsmen found them like that a couple of minutes later, both of them howling with laughter even though the cords on Phil's neck stood out from the pain.

THIRTY-FOUR

The flight back to the States on board a Douglas R4D-5 transport plane—basically the same aircraft as the Douglas C-47 "Gooney Bird" used by the Army Air Corps—was long, boring, and uncomfortable. The plane's passenger cabin was fitted out in a strictly utilitarian manner. Most of the passengers were men who were being sent back to naval hospitals stateside, it having been determined that their injuries or illnesses could be better treated there than in the hospital at Pearl Harbor.

One thing those guys were going to discover, Adam told himself, was that none of the nurses in those hospitals were as pretty as Catherine. But then, he was biased.

As one of the few healthy passengers, he felt a bit out of place, too. He found himself talking to a Marine captain who was being transferred back to Camp Kearney, just like him.

"The Eighth of the Second is already on its way out to American Samoa," the captain told Adam. "The Second of the Second is what's left at Kearney. They're called the Home Guards, from what I understand."

Adam frowned, not liking the sound of that. "You mean they're not going overseas, sir?"

"I didn't say that. At this point, I don't know, Sergeant. At any rate, you've served out here in the Pacific already, I gather. I'd think you wouldn't mind some stateside duty for a while."

"No, sir," Adam said, but he wasn't sure that was true. Catherine would be happy if he remained stationed in California for the duration. That way she would know he was safe. But when he thought about Gurnwall, Rolofson, Kennemer, Magruder, and all the other men who had been left out there on Wake Island until the Japanese overran them, he didn't like the idea of never having a chance to even the score for them. Even if they were still alive, they were prisoners of the Japs, and God only knew what hell they were going through now. There was his brother-in-law Spencer to think of, too, and all the other men who had died at Pearl Harbor. And when you looked at the big picture, the Japanese were on the same side as Adolf Hitler and the Nazis, so there were also scores to be settled there.

All in all, Adam found his current situation to be as classic a case of mixed emotions as anyone could ever want to see.

"From what I hear," the captain went on, "recruits are pouring in and have been ever since the attack on Pearl Harbor. They're enlisting so fast that we're having trouble training all of them. Not all of them go to Parris Island or Camp Pendleton anymore. We'll be getting our fair share at Kearney, too."

"So it's really a training base?"

"From what I hear, that's right. So you'll be putting your knowledge of conditions in the Pacific to good use, Sergeant."

That made Adam feel a little better. Even if he remained stateside, he would still be contributing to the war effort.

The R4D-5 landed in San Diego at last, and a master sergeant in a green Ford station wagon was waiting at the field to pick up Adam and the captain. When they reached the camp, which was surrounded by a tall fence topped with barbed wire, they were passed through the guard post at the gate and driven to division HQ. A major in the adjutant's office sent the captain who had been Adam's companion from Hawaii to see General Price, the camp's CO. Adam, being just a lowly sergeant, was given his housing assignment and told to report to Major Walton in Building A-51.

Building A-51 looked for all the world like some of the classroom buildings back at the University of Chicago, Adam thought as he went up the steps to the door and inside. Major Walton's office was down a long corridor, and sure enough, on each side of that corridor were classrooms full of recruits in green uniforms, listening intently to the officers who stood in the front of the room instructing them.

Major Walton turned out to be a short, compact Marine with white hair and a trace of a Texas accent in his voice. He glanced at the documents Adam handed him, then waved at a chair in front of his desk and said, "Have a seat, Sergeant. Welcome to Camp Kearney."

"Thank you, sir," Adam said as he sat down. "I'm glad to be here." That wasn't a complete falsehood.

Major Walton grunted. "Are you, now? I'd have thought a Marine who's already seen some action would be itching to get back into combat."

Adam suppressed a feeling of irritation. "I am, sir, but I go where the Corps sends me and do what the Corps tells me to do."

"Of course you do." Walton leaned back in his chair. "Wake Island, eh? A damned bad business. We were all upset when we heard that the relief expedition had turned back and the island had fallen."

"Yes, sir." Adam didn't want to get into that. He still had too many bad feelings of his own directed toward whoever had made the decision to recall Task Force 14. He reminded himself that given the circumstances, the reinforcements probably wouldn't have gotten there in time, anyway.

"What we do here," Walton said, "is a mixture of basic and specialized training. More basic than specialized right now, but that's going to change. There's also talk of establishing an Officer Candidate School here. So we're going to be busy." The major looked over Adam's service record again. "You started out manning an anti-aircraft machine gun position on Wake, is that right?"

"Yes, sir."

"Then Major Devereux tapped you to be one of his aides."

"Yes, sir."

"You were privy to everything that went on in the command post?"

"Most of it, sir," Adam said.

"So you've experienced not only combat, but command as well."

"I was never in command of anything except the squad at my defense position, sir."

Walton frowned. "Still and all, you've risen to the occasion and done whatever was asked of you, Bergman. If and when we get the OCS up and running here, I'd like you to consider applying for it."

Adam nodded and said, "I might be interested in that, sir." First Major Devereaux, back on Wake, and now this major. Maybe he should really take this officer stuff seriously, Adam decided.

"For now, however, you'll be assigned to Captain Crawford. He's our G-4."

Supplies? They were going to make a supply sergeant out of him?

Adam swallowed the protest that wanted to come up his throat, and said, "Yes, sir."

"You'll find him over at the quartermaster's office." Walton came to his feet, and so did Adam. When Walton said, "That's all," Adam saluted, waited until the major had returned the salute, then left the office with a bitter taste in his mouth.

The corporal on duty at the door of the building told him where to find the quartermaster's office. Adam started across the camp in that direction, growing more frustrated with every step. He had thought they would put him to work teaching these raw recruits everything he could about combat in the Pacific, and instead they were going to have him passing out underwear and prophylactics!

Maybe it wouldn't be quite that bad, he told himself. But he wasn't going to bet on it.

He had gone a couple of hundred yards along the camp's main street when he heard his name called. He stopped short, thinking that surely he was wrong. Who in this camp would know him?

"Adam! Hey, Adam! Son of a bitch, is that really you?"

There was no getting around it now, and besides, Adam thought he recognized that voice. He turned around, mouth opening in surprise as he saw the two figures hurrying toward him. At first glance, they would remind just about anyone of Laurel and Hardy, one short, thick-bodied, almost fat, while the other was tall and thin and moved with an excess of nervous energy. "Ed?" Adam said. "Leo?"

Ed Collins caught hold of Adam's hand and pumped it. "Son of a bitch!" he repeated. "It really is you!"

A head shorter than Adam, Ed had spent all his life on a farm in Iowa until he'd enlisted in the Marines. As a result of years of hard work, he might look fat but most of his bulk was muscle. Boot camp at Parris Island had sweated some of the weight off him, but he still didn't look like anyone's popular image of a Marine. That hadn't stopped him from completing basic training with a minimum of trouble.

The same couldn't be said of his companion, Leo Sikorsky. Tall, skinny, and awkward, he was a terrible shot, had blundered through the obstacle course and all the other physical training, and to top it off had a belligerent attitude that saw discrimination against him because of his Jewish heritage even where none existed. Despite all that, with help from Adam and Ed, Leo had made it through boot camp at Parris Island.

Adam hadn't expected to see either of them here at Camp Kearney. But when he looked at their sleeves, he saw division patches that were roughly arrowhead-shaped, made out of red cloth, decorated with five small silver stars arranged around a hand holding a torch with the number 2 emblazoned on it. They were 2nd Division Marines now, just like him. Soon he would be wearing a patch like that, too.

"What're you doin' here, Adam?" Leo asked. He raised his eyebrows as he noticed the three stripes on Adam's sleeve. "Oh, hell. I guess we gotta call you Sarge now. Look at that, Ed. Adam's a sergeant."

"Last we heard, you were on Wake Island," Ed said. "Me'n

Chopper figured you were a dead duck by now. Either that, or a prisoner o' them slant-eyed little fuckers."

Ed had hung the nickname "Chopper" on Leo because Sikorsky was also the name of a helicopter being developed by the Sikorsky Aircraft Division of the United Aircraft Corporation in Bridgeport, Connecticut. The inventor of the craft, Igor Sikorsky, was not related to Leo, but that hadn't stopped Ed, an aviation buff, from coming up with the nickname. Ed was also one of the coarsest, crudest individuals Adam had ever met, but to his surprise he had gotten used to Ed's language and toward the end of basic training barely noticed it anymore.

"I got off Wake before it fell," Adam said. "The brass there tapped me to act as a courier. Actually I was just a backup to an officer who was carrying some important papers, but it got me off the island anyway."

"You are one lucky bastard, let me tell you," Ed said.

"Yeah, no telling what might've happened to you if you'd stayed there," Leo said.

Adam shrugged. He didn't want to talk about that; he replayed it all in his own mind often enough without discussing it with anybody else. He asked, "What are you two doing here?"

"They sent us here for advanced infantry training," Leo said.

"Yeah, we figure we'll be in the next batch to head overseas. Some o' the boys've already gone on to Samoa." Ed got a faraway look in his eyes. "Man, just think about sittin' around drinkin' coconut milk under a palm tree while some half-nekkid little native gal fans you. Would that be the life or what?"

Somehow, Adam had a hard time imagining that the Marines who were on their way to Samoa would find any coconut milk or half-naked native girls waiting for them. There might be palm trees, but the Marines wouldn't be lounging around underneath them.

"I'm glad you boys are here," Adam told Ed and Leo. "I assumed I wouldn't know anybody once I got here."

"It don't matter," Leo said. "You're a non-com now, and we're still privates."

"Privates first class," Ed put in.

"Yeah, yeah, it don't make no difference; we're still enlisted men. Adam here, he's moved up in the world. We can't be friends no more."

"That's not true," Adam said.

"Oh, no? You just try pallin' around with us. The other sergeants'll read you the riot act, boy, and the brass will have your ass for breakfast. There's a wall between you and us now, whether any of us like it or not."

Adam frowned. He didn't want to believe that Leo was right, but what if he was? And if he was, things would only get worse if Adam went to OCS and became an officer. Maybe he could do something to get in trouble and get busted back to private. . . .

Even as the thought crossed his mind, Adam knew he couldn't do it. He had always tried to move forward in his life, not backward. He wouldn't give up a promotion just because Leo Sikorsky thought they couldn't still be friends.

"That's bull," Adam said. "We've been buddies since Parris Island. A few stripes can't change that."

"Yeah, right," Leo said, his lip curling in cynicism.

"Hey, I believe you, Adam. Put 'er there, pal." Ed stuck out his hand again.

Adam took it without hesitation and smiled. It wasn't like being with Catherine, or like being home again, but having Ed and Leo around made him think that maybe his time at Camp Kearney wouldn't be so bad after all.

THIRTY-FIVE

The hospital ship was called the U.S.S. *Solace*. Originally, it had been the S.S. *Iroquois,* a luxury liner built in 1927 by the Newport News Shipbuilding and Drydock Company. Until 22 July 1940, it served proudly as a ship of the Clyde Mallory Steamship Line. The Mallory line sold it to the U.S. Navy, which renamed it and designated it as Vessel AH-5.

There wasn't much luxurious about the ship anymore. At the Atlantic Basin Iron Works in Brooklyn, New York, its staterooms and ballrooms and salons had been converted into pharmacies and wards and operating rooms. Once its sole purpose had been the pleasure and relaxation of its wealthy passengers. Now it was literally a life saver, its crew a dedicated group of men and women who were there to take the shattered and broken and torn and make them whole again, if at all possible.

Or at least keep them alive until some place better equipped could take over.

"Well, girls, this is it," Missy Mitchell said as she stood on the dock with Catherine Bergman, Billie Tabor, and Alice Sutherland. "Our floating home away from home."

"I thought Pearl Harbor was already our home away from home," Alice said.

"Well, then, this is our home away from home away from— Oh, be quiet, Alice; you're just trying to confuse me."

All four nurses wore their white uniforms trimmed with blue and gold and brimmed caps with the insignia of the Navy Nurse Corps on them. Each of them carried a small bag, all they were

JAMES REASONER

allowed to bring with them. Inside Catherine's bag, wrapped securely inside one of her uniform skirts, was a small, framed photograph of Adam. It was all she had to remind her of him.

That, and her memories. . . .

He was back in the States, assigned to Camp Kearney near San Diego, where he was going through Officer Candidate School. Catherine had been proud and pleased when his letter arrived telling her about that . . . until she realized that the Marines wouldn't be going to the trouble of training him to be an officer if they didn't intend to make further use of him. That would probably mean sending him back to the Pacific.

Adam had been gone from Hawaii for a couple of months when the orders had arrived transferring Catherine and her friends to the *Solace*. The hospital ship was putting out to sea very soon, bound for Pago Pago, Samoa, and Catherine had been given only a couple of days to get ready to depart. She had tried to get Adam on the phone, but all the lines from Hawaii to the mainland were tied up twenty-four hours a day with official military business. She had called in some favors from a radioman she knew and managed to get a connection to Camp Kearney, but Adam was out in the field somewhere, she was told. She hadn't been able to talk to him. So with time running out, she had been forced to settle for writing him a letter telling him about her new assignment.

She hoped he wouldn't be too upset when he got the letter. They had been counting on her remaining here at Pearl, where she would be relatively safe. Now, even though the *Solace* wouldn't be right in the middle of any action, it would be a lot closer to the fighting. The embattled Pacific fleet was doing the best it could to stem the tide of the Japanese advance. The *Enterprise, Yorktown, Lexington,* and *Saratoga* had been ranging through the chains of islands in the Southwest Pacific, their fighters and bombers striking at widely scattered targets so that the Japanese wouldn't be sure where they would turn up next. At best, though, this was just a delaying action, and it hadn't really stopped the enemy advance.

Carrying their bags, the four nurses went up the ramp from

278

the dock to the main deck of the hospital ship. A colonel with the insignia of the Navy Medical Corps on his uniform was waiting for them at the top of the ramp. Catherine and the others stopped, saluted, and, as the senior member of the foursome, Catherine said, "Permission to come aboard, sir."

"Permission granted, Lieutenant," the colonel replied with a smile. He was tall, lanky, and middle-aged, with graying brown hair and a salt-and-pepper mustache. "I'm Colonel Johnston, the chief medical officer. On behalf of myself and Captain Perlman, welcome aboard the *Solace*."

"Thank you, sir."

"At ease, all of you." Johnston grinned. "Out here on deck, we have to maintain Navy protocol. Down in the wards and the operating rooms, though, it's more of a hospital atmosphere, which means you'll treat me like any other doctor."

"You mean like you were God?" Missy said.

Johnston's eyes narrowed, and for a second Catherine thought he was going to light into Missy. Then he chuckled and said, "I'll give you that one, Nurse. But *only* that one."

"Yes, sir," Missy had the sense to say.

"Chief nurse is Captain Reynolds. I'll leave you ladies to her." Johnston waved an arm to usher them toward the ship's superstructure. "Right this way."

Captain Ellen Reynolds turned out to be the same sort of typical, no-nonsense head nurse that could be found in hospitals all over the world. Even floating ones, Catherine thought. She welcomed them, showed them their quarters, then said, "We're sailing at five o'clock tomorrow morning."

Missy said, "Then since we've already reported in, can we have passes to go into Honolulu tonight?"

"You may not," Captain Reynolds said. "You're to remain on board tonight."

"Why?" Missy asked. "We'd be back in plenty of time."

For her part, Catherine didn't want to go into town. She would just as soon stay here on the ship and get settled in. But she wasn't single, either, she reminded herself.

Captain Reynolds regarded Missy with narrowed eyes. "You may have the best intentions in the world, but I know nurses and Marines and sailors. Been around 'em for a long time. I don't want any of my nurses late when it comes time to cast off in the morning, and I sure as hell don't want any of 'em late when their next period's due. There's no telling how long we'll be at sea, and we're not equipped for any obstetrical procedures except in cases of extreme emergency." Her voice had been rising as she spoke, so that she was just short of yelling as she concluded, "Do you read me, Nurse Mitchell?"

Missy stood stiffly and said, "Yes, ma'am. Sorry, ma'am."

Captain Reynolds sniffed. "All right. Carry on."

In the hallway outside Captain Reynolds's office, Missy sighed, shook her head, and said, "God, she needs to get laid."

Catherine said, "That's not the answer to everything, you know."

Missy grinned at her. "Maybe not, but it'll do until a better one comes along."

* * *

Adam stretched his legs out in front of him, crossed his booted feet at the ankles, and carefully lifted the flap on the envelope he held in his hands. Most guys just ripped their mail open, and Adam did the same thing when it was a letter from Joe Parker. But when Catherine or his mother wrote, he was extra careful opening those envelopes. It seemed fitting.

This letter was from Catherine. He caught a fleeting scent of her perfume as he unfolded the sheets of thin paper. He had come back here to the barracks early after evening chow, so that he could read the letter without having anybody hanging over his shoulder as he did so. He had been carrying it around in his pocket ever since mail call, all too aware that it was there but determined to stick to his routine.

Delayed gratification, the shrinks would call it. He didn't

care. He knew what he wanted to do. He wanted to enjoy these few moments when he felt closest to his wife.

He started to read, and almost immediately he sat up straighter on his bunk. A moment later he exclaimed, "Samoa!" His head was spinning. It didn't seem possible. He read the words again, just to make sure he had seen them right the first time.

It was true. Catherine had been transferred from the naval hospital at Pearl Harbor to the hospital ship *Solace,* which was bound for Samoa. By this time the ship would have sailed and would be well on its way to the island far to the south-southwest of Pearl Harbor.

The first emotion Adam felt was fear. Catherine was out there somewhere on the boundless ocean, easy prey for Jap submarines or bombers or battleships. And if she got to Samoa safely, there was no guarantee the Japanese wouldn't try to capture it, too, the same way they had captured countless other islands in the Pacific.

But then he remembered that some of the Second Marine Division was already based on Samoa, and scuttlebutt was that the rest of the SECMARDIV would be shipping out for there, too, as soon as they finished their training here in the States.

That training, for Adam, had meant applying for OCS and being accepted right away. The course was a hurry-up job, lasting only a month, and it was already half-over. Once he'd completed it—assuming he completed it successfully—a commission as a second lieutenant awaited him. That small gold bar on his collar would indicate that he was a thirty-day wonder, but he didn't care how many of the senior officers used the derogatory term. He was confident that he would show them all he was a good officer.

And if when he received his commission he was sent to join the Marines in Samoa, as seemed a reasonable assumption, he would have a chance to see Catherine again. The excitement he felt at that prospect almost balanced out the worry about her safety. Almost.

Quickly, he read the rest of the letter. He could tell that it had been written in a hurry. It contained no news other than that of Catherine's transfer, and she didn't go into great detail about that. Mostly she just said that she loved him and missed him and prayed for him every night and couldn't wait until they were together again. The same sort of things that he wrote in every one of his letters to her. When he was finished, he read the whole thing again, because he couldn't stand the thought of folding the sheets and sliding them back into the envelope.

With a burst of voices, the rest of the company of OCS trainees came into the barracks, returning from the mess hall. Adam sighed, put the letter into its envelope, and tucked it away in his pocket. The moment, unsettling though it had been, was gone, and he regretted that.

"Hey, Bergman, where'd you disappear to after chow?" one of the men asked.

"I know," another answered before Adam could say anything. "He came back here to read his letter from his sweetie in private. I saw him get an envelope at mail call this afternoon."

"Is that true, Bergman?"

"I could say it's none of your damned business," Adam said, but his smile took any sting out of the words.

"Yeah, and we'd ignore you and keep on pestering you until you tell us the truth."

Adam liked these guys, though he didn't feel as close to any of them as he did to Ed and Leo. He said, "Yeah, I got a letter from my wife."

"Not a Dear John, I hope!"

"No, she told me she's been transferred from Pearl Harbor to a hospital ship that's going to Samoa. She's a hell of a lot closer to the front lines than we are, fellas."

That sobered up the little group hanging around Adam's bunk. "A hospital ship, eh?" one of them said. "The Japs leave them alone, right?"

"They're supposed to—but we're talking about the Japs."

Solemn nods went around the circle. "I'm sure she'll be all

right, Bergman," one of the men told him. "And hey, when we get to Samoa, she'll be there waiting for you!"

"Don't think I haven't thought of that already." Adam lay back on his bunk and put his hands behind his head, hearing the faint crackle of paper from his pocket as he did so. "Right now, I'm just going to hope for the best—and hope it's not too long until I see her again."

THIRTY-SIX

Joe sipped his drink and listened to the music coming from the combo on the low, small stage at the other end of the room. The musicians were hacking away at "Moonlight Serenade," but even their inept job sounded pretty good to Joe. The song was a reminder of home, a reminder that somewhere on the other side of the world, a place existed that wasn't all sand and rock and scrub brush. A place where the cities might be crowded, but at least the clamor of voices was largely in English. Not like here in Cairo where there was such a mixture of tongues it was a wonder anybody ever understood anybody else.

Joe and Dale were in a nightclub called the Golden Camel. Dale was dancing with a British nurse on the dance floor in front of the stage. The rest of the room was crowded with tables. Joe sat at one in the corner, making his drink last and wondering if he ought to ask one of the girls to dance. There were English girls and Egyptian girls and Arabian girls and who knew what other kind of girls in here. He had decided that most of them weren't whores. A few of them were even pretty. Joe tossed off the rest of his drink, forgetting that he had meant to take it slow. Oh, well, he told himself. Good intentions and all that crap.

He was a little drunk, but only a little. He realized that. He was dealing with it. He was handling it just fine.

He held up a hand to signal the waiter for another round.

The waiter was a wog, which was what the British called the Egyptians for some reason. Joe had no idea where the name had come from, but he heard it all the time. He hadn't been able to tell if the Egyptians took offense at being called wogs or not. If they did, they hid it well, which made sense considering that the British were running things.

That might not last. General Erwin Rommel and the Afrika Korps were sitting there in the Western Desert, across the Gazala Line from the British, and from what Joe had heard, he had a feeling they were just biding their time until they were ready to launch a major offensive.

The line wasn't really drawn in the sand, of course. It ran from near the town of Gazala, on the Libyan coast west of Tobruk, some forty miles into the desert and then curved up like a fish hook. After Rommel had come roaring east out of El Agheila, capturing Benghazi and forcing the Eighth Army to retreat, the British had finally dug in their heels and established the defensive line. It was strewn with mines, and at intervals along it the Tommies had set up fortifications called boxes, which were strongly manned and had plenty of ammunition and supplies. The tanks of the Fourth Armoured Brigade patrolled the line as well, turning back any probes that the Germans made with their Panzers.

Joe wondered how Captain Sharp and the men of B Squadron, 3R.T.C., were doing. Little Bert Crimmens and even that obnoxious bastard Jeremy Royce, they were out there with all the other men Joe and Dale had come to know during their time in England, during the voyage on the *Leffingford,* and at the base depot here in Egypt. There hadn't been word of any major tank battles, so Joe hoped that they were all all right. He hoped that Bert was getting plenty of chances to brew up.

The waiter brought Joe's drink and gestured at the empty glasses in front of the other chairs, asking in a heavily accented voice, "Would the other gentleman and the lady care for something else?"

"You'll have to ask them," Joe said, aware that he was trying drunkenly to pronounce every word clearly and distinctly. "Come back when they've finished dancing."

"Yes, sir, of course." The waiter went away.

Joe looked at his glass of whiskey but didn't pick it up. What the hell was he doing? He didn't drink like this. He could count on his fingers the times in his life he'd been this drunk.

It was hard, though, to just sit in the tanks at the depot or in the classrooms the Eighth Army used, teaching the tankies about the M3, when what he really wanted to do was get into one of the tanks and take off across the desert to fight the Germans himself. The American instructors were teaching the British how to wage war in the Honeys, but they had never actually done it themselves.

"Do as I say, not as I do," Joe muttered to himself.

It was crazy. The United States had been at war with Germany for over four months now, and not a single GI had gone into battle yet. Over in the Pacific, the Marines had made their gallant stand on Wake Island, and they were trying their best to hold out in the Philippines. American sailors and pilots fought the Japanese every day over there. In the Atlantic, there had been clashes between American ships and planes and Nazi U-boats.

But here on the ground in North Africa, where the Nazis had their strongest presence outside of Europe, the Americans were sitting back and letting the British and the Free French and even the Canadians carry the load. It just didn't seem right. Joe sighed, picked up his drink, and swallowed some of the whiskey.

The Egyptian combo had finished "Moonlight Serenade" but were still on a Glenn Miller kick. Joe thought they were playing "Little Brown Jug," but he wasn't sure. Dale and the nurse—her name was Elspeth, Joe forced himself to recall—came back to the table. Dale jerked a thumb over his shoulder and said, "I don't see how anybody can dance to that. I'm not sure it should even be considered music!"

"It's not all that bad," Elspeth said, "but I wouldn't mind sitting down for a bit anyway. I'm rather tired."

"Rawther," Dale said.

Elspeth laughed. "You Yanks are so cute."

Dale put his arm around her shoulders. "Of course we are. Would you like to see just how cute we can be?"

"I think I might like that."

Joe said, "The waiter wanted to know if you want another drink."

"Not now," Dale said without looking at him. He kept his attention concentrated on Elspeth. "I'm busy. And I hope I'm even busier before too much longer."

The nurse laughed again. "Oh, you're a naughty one, you are."

Joe felt a little sick. He didn't know if it was from all he'd had to drink, or from the way his two companions were carrying on.

Dale finally glanced at his brother. "You want me to see if Elspeth's got a friend for you, Joe?"

"No, I think I'll go on back to the barracks," Joe said with a shake of his head. "You two kids have fun."

Dale leered at Elspeth again and said, "I think I can guarantee that." She laughed.

Joe downed the rest of his drink, got to his feet, picked up his overseas cap from the table, and settled it on his head. He was a little dizzy. Probably should have left the rest of that last drink, he told himself. He'd have to get a cab back to the depot and hope that the cabbie wouldn't try to steal him blind.

He made his way through the tables toward the door, bumping into several people along the way and muttering apologies. When he stepped out into the night, he drew a deep breath into his lungs, hoping the fresh air would help clear his head. The air wasn't all that fresh, however. It was heavily laden with the scent of spices, sewage, and other, unidentifiable odors. But at least it was a little cooler outside than it had been inside the club, and the air wasn't filled with choking clouds of tobacco smoke.

Joe looked up and down the street but didn't see a cab. Shepheard's, the famous hotel in the center of Cairo, was only a few blocks away. He would stroll in that direction, Joe decided. There was bound to be a cab up there around the hotel.

He had gone less than a block and was passing the mouth of an alley when he heard a muffled curse and then the soggy sound of a fist hitting flesh. As he stopped, someone down the alley hissed words in a language he didn't understand but thought was Arabic. Suddenly, a voice called out distinctly, "Get away from me, you thieving buggers!"

That was an Englishman, Joe thought as he turned toward the alley mouth. The light was bad, but he was able to make out the dim shapes of several struggling figures. His heart started to pound faster, and the rush of blood cleared away some of the cobwebs from his brain. An Englishman was being robbed by several Egyptians. They probably had grabbed him as he came along the sidewalk and dragged him into the alley. If Joe had come along a few minutes earlier, he might have been the victim.

This was none of his business, but he realized he couldn't just leave the guy. The thieves would probably beat him up, could hurt him badly, maybe even knife him. *Hell, the British are our allies,* Joe thought. He started trotting down the alley toward the knot of struggling figures and yelled, "Hey!"

That was a mistake, he realized a second later as one of the robbers swung around to meet him. He should have kept his mouth shut and piled into them, taking them by surprise. But at least now as one of the figures advanced toward him, he knew the man was an enemy. He didn't have to worry about picking out the Englishman in the dark.

The thief said something that was probably a curse and swung an arm at Joe. Joe ducked under it, fearing that there might be a knife in the guy's hand. He put his shoulder into the man's stomach in a diving tackle, knocking him over backward. They landed hard on the filthy cobblestone floor of the alley, but the thief was on the bottom. He seemed stunned. Joe brought his fist down, mallet-like, in the middle of the guy's face.

Close by, more blows were thudding against flesh. Joe hit his man again, bouncing the back of the thief's head off the pavement. The man went limp, and Joe pushed up off him. A few feet away, two men were trading punches. One of them was knocked back against the wall, then doubled over when his opponent buried a fist in his midsection. The man brought up a knee into his face. The one taking the beating slid to his knees, then, holding his stomach, scrambled away, narrowly dodging a kick. He made it to his feet and ran off down the alley.

"That's right, run, you bloody wog!" the man's opponent called after him, confirming to Joe that the victor in this fight was the Englishman who had been accosted by the robbers. He turned around, saw Joe standing there, and cocked his fists. "Another one, eh?"

"Take it easy, pal; I'm on your side," Joe said.

The Englishman lowered his arms. "Ah, the American cavalry, riding to the rescue just like in your cowboy pictures. Thanks, mate."

The man at Joe's feet stirred a little and let out a groan. Joe pointed at him and said, "This one's going to come to in a minute. Maybe we'd better get out of here."

"You're right." The Englishman paused for a second next to the fallen thief, long enough to draw back his leg and plant a vicious kick in the man's ribs. "There. Now we can go."

Joe didn't really blame the guy for being mad, but that kick seemed like a little too much. He didn't say anything, though, as they left the alley and turned back onto the main street, heading toward Shepheard's.

Now that they were out in the glow of the streetlamps, Joe could see that his newfound companion wore the khaki tunic and shorts of the British Eighth Army. He held out a hand and introduced himself. "Colin Richardson."

"Joe Parker," Joe said as he shook hands. Colin Richardson was a major, but at the moment he didn't seem to care about their difference in rank.

"Glad to meet you, Joe," Richardson said. "Come on down to Shepheard's and have a drink on me."

"Thanks, but I'd better not." Joe reminded himself that he'd had too much to drink already. The flurry of violence in the alley had gone a long way toward sobering him up, but it wouldn't take much to get him drunk again. "I was on my way back to barracks."

"You're one of the American tank instructors, I'll wager."

"That's right."

"Come along with me, anyway. It's early yet. What about a spot of supper? My treat, of course. Just my way of saying thanks for pitching in and helping me with those filthy wogs."

"Well . . ." Joe didn't want to offend this British officer, and besides, he was a little hungry, though he hadn't really thought about it until now. "Sure, I guess that would be all right."

"Come along, then. I know the head waiter at Shepheard's."

Richardson was telling the truth. He got them a table in the hotel dining room with no trouble, despite the fact that the place was crowded. Richardson ordered steak and potatoes for both of them.

"Can't stand the wog food," he said, patting his stomach. "Too spicy for me."

He was about ten years older than Joe, stockily built with fair hair and a high forehead. Joe felt a little uncomfortable sitting with an officer, but Richardson put him at ease.

"Pay no attention to these pips on my shoulder. Tonight we're just Colin and Joe, eh?"

"Sure," Joe said. "If that's the way you want it."

"It is. Sure you won't have a drink?"

"Just coffee."

"Right-o." Richardson ordered the coffee for Joe but had the waiter bring him a whiskey.

Richardson was already somewhat drunk, Joe decided, though he handled it well. The fact that the Englishman had been drinking probably had contributed to the ease with which the thieves had jumped him and hauled him into the alley.

Richardson mentioned that he worked at Eighth Army HQ but didn't elaborate on what his job was. He was more interested in Joe. During the meal, Joe told him about how the American instructors worked with the British tankies.

"From what I hear, you've done a spot-on job," Richardson said. "Our lads are performing quite well in the desert."

"I hope so. I just wish I was out there myself."

"Well, someday soon you will be, I expect, as soon as the old torch is lit."

Joe didn't know what he meant by that, but Richardson pushed on quickly as if he didn't want to elaborate. He had several more drinks during the meal, and by the time they were finished, he was even more drunk than he had been starting out. Joe was beginning to wonder about the wisdom of letting him wander around Cairo alone.

On the other hand, he didn't want to have to babysit some British major. The food and the coffee had finished the job of sobering up Joe. He decided that he would put Richardson into a cab and send him home, then wash his hands of the whole business.

"I've got to be getting back to my barracks," he said. "It's almost 2200."

"And I as . . . as well," Richardson said. "I've a flat not far from here." He stood up shakily, took money from his pocket, and dropped it on the table to pay for the meal and the drinks.

"We can both get cabs outside," Joe suggested.

"Good idea." Richardson belched. "I'm a bit smashed, you see."

They walked out of the hotel, Joe ready to grab Richardson's arm and steady him if the major started to sway too much. Luckily, a cab was waiting at the curb. Joe opened the rear door and helped Richardson inside. He didn't know the address of Richardson's apartment, but the Englishman managed to get it out. The Egyptian driver nodded.

Joe was about to back out of the cab and close the door when Richardson reached up and caught hold of his arm. "Listen," Richardson said solemnly. "I meant it when I said you'd get in on the action, lad. I know things, you see. We know what the Germans are going to do. Know all their plans . . . all their bloody secrets. . . . Dear old Ultra knows all. . . ." Richardson laughed. "So you'll get what you want. Got my word on that." He let go of Joe's sleeve and sank back against the cushions of the cab's backseat.

Frowning, Joe straightened and shut the door. The cab pulled away from the curb. What the hell was *that* all about? he asked himself. Who or what was Ultra, and what was that business about knowing the Germans' plans? It didn't make sense.

But he was too tired to ponder it for very long, and besides, Richardson was pretty drunk. None of his mumbling had to mean much of anything.

Joe gave a mental shrug, forgot about it, and started looking for a cab of his own.

THIRTY-SEVEN

"Okay, when I nod my head, you hit it. Got that?"

"But, Moe—"

"Just do what I tell you, you knucklehead!"

The Marines in the audience laughed uproariously, knowing full well what was coming. Many of them were still in their teens, and they had grown up watching the Three Stooges in movie theaters across the country.

But never in a theater like this. Several sheets had been stitched together and strung up on lines between trees at the edge of a large clearing in the jungle. The Marines sat on logs or rocks, and instead of a theater roof overhead, there was only the night sky over the South Pacific, dotted with an untold number of brilliant stars.

Phil Lange brushed away a couple of mosquitoes that were buzzing around his ears. Trying to keep the mosquitoes off was pretty much a waste of time, but he did it anyway. The blood-sucking little annoyances would be back again in a few seconds.

Phil smiled as Larry cried and made faces and then hit Moe over the head with a sledgehammer. Moe, being Moe, yelled and poked Larry in the eyes. Curly tried to defend Larry and got poked himself for his trouble. Phil was glad this wasn't one of the pictures with Shemp in it. He couldn't stand Shemp.

It was nice to be able to forget for a few minutes that he was in American Samoa, thousands of miles away from home. His ankle and leg didn't hurt too bad tonight. He had his right leg stretched out in front of him and his crutches propped on the log beside him. After the Stooges short was finished, the projectionist on the other side of the clearing would load up the evening's feature, some swashbuckler with Tyrone Power. And when that was done, Phil would use the crutches to stand up awkwardly and then hobble back to his *fale,* the Samoan hut where he lived. He had enough money to afford the *fale* (pronounced "folly") because he'd been lucky in a few poker games with the leathernecks from the SECMARDIV who were stationed here. Since it looked like he wasn't going to be getting back to the *Lexington* any time soon, he might as well live in as much comfort as possible, he had decided.

The broken ankle he had suffered when he and Jerry got back to the carrier was a fluke, but that didn't mean it wasn't bad. He had nearly passed out from the pain when the corpsman in the ship's infirmary unlaced his boot and pulled it off. The bone was so badly fractured that the jagged end of it was poking out whitely through the skin just below his ankle. They had given him an anesthetic, set the bone, put a cast on the ankle, and told him he'd be off his feet for a while. But then an infection had developed in his foot and started spreading up his leg, and for a while it looked like the doctors were going to have to take off his leg to save his life.

He had protested so violently against that idea that they put him on a plane and flew him to American Samoa. There was a hospital of sorts at the Marine camp at Pago Pago, but more important, an American hospital ship, the *Solace,* was due to arrive any day now. The corpsmen here at Pago Pago had taken the cast off and used sulfa drugs to try to contain the infection, and so far that seemed to be working. Phil's fever, which had risen to 104 degrees while he was on the *Lexington,* was back down to normal now. The broken ankle was wrapped securely but didn't have a cast on it. When the *Solace* arrived, the doctors on the ship could take a look at the ankle and decide what to do next.

But in the meantime, the *Lexington,* along with the three other American flattops, was still in action, roaming around the South Pacific and attempting to make life difficult for the Japanese.

Unfortunately, the American fighters and bombers were a lot like the mosquitoes that infested Samoa, Phil found himself thinking. They might be annoying the hell out of the Japs, but were they doing any lasting damage? He didn't know. All he was sure of was that he wanted to be back with Jerry and his other friends on the *Lady Lex*.

When the feature was over, Phil made his slow way back to his hut and found a corpsman waiting there for him with a jeep. "The hospital ship is in port, Lieutenant," the corpsman said. "I'll take you there."

"Tonight?" Phil asked, surprised. "It's late. I was going to turn in."

"You don't want to take any chances with that infected leg, sir. The CMO on the *Solace* said he wanted to see all the serious cases tonight. Let me give you a hand getting into the jeep."

"I can make it myself," Phil said, turning away from the corpsman's outstretched hand. He tossed the crutches into the back of the jeep while bracing himself with his other hand, then levered himself into the passenger seat. A fine sheen of sweat broke out on his forehead as he bumped his ankle against the edge of the jeep's floorboard, but he didn't cry out. This was stupid, having to go to the hospital ship tonight. It could have waited until morning.

The *Solace* was a long, impressive vessel with four main decks and a superstructure above the waterline. She was painted white with a broad red stripe running along the length of each hull except amidships, where a large red cross was painted. A smaller red cross was painted on each side of the smokestack that rose from the center of the ship. Anyone who took a good look at the vessel wouldn't have any trouble telling that she was a noncombatant.

Of course, the Japanese might not *care* about that fact. . . .

A ramp ran from the dock to a small platform on the side of the ship. From there a flight of steps led up to an open double hatch. Phil looked at the steps and frowned. He could manage the ramp all right, but he wasn't sure he could climb those steps on crutches. Not without a lot of help, anyway, and it bothered him for anyone to have to give him a hand. He didn't want anybody's pity. He already felt like a damned fool because he'd broken his ankle just by jumping down from his plane, which he had done countless times before without injury.

"Come on, Lieutenant," the corpsman said as he got out of the jeep. He came around to the passenger side, got Phil's crutches out of the back, and held them as Phil swung his legs out of the vehicle, being careful not to bump the ankle again.

Phil got the crutches under his arms and stumped across the ramp to the boarding platform. When he got there, he looked up the steps and saw a woman in a white uniform coming down them. Her white cap was pinned to short blond hair.

"I'll help you, Lieutenant," she said as she reached the bottom of the steps.

Phil shook his head. The nurse was slender and only medium height. "You're not strong enough—" he began.

"I'm stronger than I look, so let me worry about that," she said. She took hold of his left arm. "Come on. It won't be easy, but you can make it."

Phil recognized the stubborn tone in the nurse's voice and knew it wouldn't do any good to argue. He took a deep breath, then gritted his teeth and let her support him while he planted both crutches on the first step. He brought up his left foot, and the wrapped-up right one followed it.

The climb was slow going, but the two of them soon established a rhythm that helped. Steady, crutches on the next step, swing up, steady again, on and on up the steps until they reached the open hatches and went into a companionway. Phil sighed in relief.

"That wasn't so bad, was it?" the nurse asked with a smile.

Phil's ankle and leg ached, but he had to admit the climb had been easier than he'd thought it would be. He didn't have to admit it to this pretty blond nurse, however.

"What's your name?" he asked to change the subject.

"Lieutenant Bergman."

"Pleased to meet you, Lieutenant. I'm one, too. Lieutenant Phillip Lange."

"I know your name, Lieutenant. Dr. Johnston already has your medical records from the *Lexington* and from the hospital here. You were one of the cases he specifically asked to see tonight."

"It couldn't have waited until morning?"

"That broken ankle should have healed by now. The doctor was an orthopedic surgeon before he went into the Navy, so he has some expertise in this area."

Phil suppressed a groan as they walked side by side along the companionway. "Great. So this sawbones wants to experiment on me."

"I didn't say that."

They had reached an open hatchway. A voice came from inside the room on the other side of the hatch, saying, "No, this sawbones just wants to take a look at you, son."

Phil's teeth caught his lip for a second. He hadn't known that the doctor would overhear his comment. And this guy was the Chief Medical Officer on the *Solace*, too. He might be able to fix it so that Phil could never get back to his carrier.

Nurse Bergman took Phil's arm again and helped him over the riser at the bottom of the hatch in the bulkhead. They entered an examining room complete with a narrow metal table. The doctor was a colonel, Phil noted.

"I'm Colonel Johnston. Let's get you up on the table, Lieutenant."

The doctor and the nurse both helped him onto the examining table. Johnston lifted Phil's ankle, holding it gently. Phil was wearing khaki shorts, and his right foot was bare except for the white tape around his ankle. The skin just above and below the tape was an ugly, mottled red.

Johnston touched the flesh above the ankle. Phil winced. "That infection I read about in your records hasn't gone away, Lieutenant. This ankle should have a cast on it, but I don't see how we can do that until we get this swelling down."

"All I want is to get back to my ship, Doc, so do whatever you have to do."

"Except amputate, eh? I read the note from the chief corpsman on the *Lexington*. Sounds like you pitched quite a fit when they brought up the possibility."

Phil felt his face getting warm. "You can't fly a plane with one leg."

"Well, you probably could, but you're right; the Navy wouldn't let you." Johnston picked up a manila folder from a shelf, opened it, and studied the documents inside. Phil guessed those were his medical records.

After a moment, Johnston asked, "Ever hear of penicillin?"

Phil shook his head.

"It's a new drug. Well, not brand-new. It's been around for a few years. But the British have started using it to treat infections. I have a small supply of it that I can use for research purposes."

"So you *are* going to use me as a guinea pig," Phil said, then added, "Sir."

Johnston looked at him with narrowed eyes. "I prefer not to think of it that way. I'd rather say that if we can knock out that infection, we can recast that ankle and have you up and around again in a few weeks. That sounds a lot better than taking off the leg below the knee, doesn't it?"

Phil swallowed and nodded. "Yes, sir. Sorry, sir. I've just been going a little stir crazy since this happened. The Navy sent me out here to fly planes, not to sit around."

"You'll get your chance, if I have anything to say about it." Johnston turned to the nurse. "Lieutenant, prepare a hypodermic. I want to get an injection of penicillin in our dashing young aviator tonight."

"Yes, sir," Nurse Bergman said with a hint of a smile. That made her even prettier, Phil thought. She turned away from him, opened a drawer in a counter on the other side of the small room, and started working with something. A couple of minutes later, she turned around to face him again. She had a large glass syringe in her hand, and extending from the end of the syringe was the longest, sharpest, wickedest-looking needle Phil had ever seen in his life.

"Oh, shit," he said without thinking.

"This won't hurt a bit," Nurse Bergman said. She was still smiling, but Phil wasn't paying any attention to how pretty she was anymore. His eyes were riveted on the needle.

"You're lying, aren't you?" he said.

"Of course she is," Johnston said. "Now roll over, Lieutenant, and drop those shorts."

Amputation suddenly didn't seem so bad after all, Phil thought. He swallowed his humiliation, rolled over onto his stomach, and awkwardly tried to push his shorts and skivvies down over his hips. "Let me help you," Nurse Bergman said, and that made things even worse.

Then the doctor plunged what felt like a damned broadsword into his butt, and Phil forgot about his embarrassment over lying there bare-assed in front of a pretty nurse. In fact, he forgot about everything. His eyes rolled up in their sockets, and he passed out cold.

THIRTY-EIGHT

Catherine was standing beside Lieutenant Phillip Lange's bunk in the ward when the pilot opened his eyes and stared up at her. His eyes were bleary, and he looked confused. "Welcome back, Lieutenant," Catherine said.

"What the ... where ... where am I?" Lange said.

"In one of the wards on the U.S.S. *Solace*."

Lange raised his head and looked around, saw the patients in some of the other bunks, then lay back against the pillow. "How did I get here?"

"You passed out in the examining room, remember?" Catherine tried hard not to smile. She didn't want to embarrass him any more than necessary. "After the doctor gave you that penicillin injection."

Lange closed his eyes and let out a groan.

"Don't worry about it, Lieutenant," Catherine told him. "We all have our weak spots. Yours must be needles."

"I don't like 'em," Lange muttered without opening his eyes. "Never have."

"How did you make it through all the shots you got when you joined the service?"

"A couple of good stiff drinks before I went in." Lange opened his eyes and looked up at her again. "The doctors never knew I was half in the bag."

Catherine laughed. She couldn't help it. "Sorry we didn't know how to prepare you properly. Next time I'll be sure to keep that in mind."

"Next time?" Lange looked scared. "I have to have more of those shots?"

"Actually, no. The rest of the course of treatment will come in tablet form." She couldn't resist. "You don't faint at the sight of pills, do you?"

"Ha, ha." Lange looked grim. "When do I get out of here?"

Catherine grew more serious. "You don't get out of here. We're going to keep you until that infection is cured and your ankle has healed."

Lange pushed himself up in the bunk. "Wait a minute; you can't do that. All my gear is back in my hut."

"Don't worry, Lieutenant. We sent a corpsman to get your things last night."

"Last night?" Lange looked around, as if he were searching for a porthole so that he could see whether or not there was daylight outside. "I just fainted. How long have I been out?"

"Actually it's the next morning. Dr. Johnston thought it would be better if you got some rest, so since you were already out, he gave you a mild sedative, too. Then we had you moved in here."

"A sedative. Boy, you medical people just waltz in and take over, don't you?" Lange's voice held more than a trace of bitterness.

"It's for your own good, Lieutenant."

"Yeah, right." Lange turned his head and didn't look at her.

After a moment, Catherine said, "I have patients to tend to, Lieutenant. If you need anything, let one of the corpsmen know." She turned and started to walk away.

"Lieutenant . . ."

Catherine stopped and looked back over her shoulder. "Yes?"

"Sorry. Like I told the doc last night, I just want to get back to my ship and my squadron. I guess I'm a little nuts right now."

Catherine smiled. "I'm afraid we don't have a psychiatric ward. But we'll do what we can, Lieutenant. You can count on that."

*   *   *

Phil noticed before that day was over that he felt better, and when he lifted the sheet on his bunk to look at his leg, he thought the area around the ankle wasn't as red as it had been the night before. The sulfa drugs he had been given on the *Lexington* and here on Samoa had helped the infection, but that new stuff—what had the doc called it, penicillin?—looked like it was going to work even better. Maybe getting that injection and passing out would be worth it.

He wasn't too worried about his belongings. He didn't have much, and all of it would fit easily in a duffel bag. For that matter, there really hadn't been anything in his *fale* that he couldn't live without. A few letters from home, a photograph of his brothers and sisters . . . things that he didn't particularly want to lose, but nothing that couldn't be at least somewhat replaced.

If he'd had a girlfriend back home, it might have been different. But he didn't, so that was that.

As he lay there in the ward, he kept hoping that the pretty blond nurse, Lieutenant Bergman, would come back by, but he didn't see her. There were other nurses who came through the ward, and they were attractive, too, but not like the lieutenant.

She finally showed up again late in the afternoon, carrying a couple of magazines. She brought them over to his bunk and handed them to him. "I thought you might like something to read while you're recuperating, Lieutenant."

"Thanks." He glanced at the covers and saw that they were pulps. He had read a few of them when he was a kid, mostly borrowed from friends since there were never any spare dimes in the Lange family coffers for such things. These two were called *Dime Mystery* and *Astonishing Tales*. "Pretty lurid stuff."

"Pass them around to the other patients when you're through with them, okay?"

"Sure."

Lieutenant Bergman leaned a little closer to the bunk and pointed at one of the covers. "See that story by Clement Carstairs? A friend of mine wrote that."

"You know somebody named Clement Carstairs?"

"No, his real name is Joe Parker. That other is just a pen name he uses for weird menace stories, whatever they are."

Phil grunted. "I guess I'll find out. How come you know a writer?"

"We went to the University of Chicago together."

"Chicago, that's where you're from?"

"That's right."

Phil opened the issue of *Dime Mystery* to the story Lieutenant Bergman had indicated and saw a large black-and-white illustration of a beautiful woman in a torn dress tied to a table while a drooling hunchback in a lab coat loomed over her. In the background was a handsome guy—probably the hero—also tied up, writhing around on the floor as he tried to get loose.

"Doesn't really look like it'd take a college education to write this stuff."

"It's probably harder than it looks," Lieutenant Bergman said.

"I wanted to go to college. I thought I might like to be a biology teacher. I wound up in the cockpit of a Dauntless instead."

"Being a teacher would be a good thing to do after the war is over."

"Yeah, I guess so. Assuming I live through it."

Phil saw a flash of something in her eyes and knew his cynical comment had upset her. He started to apologize, but she waved it off.

"That's all right. I don't suppose any of us should be making assumptions with the world in the shape it's in these days, should we?"

Phil didn't know what to say, so he said, "Thanks for bringing the magazines. I'll read them."

"Don't forget about passing them around."

"I won't."

Lieutenant Bergman took a thermometer out of the pocket of her uniform and started shaking it down. "Now we'd better take your temperature . . ."

Later, after she was gone, Phil tried to read some of the stories in the pulp magazines, but he found his mind wandering. Ever since he had broken his ankle, he had spent most of his time wishing that it would heal so he could get back to the war. Now he was distracted by thoughts of Lieutenant Bergman. She was one of the prettiest women he had ever seen, and she had to be smart, too, or she wouldn't have been in college before the war started. Pago Pago was a pretty crappy little town, but there were a couple of restaurants that weren't too bad. Phil wondered if, once his ankle healed to the point he could get around again, Lieutenant Bergman would be willing to have dinner with him. The thought of asking her to go out with him made him a little nervous, but he told himself that it couldn't be any more frightening than landing a plane on a flattop.

Later that evening, after he'd eaten supper from the tray that an orderly brought him, another nurse he hadn't seen before came through the ward checking on the patients. She was taller than Lieutenant Bergman and not as slender, and she had dark, curly hair. She stopped at the foot of Phil's bunk, looked from him to the chart hanging on the end of the bunk and back to him, then said, "Hello, Lieutenant Lange. You're just as cute as you can be, you know it?"

The comment took him by surprise. He said, "Well . . . ah . . ."

The nurse waved a hand. "Oh, don't mind me. I sometimes just say what I'm thinking without thinking about it, you know what I mean?" She came alongside the bunk and put out a hand. "I'm Missy Mitchell."

Phil took her hand. Not surprisingly, her grip was strong. "Phil Lange."

"Broken ankle, huh? How'd you get that?"

He hesitated long enough to wonder if he ought to make up some story that would cast him in a heroic light. After all, the injury had occurred when the *Lexington* had been steaming toward Rabaul to attack the Japanese.

Then he gave a mental shrug and said, "I was jumping down from my plane. Guess I just landed wrong somehow."

"I guess so. That was a bad break."

Phil shrugged for real this time and said, "I'll get over it."

"Sure you will. You'll be back zipping around the sky in no time." She patted him on the shoulder. "Well, you just rest, honey. I'll be looking after you tonight, so if you need anything, you just let me know."

"Okay. Uh . . . what happened to Lieutenant Bergman?"

"Catherine? Oh, she's off duty now. But I can take care of you just as good as she can."

Phil nodded. "Thanks." He picked up one of the pulps. "I guess I'll read until lights-out."

"I'll be back by with your pills."

"All right."

Missy went on down the row of bunks, and Phil tried to concentrate on the magazine in his hands. He couldn't do it, though.

At least he knew her first name now, and it fit her. A beautiful, classy name for a beautiful, classy woman.

Catherine.

*   *   *

She was in her quarters—a stateroom back in the days when the *Solace* had still been the luxury liner *Iroquois*—when Missy stuck her head in the door. "Hey, guess what?" she said.

Catherine looked up from the letter she was writing to Adam and frowned. "Aren't you on duty tonight?"

"I got Alice to cover the ward for me for a few minutes. I just had to tell you this, Catherine."

"Well, what is it?"

"You know that young Navy pilot with the busted ankle? Lieutenant Lange?"

"Yes, of course." Catherine didn't bother explaining that she had helped Lange aboard the ship the night before, then assisted Dr. Johnston during the lieutenant's examination.

"I was talking to him a little while ago in the ward, and you know what?"

With an effort, Catherine contained her impatience. "What?"

"He's got a crush on you."

She put down the fountain pen and stared at Missy. "What?"

"He's sweet on you."

Catherine shook her head. "You're crazy. What makes you think that?"

"He asked about you."

"So? That doesn't mean anything."

"He asked where you were, like he was expecting to see you again, and when I told him you were off duty, he looked disappointed."

"You're imagining things." Catherine reached for the pen. "You'd better get back to the ward. Captain Reynolds likes to make surprise inspections sometimes, you know."

"Yeah, yeah. I tell you, Phil's got a crush on you. When I mentioned your first name, his eyes lit up. He liked knowing that about you."

"I don't believe it. Anyway . . . Phil? You two are already on a first-name basis?"

"Well, his name is Phillip. That's right on his chart: Lange, Phillip, Lieutenant, USNR. I couldn't help but see it. And he just looks like a Phil, don't you think?"

"I hadn't thought about it either way," Catherine said. "Really, you'd better get back."

"I'm going. Want me to take a message to Phil?"

Catherine sighed in exasperation. "Why are you trying to play Cupid? Have you forgotten, Missy—I'm married. Very happily married."

"Yeah, yeah, I know." Missy frowned in thought. "Maybe *I'm* the one who ought to make a play for him. He looks like the type I could really go for."

"You mean he's breathing?" Catherine said, then put her hand to her mouth, ashamed of herself and surprised that she would make such a remark.

Instead of taking offense, Missy laughed. "That's right, sister.

He's not only breathing, but he's got a busted ankle, so he can't run away. Damn right he's my type." She turned away from the door. "I gotta get back."

Catherine smiled and shook her head as Missy rushed off. She was sure that her friend was imagining things. During the time Catherine had been around Lieutenant Lange, he hadn't shown any signs of being romantically interested in her.

She glanced down at her left hand. She was wearing her wedding band now, but she never wore it when she was on duty. Until now, she'd never had any reason to think that perhaps she should.

And she still didn't, she told herself. Missy was wrong. The crew on board the *Solace* would take care of Lieutenant Lange until his ankle healed. Then he would go back to the *Lexington* or one of the other aircraft carriers, and that would be the end of that. Once he was gone, he would probably never even think about her again.

She picked up the pen to resume writing the letter. She wondered if she ought to tell Adam about what Missy had just said. He would probably get a laugh out of it.

For some reason, though, she decided not to.

THIRTY-NINE

Adam crouched in the bottom of the Higgins boat, helmet strapped on his head, Colt 1911A1 automatic pistol riding in a snap-flap holster on his hip, Garand M1 rifle clutched in his right hand, four grenades clipped to his uniform blouse.

And the gold bar of a second lieutenant on his shoulder and the front of his helmet.

The thirty-six-foot-long Higgins boat chugged toward shore, bouncing through the rough surf. Adam looked around at the other Marines crowded into the landing craft. Most of the men wore taut, grim expressions. A few had their eyes closed and their lips were moving, and Adam realized they were praying. Two or three were even grinning.

Ed Collins was one of them. Ed had two stripes on his wipe now, having made corporal. Beside him, Leo Sikorsky knelt, still a PFC. That didn't mean he and Ed weren't still good friends. Differences in rank stretched the bond that they had formed in boot camp, but nothing could ever break it. At least, Adam hoped so.

The bosun's mate who was driving the Higgins boat crouched at the tiller as artillery began to boom. The guns on shore opened up, sending shells screaming over the flotilla of landing craft approaching the beach. Adam kept his face expressionless as the bombardment continued. He was in charge of the men on this boat, and he wouldn't let them see that he was nervous. The enlisted men could lick their lips and sleeve sweat and sea spray off their foreheads, but not the officers. They had to peer straight ahead, calm and ready for action.

The Higgins boat was quite an innovation. Developed several years earlier by Andrew Higgins, a boat designer from New Orleans, it was a variation on the Eureka boat, which was commonly used in the Louisiana swamps and bayous. It was flat-bottomed and required very little draft. Higgins made the sides taller to give more protection to the men riding inside and added an engine and propeller at the rear. The military version was made of steel rather than wood, of course. It reminded Adam of a rectangular metal box with a wooden floor.

The most important feature of the craft was that the front wall dropped down to become a ramp. When the boats reached the beach, those ramps would fall and the Marines inside would charge out over them into the shallow water. They had gone over the plan time after time: Hit the beach running, get ashore as fast as possible, then advance, advance, advance, using whatever cover was available.

Adam glanced over at Ed, who gave him a cocky grin and a thumbs-up signal. Leo swallowed hard and tried to do the thumbs-up, too, but it didn't come off nearly as confident as Ed's gesture. Adam nodded to them, glad to have them with him today, glad that they had all been assigned to the same company.

There was no turning back now. With a rough jolt, the boat hit the sand of the beach.

The bosun's mate threw the lever that dropped the ramp. Adam straightened his legs and came up out of his crouch. The carbine was in both hands now, held slantwise across his chest. Giving a yell that blended with all the other yells coming from Marine throats at this moment, he charged forward, pounding down over the ramp and into the surf.

Adam's first thought was that he hadn't expected the landing to be this *noisy*. The shouting of the Marines, the thud of their boots against the metal ramps, the rumble of the surf, the roar of the artillery, the crackle of machine guns opening up from emplacements just beyond the beach, the sharp snap of rifle fire—it was chaos, pure chaos, and the tumult made it hard for Adam to keep his wits about him.

He forced himself to concentrate on the objective and not think about what might go wrong. As he came out of the water onto the damp sand, he spotted a large piece of driftwood ahead and to his right. Veering toward it, he flopped onto his belly, landing hard enough so that some of the breath was knocked out of his lungs. He gasped for air as he wriggled on the sand, getting more of his body behind the protection of the driftwood. He lifted his rifle, smacked the butt stock hard into his shoulder, and squinted over the sights, searching for a target.

To his left, Ed Collins suddenly rushed past, whooping exuberantly as his stubby legs carried him with surprising speed toward the machine gun nests. "Ed! Get down!" Adam shouted at him, but Ed ignored the warning. He jerked one of his grenades loose and threw it toward the nearest machine gun nest, a perfect toss, high and overhand, that carried the grenade into the emplacement. Adam saw the men who had been manning the machine gun bail out, making desperate leaps that carried them away from the grenade.

Leo stumbled past Adam, following Ed. Adam bit back a curse and came to his feet. His men were attacking the enemy, and he couldn't very well cower here behind a piece of driftwood while they were charging ahead. He yelled and ran after them. From the corners of his eyes, he saw the rest of the company swarming across the white sand of the beach, and farther along, so were the men from the other landing craft. It was like a high tide of Marines sweeping ashore. Ed was still at the point of the attack, flinging grenades right and left until he didn't have any more. Leo was right behind him, keeping up somehow. Adam caught up to Leo, threw his own grenades, then bounded into one of the machine gun nests, swinging the muzzle of his rifle around so that he could cover the men clustered around the gun. With the threat of the machine guns neutralized, the rest of the invasion force swept on toward the artillery bunkers, and within a few minutes, those were captured as well. The big guns fell silent.

Adam stood there on the earthworks surrounding the

machine gun nest. The yelling died away, and an eerie calm fell over the beach.

It was so quiet he could hear the cars and trucks swishing by on the road a couple of hundred yards inland, the usual heavy traffic between Los Angeles and San Diego. He looked around in satisfaction. The beach at La Jolla, California, was now under the control of the United States Marines.

General Price came striding along the edge of the beach, which was dotted with tufts of grass next to the parking area where tourists left their cars when the place wasn't closed off for military exercises. He walked over to Adam and said, "What's your name, Lieutenant?"

"Bergman, sir, Adam J."

Price pointed to Ed and Leo, who stood close by waiting with looks of anticipation on their faces. "Are those your men?"

"Yes, sir."

"You should be proud of them. They were the spark plugs of this entire landing. Without their bold action, you might have all been pinned down on the beach."

"Yes, sir."

"Of course, if those guns had been firing live ammo, they probably would have been killed."

Adam nodded. He knew the general was right.

Price moved on down the beach, speaking to the other officers who had come ashore in the mock landing. Adam walked over to Ed and Leo and said, "Good job, fellas. But you heard what the general said?"

"About us gettin' our asses shot off?" Ed asked. "Yeah, but I figured we had to get them machine guns knocked out. We never would've had a chance as long as they were chewin' us up."

Adam couldn't make any reply to that, and for the first time he realized what a fine line an officer had to walk. He wanted to do his best to protect his men, but at the same time their lives were expendable, human cash to be spent attaining a goal, in this case the establishment of a foothold on an enemy-held island. Sure, today it was La Jolla, a few miles up the coast from San Diego, and today the machine guns had been firing blanks and the shore batteries had deliberately fired over the landing craft, but soon enough they would be in the South Pacific, facing the real thing.

He patted Ed on the shoulder and muttered, "Good work." When the time came, maybe they would be lucky. Until then, all they could do was train as much as possible so they would be prepared for whatever they might face.

Adam had a feeling, though, that when the real thing came, no amount of training could fully prepare them for it.

Nobody got to practice dying.

After gathering up the dummy grenades, the Marines returned to Camp Kearney in the backs of deuce-and-a-half trucks, laughing and talking excitedly most of the way. Today's mock landing had been the first such exercise, and they had all been either looking forward to it or dreading it. Now that it was over, however, the reaction was the same: relief, almost giddiness. There would be more mock landings before they shipped out for the South Pacific, but now they all knew what to expect.

After the men had gone back to the barracks and cleaned up, mail call was held in the late afternoon. Since graduating from OCS and being assigned to a company, Adam shared the barracks with those men, though he had private quarters, as well as a small office, at the far end of the long building. The four company sergeants had rooms at the other end of the barracks, with the rows of bunks for the enlisted men in between. There was a letter from Catherine in the mail bag, and after claiming it, Adam took it back to his office to read it.

The *Solace* was leaving its current port, Catherine reported in the letter, and by the time Adam was reading this, the hospital ship would be steaming toward its new destination. She didn't include any details because new censorship regulations had gone into effect, and even if she had mentioned the names of the places involved, the military censors would have blacked them out.

Adam didn't have to know the exact details to be worried. Wherever the *Solace* was, it wasn't far from the action in the South Pacific.

The letter was chatty, mostly about Missy and her crush on a young Navy aviator who was a patient on the hospital ship. Catherine didn't say what was wrong with him, but clearly it wasn't anything too serious or Missy wouldn't be interested in him. Adam sensed that there was something else about the situation Catherine wasn't saying, but he couldn't put his finger on what it was. He finally shrugged and told himself not to worry about it.

The door of his office was open a couple of inches. When someone knocked on it, Adam put the letter on the desk and said, "Come."

Leo Sikorsky pushed the door open and stepped into the office. "Am I disturbing you, Lieutenant?" he asked formally.

"Not at all. Come in, Private, and shut the door."

When Leo had stepped into the office and pushed the door closed behind him, Adam said, "What is it, Chopper? Something wrong?"

He knew he shouldn't be so familiar with an enlisted man now that he was an officer, but it was hard to remember that where an old friend was concerned. Leo came closer to the desk, nervously rubbed his chin, and said quietly, "I heard what the general said today, Adam. He said me and Ed would've been killed if that was the real thing."

"He said you might have been killed. There's no way of knowing what would have happened."

"That Ed, he's crazy. If those guns had been firing real bullets, he'd have done the same thing."

Adam nodded. "I know."

"When we get out there, he's gonna get himself killed, Adam. Worse yet, he's gonna get *me* killed. You gotta talk to him."

"And tell him to do what? To be careful?"

"Well . . . yeah. He can't just go chargin' around like he's Superman or something."

Adam took a deep breath. "Let's say it was real. We might have gotten trapped on that beach, and then the machine guns would have chewed up the whole company. We might have all gotten killed."

Leo squinted at him and said, "So you're sayin' it's better for a couple of guys to die, instead of a whole bunch of guys."

"That makes sense, doesn't it?"

"But what if the two guys who die are friends of yours?"

Adam put his hands on the desk and shook his head. "Don't do this, Leo. The situation may be completely different when we go ashore for real."

"But if it ain't . . . or even if it is . . . you don't really care who gets killed as long as we take the beach, right?"

Adam's jaw was so tight it was almost painful. "That's our job," he said.

Leo stared at him for a long moment, then nodded. "Yeah, you're an officer, all right."

Adam came to his feet. "What the hell does that mean?"

"It means you ain't the same guy we knew in boot camp anymore. You don't give a shit about anything except duty."

That wasn't true, but Adam couldn't let Leo see that. He said, "I think that's all, Private Sikorsky."

"Yeah. That's all." Leo came to attention and saluted, then turned on his heel, jerked open the door, and walked out of the office without waiting for Adam to return the salute.

Adam's face was hot with anger. Leo didn't understand what it was like to be an officer, to have to risk not only your own life but the lives of men you cared about. Adam was only beginning to comprehend that burden himself.

He looked down at the letter from Catherine lying on his desk. He didn't feel like reading any more of it now, so he folded it and put it back in the envelope. He would get back to it later. Slowly, he sank into his chair.

And wondered whatever had possessed him when he decided to become an officer in the first place.

FORTY

Joe came out of the showers with a towel wrapped around his waist and started down the long aisle in the center of the barracks. He stopped short as he saw the man standing beside his bunk with his back to him. The man wore the uniform of a British officer, and there was something familiar about him, even though Joe couldn't see his face.

"Looking for me?" Joe asked.

The officer turned around, and Joe recognized him as Colin Richardson, the major he'd met in a dark alley, in company with a couple of Egyptian thieves, several weeks earlier.

"Corporal Parker," Richardson said. "I was hoping I'd find you here. Your commanding officer told me that you were already back from today's training."

"That's right," Joe said. He glanced around the barracks. He and Richardson were the only ones in the building, and something in the major's eyes made a tingle of nervousness go through Joe.

"Hope you don't mind." Richardson held up a bottle of whiskey. "I brought this for you."

"Okay. Thanks." Joe didn't make any move to take the bottle from Richardson. In fact, he edged back a step or two. He was acutely conscious of the fact that he was wearing just a towel.

Suddenly, Richardson laughed. "Don't worry, Joe," he said. "I'm not one of those English faggots you've no doubt heard about. In fact, I'll be quite happy to turn my back while you get dressed."

"Okay," Joe said again, a little relieved but not ready to relax just yet. He didn't see any reason why Richardson should have shown up like this with no warning.

Richardson turned around while Joe hurried into clean skivvies and khaki trousers and shirt. Still bare-footed, he said, "All right."

Richardson swung back to face him and held out the bottle. "A token of my appreciation. For helping me that night, you know."

"You already bought me dinner," Joe said.

"That was for pitching in when those bloody wogs jumped me. This is for your discretion later on when I was a bit, ah, under the influence."

Richardson had been more than a bit under the influence, Joe thought. He'd been stinking drunk. Clearly, though, he remembered some of what had happened at Shepheard's. He proved that by continuing, "If you hadn't put me in a cab, I might not have ever made it back to my flat."

"I'm sure you would have been fine," Joe said.

Richardson wagged the bottle back and forth and said, "Just take the bloody thing, all right? I don't want to have to make it an order."

Joe reached out and took the bottle from him. "Thanks," he said.

"You're welcome. Now, be a gent, why don't you, and offer your visitor a drink?" Richardson grinned.

"There aren't any glasses around here. I've got a canteen cup—"

"Any old port in a storm, as the saying goes. I'll just have a jot, anyway. The cup'll do me fine."

Still not convinced that Richardson had brought the whiskey as a gesture of thanks, Joe found his canteen and unscrewed the top that also served as a cup. He broke the seal on the bottle, looking at the label as he did so. He was no expert on booze, but this looked like the good stuff. He poured a couple of fingers into the canteen cup and handed it to Richardson.

"Cheers," the major said, holding up the cup and waiting. Joe tapped the bottle against the cup and then lifted it to his lips.

The whiskey was pure, clean fire, all the way down to his gut. He caught his breath but managed not to cough and sputter. Richardson tossed off his drink and seemed completely unaffected by it.

"You know," Richardson said, "I didn't come here today just to express my gratitude."

Joe looked at him but didn't say anything.

"I've been mulling over this quite a bit. I was wondering about that night, you know. The night we met."

"What about it?" Joe asked.

"Well, I was rather smashed, wasn't I?"

"You'd had a lot to drink," Joe said.

"I may have said some things . . . things I shouldn't have said . . ."

Joe felt a chill race through him. He had given some thought to Richardson's comments about knowing what the Germans' secret plans were, as well as his mention of Ultra. Joe didn't have any idea what that was, but it had to be something important. The look in Richardson's eyes now confirmed that. The major still wore a congenial expression, but in his eyes was nothing except cold menace.

Joe shook his head and said, "I'm afraid I don't know what you're talking about, Major."

"I think you do. I'm sure you must have wondered—"

"I didn't wonder about anything." Joe kept his own face carefully expressionless. He was worried, even scared, but he didn't want Richardson to see that.

"Well, I must say I'm glad to hear that," Richardson said after a moment. "You see, there are places back in England—private sanitariums, you know—where we sometimes have to put people who have too vivid an imagination and start questioning things they shouldn't question. It's all for their own good, of course."

"Of course," Joe said.

"I wouldn't have wanted to take such steps in your case, because I feel a certain debt of gratitude to you. After all, it's possible those wogs could have injured me, perhaps even killed me."

"I suppose they might have," Joe said carefully. "I can see where it would be . . . awkward . . . to have to do what you're talking about."

He left unsaid the rest of what he was thinking: If Richardson tried to put him on ice for knowing things that he shouldn't, then he ran the risk of Joe revealing where he had heard the secrets in the first place. Joe didn't think the major wanted to admit that he had gotten drunk and spilled the beans—whatever the beans were—to the first friendly face he saw.

It would be far safer for Richardson, Joe suddenly realized, just to kill him.

That was the pulp writer in him talking, he told himself. Surely something so bizarre and far-fetched couldn't really happen. This British major—who probably worked in Intelligence—hadn't come here today to kill him. How could Richardson hope to get away with such a thing in broad daylight, in the middle of an American barracks where someone could come along without warning at any second?

Joe wished someone *would* come along.

"I'm glad you understand," Richardson said. He tossed the canteen cup to Joe, who caught it without thinking. Only then did Joe realize he now had both hands full. If Richardson jumped him, the major would have at least a momentary advantage. . . .

"So I'll bid you good day," Richardson went on, turning toward the door of the barracks.

Let him go, Joe told himself. *You dodged a bullet just now, so just let him go.*

Richardson paused at the doorway and looked back at him. "Corporal Parker?"

"Yes, sir?"

"You strike me as quite an intelligent young man, and moreover, one who can be trusted. It could well be that somewhere along the line, the service I work for might have some use for a young American officer such as yourself. So don't be surprised if someday I contact you again."

The look in Richardson's eyes told Joe that there was now a pact of sorts between them. They knew some of each other's secrets, and each of them, to a certain extent, was at the mercy of the other.

Joe nodded and said, "All right."

Richardson sketched a salute and went out. Joe waited until he was gone, then took a deep breath and let it out in a sigh. A part of him wondered if he had imagined the whole thing. Surely the major hadn't come in here and threatened him with imprisonment or even worse, then told him that someday British Intelligence might want to make a . . . a spy out of him! That was crazy. If he wrote this up as a story, even the pulp editors would bounce it as being too unbelievable.

But then he looked down at the open bottle of whiskey in his hand and knew it was true. Unlikely as it sounded, it was all true.

He lifted the bottle to his mouth and took a drink to steady his nerves. There was one thing about this whole mess that he knew for sure:

He wasn't going to tell Dale about it.

FORTY-ONE

The *Solace* was bound for the Tonga Islands, the main island, Tongatapu, specifically. The group was approximately 500 miles south-southwest of American Samoa and was under the control of the U.S. Navy. In the future, of course, the Japanese might have something to say about that. But for the moment, it constituted a safe harbor.

Lt. Phillip Lange, USNR, was still aboard the hospital ship. The infection in his foot and leg was gone, cured by the penicillin. The broken ankle had been recast, and after several weeks of letting it heal, he was getting anxious to have the plaster off his leg. A guy could only lie around and take it easy for so long without going nuts.

But when the cast came off and his ankle was all right, that would mean the time had come for him to leave the *Solace* and return to the *Lexington*. At first Phil had been itching for that to happen, but now he wasn't so sure. Leaving the hospital ship meant leaving Catherine.

He knew he shouldn't feel like that. She hadn't given him any indication that she was interested in him. In fact, it seemed as if she'd gone out of her way not to be around him ever since his first couple of days on board. He hadn't seen her more than a handful of times since then, and always only for a few moments. Of course, it was a big ship, with a lot of wards, and he told himself that it was just a matter of her duties keeping her elsewhere. She wasn't really trying to avoid him. At least he hoped not.

His plans to ask her out to dinner in Pago had been scotched by the ship's abrupt departure from that port. Phil didn't know much about Nuku'alofa, the capital city located on Tongatapu, but surely there would be a decent restaurant or café somewhere in the city. And he was getting around a lot better now on his crutches. He could keep up with Catherine unless she wanted to go dancing or something like that. He didn't think he was quite ready for a jitterbug.

He was sitting in one of the armchairs in the salon in bathrobe and pajamas, his right leg propped on a footstool in front of him, when Catherine came in. Phil was reading one of the pulp magazines she'd given him. He was on his second time through the magazine, in fact, and it had also been handed around the ward, so it was getting pretty ragged. He lowered it to his lap, looked up at her, and grinned. "Hi there, stranger."

She stopped and looked surprised to see him, as if she hadn't expected to see him there. "Hello, Lieutenant," she said.

He was determined that she wasn't going to dash off this time, the way she usually did. There was an empty chair beside him. He reached over and patted its cushion, saying, "Why don't you keep a lonely sailor company for a while? Unless, of course, you're on duty."

Catherine hesitated, then shrugged and said, "As a matter of fact, I'm not." She came over to the chair and sat down. "How are you feeling, Lieutenant?"

"Peachy. I think this ankle is just about well."

"You'll need at least another week in the cast, and then you'll have to get your strength back in the ankle." She smiled. "But it won't be much longer before you're on your way back to your ship."

"I don't know if I'm glad to hear that or not."

"Well, then, you've certainly changed since you got here. At first that was all you wanted."

"Back then I didn't have any reason to want to be here."

Catherine frowned, then pointed to the magazine in his lap. "Still reading that, I see."

It was the copy of *Dime Mystery*. Phil lifted it and said,

"Rereading it, actually. You know, I read that story by your friend. It wasn't bad. Pretty creepy."

Catherine laughed. "I'll be sure and tell Joe next time I write to him."

"You write him pretty often?"

"Oh, probably not as often as I should. He and his brother are in . . . well, they're somewhere overseas. We're not really supposed to know any more, what with all the new regulations."

Phil took a deep breath, then decided to be bold. "This guy Parker . . . is he your boyfriend or something like that?"

"Oh, no, nothing like that." Catherine looked steadily at him. "In fact, he's my husband's best friend."

For a second, Phil thought he had heard her wrong. She couldn't have said "husband." But then he knew his ears hadn't made a mistake. He suddenly felt utterly stupid and even a little bit sick.

"That's nice," he forced himself to say. "I didn't know you were married."

Catherine glanced down at her left hand. "I don't wear my wedding ring when I'm on duty. I guess I should."

"Your husband . . . is he in the service?"

"He's in the Second Marine Division."

Phil was surprised. "Those guys are in Samoa. Was he there while we were?"

Catherine shook her head. "No, he's back in the States with the troops that haven't come over yet. He's already seen action, though. He was on Wake Island."

Phil sat up straighter and repeated, "Wake? But those guys didn't get off the island, did they?"

"Adam did. One of the few after the Japanese started bombing it."

"Lucky son of a gun," Phil said, and meant it more than one way.

If Catherine realized that, she didn't give any indication. With pride in her voice, she said, "He went through OCS when he got back, and he's been commissioned a lieutenant. He'll be an officer the next time I see him."

"Congratulations. I'd like to meet the guy sometime."

"Maybe you will. I hope so." Catherine hesitated, then said, "Lieutenant . . . I hope you didn't get the wrong idea about any-thing—"

Phil didn't let her go any further. "What would I get the wrong idea about?" He shook his head. "No problem here, Lieu-tenant."

"Well, that's good." Catherine stood up. "I've got to be going now. I'll see you later."

"Sure," Phil said. "Back in the ward."

Catherine nodded. "That's right. Back in the ward."

She smiled, then left the salon. Phil settled back in his chair, staring straight ahead.

Son of a bitch. He had almost made a gold-plated fool of him-self. Catherine was a smart woman. She had known what he was getting at. Thank God she had stopped him before he asked her out on a date or something, and her a married woman!

Still, he felt a pang of loss inside. He had really liked Lt. Catherine Bergman. Hell, he still liked her! It was just that noth-ing could ever come of it, now that he knew she was married.

Adam Bergman, that was the guy's name. Phil felt a twinge of jealousy.

No matter how you looked at it, some guys had all the luck.

Missy walked quietly through the dimly lit ward on her rubber-soled shoes. Most of the patients were asleep. She spoke softly to the ones who were awake, comforting those who were in too much pain to sleep. This ward had all kinds of cases, from the serious to the not-so-serious.

One of the latter was Lt. Phil Lange, at least at this point in his recuperation. He could get up and get around better than anyone else in the ward. Still, Missy was surprised when she came to his bed and found it empty.

She looked down at the other end of the ward where the head was located. Maybe he had gone down there. Since she had the night duty, he was her responsibility, so she wanted to be sure he was all right. She walked down to the open door of the head and called softly, "Lieutenant Lange? Are you in there?"

There was no answer. Missy hesitated, then stepped into the head. She was a nurse, after all, and it wasn't like she was going to see anything she hadn't seen a thousand times before. But the head was empty, with no sign of Lieutenant Lange or anybody else.

Where could he be? Missy was starting to get worried now. She went from the ward into the central companionway that ran nearly the entire length of the ship. The ward was located on C Deck, just aft of amidships. Another nurse was coming out of one of the other wards, so Missy asked her, "Have you seen a patient on crutches out here in the past few minutes, Louise?"

"No, but I thought I heard somebody go by, heading back toward the stern." The other nurse grinned. "Have you got a runaway, Missy?"

"I don't know, but I'll check it out. Could you keep an eye on my ward for a few minutes?"

"Sure, I suppose so."

"Thanks."

Missy walked down the companionway to a hatch that led onto the rear deck. As she swung it open and stepped out, Missy spotted the figure standing at the railing, looking out over the wake left by the ship's passage. The water bubbled and glowed with phosphorescence. The moon was bright. Missy had no trouble seeing the crutches and the white plaster cast on the right ankle.

"Lieutenant Lange," she said.

He jumped a little, surprised to hear her voice. As he swung away from the railing, he said, "I'm sorry. Am I breaking a rule or something by being out here?"

"You're supposed to be in your bed after lights-out." She let herself sound angry, even though she really wasn't. "What if you fell overboard? Nobody would even know about it."

"I'm not going to fall overboard."

"What were you doing, then?" Catherine had told her about breaking the news to Phil that she was married. Even though he didn't strike her as the type to take a lover's leap, she asked, "Getting ready to jump?"

"Of course not!"

She moved closer to him. "Come on; we'd better get you inside—"

"I just came out here for a breath of fresh air," he said. "We're in the tropics, Nurse Mitchell. Doesn't that mean anything to you?"

"It means it's hot as blazes most of the time."

"Well, it's a beautiful night tonight." Phil tipped his head back and looked up at the moon floating in the dark sky above them. "Just beautiful."

"Yeah, I guess it is." Despite her best intentions, Missy found herself drifting over to the railing. She rested her hands on it and looked up at the moon and stars. Beautiful was the word, all right.

Phil moved to the rail beside her. "On a night like this, it's hard to believe that the world's at war, isn't it?"

"If it wasn't, we wouldn't be out here." Missy sighed. "But I know what you mean. It all seems a million miles away, doesn't it?"

"At least." He chuckled. "You know, the guys back home would probably be jealous if they could see me right now, broken ankle and all."

"Why?"

"Well, here I am, cruising along on a ship in the moonlight with a pretty girl . . ."

" 'I was sailing along,' " Missy said, " 'on Moonlight Bay. . . . ' "

"Yeah, something like that."

They were both quiet for a moment, so quiet that Missy thought she could hear the pounding of her own heart. From the moment she had first seen him, she had been attracted to Lt. Phil Lange. But he was interested only in Catherine, no matter how much Missy flirted with him.

Now that Catherine finally had let him know she was off-limits—something that she should have done sooner, in Missy's opinion—Phil was hurting. He was on the rebound, ripe for comforting.

But at the same time, the whole situation was a little insulting, Missy told herself. She hadn't been good enough for Phil to pay any attention to until Catherine had let him know he wasn't going to get anywhere with her. Now, suddenly, things had changed.

What she ought to do was tell Lieutenant Lange to go to hell, then drag his ass back into the ward and order him to get into bed where he was supposed to be. That would serve him right.

Phil straightened on his crutches and said, "I'd better get back to the ward. Sorry I made you come out here looking for me, Nurse Mitchell."

She turned and put a hand on his arm. "No, wait. It's Missy."

"I know." He looked at her and said her name. "Missy."

Oh, the hell with it. They were in the middle of the South Pacific on a warm, moonlit night, and suddenly she didn't care if he was on the rebound or not. All she cared about was stepping closer to him and sliding an arm around his waist. He put a hand up to her face, and even though the crutch that was under that arm clattered to the deck, neither of them paid any attention to it. She was almost as tall as he was, so she had to tip her head back only a little for him to be able to kiss her.

Like she had said, the war seemed a million miles away, and for now, it could stay there.

FORTY-TWO

All through the spring of 1942, the stalemate along the Gazala Line had continued in the Libyan desert. There had been numerous skirmishes between the British Eighth Army and the Deutsche Afrika Korps, but no major battles. Each morning, the American-made General Grant M3 tanks, known to their British crews as Honeys, dispersed from their leaguers to patrol the line. Most days, all the tanks returned to leaguer in the evening.

Most days . . . but not all.

Bert Crimmens peered into the guts of the damaged wireless set and then wearily rubbed a hand over his sweating, beard-stubbled face. The radio had taken a piece of shrapnel during a minor dust-up with a German armored car earlier in the afternoon, and it had been useless ever since. If Joe Parker had been here, Bert was confident that the American could have repaired the wireless set. The damage was beyond Bert's abilities to fix, however.

The radio wasn't the only casualty of the brief battle. Sitting on the floor of the tank's crew compartment, close by Bert's seat, with his back propped against one of the ammunition lockers, was Captain Neville Sharp, old Hell-on-Treads himself. Sharp's shattered left shoulder was heavily bandaged, and he was pale from blood loss. Bert had thought that the commander was going to bleed to death before he and the other two members of the crew got the bleeding stopped. At the moment, Sharp's eyes were closed. Bert didn't know if he was asleep or if he had passed out.

"Can't you raise anybody on that sodding thing?"

Bert looked up into the turret, where Jeremy Royce's raw-boned face was peering down angrily at him. You would think that after this long in the desert, no one would sunburn anymore, but Royce did. His face was always a painful-looking shade of red.

"The wireless is ruined," Bert told Royce, who had appointed himself temporary commander after Captain Sharp was wounded. Tom Hamilton, the gunner, had taken over Royce's job as driver. "If we can get back to leaguer," Bert went on, "one of the other lads may be able to fix it, but I can't."

"How are we going to get back to leaguer without the bloody wireless? Do you know where we are?"

Bert shrugged and couldn't resist saying, "No, I don't know. You're the commander now. I suppose you'll have to figure something out."

For a second he thought Royce was going to drop down from the turret and pound him. Royce could do it, too; he was a lot bigger than Bert. And Hamilton, a surly sort of fellow who never involved himself in other people's affairs, probably wouldn't step in to put a stop to it. But then Royce must have thought better of the impulse, because he muttered, "Keep trying to raise someone," then straightened to look out the turret once more.

Bert didn't know how the stupid git expected him to keep trying to raise someone on the wireless when the thing was smashed. Arguing with Royce was a waste of time, though. He sighed and went back to staring at the radio as if that would miraculously do some good.

The tank was sitting in a slight depression on the desert in the position known as hull-down, with only the upper portion of the turret and the barrel of the 37-mm cannon visible from the surrounding countryside. As long as the Honey wasn't moving, it would be very difficult to spot. After Sharp was wounded in the battle with the armored car, Royce had taken over and got them into this depression before calling a halt, unsure what to do next. Bert was thankful that Tom Hamilton had managed to put a shot into the armored car's petrol tank, blasting it into a flaming hulk, just as the Honey was hit. Perhaps the Jerries hadn't had time to get on their own wireless and call in any help.

But the burning armored car had given off quite a bit of smoke, and there was no telling when a Panzer prowling through the area might decide to come over and investigate. Bert hated to think about what they might do if they had to go up against one of those German monsters without Captain Sharp in command.

Maybe they would be lucky, he thought. Maybe one of their own tanks would find them first and lead them back to the rest of the squadron.

Suddenly, Royce dropped down out of the turret. His suncracked lips were pulled back from his teeth in a grimace. "I hear an engine," he said. "Something's coming!"

Bert's pulse began to race. Was it one of the Honeys from the squadron—or a Panzer?

"Well, don't just stand there," he said to Royce without thinking. "Get up there and see what it is."

Royce took off Captain Sharp's binoculars, which he had slung around his neck on their leather strap, and thrust them into Bert's hands. "You take a look, you're such an effing expert on everything!"

Bert was about to protest, but then he decided to do as Royce said. He could certainly recognize a Panzer if he saw one. The massive shapes of the Mark III and Mark IV were unmistakable.

He hung the binoculars around his neck and scrambled into the turret, using the grab irons to pull himself up. He lifted his head through the open hatch and peered around. Nothing but sand and rock as far as the eye could see . . . but he heard the distant growling of an engine, and then suddenly he saw a small dark shape moving over the desert, coming toward the depression where the tank was concealed.

Bert's heart pounded as he settled himself on the commander's seat and lifted the binoculars to his eyes. The moving shape was coming on fast, too fast to be a tank, he judged. He squinted through the glasses, trying to locate whatever it was, and when a familiar image leaped into focus, he couldn't stop himself from loosing a small cry of relief.

"It's a petrol lorry!" he called down into the tank.

"One of ours?" Royce asked.

Bert frowned. He hadn't thought about that. The Germans had tanks operating in this area, too, which meant that their rear echelon forces, including petrol lorries, might well be out and about, as well. And since the one he was peering at through the glasses was coming toward them almost straight on, he couldn't see any markings on the sides of it.

"I don't know," he said.

Tom Hamilton said, "I'd best move the tank so we can use our gun if need be." The engine cranked, then started with a rumbling roar. Hamilton shouted something else, but Bert couldn't make it out. He looked down into the crew compartment and shook his head at Royce, pointing to one of his ears.

Royce pointed at the earphones lying on the shelf just inside the turret. Bert felt foolish as he picked them up and put them on. He should have thought of the interphone. It still worked, even if the wireless set didn't.

"You there, Bert?" Hamilton's voice asked in his ears.

"I'm here."

"Tell me how much to turn."

Bert studied the oncoming lorry for a second, then said into the microphone, "Try about ten degrees."

The Honey lurched into motion, its left track turning faster than its right as Hamilton shoved that throttle forward. Bert didn't know why Royce didn't take over the driving again, since that was normally his job. Hamilton could shift back over to the 75-mm cannon.

But that left him in command, Bert thought. And he wasn't qualified to command a tank. Not by any stretch of the imagination. Royce was just standing there not doing anything. Why the bloody hell didn't he get back up here in the turret?

Because he was afraid, Bert realized. For all his bluff, bullying attitude, Royce was scared. For some odd reason, that made Bert feel a bit better—but only a bit.

The barrel of the cannon came in line with the lorry, which was now only a few hundred yards away. "That's good," Bert called through the interphone, and the tank came to a stop. He said, "Someone get on the gun."

"I'll do that," Hamilton said. "Royce, take the controls again."

Royce gave a little shake of his head, not arguing with Hamilton but rather as if he were coming out of some sort of trance, and turned to take the driver's seat while Hamilton shifted back over to the gunner's position. Bert leaned down and glanced at Captain Sharp, hoping against hope that old Hell-on-Treads had come to enough to take command once again. Unfortunately, the captain was still unconscious.

"Can you tell yet if it's the Jerries?" Hamilton asked over the earphones.

Bert straightened and put the glasses on the lorry again. It just looked like the front of any large truck with a big petrol tank on the rear. There was nothing distinctive about it whatsoever.

"I don't know," he said.

Royce's voice came over the earphones. "Put a shell in 'em anyway, Tom. Blow the buggers up. That's the only safe thing to do."

"Hold on!" Bert said. "We can't do that. What if it's one of ours?"

"We can't take that chance."

"Why not? It's just a petrol lorry. At most they have a couple of small hand machine guns in the cab. They can't hurt us."

"If they have a radio, they can call in the Panzers."

"If they're one of ours and they have a radio, they can call the squadron for help," Bert said. "We have to wait."

"Don't listen to the little bastard," Royce said to Hamilton. "Put a shell in 'em, Tom—*now*!"

Bert felt anger flooding through him. Royce had taken over earlier without consulting anyone, his natural arrogance making him think he was best suited to replace Captain Sharp. But when he'd been faced with the first real sign of possible danger, he had abdicated his position to Bert. Now Royce was trying to take charge again, only he was acting out of fear and stupidity rather than any sort of command sense.

"Hold your fire, Tom," Bert said into the microphone. "I'll let you know when to fire."

Royce began, "Why, you bloody little—"

"Shut up, Royce." The lorry was only a hundred yards away now and still coming on at a good clip. Bert wanted to concentrate on it, rather than on Royce's rabble-rousing.

The men in the cab of the lorry were bound to spot the tank any second now. If they were Germans, they would likely slam on the brakes and try to turn around. They wouldn't want any part of a British M3. That would be the time to order Tom Hamilton to open fire.

Instead, the lorry continued on toward the depression. When it finally began to turn, the maneuver was slow and deliberate, so that it came to a stop turned side-on to the tank, about twenty yards away. Bert, who hadn't realized that he was holding his breath, started breathing again as he saw the markings of the Eighth Army stenciled on the door.

"It's one of ours!" he called down to the others. A sense of relief went through the crew compartment.

The doors of the lorry opened and three men got out. They were Australians, Bert thought, recognizing the hats with the brim pinned up on the left side. One of the men came down into the depression, slogging through the sand toward the tank. The other two waited by the lorry.

Bert felt a sudden twinge of alarm as the man came closer. What if these were Germans masquerading as Aussies? The lorry and the uniforms could have been captured by members of the Afrika Korps . . .

"Hello, there! Need a hand?"

The voice that came from the stranger was not Australian at all, not even close. But the accent wasn't German, either.

It was *American*.

And when the man reached the tank, took off his hat, and grinned up at Bert, Bert recognized him immediately.

Dale Parker.

FORTY-THREE

"Hey, Bert, is that you?" Dale called up when he recognized the face of the man goggling down at him from the turret of the tank.

Bert Crimmens yanked the earphones off his head and scrambled out of the turret. He dropped down to the hull and then to the ground. "Dale?" he said. "Dale Parker?"

"Yeah," Dale said with a grin as he shook Bert's hand. "I'll bet you're surprised to see me out here."

From the turret, another voice said, "What the bloody hell—Parker?"

Dale looked up and wasn't nearly as happy to see Jeremy Royce as he had been to recognize Bert. Royce started climbing out of the tank, too.

The Honey's engine was still running, so Dale gestured at it and said, "I know you're not out of gas. Why are you just sitting here? Did you throw a track or something?"

Bert shook his head and jerked a thumb at the tank. "Captain Sharp's in there. He's been wounded. We had a bit of a scuffle with a Jerry armored car earlier today."

"Is Sharp hit bad?"

"He's got a busted shoulder. He's unconscious, though; that's the main thing right now. We found ourselves without a commander."

Royce jumped down from the hull. "I took command," he said. "I'm senior man in the crew."

"Then why didn't you head back to leaguer?"

Bert said, "Because he doesn't know how to get back," and

drew a filthy look from Royce. Bert shrugged and went on, "Neither do I, actually. And our wireless is out of order, so we can't call for help."

Dale glanced up at the sun. There was an hour of daylight left, maybe a little more. It would be good to get back to the squadron's base camp before dark, rather than being stuck overnight alone out on the desert. He was pretty sure he could find the way.

"I'll stay with you guys," he said. "You can top off your gas tank; then we'll head back."

Royce's lip curled in a sneer. "I don't reckon we need any help from an effing American who's not supposed to even be out here."

"Why *are* you here, Dale?" Bert asked. "I thought you were at base depot back in Cairo."

Dale grinned. "I'm just off on what you guys call a lark. I thought it was time I saw for myself what's going on up here at the front, so when I got a three-day pass, I sneaked a ride with a buddy who was coming this way. He's an Aussie who works with the rear echelon forces, so he got me this uniform and told me to keep my mouth shut so nobody would be the wiser."

"Well, I'm glad you're here," Bert said. Royce glared at Dale, clearly not sharing that sentiment.

Bert called through the driver's port to the guy at the throttle, who sent the M3 up out of the depression and stopped it next to the gasoline truck. In a matter of minutes, the two real Australian soldiers had filled the Honey's fuel tank.

"I'm gonna go with these guys back to leaguer," Dale told them.

"Are you sure about that?" one of the Aussies asked. "The officers are sure to find out you're an American."

Dale shrugged. "They need a hand, and I'm not gonna go off and leave them out here."

"We can call for aid on the wireless."

"Nah, it'll be quicker if I just ride on the tank."

Both of the soldiers from the truck shrugged as if to say, "Suit yourself, Yank," and drove off in search of any other British tanks that might be running low on fuel. Dale waited until Royce and Bert had climbed back into the tank, then pulled himself up onto the outside of the turret.

"Head that way," he said to Bert, who sat on the seat inside the turret and put on the earphones. Dale pointed to indicate the direction, and Bert relayed the course to Royce, who had taken the controls.

The tank rolled away from the depression where it had been hiding. After it had jolted along for a few minutes, Dale asked the question that had been bothering him ever since he and his companions on the gasoline truck had stumbled onto this situation.

"Why didn't you just follow your own tracks back to your camp?" He raised his voice to be heard over the rumble of the tank's engine and treads.

Bert shook his head and waved a hand toward the ground. "Tanks have been all over this part of the desert. There are too many tracks. It's all a jumble. We couldn't tell which marks we'd made and which ones were already there. We thought we might get lost and wind up behind the German lines."

Dale shrugged. He supposed that was possible, but unlikely in his opinion. "You can tell directions from the sun. You would have known if you were going west."

"I reckon that's right." Bert shook his head. "But after the captain was hit and with the wireless smashed, we simply weren't certain what the best course of action would be."

Dale didn't say anything, but he thought this was a perfect example of how the British soldiers relied too much on their officers. Bert and the others could have wandered around out here in the tank and probably found their way back to their camp. It might have taken a while, and there might have been some wrong turns, but Dale was confident that sooner or later they would have wound up in the right place just by using some common sense.

But without an officer to tell them what to do, they had hunkered down and done nothing.

He told himself not to feel too superior. The British Army had been around for a hell of a long time, and they were used to doing things a certain way. They might not have the talent for improvisation that the American military did, but that wasn't their fault. And if good old logical Joe was here, he'd probably be saying that the British also didn't usually get themselves in trouble by taking reckless chances, either, the way Americans sometimes did. Dale grinned as that thought went through his head.

As if Bert had picked up on what he was thinking, the Englishman asked, "Does Joe know you came up here to the front?"

"Nah, he knows I got a pass, but he thinks I'm holed up in a Giza whorehouse. He'd give me hell if he knew where I really was."

"Well, I for one am quite glad you came out on this lark."

Dale slapped Bert on the shoulder and grinned at him. "Yeah, me, too."

The tank rolled on to the south, and they had gone several miles when movement to the west caught Dale's eye. The sun was lowering and casting a red glare over the arid landscape, and he almost didn't see anything. But when he did, he tapped Bert on the shoulder, pointed, and said, "What's that?"

Bert squinted through the binoculars for a few seconds, then suddenly exclaimed, "Oh, my God!"

Dale didn't like the sound of that. He leaned closer to the turret and asked, "Germans?"

"A Mark IV. A Panzer tank."

"Shit," Dale said. "You think he's seen us?"

Bert studied the German tank through the glasses for a moment, then said, "I'd say so. He's changed course to intercept us."

"How far away is he?"

"Half a mile, no more."

"Can we outrun him?"

"We can try. But it'll be bloody difficult to outrun that seventy-five-millimeter cannon on its turret."

Dale clenched his right hand into a fist and thumped it on the turret. "Well, then, we can fight. We've got a seventy-five-millimeter gun, too."

"Yes, but it's mounted on the hull, which means the Panzer is more maneuverable. And the shells from the thirty-seven-millimeter just bounce off its armor." Bert wiped the back of his hand across his mouth. "Those Panzers have so bloody much armor even our seventy-fives don't always dent them."

Dale thought furiously. "Yeah, but they're slow sons of bitches. Let's head east and see if we can get away from him."

Bert nodded in agreement with the suggestion, since there was nothing else they could do except make a stand. He relayed the order to Royce, who swung the tank into a ninety-degree turn and sent it due east at top speed.

That put the Panzer to their right, rear. Dale twisted his head to look over his shoulder at it. The turn had increased the gap between the two tanks, but not by much. However, given a chance the M3 might be able to pull away. Also, the Panzer's commander might not want to wander too far in this direction, which for the Germans was behind enemy lines.

Dale happened to be looking back when smoke and flame belched from the Panzer's cannon. A second later, an explosion about a hundred yards to the left threw dirt and rocks high into the air. For an opening shot, that was too blasted close, Dale thought. Fear and excitement had his heart pumping now, and all his senses seemed keener than usual.

The German crew was efficient. Their cannon blasted again, and this time the shell exploded ahead and to the right of the fleeing British tank. "They've got us bracketed!" Dale shouted to Bert as he clung to the outside of the turret, feeling terribly exposed. "The next one's liable to be right up our ass!"

Bert's eyes were wide with terror. He was trying his best to hold up under the strain of the pursuit, but he wasn't used to command.

Neither was Dale, but somebody had to do something. He said, "Gimme the earphones! You go down and load for your gunner! I'll see what I can come up with!"

Bert hesitated, then jerked his head in a nod. He pulled the earphones off his head and thrust them toward Dale. Dale took them, and Bert dropped out of the turret into the crew compartment.

Dale stood up, hanging on so that he wouldn't get pitched off the tank, and swung a leg into the turret. He climbed in and settled himself on the seat, then clamped the earphones over his head. Before he could say anything, a huge explosion threw him forward. He grabbed the front edge of the hatch opening and managed not to fall off the seat. His ear stung like blazes. When he reached up and touched it, his fingers came away bloody.

He twisted his head and saw the crater in the earth that was falling behind the tank. The German shell hadn't hit the M3 itself, but it had landed only a few yards behind it. Some shrapnel or a bit of gravel had nicked his ear, Dale decided. A few inches to the left and it would have bored into the base of his brain, no doubt killing him instantly.

He swallowed the feeling of sickness that welled up in his throat. It had been a close call, but he was still alive and the tank seemed to be undamaged. He said into the microphone, "Royce! Hard right!"

Royce was a bastard but he followed orders. The tank swung to the right. "Hard right! All the way around!" Dale said. "Gunner, you ready?"

"Ready," the man's voice said in Dale's ears.

"Full ahead!" Dale called as the M3 came in line with the Panzer that was rushing after it. He didn't know anything about elevations or ranges or anything else about how to fire a cannon, but he assumed the gunner did. "Fire whenever you're ready!"

A couple of seconds later, the 75-mm cannon on the hull roared. Dale felt the jolt of its firing through the body of the tank. At almost the same instant, the Panzer fired again, but the Honey's quick turnaround had spoiled the aim of its gunner. The German shell whistled harmlessly overhead and burst a good seventy-five yards to the rear. The British round, on the other hand, slammed up dirt less than ten yards in front of the Panzer.

Dale let out a whoop. "That threw some sand in their eyes! Left, Royce, turn left!"

Dale swayed in the turret as the tank made the sharp turn. He looked down inside the turret and saw the pistol grip that controlled the .30-caliber machine gun mounted just above the 37-mm turret cannon. He didn't know how to fire the cannon, but he figured he could squeeze the trigger of the machine gun if they got close enough to the Panzer for it to do any good.

"Right, hard right!"

That turn put them on the Panzer's flank, less than half a mile away now, and the distance was shrinking by the second. The Panzer swung toward them, and Dale called, "Give it all she's got, Royce!" A second later, as the M3 lunged ahead, the German gunner fired again, just as Dale was expecting. The round exploded forty yards behind them.

That was close enough for debris to pepper the tank with sharp pinging sounds. Dale ducked instinctively. He straightened in the turret and yelled, "Left!" If they continued on the way they were going, that would take them across the front of the enemy tank in a straight line, and that would be an easy shot.

The turn to the left took them still closer to the Panzer, however. No more than a quarter of a mile separated the two tanks as Royce made the turn and sent the M3 rocking ahead. Up in the turret, Dale grinned tightly. That German commander was probably getting frustrated as hell at the way his prey was jitterbugging around.

Dale figured they were still out of range, but he fired off a machine gun burst anyway, just to give the Krauts something else to think about. "Left!" he shouted over the interphone.

"That puts our back to them again!" the gunner protested.

"Do it, Royce!"

Royce made the turn, which headed the British tank toward a long, low ridge that would give them some cover if they could reach it before the Panzer blew them up. Dale glanced back at the German tank. It was still speeding after them, but its cannon was silent now. The commander probably wanted to get close enough to make sure of them before he ordered another round.

Dale swallowed hard as the tank reached the ridge and

roared up the slope. They would make a hell of a good target when they got to the top. He kept his eyes straight ahead now, not wanting to see the shell that was going to blow him to bits.

The tank crested the rise and dropped down on the far side. Dale started breathing again as he realized they hadn't been hit. Maybe the Panzer's cannon had jammed; maybe its commander wanted to get closer; maybe it was just a goddamned miracle—Dale didn't care. All that mattered was that fate had just dropped one last chance in their lap.

"Turn around, then stop!"

"What! Are you bloody insane? We've got to run—"

"Turn around, then stop!" Dale shouted again. "Do it!"

A new voice, full of pain, rasped in the earphones, "Do what the Yank says."

Dale's eyes widened. That voice could only belong to Captain Neville Sharp. The tank's real commander had regained consciousness at last, and Dale was ready to let him have his command back.

But before he could say anything to the captain, Sharp said, "It's all yours, Yank. Carry on."

"Oh, hell," Dale muttered as the tank made its broad turn and then came to a halt facing back up the slope. He said, "Yes, sir," then asked, "Ready, gunner?"

"Ready."

"You get one shot as they come over the top. Make it count."

The M3's engine was idling loudly, but Dale could still hear the rumbling and clanking from the Panzer as it approached the top of the ridge. The little valley formed by the ridge was already in shadow from the gathering dusk, and Dale was counting on that to give them a second's advantage. The sky above the ridge was still light but growing rosy with the approach of sunset.

Suddenly the Panzer was there, looming over the crest like some sort of prehistoric behemoth, and Dale yelled, "Fire!" Flame licked from the muzzle of the Honey's cannon as it launched the 75-mm shell. Dale saw it fly straight and true into the underbelly of the Panzer.

The explosion seemed to lift the Panzer off the ground for a second before it settled back down. Thick black smoke poured out through its hatches and ports. Dale wrapped his hand around the pistol grip of the machine gun in case any of the crew came out and tried to keep fighting. No one emerged from inside the Panzer, however, and after a few minutes of the furious blaze inside the German tank, Dale was convinced that no one ever would.

He let out his breath and suddenly felt shaky. If that shot had missed, or if it had failed to knock out the Panzer, he and his companions would be the ones roasting inside a burning tank. It had been a gamble, pure and simple, with the highest stakes of all.

Someone tugged on his foot. He looked down and saw Captain Sharp gazing up at him. "Who the bloody hell are you?" Sharp asked.

"Dale Parker, sir."

"Well, you did a good job, Parker, but that's my seat. Kindly remove yourself from it."

"Yes, sir." Dale took off the earphones and climbed out of the turret.

Carefully, assisted by Bert Crimmens, Sharp climbed into the commander's seat. He looked at Dale and said, "You're bleeding, you know."

Dale touched his ear. "Yeah, I got a little scratch back there."

"You're not supposed to be here, are you?"

"No, sir."

"You're one of those American instructors from back at base depot, aren't you? I seem to recall seeing you there."

"Yes, sir."

"What are you doing out here on the Gazala Line usurping command of a British tank?"

"Well . . . sir . . ." Dale thought furiously, but at last all he could do was say helplessly, "It seemed like the thing to do at the time."

Sharp looked at him for a moment, then smiled. "I'd say we were bloody lucky that I asked you to come along as an observer on this jaunt, wouldn't you, Parker?"

Dale realized what the captain was saying: Sharp was going to cover for him with the brass, both British and American. Everyone would probably suspect what Dale had done, but as long as Hell-on-Treads Sharp was vouching for him, he wouldn't get into too much trouble.

"Yes, sir, I'd say we're all pretty lucky."

Sharp nodded, then said into the microphone, "Steer around that burning tank, Royce, and set course for leaguer. Let's get out of here before more Jerries come to call."

FORTY-FOUR

Not as confidently as he meant to, Phil Lange put his weight on his right ankle and waited to see what was going to happen. He felt a little pain, but not much, and the ankle, indeed the whole leg, seemed sturdy enough. It gave no indication of wanting to buckle beneath him.

"Walk across the room," Dr. Johnston said.

Phil did so while the doctor, as well as Missy Mitchell and Catherine Bergman, watched him. He turned around and walked back, then looked up at Johnston and the nurses and said, "It feels okay."

"It should. We do good work here." Johnston nodded in satisfaction. "Be careful when you're jumping down from planes in the future, and you should be all right."

"Yes, sir," Phil said, suppressing a surge of irritation. It wasn't as if he had been careless when he broke his ankle. It was just bad luck.

Johnston picked up a manila folder from the desk in his office. "Here's the worst of it: the paperwork. The forms in here clear you for return to active duty, Lieutenant, and contain orders transferring you back to the *Lexington,* which at this moment is returning to the South Pacific from Pearl Harbor."

Phil's eyebrows lifted. This was the first he'd heard about the *Lady Lex* going back to Pearl.

Johnston saw the reaction. He chuckled and said, "That's right, Lieutenant. By breaking your ankle and then developing that infection, you missed your chance at the fleshpots of Honolulu."

Phil glanced at Missy and murmured, "Yes, sir." He was surprisingly embarrassed by the doctor's comment.

Catherine came over to him and held out her hand. "You've been a fine patient, Lieutenant. Good luck."

"Thank you, ma'am," Phil said as he shook hands with her. "Good luck to you, too, and to your husband and that writer friend of yours."

Catherine smiled and nodded as she let go of his hand. He turned to Missy, who said, "Come on, Lieutenant, and I'll help you get your gear together."

"Thank you, Nurse," Phil said formally.

Johnston said from the desk, "There's a PBY leaving the air station here at 1100 hours that'll rendezvous with the *Lexington*. Don't miss it, Lieutenant."

"I won't, sir. Thank you."

Phil and Missy left the doctor's office and started down a companionway toward the ward. They took a detour before they got there, stepping into a narrow passage that led to a stairway. Even on a busy ship such as the *Solace,* there were nooks and crannies where people could be unobserved—and by this time Phil and Missy knew most of them.

She was in his arms in a second, her arms around his neck and her lips on his. He held her tight against him, so tight that he could feel the pounding of her heart as well as his own. Her tongue slid into his mouth, making the desire he felt for her spike upward.

When she finally took her lips away from his, she whispered, "I can't believe this. I can't believe you have to go."

"We knew this day was coming. It had to."

"But we haven't had enough time . . ." Her words trailed off into a sob, and she buried her face against his shoulder.

Phil felt the sting of tears in his own eyes. A couple of weeks had passed since that night on the fantail of the ship when Missy had come to him in the moonlight. The time seemed to have passed in the blink of an eye, and yet he felt as if he had known her forever. Had loved her forever.

She had told him later, once they knew each other better, about her hesitation that night. She had worried that he was on the rebound, that he was turning to her only because he was hurting from Catherine's rejection.

"It wasn't really a rejection," he told her. "I mooned over her for a couple of weeks until I found out she's married, that's all. It never really amounted to anything except wishful thinking on my part."

"And you never even looked at me in all that time," Missy had said, punching him playfully on the arm.

"Oh, I looked at you, all right. I looked a lot."

"Don't lie. I know when a guy's looking at me."

"I was careful about it."

He'd been kidding her a little, but it was true. He really did know how pretty and sexy she was, even when he was smitten with Catherine. A guy would have to be blind not to be aware of Missy Mitchell's sensual appeal. Blind, deaf, and not even able to smell her perfume. When she first came into his arms and kissed him, the impact was like a thunderbolt. Maybe he was lucky, he thought, that Catherine had turned out to have a husband.

Now, a couple of weeks later, he knew he was lucky. His feelings for Missy were stronger than he had experienced for any girl since high school. And none of the girls he'd dated back in New York were any match for Missy.

He leaned back against the bulkhead behind him and stroked her dark hair as he held her. "Don't worry," he said. "The *Solace* is going to be here in the South Pacific for a while, and so is the *Lexington*. We'll see each other again."

"Only if you get hurt!"

"Not necessarily. The carriers put into port sometimes, and the guys get liberty. It could be here at Tonga."

Missy looked into his eyes. "We don't know that. We don't know that we'll ever see each other again after today."

"We'll write—"

"The hell with that! It's not enough." She reached up and touched his cheek with her fingertips. "We never even made love."

"Missy . . ."

"I love you, Phil. I want to *make* love with you."

"We can't. There's no place, no time—"

"Damn it! There's got to be. I'm not going to let you go without it, even if I have to break your other ankle!" She stepped back and took his hand. "Come on."

"Where are we going?" he asked as she led him out of the passage and back into the main companionway.

"To my quarters."

"You can't be serious! There are other nurses in there."

"I'll kick 'em out. I'm tired of your excuses, Lange. You're gonna have your way with me, whether you like it or not."

"We'll both get thrown in the brig, maybe even dishonorably discharged."

She paused and looked back over her shoulder at him. "It'll be worth it," she promised.

Somehow, Phil didn't doubt her.

*　　★　　★*

She found it very hard to believe. A handsome young pilot like that, and she'd been his first. His very first. But afterward, she was the one who'd cried and clung to him like a deflowered virgin, and he had to hold her and pat her on the back and tell her that everything was going to be all right. He told her he loved her and that he would be with her again and everything would be all right.

Missy wanted to believe him. She wanted to believe so much that it was a sharp ache inside her.

But she couldn't bring herself to go up on deck and watch the PBY taxi across the harbor and take off. She stayed in her quarters, sprawled on the bunk, clutching the pillow tightly to her and doing something she had thought she would never do again.

She prayed. Prayed for Phil, and for herself.

But mostly for Phil.

While the *Lexington* was back in Pearl Harbor for repairs, the *Enterprise* and the *Hornet* had steamed northward on another mission, leaving the *Yorktown* as the lone carrier in the Southwestern Pacific. Taking off from the *Hornet,* a flight of U.S. Army Air Corps bombers under the command of Lt. Col. James H. "Jimmy" Doolittle had struck at Tokyo itself, taking the Japanese completely by surprise. Though the bombing raid shook the Japanese and did wonders for American morale, it also meant that the two carriers involved were too far north to become involved if any more hostilities broke out in the South Pacific, which was inevitable considering the way the Japanese Army was sweeping through the Solomon Islands, northeast of Australia.

The Japanese had already captured New Britain, Bougainville, New Georgia, Savo, Guadalcanal, and much of New Guinea. Their objectives now were the city of Port Moresby, near the eastern tip of New Guinea, and the island of Tulagi. Before pressing on, however, the Army commanders requested carrier support, because they knew from reconnaissance flights that the American Navy had carriers in the area. The Imperial Navy agreed, sending three carriers to the Coral Sea, between the Solomons and Australia.

Once Tulagi and Port Moresby fell, the Japanese would have succeeded in cutting off Australia from the rest of the Pacific. Then, according to their commanders, it would be only a short time before the Army crossed the Coral Sea and invaded Australia itself, allowing Japan to take another step on the path to the divine destiny that awaited it.

The old girl looked *good,* Phil thought as the PBY approached the *Lexington*. The flight had taken several hours, and although that time had done little to dull the ache of leaving Missy, he felt his heart speed up as he looked over the carrier. The flying boat landed and taxied up next to the *Lexington,* which had stopped its engines for the rendezvous.

One recuperated flier wasn't the only reason for the PBY meeting the carrier. Several other men who had been patients on the *Solace* were being returned to duty, and more injured and sick men would be flown back from the carrier to the hospital ship. A lighter ferried the passengers between the PBY and the *Lexington*.

Phil went up a ladder to a hatch that led onto the hangar deck. A small delegation was on hand to greet him and the other men who were returning to duty. Phil and his companions saluted, requested permission to come aboard, and then were welcomed with handshakes and slaps on the back.

Jerry Bennett was waiting for Phil, a big grin on his round face. "Partner!" he said as he threw his arms around Phil for a bear hug.

"Careful," Phil warned him with a smile. "This ankle of mine just healed up. You don't want to break something else."

Jerry stepped back, put his hands on Phil's shoulders, and looked him over. "They must have taken good care of you on that hospital ship."

Phil tried not to think of Missy and what had happened this morning as he said, "Yeah, they took real good care of me."

Jerry didn't help matters by asking, "Were there a lot of pretty nurses on board?"

"Yeah, they all looked like Carole Lombard," Phil said, knowing how Jerry felt about her.

Jerry rolled his eyes. "Oh, man! You lucky stiff. Lazing around with a bunch of gorgeous nurses to wait on you, while the rest of us were out here sweating and fighting Japs."

"Is that so? Seems to me I heard something about three weeks at Pearl Harbor . . ."

"Don't believe it. Don't believe a thing you hear, especially if it has anything to do with me and three nineteen-year-old Polynesian girls." Jerry threw an arm around Phil's shoulders. "Come on; let's go look at the plane."

They made their way past the other planes stored on the hangar deck until they came to the SBD Dauntless that Phil had flown. He recognized it immediately, even though some work had been done to it while the carrier was in Pearl Harbor. He frowned as he touched the metal skin of the fuselage.

"This looks like somebody patched up some bullet holes."

"Well, yeah," Jerry said. "The plane was up on deck one day when a Zero strafed us, before we went up to Pearl. She took a few slugs. No real harm done, though."

Phil patted the airplane. "Sorry," he muttered. "If I'd been here, I wouldn't have let that happen."

"Hey, there was nothing I could do!" Jerry said.

"Who's been flying her?"

"Different guys. I've been riding shotgun, though, every time, just to make sure everything's all right."

Phil nodded. "Thanks. It'll be good to get back up in the air."

"They're going to let you fly again? You're all clear?"

"All clear," Phil said.

Jerry clenched a fist and grinned. "Man, oh, man, we're back in business! Just in time, too."

"Just in time? What does that mean?"

"You haven't heard? This was our last stop. From here we're headed to the Coral Sea. They say the Japs have some carriers on their way down there, and we're gonna be there to give 'em a nice warm American welcome."

FORTY-FIVE

Phil tugged the leather flying helmet down over his ears as he hurried along the companionway to the ready room. Jerry and half a dozen other pilots and observers were with him. It was the morning of 7 May 1942, and a few minutes earlier the alarm had sounded as the men were finishing up breakfast.

"This is it," Jerry said in a low voice to Phil as he struggled to buckle the strap of his helmet under his chin. "This time we go get 'em for sure. That's what my gut's tellin' me."

Phil nodded, but he wasn't sure if he really agreed with Jerry's instincts or not. There had been some close calls before.

A few days earlier, Japanese forces had captured the island of Tulagi. Admiral Frank Jack Fletcher, commander of the carrier group in the Southwestern Pacific, had sent planes from the *Yorktown* to attack the Japs on Tulagi. The pilots expected to find one of the Jap carriers there, but they saw no sign of one. Their attack sank several smaller Japanese ships, however, and Fletcher declared the engagement a victory.

If there were Japanese carriers in the area, the raid on Tulagi would surely draw them out, Fletcher reasoned, and it also stood to reason that they would steam between New Guinea and Bougainville into the northern part of the Coral Sea. Accordingly, he ordered the *Yorktown* and the *Lexington* to proceed northwest, past the eastern end of the Solomons. That put them practically on a collision course with the Japanese carriers.

So the level of readiness on the American ships had been high for the past couple of days, and so had the level of tension. They

JAMES REASONER

were here to carry the fight to the Japs for a change, and everyone was anxious to get started.

The pilots and observers filed into the ready room. Captain Frederick C. "Ted" Sherman, the skipper of the *Lexington,* stood beside a table at the front of the room, with several maps on the wall behind him. There were also maps on the side walls of the room.

Rows of wooden-backed seats that always reminded Phil of seats in a movie theater filled the room, enough for forty men. Some of them were already occupied. Phil and the rest of the fliers with him sat down, and soon every seat in the room was filled. All the men wore flying suits, leather flight jackets, and most had already donned their leather helmets. Goggles dangled on rubber straps around their necks.

Sherman began by picking up a pointer and indicating a spot on the main map behind him, which was a map of the Coral Sea and the surrounding area, including New Guinea and the Solomons as well as the northeastern coast of Australia. He said, "A short time ago, Japanese fighters and dive bombers attacked the destroyer *Sims* and the fleet oiler *Neosho,* here and here." He tapped the pointer on spots on the map not far south of the current positions of the *Yorktown* and *Lexington,* which were marked by small flags attached to push pins. "The *Neosho* suffered considerable damage. The *Sims* was struck by several bombs and sank."

Sherman paused to let the seriousness of that news settle in. That didn't take long. Every man in the room knew that if the *Sims* had gone down, then many of her crew had gone down with her.

The skipper continued, "We've also received word that one of the SBDs from the *Yorktown* located two Japanese carriers and four cruisers some two hundred and twenty-five miles northwest of here. It's a safe bet the planes that attacked the *Sims* and the *Neosho* came from those carriers."

Phil sensed the anger in the room, but no one said anything. The time for muttering curses was long since past. Now they finally had their chance to fight back.

"Admiral Fletcher has ordered us to launch a deck-load strike," Sherman said. "Here is the course you'll follow."

Quickly, using the pointer, he sketched the route the dive bombers, torpedo planes, and fighters would take. Phil slid a small notebook and a pencil from the pocket of his flight jacket and jotted down the course in case he had to refer to it later. He didn't think that was very likely; everything Sherman had said was burned into his brain.

"The *Yorktown* will launch a flight to follow ours and mop up," Sherman went on, "but you boys have the honor of getting in the first licks. Make them count."

All the men in the room nodded their agreement. They were ready to go.

Sherman dismissed them, and they left the ready room. A short climb up one of the ship's ladders brought them to the hatch that led from the superstructure out onto the flight deck. They found that the elevators had already brought up all their planes, and the flight crews had wheeled them into position and chocked the wheels. The fighters—Grumman F4F-3 Wildcats—would take off first, followed by the Dauntless dive bombers and finally the torpedo planes, Douglas TBD Devastators.

They would follow that same order in establishing a three-tiered formation once they were in flight. The Wildcats soared the highest, above 16,000 feet, where they could give cover to the dive bombers and torpedo planes if they happened to run into a flight of Japanese Zeros. Next, at around 12,000 feet, would come the Dauntlesses, and lowest of all, at less than 10,000 feet, would be the Devastators. Each group of planes flew at the altitude that would be most effective in combat.

Phil had been through countless practice runs, but today he sensed immediately the difference between those and the real thing. He was scared, but not overly so. Takeoffs and landings on a flattop always had their dangers, even in peacetime. What he felt today was the anticipation of actually accomplishing something. Maybe he would never know the satisfaction of standing in front of a classroom and teaching, but he could still do something today to make the world a better place, a safer place. Breathing deeply, he shook hands with Jerry, then patted the metal skin of the airplane as he climbed up into the cockpit.

After that, there wasn't really any time for thinking or worrying. He and Jerry carried out all their pre-flight checks. The Wildcats in the front ranks began taking off. After the airedales removed the chocks, Phil started the Dauntless's engine and taxied forward slowly, keeping his place in line. In what seemed like only a matter of seconds, there was nothing in front of the plane except open deck, with the carrier's superstructure rising to the right and the open sea beyond the end of the deck. As the ship rose on a swell, the launching officer waved Phil ahead with his flag, signalling that he was cleared for takeoff. He pushed the throttle forward.

Taking off from a carrier required a pilot to build up flight speed in a hurry. Phil poured the power to the engine, calling on all 1200 horses. The acceleration pushed him back against the seat, slackening the web harness around him for a second.

Then the deck dropped out from under the plane, and Phil felt his heart thudding wildly at the sickening lurch, as it always did. But the stick responded and the Dauntless lifted, and Phil began to breathe easier. He said to Jerry, "All right back there?"

"Yeah, doin' fine."

Phil banked the plane into a wide, climbing turn that brought it into the formation. He tipped his head back to look for the Wildcats, but they were so high already that he could barely see them. He climbed to twelve thousand feet, which took almost ten minutes, then leveled off and throttled back to cruising speed. He could see some of the other dive bombers on both flanks, so he knew he was in the right place, but he checked his instruments anyway, mentally noting the compass and course headings.

The heat of sea level had disappeared. It was cold up here, making Phil grateful for the fleece-lined flight jacket. There were a few high clouds, but for all practical purposes, the ceiling was unlimited, and so was visibility. Phil looked around, seeing nothing but endless ocean.

"Well, it's up to you and the other spotters now," he said to Jerry. "Find those Japs for us."

"Aye, aye, Cap'n."

Despite what he had just said, Phil wasn't going to rely totally on Jerry's eyesight. He had a small pair of binoculars in the side pocket of the seat. When they reached the area where the Jap ships were supposed to be, he would have a look for himself. The Dauntless wouldn't fly itself, but the controls could spare him for a few minutes at a time.

As the sun rose higher in the sky, it reflected more off the ocean, making it even more difficult to see. Spotting ships from this high wasn't easy to start with. The glare made it even harder. Of course, cloud cover brought its own problems with it, Phil thought. No two ways about it, they were faced with quite a task.

The planes droned on, heading northwest. Just past mid-morning, Jerry said, "Uh-oh."

"What is it?"

"Word from the *Lex* is that *Yorky*'s scouts sent the wrong message earlier this morning. They didn't spot any Jap flattops after all, just some cruisers and destroyers."

"Damn! Are we going to hit them anyway?"

"If we can find them."

Phil saw one of the Dauntlesses climbing and recognized it as the plane being flown by Lt. Cmdr. W. L. "Ham" Hamilton. Ham was trying to get a better vantage point, and it paid off a short time later. Over the radio, Phil heard the report that enemy ships had been spotted twenty miles to the north.

Phil felt his pulse begin to beat a little faster, but he cautioned himself not to get too excited just yet. "It's probably just those cruisers and destroyers."

"Maybe. We ought to know in a few minutes."

Phil got out his binoculars and started searching the vast ocean below. For several minutes, he didn't see anything except water, but then, as he swept the glasses from side to side, something suddenly flashed into view. It was just as suddenly gone. Phil leaned forward and tried to bring the binoculars back to where he had been looking a second earlier, compensating for the forward motion of the plane. It was a tricky business, but then, abruptly, there it was again, a flash of light. That light had to be reflecting off something big and flat down below, something besides the ocean.

"There it is! There it is! My God, I see it, Phil! It's a flattop, a Jap flattop!"

"I see it, too," Phil told Jerry, his voice shaky with excitement.

On the radio, Phil heard the other pilots and observers chattering about the Japanese carrier. Orders were passed around. The Dauntlesses and Devastators would coordinate their strikes, attacking the carrier at the same time. They began dropping to lower altitudes as they approached the carrier.

Phil could see the flattop without the binoculars now. That meant the Japs could probably see the flight of American planes, too, and down there on the ship they would be scurrying frantically to their posts, trying to get ready to fight off the attack. It was his job, and the job of the other American flyboys, to see that they didn't have time.

The order to dive sounded in Phil's earphones, and he called, "Here we go!" to Jerry. He shoved the stick forward and used the left rudder to kick the plane into a half-roll that dropped the nose. Air began to shriek around the cockpit as the Dauntless built up even more speed, held back only by the perforated surfaces of its opened dive flaps. The flight of bombers hurtled down out of the sky, aimed straight at the Japanese carrier as if they intended to crash into it.

Several thousand feet below them, the Devastators flew directly at the ship, too, only on a level course. Each of the Devastators carried a single, thousand-pound torpedo. When they were close enough, the pilots launched the torpedoes, sending them splashing into the water, then peeled off to make way for the dive bombers.

The Japs were putting up a fight. Even in the brilliant midday sun, Phil saw tracers coursing out from the muzzles of machine guns mounted on the deck, and rounds from the anti-aircraft guns burst in the sky, blossoming into innocent-looking black puffs that were really full of deadly shrapnel. From the corner of his eye, Phil saw an anti-aircraft round blow off the right wing of one of the Dauntlesses and send it spinning crazily out of control in a fall that would take it into the ocean.

Phil's jaw tightened. He wrapped the fingers of his left hand around the stick and placed his thumb on the button on top of it that would release the plane's bomb. Not yet, he told himself, holding the plane in its dive. Not just yet. . . .

The flight deck of the Japanese carrier seemed to rush up at him. He saw the planes parked on it, ready to take off and deal more death and destruction. Small figures ran to some of the planes, pilots, no doubt, who thought they might be able to get their craft off the deck and into the air before the bombs hit.

They were going to be disappointed.

Like a falling rock, the Dauntless kept plummeting toward the ship. Phil shook off the hypnotizing power of the dive and yanked back on the stick at the same time as he released the bombs under the wings. Freed suddenly of its nearly two thousand pounds of bombs, the SBD leaped up. The sudden change in direction was sickening. Phil swallowed the nausea and kept the plane climbing. Even over the howling of the engine, he heard the explosions below as the bombs found their target.

Jerry had the best view of the show. He whooped. "We got 'em; we got 'em! Man, oh, man, those Japs don't know what hit 'em!"

Phil twisted his head around and craned his neck to watch the destruction going on below. He saw flames on the carrier's flight deck, and smoke came from somewhere inside the ship. The carrier must have taken direct hits from several bombs and torpedoes, and more were coming. The flight from the *Yorktown* would be here within minutes.

"Damn, I wish we could hang around to watch," Jerry said. "She's gonna go down; I just know she is."

Phil agreed with that assessment, and he wouldn't have minded seeing the carrier sink, either. But they didn't want to be in the way as the rest of the attack was carried out. "Time to go home," he said.

"Yeah, I guess so." Jerry paused. "I thought you were gonna fly right down their smokestack. I don't mind tellin' you, I was gettin' a little worried back here. You haven't gone and developed a death wish, have you?"

Phil thought about Missy Mitchell. He had more reason to live now than ever before. "Nope," he said. "I just wanted to make sure we put those bombs right where they were supposed to go."

"We sure did."

Phil joined the rest of the Dauntlesses and Devastators flying southeast toward the spot where they had left the *Lexington*. Less than half an hour later, while they were still in the air, the radio brought the news that the Japanese carrier, tentatively identified as the *Shoho,* had indeed gone down with all of her crew. The initial engagement of this battle was a definite American victory, the first one in what seemed like a long, long time.

And every man from the *Yorktown* and the *Lexington,* from the pilots to the machinist's mates in the engine room, was determined that it wouldn't be the last.

FORTY-SIX

That evening, a flight of Japanese Val dive bombers and Kate torpedo planes, searching for the American carriers, almost literally ran into four patrolling Wildcats from the *Lexington*. Phil heard all about the dogfight from Lt. Cmdr. Paul Ramsey, who had been flying one of the American fighters. Though outnumbered, the Wildcats had torn into the Japanese planes with a ferocity worthy of their name. Reinforced by more F4F-3s from the *Yorktown,* the Americans wreaked havoc among the enemy bombers, which were unaccompanied by Zeros that might have provided protection for them. Nine of the Vals and Kates went into the ocean before the Wildcats broke off the attack.

In fleeing, the surviving Japanese pilots flew over the *Yorktown* without knowing it, mistaking it in the dark for one of their own carriers. One of them was shot down by anti-aircraft fire from the American flattop. The other planes roared off into the night, wanting no part of a fight now. The story was greeted with triumphant laughter as it was passed around the crews of both carriers.

Phil's sleep that night was restless. His dreams were a jumble of images: Missy, the flight deck of the Japanese carrier as he dove at it, the Dauntless he had seen shot down, one of several that had been lost in the attack. He woke up more than once, sweating, his heart pounding, the scream of air past the cockpit in his ears. No amount of training could really prepare a man for his first time in combat, he thought. It was something that had to be experienced for itself. Men who had been through it could talk about it, and their words would ring true, but even hearing the truth was nothing like living it.

Over breakfast the next morning, most of the pilots were subdued. The battle the day before had been the first action for many of them. They looked at each other over the tables in the officers' mess and knew they shared a bond that nothing could ever break.

Reconnaissance flights had taken off at dawn, and the word wasn't long in coming back from them. Two Japanese carriers had been spotted 175 miles away, to the northeast this time instead of the northwest, not far from the island of Guadalcanal. The call to arms sounded, and within minutes Phil and Jerry, along with the other Navy aviators, were on their way to the ready room.

Strikes would be launched from both American carriers, Captain Sherman explained. The pilots listened intently during the briefing, with Phil, among others, taking notes as he had the day before. Then they headed up to the flight deck to claim their planes.

The whole thing had taken on an air of familiarity, though by no stretch of the imagination did any of the men consider any of it routine. But they had been through it once, and now they knew what to expect. Phil felt a slight tingle of impatience as he and Jerry ran their pre-flight checks and then waited for their turn to take off. He wanted to be in the air.

Soon enough, he was.

"Think we'll get another flattop today?" Jerry asked as Phil put the Dauntless into its climb.

"I wouldn't say *we* got that one yesterday," Phil said. "There were a lot of guys out there dropping bombs and launching torpedoes."

"Yeah, but you know one of ours hit. I saw it land right there on the flight deck. Blew the hell out of a couple of Kates and left a big hole in the deck. Who knows how much other damage it did."

Phil figured it was more likely some of the torpedoes from the Devastators had been responsible for sinking the Japanese carrier, but he didn't say anything. There was nothing wrong with Jerry being proud of what they had done. He was pretty proud himself. He was going to write a letter to Missy and tell her all about it.

The formation was the same as the day before. The major difference was the weather. There were a lot more clouds today, and they seemed to be growing thicker all the time. The American planes flew on to the northeast, toward the Solomons, but as the clouds increased and visibility decreased, Phil began to worry that they wouldn't be able to find the Jap flattops. After a while, it was so bad he was having trouble seeing even the other planes in the formation.

"This is no good, Phil," Jerry said. "If this keeps up, we may have to turn ba—. Wait a minute! The guys from the *Yorktown* have spotted the Japs! They're going in!"

Phil had just heard that for himself on the radio, though the transmissions were garbled and full of static. "Did you hear any coordinates?" he asked.

"Damn it, no! I don't know where they are!"

Phil looked at the clouds for a moment, then said, "I'm going down some." He dropped the Dauntless into a gentle descent. He wasn't sure if he was breaking formation or not. For all he knew, some or all of the other planes could be trying to drop out of the clouds, too.

Ten minutes passed, then a quarter of an hour, and still the gray-white clouds were thick around the plane. Phil leaned one way in the cockpit and then the other, searching for any sort of break that would give him a view of the ocean. He saw a flash of blue far below and called out to Jerry, "Down there!"

"I see it! Can we get a little lower?"

Phil thought about it. A dive bomber had to have height in order to be effective. Still, if they couldn't find the target, it wouldn't really matter, would it? He edged the stick forward and sent the Dauntless lower.

The clouds thinned and then parted. The ocean spread out below them. Jerry said, "Yeah! Now we can see what we're doing!"

Phil's eyes widened a little behind his goggles as he peered out through the Plexiglas canopy. "Carriers dead ahead!" he called.

The battle was already going on. He saw Wildcats and Zeros swooping in and out of cloud banks in their deadly, high-speed dogfights. Waves of torpedo bombers and dive bombers from the *Yorktown* were going in, targeting a Japanese carrier. Off in the distance, Phil spotted another ship that he thought might be a carrier, but he couldn't be sure about that. The one right in front of him was closer, so that was the one he was going for.

The carrier was twisting and turning in the water, changing course constantly, and as Phil closed in he realized the flattop was dodging the torpedoes launched by the Devastators. He bit back a curse as he saw several of the torpedoes race harmlessly past the Jap carrier. The ship's commander was good; you had to give him credit for that. As Phil watched, the carrier even managed to dodge several of the bombs being dropped by the Dauntlesses.

One of the SBDs launched itself in a screaming dive like a comet falling from the heavens. Phil watched as the pilot sent his plane almost straight down at the carrier. He kept expecting to see the bombs drop and the plane lift back up, but it didn't happen. He found himself muttering, "Release! Release, damn it!"

Finally, when Phil estimated that the plummeting Dauntless was less than two hundred feet above the flight deck of the carrier, the bombs fell. "Pull up!" Phil screamed as explosions slammed the carrier. "Pull up!"

The Dauntless's pilot tried, but he was too low. Even with the lessened weight, the plane's nose wouldn't come up. It smashed into the ocean only a few yards from the hull of the Japanese carrier, throwing water high into the air in a huge splash. Phil squeezed his eyes shut in horror, knowing all too well that the two men in that Dauntless had just given their lives to inflict damage on the enemy vessel.

He opened his eyes after only a second, gave a little shake of his head, and called out to Jerry, "Hang on!" He was already lined up for his dive. He shoved the stick ahead.

The plane dropped, whistling toward the sea between puffs of anti-aircraft fire. Phil was aware that Jerry was muttering, "Oh, shit, oh, shit," but he didn't pay any attention. He kept the Dauntless in its dive. Acceleration pressed him back in the seat like a giant hand.

He wasn't following the example of the pilot who had crashed into the ocean. He fully intended to pull up in time. But he wasn't going to miss with his bombs, either. He readied himself for the release.

Five hundred feet . . . four hundred . . . the needle on the altimeter dropping like a rock . . . Phil saw every detail distinctly now: the fires on the flight deck, the Japanese sailors scrambling for cover or for another defensive position, the little black clouds of anti-aircraft fire on both sides of the Dauntless. Three hundred feet . . . two-fifty . . .

Now.

He released the bombs and pulled back on the stick. The flight deck that had filled his vision a split-second earlier was gone and now he saw only the water rushing at him. Someone yelled in terror. Phil didn't know if it was him or Jerry, didn't care. Water . . . horizon . . . sky—the nose came up.

With a shrieking roar from its engine, the Dauntless lifted into the air, whipping past the carrier so close that Phil could see the sailors on board the ship staring goggle-eyed at him. Phil kept the plane climbing until it was well out of range of the anti-aircraft fire. Then he started to circle, banking a little so that he could look down at the carrier.

The attack had done a lot of damage, but he wasn't sure it had been enough to sink the Jap flattop. It was still steaming along despite the fires on its flight deck and the smoke coming from inside it. It wasn't even heeling over.

"Damn," Phil said. "We should have hit it harder."

"Hit it . . . harder . . ." Jerry said, wheezing a little. "My God . . . we were so close we could've thrown a fuckin' rock at 'em! There's nothing else we can do, Phil."

"I know." Phil checked the compass and put the plane on a heading that would take it back toward the *Lexington*. "We took our best shot. That'll have to be good enough."

The Dauntless had climbed back into the clouds. There were no formations any longer, just individual planes either heading back home or trying to get in an attack on the Japanese carriers. Phil kept an eye out all around him and told Jerry to do the same. With the planes scattered the way they were, he didn't want to fly right into one of them.

After an hour, when he judged that they were getting close to the point where the *Lexington* should be, Phil began dropping to a lower altitude again. The clouds thinned and broke apart, and the plane suddenly emerged into dazzling sunshine. Phil blinked behind his goggles.

"You see the ship?" he asked Jerry.

"No, not yet. We're not lost, are we, Phil?"

Phil checked the instruments. He knew within a few miles where they ought to be, and the *Lady Lex* ought to be coming within sight any minute now. "We're okay," he said.

The Dauntless carried more fuel than either the Devastator or the Wildcat and had a range of 1100 miles under normal operating conditions. Phil had put a strain on that today. Still, the gauge on the instrument panel showed that the fuel tanks were half-full. He had plenty of gas to cruise around for a while and look for the *Lexington*.

"You hear any chatter on the radio?" he asked Jerry.

"The radio's dead. I think it died of fright during the dive you pulled."

Phil frowned. He didn't like being out of radio contact. That could lead to all sorts of problems, even mistaken identity when he tried to land. He sure didn't want the gunners on the ship thinking that he was a Jap. That would be a hell of an ending to this mission, to be shot down by his own guys.

A few minutes later, he spotted smoke on the horizon. "There's something," he said, "but it doesn't look too good."

He increased the speed and roared toward the south. The

dark speck at the base of the rising smoke soon resolved itself into a familiar shape, and as Phil realized what he was looking at, his heart seemed to drop all the way into his belly. "Jerry," he said in a choked voice.

"What is it?"

"The *Lexington*. She's on fire."

FORTY-SEVEN

The Dauntless flew on toward the carrier. Jerry said, "Better buzz 'em first and give 'em a wing waggle, so they'll get a good look at us."

"I was just thinking the same thing," Phil said. Everyone on the ship was familiar with the shape of the Dauntless. They would recognize the approaching plane as one of their own.

But it might not matter, because they might not be able to land anyway. The flight deck was clear, but grayish-black smoke drifted from the superstructure along its edge. As the plane came closer, Jerry exclaimed, "Look at the smokestack! Something hit it!"

"The Japs must've found the *Lex* while we were bombing their carriers." Phil pointed. "There's the *Yorktown,* about a mile off to starboard."

"Doesn't look like she's been hit. We may have to land over there."

Phil nodded. He was prepared to land on the other carrier if necessary, even though he had never done so, even in practice. But one flattop was pretty much like another, he told himself.

That didn't explain the lump in his throat or the tightness in his chest when he looked at the *Lexington* and saw the damage to the old girl. Whatever was happening down there, he hoped the crew was able to get it under control soon.

The Dauntless buzzed past the flight desk at low altitude, as slowly as possible. Phil wagged the plane's wings in a signal to let the men on the carrier know he was friendly. A couple of men ran out onto the flight deck from the superstructure. Phil looked at them, pointed at his ear, and shook his head. He hoped they got a good look at him through the canopy over the cockpit and understood that he was trying to tell them the radio was out. He looped around and started back again.

Jerry put his binoculars on the deck and said, "They're using the paddles to tell us to come on in. Even with the damage, they've got flight operations up and running."

Phil nodded and started lining up the plane for a landing. "Will do."

He greased the landing, bringing the Dauntless in perfectly. The hook caught the cable and brought them to the usual jolting halt. Phil killed the engine and popped the canopy.

Members of the flight crew ran out to meet them as they climbed onto the wing of the plane. "What happened?" Phil asked, even though he already knew the answer.

"The Japs hit us about an hour ago!" one of the airedales replied. "The Kates got us with a couple of torpedoes, and a couple of bombs from the Vals hit us, too. Most of the damage is under control, though."

Phil felt a wave of relief go through him. When he'd first sighted the *Lexington* and realized the carrier had been hit, he was afraid that it might sink. Now it appeared that wasn't going to be the case.

He pulled off his goggles and helmet and unzipped his flight jacket. The air on the flight deck stunk of smoke. He asked the airedales, "Can you get the plane down to the hangar deck?"

One of the men shook his head. "The elevators are out. We'll have to just put it out of the way up here until we can get them fixed."

Phil shrugged. He would have preferred that the Dauntless be taken down to the hangar deck so that it would be safer in case the Japs came back for another bombing run. If the elevators didn't work, though, there was nothing that could be done about that.

He and Jerry went aft to one of the other hatches, away from the worst of the smoke, and clattered down the ladders to the main deck where the ready rooms and their quarters were located. Phil wanted to get out of his flight suit and back into a regular uniform. He wouldn't have minded a shower, but with everything else that was going on that was probably out of the question.

The commander who headed up the group of Dauntless dive bombers was waiting in the ready room to take their reports. In clear, concise terms, Phil and Jerry told him everything they had seen and done during the engagement with the Japanese carrier. All that information would go into the after-action report. While they were doing that, more of the returning planes came in and landed, and soon the edges of the flight deck began to grow crowded with parked airplanes. The elevators being knocked out was starting to be a problem.

Phil and Jerry hung around for a while in the ready room as the other pilots came in to give their reports, and the thing Phil had worried about was confirmed: The Jap flattop they'd bombed had not gone down, despite the extensive damage it had suffered. However, both Japanese carriers and the accompanying smaller vessels in their group had turned around and were steaming back north as fast as they could.

"We whipped 'em," Jerry said as he and Phil started toward their quarters. "They're running off with their tails between their legs."

"That's what it sounds like, all right," Phil said. "But we may have lost more—"

He never finished his sentence, because at that moment, the deck under their feet suddenly shuddered violently. From somewhere deep in the ship, a low rumble sounded.

"That was an explosion!" Jerry said as he and Phil steadied themselves. "Were we hit by another torpedo?"

"I don't think so. There wasn't any alarm."

That was no longer the case. Klaxons began to blare all over the ship. Helmets and goggles in hand, Phil and Jerry hurried back up toward the flight deck. As they climbed one of the ladders, it swayed and shook from another explosion down below.

"What the hell's happening?"

Phil shook his head. "I don't know, but it can't be good."

They emerged from the island and trotted out onto the flight deck to find dozens of pilots and crewmen milling around in confusion. Phil caught hold of another pilot's sleeve and asked, "Do you know what's going on?"

The harried-looking pilot shook his head. "No, but we're not under attack. I'm sure of that."

Phil looked up at the sky. It was clear, all right, not a plane in sight. The Japs might be indirectly responsible for the explosions that were rocking the carrier, but the blasts weren't direct results of a bomb or torpedo strike.

There was nothing to do but stand around and speculate. Ten minutes passed during which no more explosions were heard, and Phil began to hope that the worst was over. But then another blast made the flight deck shiver under his feet. Men yelled curses and questions, but there were no answers.

The smoke had almost stopped coming from inside the ship earlier, but now it began to billow out again, thick, dark choking clouds that forced the pilots and flight crews away from the island. Down in the bowels of the carrier, probably in the engine rooms, terrible fires had to be raging to produce that much smoke, Phil thought as he made his way to the railing and blinked away tears from the stinging smoke.

One of Captain Sherman's aides came down from the bridge and stumbled along the flight deck, calling out, "Get these planes in the air! We're going to have to abandon ship!"

Abandon ship. Those were the words every Navy man dreaded the most. Phil felt their impact like a blow from a fist. Except for the time he had spent on the *Solace,* the *Lexington* had been his home for the past two years. Hearing that she was going to go down was like being told that a family member was about to die.

But at least some of the planes could be saved. Phil tugged on his helmet, then glanced over at Jerry. Jerry looked just as aghast as

Phil felt. Phil touched his arm. "Let's go," he said. "We've got to get in the air."

Jerry jerked out of his daze and nodded. "Yeah. Let's go."

The usual routine was forgotten now. All over the flight deck, men scrambled into their planes, ran through their checks as quickly as possible, then started engines and taxied into position to take off. Nobody cared about proper formations. All that mattered was getting the planes off the *Lexington* while they still could.

And what about all the sailors on board? Phil asked himself as he waited for an opening to take off. He and Jerry could escape easily enough and fly the Dauntless over to the *Yorktown*. The other carrier would be crowded with planes if it took on all the *Lexington*'s refugees, but they could manage. The carrier's regular crew, though, would have to go into the drink.

A few minutes later, the SBD soared off the flight deck and into the air with Phil at the controls. Glad that the Dauntless still had plenty of fuel, he joined the other planes circling above the *Lexington* and the *Yorktown,* waiting for his turn to land. The smoke coming from the *Lexington* grew worse. The gray cloud was so thick amidships Phil could barely see the carrier's towering superstructure.

Sailors began to crowd onto the flight deck toward the bow. The order must have been given to abandon ship, Phil thought as he watched. Ropes were tied to the railing around the flight deck and dropped over the side, and the sailors began to scramble down them. Some lost their grip and fell before they made it all the way to the water. Some of the men wore life preservers, but others didn't. Small boats were already moving in from the *Yorktown* to rescue the men who were fleeing from the *Lexington,* but not all of them would make it, Phil thought. Some would drown before they could be picked up. And inside the carrier itself, many other sailors had surely died in the explosions or fighting the fires that resulted. The loss of life was going to be in the hundreds—if they were lucky.

When Phil's turn came, he brought the Dauntless down on the deck of the *Yorktown*. When the plane had been yanked to a stop, he and Jerry climbed out and let the deck crews take over. The *Yorktown* appeared to have been unhit during the earlier Jap raid, so all of her elevators were working. The hangar deck was going to be packed like a sardine can before this day was over, Phil thought.

He and Jerry gathered with the other aviators from the *Lexington,* and they were joined by some of the officers from the *Yorktown*. Finally, they found out what had happened. The damage inflicted by the Japanese bombs and torpedoes had caused a fuel spill somewhere inside the *Lexington,* and the fumes had built up to the point that a stray spark from a generator set them off. That explosion caused another and another, and the fires set off even more of the fuel.

"Your captain's already over here talking to Admiral Fletcher about scuttling her," one of the *Yorktown*'s officers told the men from the *Lexington*. "Sorry, fellas. I know that's the last thing you want to hear."

By late afternoon, as the fires still burned furiously within the *Lexington,* all hands had abandoned ship and everything that could be salvaged from the carrier had been taken off her. Many of the rescue boats were still in the water, packed with survivors who had been pulled from the sea. The *Yorktown* and the other ships in the carrier group pulled back, leaving only the destroyer *Phelps* close to the burning *Lexington*. The gunners on the Phelps readied torpedoes, and when the order came, they launched several of the deadly metal fish.

Phil, Jerry, and the other fliers from the *Lady Lex* stood at the railing of the *Yorktown* and watched with tears in their eyes as the torpedoes cut through the water and then slammed into the carrier. The explosions shook the *Lexington* and blew several large holes in the hull below the waterline. Slowly, the embattled carrier began to settle in the water. It was only a matter of time now until it sank completely.

"Those damned Japs," Jerry said as he watched, tears running down his face. "They'll pay for this. By God, they'll pay."

Phil didn't say anything, but he knew a day of reckoning was coming.

And he hoped he was there when it did.

FORTY-EIGHT

Karen was singing "Over the Rainbow." In the movie with all those midgets running around, that Judy Garland kid had sung it as a wistful ballad about homesickness. Here in the Dells, with Karen's sultry pipes wrapping themselves around the words, the song became a torch number instead, a smoky ode to heartbreak and loneliness. Mike Chastain lit a cigarette and marveled at Karen's ability to take just about any song and turn it into the blues.

She was good. He was no expert on music, but he knew she was damned good. With his eyes half-closed, he smoked and listened to her sing. She made him forget. . . .

Which was why he wasn't happy when a hand came down hard on his left shoulder and squeezed.

"Mike Chastain?"

Mike had the cigarette in the fingers of his left hand. His right moved instinctively toward the lapel of his coat, but he stopped the gesture after only a couple of inches. He wasn't carrying a gun, and besides, even if he had been, he couldn't start blazing away here in this ritzy nightspot. If he killed a guy and got blood on the floor, they'd never let him back in.

Trying to move casually and nonchalantly now, he turned his head and looked up at the man who was standing behind him. "Yeah?"

"Are you Mike Chastain?" The guy was big; Mike could tell that much even in the dim light of the club. And he had a voice like something being dragged down a gravel road.

"Who the hell wants to know?"

"Name's Carl Bowden. And you don't have to answer. I know you're Chastain. You been pointed out to me."

Mike looked down at the hand on his shoulder. "You want to move that before you wrinkle the fabric?"

Bowden lifted his hand, which had long, thick fingers with prominent knuckles. It looked like a prizefighter's hand, but he was no palooka, Mike decided. Everything else about him screamed cop.

Bowden moved around the table, followed by another, shorter guy. The second man was heavyset, wearing thick glasses with dark, square frames. Both men wore cheap suits and fedoras. Bowden pulled back a chair and sat down without asking if it was all right. The other guy hesitated for a second, then sat down, too.

"You want to see some badges," Bowden asked, "or will you take our word for it that we're cops?"

"I'll take your word for it," Mike said. "You start flashing badges in here, you're liable to give heart attacks to some of the customers. They're upper crust, so they're not used to flatfeet bargin' in."

"We're not barging in anywhere. You invited us to join you, didn't you, Chastain?"

Mike shrugged. "It wouldn't do any good if I said different, would it?"

"Not a damned bit. You're a cool character, you know that? You must really be used to being rousted by the cops."

"Nobody gets used to being harassed. If you've got something to say to me, Bowden, say it."

Bowden clasped his knobby-knuckled fingers together on the table. "What I've got for you is a question: Where were you an hour ago?"

Mike took a drag on the cigarette, blew out the smoke. "Right here," he said. "And I can prove it."

"You weren't down on the South Side trying to hijack a refrigerated truck full of meat?"

"Of course not."

"You know a guy named Roger Hale?"

"I play poker with him sometimes."

"You're not in business with him?"

Mike smiled. "My only business is playing cards and taking life easy."

Bowden suddenly leaned forward, his beefy face contorting with anger. "You slimy little son of a bitch! Don't you sit there and smirk at me!"

His partner reached over and put a hand on Bowden's arm. "Take it easy, Carl," he said. "Losing your temper's not going to help anything."

Mike couldn't help it. He laughed out loud. He said to the second cop, "Now you try to convince me that you'll keep a tight leash on Bowden here if I'll just cooperate with you, right?"

The second cop reached up, took his glasses off, and pinched the bridge of his nose for a moment. Then he put the glasses back on, looked across the table at Mike, and said, "I'm not trying to convince you of anything, you asshole. I'd rather take out my gun and blow a hole in your head than sit here and argue with you."

For a second Mike was frozen with shock that anybody would talk to him like that. Then rage flooded through him and it was all he could do not to throw himself across the table and wrap his fingers around the second cop's thick neck.

"Take it easy, Pete," Bowden said with a smile. "You've upset Mr. Chastain."

"Ah, I just don't like the guy," the second cop said. "I don't like any crook."

Breathing shallowly, Mike asked, "What's your name?"

The second cop said, "Pete Corey. Detective Peter Corey."

"I'll remember you, Detective."

Corey smiled. "I'm shakin' in my little booties."

With an effort, Mike got control of his emotions and said, "Look, I told you where I was tonight; I told you I don't have any connection with Roger Hale except for an occasional card game; I told you I don't know anything about any meat truck getting hijacked. What else do you want from me?"

Bowden said, "We have it on good authority that you and Hale are partners in a scheme to sell stolen meat on the black market, and maybe other goods, too. I don't like black marke-teers, Chastain. The Germans gassed me at Belleau Wood back in the First World War. The way I see it, anybody who goes against our government now is helping those Kraut sons o' bitches."

"I'm an upstanding American citizen, Detective. If you think you know different, then you'd better be able to prove it."

"We will." Bowden put his hands flat on the table and pushed himself to his feet. "I don't imagine you'll be playing cards with Roger Hale any time soon, Chastain."

"Oh? Why's that?"

Corey stood up, too, and said, "Because he got himself shot tonight when he tried to boost that truck."

Trying to sound idly curious, Mike asked, "Was he hurt bad?" He halfway expected them to tell him that Hale was dead.

"Don't know; we couldn't nab him." Bowden slipped a cigar from his vest pocket and put it in his mouth. "But judging by the amount of blood he left behind, it was more than a scratch. A hell of a lot more."

Mike shrugged. "Sorry to hear that."

"Yeah, I'll bet."

Both detectives glared at him for a second, then turned and walked off. Just one of his shoes cost more than their suits, hats, and shoes put together, Mike thought.

Damn that Hale! He'd gotten greedy. The warehouse was full of meat; they didn't have any place to put any more. You couldn't just dump a few tons of steak and roast on the market at once, not without attracting too much attention. You had to sort of space things out. Mike had tried to explain that to Hale when he said they didn't need to hit any more shipments for a while. Obviously, Hale hadn't listened and had tried to hijack the truck by himself. Either that, or he had hired some goons who'd turned out to be bad at their jobs. Hale wouldn't have gotten himself shot if he'd had some decent help. He wouldn't have gotten shot if Mike had been there.

Mike wondered if Hale was dead or just holed up someplace. He ought to try to find out, he supposed. A dead partner was no threat, but a live one in trouble could be.

Karen had finished her set. She came over to the table, leaned over Mike, and kissed him as he tipped his head back. "Hi," she said.

"Hi yourself."

"How was the show?"

"Great, just like always."

"I noticed a couple of guys sitting here with you but didn't recognize them. Who were they?"

Mike butted out his cigarette in an ashtray. "Just some guys." Normally he didn't like people asking him questions, but what could he do? It was Karen.

"They looked like cops to me."

She was too damned observant, and too smart, as well. It wouldn't do any good to lie to her. "They were cops."

"What did they want?"

"Ah, just the usual garbage. They got a crime they can't solve, so they figure they'll pin it on me."

"Something to do with Roger Hale?" Karen knew Hale, knew that Mike had something to do with him, and didn't like it.

He answered her question indirectly by saying, "I told them I didn't know what they were talking about and that I'd been here all evening listening to you sing. You can vouch for that, can't you?"

"Of course I can. It's the truth." Her voice dropped a little. "You know that no matter how many people are here, I'm always singing to you, Mike."

He took a deep breath. When she said things like that, it got to him. At times like this, he sometimes thought she deserved better than him. He knew that he sure as hell didn't deserve her. But he was going to hang onto her anyway.

He reached for her hand. "What say we get out of here?"

"I'm done for the night. That sounds fine to me."

It was a warm night. He didn't need an overcoat, and she wore only a light sweater over her sleeveless gown. They walked down the street to the place he'd left his car, then drove back to the apartment. As they cruised along beside the lake, Karen slid close to him and rested her head on his shoulder. The aroma of her perfume mingled with the clean scent of her hair and made the blood race faster through his veins. So did the touch of the hand that she dropped casually onto his thigh as he drove.

The only thing he was thinking about was getting her up to bed and making love to her. He was aching to wrap his arms around her and bask in her heat. He wasn't sure she completely believed him about his conversation with the cops, but he forced that whole subject out of his head. He would worry about Hale's botched hijacking attempt and those two detectives tomorrow.

When they reached the apartment house, the doorman promised to put the car away in the garage around the corner where Mike kept it. Arm in arm, he and Karen went through the lobby and rode up in the elevator. The sleepy operator grinned at them and then grinned even bigger when Mike tossed him a half-dollar.

"I think I'll call back down to the lobby and have the doorman rustle us up a bottle of champagne," Mike said as he unlocked the door to the apartment.

"Champagne? What are we celebrating?"

"Any night I'm with you is a reason to celebrate." He knew it sounded hokey as hell, but he meant it. He really meant it.

The door swung open and they stepped inside. Mike hit the light switch at the same time as he used his heel to push the door closed behind them. The subdued lighting in the foyer and living room came on, and the first thing Mike saw were the ugly, dark red splotches on the carpet. The second thing he saw was the figure with the gun in its hand coming toward him from the darkened hallway that led to the bedroom. Karen let out a startled cry as he grabbed her and thrust her behind him. He didn't have a gun, but he would do what he could to protect her from whoever was after him. If he could just get his hands on the bastard, even if it meant he had to take a slug . . . !

Then the figure stumbled into the light, left arm clenched across a blood-soaked midsection. "Mike," Roger Hale croaked. "You gotta help me—"

Then he pitched forward onto his face, getting still more blood on the carpet, and Karen started to scream.

FORTY-NINE

Mike came out of the bedroom, trying to wipe the blood off his hands with a handkerchief. It didn't want to come off. He balled up the handkerchief and tossed it away from him.

From the comfortable sofa by the window that overlooked the Loop and part of the lake, Karen asked, "How is he?" Smoke drifted up from the cigarette in her hand. The lights were dimmed, so that the coal on the end of the smoke glowed red as she inhaled.

Mike walked over to the window and put his hands on his hips as he looked outside. "Alive. He's in pretty bad shape, though. Looks like he took at least two slugs in the belly."

"You'll never get the blood off those sheets. You'll have to burn them."

"Yeah, I know."

Mike hated having to put Hale in his bed. That was the best place for him, though. He had to rest while waiting for the doc to show up.

"And it'll be hard to get it off the carpet. You may have to pull it up and have new put down."

"I know." Mike felt a surge of impatience with Karen. She was pointing these things out because she was mad at him. She wanted to make sure he understood how upset she was that the violence of his business had intruded into their lives.

Hell, he understood that. He was upset, too. It wouldn't have broken his heart if Hale had just crawled off into an alley and died after that shoot-out. But that wasn't what had happened. Hale had come here and gotten into the apartment somehow, and now that he had, he was Mike's responsibility. Karen would just have to understand *that*.

"Did you call that number I gave you?" he asked her.

"Yes. The man who answered sounded surprised to hear your name, but he said he would be right over. Who was he?"

"A doctor."

"Somebody you know from before?" She didn't have to say from before when.

"Yeah." Mike reached up, loosened his tie, pulled it off. He unbuttoned the collar of his shirt.

Karen leaned forward and put out the cigarette in a heavy glass ashtray on the coffee table. She stood up. "I'm going home."

"Back to your place, you mean?"

"That's right. I'm just in the way here tonight."

Mike thought about telling her just how much he had wanted her, how much he had looked forward to making love to her when they got back here. But this wasn't the time, he sensed. She was too mad to really hear anything he could say to her.

"You're never in the way," he said, "but it might be better this time if you left. I'll call the doorman and have him get you a cab."

"Thanks." She reached for her sweater, which she had tossed on the back of the sofa.

Mike got it first and helped her into it. She pulled away from him a little as he did so, and he wondered if it was because of the bloodstains on his hands. He should have backed off, he told himself. Karen needed some time to get over her anger. Once she thought about it, she would see that he hadn't had any choice except to help Hale.

She walked to the door, her heels clicking on the tile of the foyer. Mike followed her, knowing that he ought to let her go but for some reason unwilling to. "I'll see you tomorrow night," he said.

"Will you?" she asked without looking at him.

"Sure. I always come to the club when you sing, don't I?"

"Except when you have to go out and be a criminal."

Mike's jaw tightened. "You shouldn't say things like that."

"Why not?" Now she looked at him, and her eyes blazed with anger. "That's what you are, isn't it? A criminal? I know about you and Hale and the black market. That's why those cops were at the table tonight, wasn't it?"

"Those cops were just trying to roust me—"

She hit him hard in the chest, not hurting him but taking him by surprise. "Don't lie to me, you bastard! I've watched you for months now, getting deeper and deeper back into the rackets. You gave all that up, Mike. You can't go back to it now; you just can't. You have to give it up. . . ." Her face crumpled into tears.

He reacted instinctively, reaching out to put his arms around her. Instead of letting herself be drawn into his embrace, she pushed him away. "Don't touch me! I'm going home."

He was helpless to say or do anything except repeat what he had said earlier. "I'll have the doorman get you a cab."

"You do that," she said, and then she was gone, jerking the door open, stepping out into the hall, and slamming it behind her.

Mike stood there a minute, gave a little shake of his head, then went over to call the doorman. The doorman told him that an old guy had just come into the building asking for him. That would be the doc, Mike knew.

"Send him up. And Miss Wells is on her way down. See that she gets in a cab all right, will you?"

"Sure thing, Mr. Chastain. Nothing's too good for you, Mr. Chastain."

You have to give it up, Karen had said. But what if he couldn't? What if this was just the way he was? Would she leave him?

Mike hung up the phone and stared at it while waiting for the doorbell to ring, announcing that the doctor had arrived.

Dr. Gerald Tancred sat in his study, finishing his notes on the patients he had seen that day. None of them had been seriously ill. Since his practice was confined for the most part to the wealthy inhabitants of Chicago's Gold Coast, he seldom saw anyone with a complaint more serious than bronchitis or gout. And when he did, he referred the cases to a specialist right away. He was a general practitioner, nothing more.

Perhaps he should have been a psychiatrist, he told himself as he put down his pen and rubbed his eyes. Perhaps then he could have helped his wife.

Most days she was better than she had been back in the winter, in those terrible days and weeks after Pearl Harbor. She seemed to have grasped reality: Spencer was dead. She still grieved for him, of course. At times even Tancred still caught himself thinking that he heard the slamming of a door and the loud, cheerful voice of his son. But he knew that Spencer was gone and that life had to move on, and most of the time, so did Elenore.

But then she caught him by surprise, telling him that she had just had the nicest talk with Spencer, or asking him what he thought Spencer would like for dinner, or wondering aloud when Spencer was coming home. At such moments, Tancred felt a sharp pain deep inside his chest, and he was unsure whether it was physical or emotional. Some of both, he supposed.

He had considered hiring a nurse for Elenore, someone who would care her for her not so much physically, but who would be there to keep an eye on her. Tancred refused to believe that his wife would ever harm herself, but he was not as convinced of that as he once had been. Still, she was his wife, and he hated the idea that he could not care for her himself. The cook and the housekeeper were there during the day, while he was at his office, and it had been years since he had been called out on an emergency in the evening.

The sound of a footstep in the hallway just outside the open door of his study made him glance up in surprise. He thought Elenore was upstairs in bed, and there was no one else in the house. At least, there shouldn't be. He pulled open the center drawer in the desk and glanced down at the small pistol lying there. He kept the pistol in case of intruders who might know he was a doctor and come looking for drugs. He dropped his hand onto the butt of the gun.

Elenore stepped into the doorway, wearing a white dressing gown that contrasted nicely with her dark hair. "Gerald?" she said. "Am I disturbing you?"

He smiled, took his hand off the gun, and closed the drawer. "Not at all, my dear. I was just finishing up my notes. I thought you were upstairs asleep."

She shook her head. "I couldn't seem to doze off."

That was surprising, considering that she had had several drinks after dinner, he thought. Usually that made her sleepy. She might listen to the radio for a short time, but then she went up to her room.

Tancred got to his feet. "Do you feel all right?" he asked as he started out from behind the desk. Elenore's eyes looked clear, and she didn't have the distracted expression that was common when she slipped into her grief-haunted unreality.

"I'm fine," she said. "I was just thinking about something."

He came up to her, still smiling indulgently, and put his hand on her arm. "And what would that be?"

"I was thinking about Spencer. . . ."

Tancred stiffened. He was tired. He didn't want to deal with this tonight. But how could he turn his back on her? She was, after all, his wife.

"Yes?" he said.

"I think you should start a clinic."

"What?" he asked, frowning.

"A clinic. For poor people. We could call it the Spencer Tancred Memorial Clinic."

He was thrown. Clearly, Elenore was not delusional at the moment. She knew that Spencer was dead; otherwise she would not have mentioned a memorial. But the idea was ludicrous.

"That's nice, dear," he made himself say, "but I'm afraid I don't have the time. My practice—"

"Your practice is nothing but rich, lonely women who convince themselves they're sick so they can have you pet them and fuss over them. You're a good doctor, Gerald, but you're wasting your time on those people. You should be somewhere where you can really do some good."

"I help people in my practice," he said, offended by her statement that he was wasting his time. "And it's quite lucrative—"

"That's just it. You've made plenty of money. You could afford to establish a clinic and give up one or two days a week there—"

He shook his head. "No. It's out of the question."

She caught hold of his right hand with both of hers. "Why? You could do it, Gerald; I know you could."

"Why in heaven's name would I want to?"

"To help people, and so Spencer's name would be remembered."

"It's a fine sentiment, but I can't—"

"You *can*." She brought his hand to her face and rested her cheek against it. "Please, Gerald. It would mean so much to me."

"Well . . ."

"I know I've been . . . difficult lately. . . ."

"Not at all," he lied.

"Yes, I have. But I think this would help. I could help you run the clinic, and it would give me something to do." Her excitement grew as if she sensed his resolve weakening. "I was talking to Agnes today, and she told me about a building she knows that's for rent."

He had to think for a second to remember that Agnes was the name of the housekeeper. "I'm sure it would be quite expensive—"

"No, the place is sitting there empty, and Agnes said the landlord would probably be willing to negotiate on the price. Please consider it, Gerald. Please."

He took a deep breath. "All right. I'll think about it." The promise was harmless, he thought. He wasn't committing himself to anything, and he was sure that Elenore would forget about this crazy scheme. Perhaps even by morning, it would be gone from her head.

"Thank you, Gerald." She rose up on her toes and kissed him, something she hadn't done in a long time. "I knew I could make you understand." She slipped her arms around his waist and hugged him.

Tancred returned the embrace, and as he did so, he felt a pang of longing go through him. For all these long months, Spencer's death had been a wall between him and his wife. He missed her more than he liked to admit. If thinking about her idea for a clinic would help mend the breach between them, it was surely worth it, he decided. He wouldn't have to actually *do* anything. . . .

They stood there just inside the door of the study holding each other. After a moment, Tancred reached up and touched her hair.

Kenneth Walker sniffed the air. *Sweatsocks.* The odor was faint but unmistakable. You would think that the government could find a more suitable place for such important work than one that smelled, even faintly, of sweatsocks.

He rested his hands on the metal railing and looked down at what had been a squash court. The lines that had once marked off the court were still visible in places, even though it hadn't been used for that purpose for quite a while. Now, instead of the slap of rubber balls and the shouts of triumph or dismay from the players, the room echoed with the voices of the workers who had begun the delicate task of assembling the world's first man-made nuclear reactor.

At least, that was what it was supposed to be. At the moment it looked like the bottom part of a big box constructed of cinderblocks. In time, when those thick walls were completed, they would be surrounded by another layer made of heavy wooden beams. Inside the box would be the pile of graphite blocks and rods itself, designated CP-1. Ken had seen the plans and had a pretty good idea what it would look like.

It wouldn't be very impressive, he thought, and it certainly wasn't located in impressive surroundings. This abandoned squash court was underneath the west grandstands of Stagg Field. There were several such courts down here. During his days as an undergraduate at the university, Ken had played squash, but he couldn't recall if he had ever played on this particular court. He thought he probably had.

In those days, spectators watched the games going on below from the railed balcony that ran above the courts. Now, instead of cheering for their friends, the observers who would someday cluster at the railing would no doubt stand there in awed silence. Instead of college students, the group would consist of the world's leading physicists and engineers. And instead of a game, they would be there to witness the first controlled nuclear chain reaction in history.

That is, if all went as planned. The workers were just beginning the construction of the pile. There were still months to go before they would be finished and the great experiment could proceed.

Someone came up to the railing beside Ken. He glanced over and saw that the newcomer was Dr. Enrico Fermi. "It doesn't look like much, does it?" Fermi asked, as if he had been reading Ken's mind as he approached.

"Not yet."

"Sometimes the greatest events in history take place in the most mundane surroundings."

Ken looked at Fermi. "Do you think what we're doing here will go down as a great event in history, Doctor?"

"In the history of science, certainly it will, if we're successful."

"And in the history of the world as well?"

Fermi smiled. "That depends on what we do with it, doesn't it?"

Ken couldn't argue with that. He knew that the ultimate goal of the project dubbed the Metallurgical Laboratory, or Met Lab for short, was to harness the power of a nuclear chain reaction and use it as the basis for a weapon unlike any the world had ever seen. He didn't know if that was possible, but if it was, the prospect didn't bother him. He knew, as did all the other scientists working on the project, that it was very likely Adolf Hitler had his Nazi physicists working on the same problem at this very minute. Assuming it was possible to produce a nuclear weapon, Ken didn't want the Nazis to be the first to do so. That could lead to the destruction of the entire world.

Of course, that was what some people theorized would happen anyway if a chain reaction ever started. Atoms would just keep on splitting and splitting, with no way of stopping them, until the resulting release of energy was so great that the planet would be shattered. Ken didn't believe that. Nothing he had seen in the research of Dr. Fermi, Dr. Szilard, Dr. Bohr, and the other scientists who dealt with nuclear fission indicated such a thing to him.

Yet he knew it was going to be an awe-inspiring, even frightening, moment when the final switches were thrown.

"There's talk that there may be some changes made in the next few months," Fermi said.

"Really? I thought everything was going well."

"It is. Well enough so that the Army believes it's time for someone from the military to step in and begin coordinating the various phases of the project. Do you mind working for the Army, Kenneth?"

"No, sir."

"I'm glad to hear that. You know, for a time I thought you might be working for the Army in another capacity. You were ready to hang up your lab coat and pick up a rifle."

"Enlist, you mean?"

"Don't tell me you didn't think about it."

It was true. He had thought about it a great deal in the days after the Japanese attack on Pearl Harbor. With most of his friends in the service, it would have been logical for Ken to go, too. And besides, there was a debt to be paid. Catherine Tancred's brother had died at Pearl Harbor, he'd heard, and one of Joe's letters had told him how their British friend, Arthur Yates, had been blinded in one of the German bombing raids on London. Arthur's fiancée had been killed in an earlier raid. For those and the thousands like them who had already fallen victim to the naked aggression of the Axis, the score had to be settled.

But not by him, Ken had decided. Not by enlisting in the Army, at any rate. He would do his part here, in the labs under Stagg Field.

"You wouldn't have been able to go, you know," Fermi said quietly.

Ken nodded. "Yes, sir, I know." He had been privy to too much confidential information. He would be a security risk if he left the Met Lab project, and the government couldn't allow that. So in that way, if not in any other, his decision had been an easy one.

"Well," Fermi said as he rubbed his hands together, "shall we roll up our sleeves and get to work?"

"Yes, sir," Ken said. History was waiting for them.

FIFTY

"You're sure about this," Joe said as he and Dale walked into the bar at Shepheard's in downtown Cairo.

"Of course I'm sure." Dale pointed across the crowded room at a group of British officers sitting at one of the tables. "There they are now."

Joe frowned. True enough, one of the men had spotted Dale and was waving him over. But why would a bunch of British officers want to have a drink with a couple of American non-coms?

They made their way across the room, and as they came closer to the table, Joe recognized the officer who had waved as Captain Neville Sharp. The British tank commander had his left arm in a black silk sling under his uniform jacket. The sling made him look even more dashing than usual.

Sharp stood up to greet them and put out his right hand to Dale. "Sergeant Parker," he said. "Congratulations on your promotion."

"Thank you, sir."

"I'm sure it was richly deserved." And then Sharp did something that caught Joe completely by surprise.

He winked at Dale.

What the hell? Joe thought. That was definitely a conspiratorial wink. What sort of secret could Dale share with one of the leading tank commanders in the Eighth Army?

"This is my brother Joe," Dale said, pointing a thumb at Joe. "I don't think you've met."

399

"The second Sergeant Parker, eh?" Sharp said as he shook hands with Joe. "Pleased to meet you, Sergeant."

"Thank you, sir," Joe managed to overcome his confusion to say. "It's an honor."

"Not at all, not at all." Sharp waved at the empty chairs. "Sit down, lads, and I'll introduce you around."

Joe and Dale lowered themselves into the chairs, and as Joe sat down, he looked across the round table into a familiar face. The pale gray eyes of Colin Richardson gazed back at him. Richardson's expression was carefully neutral, as if he had never seen Joe before in his life and was only politely interested in him. Joe tried to keep his own face equally expressionless.

There were half a dozen officers at the table besides Sharp and Richardson, each of them either a captain or a major. Joe shook hands with all of them and tried to file their names away in his memory, but he wasn't sure it would matter whether he remembered them or not. He didn't think he would ever see any of them again after tonight.

Unless it was Richardson, who had indicated at their last meeting that he might have some use for Joe in the future. Joe still wasn't sure what that meant, but since he'd decided that Richardson probably worked in Intelligence, he wasn't going to rule out anything.

Dale was sitting to Sharp's right. Sharp clapped a hand on his shoulder and said, "This is the fellow I told you about. Saved my bacon, he did, and that of my crew as well."

The other officers congratulated Dale. Joe turned his head to stare at his brother and asked, "What's he talking about?"

Sharp leaned forward so that he could look past Dale at Joe. "Didn't Dale tell you? When I was knocked out—" he patted his left shoulder, which was bulky with bandages under his coat "—he pitched in and took command of my tank. Did a bang-up job, too. Knocked out a bloody Panzer."

Joe stared at Dale, eyes widening in disbelief. "What?"

Dale shrugged and looked uncomfortable. "It wasn't really that big a deal."

400

"Not that big a deal?" Sharp said. "Bert Crimmens told me all about what happened while I was out cold. Just some of the canniest maneuvering under fire the Western Desert has seen so far."

"Bert?" Joe said. "What was Bert doing there? What were *you* doing there?"

"Bert was a member of the tank crew," Dale said. "And as for me, well, I was just visiting." He leaned closer to Joe. "Remember that time last month when I had that pass, and you thought I'd gone to one of the whorehouses in Giza . . . ?"

"You mean you snuck up to the *front*?"

"Shh," Dale said. "Don't announce it to the whole world, Walter Winchell."

Joe sat back in his chair. He had been flabbergasted only a few times in his life, and Dale had been responsible for most of them. Tonight was going on the list.

"Tomorrow I'm going back up to the line myself," Sharp said, "so I thought I'd get together with a few of the lads and have a drink first. That's why I invited you and your brother to join us, Dale. I want to say thank you for saving my tank." He snapped the fingers of his right hand to attract the attention of a waiter. "We'll have that bottle of champagne now."

The Egyptian waiter nodded and went off to fetch the champagne.

Dale said, "This is nice, but it really isn't necessary, Captain—"

"Of course it is. I don't believe in letting heroism go unrewarded. If I could, I'd tell the Auk himself what you did."

Dale shook his head. "Please don't, sir. I've got a master sergeant who'd have my ass for breakfast if he knew I'd gone off to the front like that. I don't think your brass would be too happy about it, either." He looked around worriedly at the other officers at the table.

"Don't worry about these lads," Sharp assured him. "They're sworn to silence, and I trust each and every one of them. We won't divulge your secret, even if it should be told."

"Thank you, sir."

The waiter came back to the table wheeling a large ice bucket with a magnum of champagne in it. Another waiter carried a tray with crystal glasses on it. With smooth, practiced efficiency, the first waiter uncorked the champagne and offered the cork to Sharp, who waved it away. "What do you think I am, a bloody Frenchman?" Sharp asked. "Just pour the drinks."

If discretion was the idea, Sharp wasn't going about it very well, Joe thought as the waiter set glasses of champagne before the men seated at the table. They were in the middle of the busiest watering hole in Cairo, and someone was bound to notice the two Americans sitting at the same table with the British officers. He supposed that if anyone asked him, he could say that Sharp had asked him and Dale here to consult with them about some technical matter regarding the General Grant tanks. After all, the American instructors were supposed to make themselves available to the British to answer any of their questions. Yeah, that story might go over all right, he decided.

When everyone had a glass of champagne, Sharp raised his and said, "To the members of the Fourth Armoured Division."

Everyone echoed the toast and drank. Sharp continued, "And to the Yanks who give us a helping hand."

"Here, here," Colin Richardson said.

Joe sipped his champagne while Dale took a healthier slug of his. Dale lowered his glass and asked, "How's the shoulder, Captain?"

"Much better, but I'll still be on non-combatant status for a bit. Now that I'm out of hospital, General Ritchie has had me transferred to his staff temporarily." Sharp lowered his voice. "Word has it that the bloody Desert Fox is going to make another push any day now, so we're getting ready."

Joe happened to be looking across the table at Richardson as Sharp spoke, and he saw how Richardson's eyes narrowed in anger for a second. The reaction was fleeting, but Joe was sure Richardson wasn't happy that Sharp was discussing such things.

Richardson was a fine one to worry about secrecy, Joe thought. After all, Richardson had gotten drunk, mugged, nearly killed, and had followed that up by telling his rescuer that British Intelligence was listening in on the German radio transmissions and decoding them somehow. That had to be what he meant when he talked about knowing all the Germans' secrets.

Joe had read plenty of spy stories in the pulps. This was just the sort of stuff that Operator 5 or Captain John Vedders or Major Hugh North got into. If Joe's theory was correct about the British breaking the German codes, then he could understand why it was such a secret—and why Richardson had been upset with himself for blabbing it.

"If Rommel attacks, we'll be ready for him," one of the other officers said. "He won't push us back any farther. The Gazala Line will hold."

Sharp drank more of his champagne. "I hope you're right, Rollie. I bloody well hope you're right."

Dale said, "I just wish we could get in on the fighting. I don't understand why the United States isn't doing anything."

"You're providing us with some fine tanks and men such as yourself to teach us how to use them," Sharp said.

Dale shook his head. "That's not enough. We need to be part of the action, for real. Hell, if we landed a few divisions in North Africa, it'd make a difference."

"Don't you worry about us," another of the Englishmen said. "We'll take care of those Nazis."

"Yeah, but I want to lend a hand." Dale tossed off the rest of his drink. "I can drive a tank or handle the guns, and Joe here is one of the best wireless operators you'll ever see."

Richardson leaned forward slightly. "Good with a radio, are you, Parker?"

Joe said, "I, ah, don't really know anything except what the Army has taught me, sir."

"He's good at it," Dale insisted. "You wouldn't think it if you'd grown up with him like I did. Always had his nose stuck in a book. He never built a crystal set or a short-wave radio like Frank and Joe Hardy did."

"Frank and Joe Hardy?" Sharp said.

"Yeah, the Hardy Boys. They went around solving crimes all the time with their chums."

Baffled looks around the table.

Joe stepped in, since Dale seemed to be getting a little giddy from the champagne. "They're just characters in some books that boys read in the States."

"Ah, like our boys' papers." Sharp nodded. "I read 'em all when I was a lad. Never thought I'd be living through such exciting times myself."

That comment led to more discussion of the build-up by the Afrika Korps along the Gazala Line. While that was going on, Joe excused himself to pay a visit to the restroom, and when he stepped out a few minutes later into the passageway that also held a pair of telephone booths, he found Colin Richardson standing there lighting a pipe.

"Thanks for not letting on about our previous meetings, Parker," he said.

"There was nothing really to say about them, was there?"

The pipe caught as Richardson puffed on it, and smoke wreathed his head. He took the stem out of his mouth and said, "I suppose not. I would like to talk to you sometime, though, about this business of your expertise with wireless."

"Dale exaggerates," Joe said with a shake of his head. "I'm not really that good."

"Nonetheless, I have a feeling that you're a talented young man. I'll be in touch. Now if you'll excuse me, I'm going to the loo."

Richardson pushed open the restroom door and went inside. Joe wasn't fooled for a second. Richardson had come over here to corner him when he came out and drop some more hints about recruiting him for intelligence work.

Well, would that be so bad? Joe asked himself. He liked to think of himself as trustworthy, and he wasn't an absolute dope. He wasn't sure he wanted to work for the British when the American forces in North Africa would probably be increasing in the coming months, but surely Army Intelligence had some agents working for them as liaisons to the British. *Joe Parker, American Agent*. It had a nice ring to it.

"Oh, hell, I know that look," Dale said from beside him, startling him. "You're dreaming up another pulp story, aren't you?"

"Uh, yeah, I guess so." Joe smiled. "It was a pretty far-fetched idea; that's for sure."

"I don't know where you writers come up with all that crazy stuff." Dale inclined his head toward the arched doorway leading to the hotel lobby. "The party's over, so we can head back to the barracks."

"You said goodbye to Captain Sharp?"

"Yeah, but I hope I see him again. Out of all the limeys I've met, he's the only one I'd like to serve under."

They started out of the hotel, walking side by side. "You know," Joe said, "you've got to tell me all about what happened on the Gazala Line when you were there."

"Like the captain said, I took command of his tank, saved the crew, and blew the hell out of a Panzer."

"And you say writers come up with crazy stuff. . . ."

FIFTY-ONE

The newspaper headline read in bold letters JAP SUB SPOTTED OFF CATALINA ISLAND. Adam didn't doubt it for a second. The talk in the barracks these days was about equally divided between the subject of the 2nd Marine Division going to war and the possibility of a Japanese invasion of California.

Adam was convinced the SECMARDIV was bound for the Jap-held islands of the South Pacific. Otherwise why would they have spent a month practicing landings under fire on the beaches of La Jolla?

Given the climate of fear in California these days, it wasn't surprising that some people had mistaken the Marine "invasions" for the real thing. The SECMARDIV was using three converted passenger liners—the *Hayes,* the *Jackson,* and the *Adams*—as troop ships, and every time the liners steamed along the coast and disgorged their Higgins boats full of Marines, the switchboards at all the local police stations lit up with reports that the Japs were coming ashore. A couple of times, civilians armed with pistols, shotguns, .22 rifles, and the like had rushed to the beach to try to repel the landing. It had taken some quick-talking Marine officers to convince these locals that the men splashing ashore were actually good old American boys. The whole thing had been a comedy of errors on occasion, but it could have turned deadly easily enough, Adam thought.

And the worst of it was that it was entirely possible the Japanese *would* try to invade the United States. Conventional wisdom had it that they would attempt to capture Hawaii first, but what if the Japs crossed up everybody, bypassed Hawaii, and set their sights instead on Los Angeles or San Francisco? It could happen.

"Say, when you're through with that paper, pass it over, would you?" Ed asked from the other end of the rec hall sofa. "I want to read the funnies and see what Smilin' Jack and Terry and the Pirates are up to."

"Sure," Adam said. "I'm almost finished." He looked over the rest of the newspaper's front page, then handed it to Ed. The paper was three days old, but any news was better than none. The front page, of course, was almost all war news. In North Africa, the British Eighth Army was holding the line against Rommel's Afrika Korps. In the Pacific, the Navy was trying to recover from the loss of the aircraft carrier *Lexington* at the Battle of the Coral Sea. In the Philippines, the grim fortress of Corregidor had finally fallen after a lengthy siege and bombardment by the Japanese, and American resistance in that island nation had ended. So most of the news was bad, which was no different from the previous six months. But the tide had to turn eventually. Adam was convinced of that.

Leo came into the rec hall and spotted Adam and Ed on the sofa. He came over to them, stared down at Adam, and said, "Shouldn't you be at the officers' club, Lieutenant?"

Adam looked at him with narrowed eyes. "Are you telling me I'm not welcome here, Private?"

Ed spoke up, saying, "Ah, hell, that's not what Chopper means—"

"Yes, it is," Leo said. "This place is for enlisted men. You may have been one of those not long ago, but you ain't now, Lieutenant."

Adam reined in his temper. The bad part about it was that Leo was right. He *was* out of place here, now that he had been commissioned, and he had spotted more than one of the men in the room looking at him with resentment. He was intruding, and although they wouldn't say anything, they didn't like it.

Nor was that feeling confined to the enlisted men. Just as Leo had predicted, some of Adam's fellow officers had tried to tell him that he shouldn't spend so much time with his old friends. Maybe they were right. Maybe it was detrimental to the system of discipline and command that was necessary for the Corps to function. Maybe, nothing—he was sure they were right. But it was hard to break the bonds of friendship.

Still, he hadn't signed up to weaken the Corps. He got to his feet and said, "Thank you, Private, for pointing out what should have been obvious to me. Carry on." With a curt nod, he started toward the door.

Behind him, Ed said, "Damn it, Chopper, look what you done. You ran off Adam."

"He's not Adam anymore. He's Lieutenant Bergman. The sooner you get used to that, the better, Ed."

As Adam went out and let the rec hall's screen door slam behind him, he realized sadly that Leo was right: The sooner they all got used to the changes in their lives, the better.

"The scoop is, we're headed for Samoa," Lt. Theodore Nash, USMCR, said as he lifted a mug of beer. "From there it'll probably be the Solomons."

Adam sipped his own beer and leaned an elbow on the bar in Camp Kearney's officers' club. In the corner of the room, a Cole Porter tune came from a record player. Adam remembered dancing to it with Catherine in a Chicago nightclub before they were married.

"What do you think, Bergman?"

Adam gave a little shake of his head as Ted Nash's question broke into the sweet memories. "What?"

"I asked which of the islands do you think we'll invade first."

"I don't know. Whichever one they tell us to, I guess."

Nash rolled his eyes and shook his head. Clearly, he was regretting starting this conversation with Adam.

Nash was from Connecticut, the oldest son of a wealthy family, and had been pre-law at Yale when the war started. That background gave him at least a little in common with Adam, who had been pre-law at the University of Chicago. But nothing in Adam's modest life matched up with Ted Nash's extravagant one.

Still, they were both Marines now, the ultimate common ground. Adam tried to be friendly by saying, "If I had to guess, I'd say New Guinea. That's where the Japs have the most men, isn't it?"

"I think it'll be one of the smaller islands. That's what I'd do. Take one of the small islands and set up an air base on it so that we can bomb the other islands."

"Well, that makes sense, all right," Adam said. "Maybe you should be in charge of planning the invasion, Ted."

"They could do worse," Nash said with a smile. "A legal-trained mind can see things more clearly than anyone else's."

Adam wasn't so sure of that, but he didn't argue. He had come over here to kill the rest of the evening after the clash with Leo Sikorsky had prompted him to leave the rec hall. He could go back to the barracks, but he was afraid that if he did, he would spend the evening thinking about Catherine and brooding over their separation.

He had gotten a letter from her a couple of days earlier. She hadn't said where the *Solace* was, but the letter had sounded like the hospital ship was still in the same port where it had been for a while. That was somewhere in the South Pacific. Catherine's letter mentioned that the ship had received patients from the Battle of the Coral Sea, so the *Solace* couldn't be too far away from there. Samoa was a possibility. So were Fiji and Tonga. No matter where the *Solace* was, once the 2nd Division shipped out, they would be heading for some place a lot closer to the hospital ship. Adam didn't know if he would have a chance to see Catherine or not, but he was keeping his fingers crossed.

"Damn it, there you go again," Nash said. "Your mind's a million miles away, isn't it, Bergman?"

"No, not a million," Adam said. "Just a few thousand."

*   *   *

Catherine stepped out onto the fantail of the *Solace*. The sun had set a short time earlier, but an arc of its red glow was still left in the sky to the west. Back in the States, it was already night, even in California, Catherine thought. She wondered if Adam was looking up at the stars and thinking of her, the way she was thinking of him at this moment.

No, probably not, she decided. That would be too much of a coincidence. But it didn't stop her from seeing him in her mind's eye anyway.

She moved over to the railing and leaned on it, glad for the momentary respite from her duties. She lifted her right foot to ease the muscles in her leg, then repeated the movement with the left. You'd think after all these months as a nurse, she would be used to standing on her feet all day, she thought, but that wasn't the case. She still ached with weariness. The influx of patients after the Battle of the Coral Sea had left the nurses busier than ever.

A soft step on the deck behind her made her turn her head and look over her shoulder. A figure in white had come out of the hatch leading onto the fantail. The newcomer's face was still in shadow, but Catherine recognized the shape of Missy Mitchell.

"Hi," she said. "Are you out for a breath of fresh air, too?"

"Ah, no, that's all right." Missy lifted her hand to her eye and, unless Catherine was mistaken, wiped away a tear. "I didn't mean to intrude."

Catherine heard the strain in her friend's voice. "You're not intruding," she said quickly. "Come on over here and take it easy for a minute. The war can get along without us for a little while."

Missy hesitated, then came over to the railing. She grasped it with one hand, her fingers tight around the metal.

"What's wrong?" Catherine asked.

"Wrong?" Missy turned toward her and smiled. "Nothing's wrong. Why should anything be wrong?"

411

"Well, we're in the middle of a war. . . ."

Catherine could see the streaks where tears had rolled down Missy's cheeks. Missy looked down at the water beyond the ship's fantail, hiding her face. She said, "You don't have to remind me."

Catherine reached out to touch her shoulder. "Missy, what is it? Is it Phil?" She knew how her friend felt about the young Navy aviator. But Phil had come through the Battle of the Coral Sea unharmed. In fact, he had distinguished himself during the battle by dropping a bomb on one of the Japanese carriers. Catherine knew all that because Phil had told Missy about it in his letters, and Missy had shared those parts with her.

Now Missy shook her head. "It's not Phil," she said. "I was just . . . remembering something."

"You want to tell me about it?"

"No, it's not important." Missy straightened. Her eyes were dry now. She said, "I've got to get back to the ward."

"You're sure?"

"Of course I'm sure. The patients need me. I'm not going to neglect my duty."

"Of course not," Catherine said.

Missy mustered up a smile. "I'll see you later."

She turned to go back into the ship, thrusting her hands into the pockets of her uniform as she did so. But as she did, something dropped to the deck. She didn't notice it, but Catherine did.

Catherine started to call out to Missy and tell her she had dropped something, but for some reason, she didn't say anything. She waited until Missy was gone, then bent over and picked up the thing that had fallen to the deck. It was a wadded-up piece of paper.

"You ought to be ashamed of yourself," she said aloud. *This is none of your business, Catherine Bergman. You ought to march right in there and give this back to Missy, whatever it is.*

Instead of following her own mental admonishment, Catherine started unfolding the paper and smoothing it out so that she could read what was written on it in the rapidly fading light.

Or at least, she could try to read it. The paper was a newspaper clipping. It was old, and it had been folded and refolded so many times that it felt more like a thin piece of fabric than paper. Catherine squinted at the printing on it but was only able to make out the headline: LOCAL MAN KILLED IN TRAINING ACCIDENT.

Intrigued, Catherine moved closer to the hatch. A few feet down the companionway, light came from an electric bulb enclosed in a metal cage. She turned the paper so that she could read the words on it.

The next thing she noticed was that the clipping was from a newspaper in Lincoln, Nebraska. Missy was from Lincoln, Catherine recalled from previous conversations with her friend, although Missy had never been very forthcoming about her background. This clipping, then, might be about one of her family, or a friend.

She read on, seeing that the story was about a young man from Lincoln, John Stevens, who had been a private in the Army when he was killed by inadvertent live fire during a training exercise at Fort Bragg, North Carolina. He was survived by his parents and a younger brother and sister, all of Lincoln. Catherine looked up at the date on the top of the clipping: May 30, 1941.

One year ago today, she thought.

Questions went through her mind. John Stevens must have been someone special to Missy, or she wouldn't have carried around this clipping for a year. Exactly a year. That was important, too, because Missy had been crying, and she wouldn't have cried over such an anniversary unless it was important to her. Catherine felt tears of sympathy in her eyes as she looked down at the clipping. John must have been Missy's boyfriend, maybe even her fiancé. Missy had never said what prompted her to enlist in the Navy Nurse Corps. It could have been the death of a lover.

Ever since Catherine had known her, Missy had acted carefree, more than a little man-crazy, even promiscuous. Maybe that was all an act to cover the pain and grief of losing John Stevens to a tragic, senseless accident.

But there was another question in Catherine's mind: If she was right about Missy and John, why had Missy crumpled this

413

newspaper clipping? After carrying it around, obviously carefully preserved, for a year, why ball it up as if she were about to throw it away?

Maybe that was exactly what she had intended to do when she stepped out onto the fantail, Catherine thought. If Missy had found the fantail deserted, as it often was, she could have tossed the clipping overboard without anyone knowing about it. She'd probably had the ball of paper in her hand when she came over to the railing, and Catherine recalled now that she had kept one hand clenched while they were talking.

"I'll take that back now, if you're through with it."

Missy's voice was as cold and hard as the metal plates of the ship's hull. Catherine gasped and looked up to see Missy standing there in the companionway, under the caged light. Missy's face was taut with anger.

"I . . . I'm sorry," Catherine said. "I saw you drop something, and I thought I should see what it was. . . ."

"You mean you thought you should snoop in my business. I wouldn't answer your questions, so you took it on yourself to find out what was going on."

"It wasn't really like that—"

Missy came closer and held out her hand. "I don't care what it was like. I want that back."

"Of course." Catherine gave her the newspaper clipping.

Missy crumpled it again, closing her hand so tightly into a fist that her arm trembled a little. She brushed past Catherine and walked across the fantail to the railing. Her arm came back, poised to throw the wadded-up clipping out away from the ship and into the gently lapping water that was growing dark with the fall of night.

For a long moment, Missy stood that way as if frozen, then slowly lowered her arm without throwing the paper overboard. Her shoulders slumped and began to shake. "I can't do it," she said, her voice miserable. "Why can't I do it?"

Catherine hesitated. Missy had been furious with her, and with good reason. She *had* been snooping. But Missy was her best friend, and if that didn't excuse a little snooping, then what did, Catherine wanted to know.

She moved across the fantail, coming up on Missy's left so that she could put her right arm around Missy's shoulders. Missy turned toward her with a sob, and Catherine put both arms around her friend. "It's all right," Catherine said. "It's all right."

"No, it's not! Johnny's dead! Why can't I just . . . let go of him?" Missy began to cry harder.

"It's hard to let go of the people we love," Catherine said. She patted Missy's back and thought about her brother Spencer. The memories—and the pain—were still so sharp inside her whenever she thought about Spencer. That grief was so bad she couldn't even begin to imagine what it would be like if she ever lost Adam.

"We . . . we were engaged," Missy said, sniffling. "We were going to get married . . . when he was on his leave after basic training. Then . . . then . . ."

"I know. I read the clipping."

"It's not *fair*! He . . . he didn't even go off to war, and he still got shot! Damn it, it's just not fair!"

"No," Catherine agreed, "it's not."

"With . . . with Johnny gone, I figured it didn't matter what I did anymore. But I couldn't stay in Lincoln, so I joined the nurse corps . . ." A hollow laugh came from her. "And here I am."

"Doing a lot of good."

"Yeah. Maybe. I even managed to forget about it part of the time . . . until Phil came along." Missy stepped back and looked at Catherine. "Why the hell couldn't you have just had an affair with him, the way he wanted? Why'd you leave him for me to comfort and . . . and fall in love with?"

"Oh, honey, I'm sorry." And even though she was, Catherine started to laugh. She couldn't help herself. Missy had asked that absurd question so seriously.

Missy laughed, too, and they hugged each other again. "I'm sorry," Missy said. "That wasn't fair, either. I know you'd never cheat on Adam. I just . . . I just wasn't ready to start caring about somebody so much again."

"Love doesn't ask us if we're ready," Catherine said. "It just barges in on us."

"Yeah." Missy grew more serious. "I thought the thing to do was to get rid of this clipping. It's been a year. It's time to move on, to think about Phil instead of Johnny. So I thought I'd throw it overboard. But I can't."

"You don't have to. You can remember Johnny and still love Phil."

"You think so?"

"Of course you can."

"Maybe . . . I hope you're right. But what if I'm a jinx?"

"What?" Catherine asked with a frown.

"A jinx. You know, bad luck. Johnny was engaged to me, and then he got killed. Now that Phil and I . . . since we, you know . . ."

"You don't have to say it," Catherine told her.

"Yeah, well, what if that jinxed him? What if everybody I fall in love with gets killed?"

Catherine shook her head. "You're getting way ahead of yourself. Phil came through that battle in the Coral Sea just fine. He told you so himself in his letters. He's a very good pilot."

"What about that broken ankle? That was a fluke, he said, but what if it wasn't?"

"I don't have the slightest idea what you're talking about."

Missy began to pace back and forth in agitation. "Suppose that it was fate he broke his ankle, so he'd meet me here on the ship, fall in love with me, and then go off to get himself killed. Suppose it's all tied together."

"That's crazy."

"I know! But I keep on thinking things like that."

Catherine took hold of Missy's upper arms. "Listen," she said. "I don't know about fate, or bad luck, or jinxes. But I do know you can't do anything about it if you and Phil are in love. That's just the way things are. You have to accept it and get on with your life. Write to him; think about him; pray for him. I'm sure he'll do the same. And hold on to the thought that someday the war will

416

be over and the two of you will be together. Hold on tight to that."

"You sound like you're speaking from experience."

Catherine smiled. "That's right."

Missy took a deep breath. "I know you're right. It's just . . . hard."

"War is hard. So is love."

"Yeah." Missy hugged her and said, "Thanks, Catherine. You really are a good friend . . . even if you are a snoop."

Arm in arm, they started back into the ship. "Where is Phil now?" Catherine asked.

"On the *Yorktown*. He said in his last letter he thought something was up, but he wasn't sure what."

"Do you know where the carriers are?"

Missy shook her head and waved her free hand toward the Pacific. "Somewhere out there, that's all I know."

FIFTY-TWO

The water pipes banged and groaned, but only a trickle of hot water came out of the faucet. Dale cursed as he held his razor under it. Sometimes back in Chicago it had been difficult getting enough hot water for bathing or shaving, but Dale didn't remember it that way. Instead he grumbled to himself about their accommodations here in Egypt.

It was early morning, and Dale was the only one in the barracks latrine. He wasn't used to being the first one up. That honor had usually gone to Joe, since he was the real go-getter in the family. Dale, on the other hand, had to be dragged out of bed most of the time. Months in the army had taught him to get up when reveille sounded or face the consequences, but this morning he was out of bed even before that. He hadn't slept well the night before, tossing and turning restlessly instead of lying in his bunk like a log.

He finished scraping lather off his face and reached for a towel. What the hell was wrong with him these days? Back home, he had never been a worrier.

But he was thousands and thousands of miles away from home, he reminded himself, and there was a war going on. A guy would have to be a fool not to be worried.

Dale turned around as Joe stumbled into the room, also awake before reveille. Joe stopped and looked at his brother in surprise. "What are you doing up?"

"Couldn't sleep," Dale said with a shrug.

"You? Rip Van Winkle himself?"

Dale felt anger flare inside him. "Are you calling me lazy?"

Joe moved past him, heading for the showers. "If the shoe fits . . ."

Dale reached out and caught hold of Joe's shoulder. "Wait just a damned minute," he said. "You can't talk to me like that anymore. We're not back home, and I'm not your foul-up little brother anymore."

Joe jerked free of Dale's grip, and his eyes flashed with some anger of his own. "Oh, no? What the hell do you call it when you go sneaking off to the front and wind up in the middle of a tank battle, for Christ's sake?"

Dale drew himself up straighter and said, "Captain Sharp seemed to think I did all right."

"You were lucky," Joe said, his voice dripping with scorn. "You could have just as easily got yourself and all those tankies killed."

A part of Dale's brain knew that Joe was right. But Dale didn't want to think about that. It didn't matter what could have happened, only what had. And whether Joe liked it or not, Dale was the closest thing to a hero in the Parker family.

"You're just jealous," he said as he started to turn away.

"Jealous?" Joe repeated. He laughed in derision. "Jealous of what?"

Dale faced him again. "My success. You thought when you made sergeant that you could lord it over me for a while, but less than two weeks later, I was a sergeant, too. And you're jealous because I'm a hero, like the guys in your pulp stories, and you're not."

Joe stared at his brother. "A hero?" He shook his head. "Like I said, you're just lucky."

Once again, Joe started toward the showers. Dale grabbed his arm, roughly this time, and hauled him around. "Take that back!"

"Go to hell!"

Anger blazed up inside Dale. Without thinking about what he was doing, he threw himself forward, tackling Joe around the waist and sending both of them sprawling on the tile floor of the latrine.

Joe was taken by surprise. He and Dale had wrestled some as kids, usually out of sheer exuberance but occasionally in anger as all brothers will. Now, as Joe slammed into the floor and pain from the impact went through him, he grabbed Dale's shoulders and heaved him to the side. "Get off of me, you bastard!" he yelled.

Dale rolled over and caught himself, then scrambled after Joe, latching onto a leg. His other hand reached for Joe's throat. Joe knocked it away and tried to pull free, but Dale's grip was too strong. Joe got hold of Dale's arm and bent it back. Dale yelped and let go, but before Joe could put some distance between them, Dale had twisted around and caught him in a scissors hold with his legs.

This was ridiculous, Joe thought. Here they were grown men—well, almost—both of them sergeants in the Army, and they were rolling around on the floor of the latrine in an Egyptian barracks like a couple of twelve-year-olds scuffling in a school bathroom. But he had to fight back, Joe knew. Dale was too mad to listen to reason. Joe was mad, too, whether he wanted to admit it to himself or not. It wasn't fair that Dale got all the glory—*again*!

For months back home, Joe had watched as Dale won race after race in the car he and Harry Skinner had souped up. Dale drove around dirt tracks like a maniac and brought home more in prize money than Joe had earned in years of hard work at a variety of menial jobs. Dale got his picture in the paper and had people cheering him on. Meanwhile Joe toiled away in school and at work, using his spare moments to grind out stories that were published under pseudonyms or house names; even if he'd gotten credit for them, it wouldn't have mattered because everybody knew that the pulps were just lurid trash and the stories weren't worth the paper they were printed on. . . .

Joe kicked free, came up on his knees, and swung a punch as Dale started up, too. Joe's fist smacked into Dale's jaw and sent him over onto his back. Dale slid a couple of feet on the tiles before coming to a stop.

Joe stared down in horror at his hand, still clenched into a fist. He looked up at Dale, who propped himself up on one elbow and used his other hand to take hold of his jaw and work it back and forth. "Good one," he said. "I didn't know you had it in you."

"I . . . I didn't . . . Oh, hell, Dale, I'm sorry—"

"Don't be," Dale said. "I've wanted an excuse to do this for a long time."

With that, he launched himself at Joe again.

Joe didn't defend himself when Dale crashed into him and knocked him over on his back. Dale started pummeling his mid-section, and still Joe didn't fight back. After a moment, Dale stopped throwing punches and pushed away from Joe. "Damn it, don't just lay there and take it!"

"I can't believe it," Joe said, as much to himself as to Dale. "I punched my own brother."

"Aaaargh!" Dale came to his feet and threw his clenched fists into the air in frustration. "Saintly Joe Parker, kind to animals and his numbskull little brother! Do you have any idea how crazy that makes me?"

Joe caught hold of one of the sinks and pulled himself upright. "I'm sorry, Dale," he said again. "I don't know what happened. I guess you're right. I'm jealous of you."

That admission took Dale by surprise. "Really?"

"You were so successful back home, the last year, and now the British think you're a hero—"

"Hey, I didn't really mean all that," Dale broke in. "You were right; it was just pure dumb luck, what happened up there at the front." He shook his head. "As for what went on back in Chicago, I was so damned successful I got us both in such a jam that we had to enlist to get out of it. You're the success story in the family, big brother. You're the writer."

"Are you kidding? I'm a hack."

"No, you're not. Everybody who reads your stories likes 'em. And you're smart enough that you'll wind up as an officer. You just wait and see. You've already got something going on with the British."

Joe stiffened as he thought about Colin Richardson. "What do you mean?" He hoped he wouldn't have to tell Dale an out-and-out lie, but he couldn't reveal his fledgling connection with British Intelligence.

Or could he? Dale *was* his brother. They had been through a hell of a lot together, Joe thought. Maybe he could trust Dale with what was going on.

"I don't know," Dale said with a shrug. "I just thought I saw one of those limey officers looking at you like you and him were buddies."

Joe shook his head. "No, I'm not friends with any of them." That was true enough. He didn't consider Richardson his friend, not by any stretch of the imagination.

"Okay, maybe I was wrong. But there's no getting around the fact that you're going to go a lot farther in the army than I ever will. We may both be sergeants now, but it won't stay that way long. Sooner or later there'll be a lot of our guys over here, and when that happens, they're going to put you in charge of something. You just wait and see."

"I don't know . . ."

"I do." Dale's face was solemn now, and his anger seemed to have vanished, just as Joe's had. "Listen. I'll deny this if you ever repeat it, but . . . I'm scared, Joe."

"You? Scared?" That seemed impossible to Joe. Dale had always been the daredevil, the brother who would plunge into anything without fear while Joe hung back.

Dale said, "Yeah. I don't just mean about the war, either. Think about it, Joe. We've always done almost everything together, even getting in trouble. We even got sent over here together. What do you think the odds are of that happening?"

Joe shook his head. "Pretty slim."

"Yeah. So I thought it meant something, like . . . like fate or something. But now . . . I tell you, Joe, you're going to go one way, and I'm going the other. And it *scares* me."

"No, it's not going to work out that way—"

"How do you know? You don't know what the Army's going to do. None of us do. Hell, Adam thought he'd be the one going to Europe when he joined the Marines, and he wound up on the other side of the world!"

Joe nodded. "That's true."

"So we can't count on being together. We can't count on . . . anything."

"That's just because of the war—"

"No. That day's always been coming, war or no war. I've tried not to think about it too much." Dale chuckled. "Hell, you know me; I never clutter my brain up with any unnecessary thinking. But I've still known in the back of my head, all along, that we had to grow up. It's just . . . hard, Joe. It's really hard."

With some difficulty, Joe swallowed. Dale was right. Maybe it had just started, but they were going in different directions now, for the first time in their lives. And there was no way of knowing how far apart they might wind up.

"Listen," Joe said. "It doesn't matter where we are or what job we're doing; we're still brothers. We're always going to be brothers. Nobody can change that, not Roosevelt or Churchill or Adolf Bloody Hitler. We're brothers."

"Yeah, but—"

"No buts about it," Joe said. "They can split us up. Maybe it'll come to that. But when you get right down to it, we'll be there for each other, just like we always have been."

"I wish I could believe that."

"You can." Joe put out his hand. "Shake on it."

Dale hesitated, then took Joe's hand. He pulled Joe into a hug and started pounding on his back with his other hand.

"Blast it, stop that!"

"You're the one who got all sloppy and sentimental," Dale said. "Now you have to put up with the result."

Joe laughed and said, "No, really, let me go."

"Nope, can't do it."

Joe started trying to pull away. "I'm not kidding, Dale—"

"Neither am I. I'm gonna hug you until I'm good and ready to let you go."

"The hell you are!" Joe got his foot behind Dale's ankle and twisted, trying to trip him. Dale grappled harder in an attempt to retain his hold.

Both of them fell down and rolled under the row of sinks along the wall, wrestling furiously as reveille began to sound over the loudspeakers in the barracks.

FIFTY-THREE

Like Wake, Midway was a coral atoll which seemingly shouldn't have amounted to much in the great scheme of things. The two islands which formed it, Eastern Island and Sand Island, added up to only three square miles of land area. The islands were surrounded by a coral reef which formed a large lagoon to the north. Three long, intersecting runways on Eastern Island, along with the other facilities of the air station located there, made the place important. If the Japanese could capture Midway, it would make a perfect jumping-off spot for an invasion of Hawaii, only 1,136 miles away to the southeast.

Launching an attack on Midway would serve another purpose for the Japanese. Ever since the attack on Pearl Harbor, the surviving ships of the U.S. Pacific Fleet had been playing hard-to-get. They were scattered across the ocean, and although their hit-and-run raids were an annoyance, they had done little real damage to the Japanese other than wounding their pride at the Battle of the Coral Sea. The Japanese Navy still wanted to crush their opponents, and it seemed likely that if Midway were captured, the U.S. fleet would be forced to come together to try to retake the atoll. That would give Admiral Yamamoto's ships the chance to destroy the enemy once and for all.

A diversionary strike would come first. The Japanese would make it appear that their real target was the Aleutian Islands, far away in the North Pacific. Once the American fleet had been drawn off by this feint, the Japanese would sweep in, capture Midway, and lie in wait for the American ships to return. There was only one problem with Yamamoto's plan.

The United States Navy knew exactly what he was up to.

For weeks during the spring of 1942, the Navy's Combat Intelligence Unit at Pearl Harbor had worked like demons at intercepting Japanese radio transmissions and breaking the code in which they were sent. The leader of the effort was Commander Joseph J. Rochefort, Jr., probably the leading cryptographer in the world. The Japanese code, dubbed JN-25, was no match for Rochefort's efforts, which first began to pay off when his radio intercepts tipped the Navy to what the Japanese were up to in the Coral Sea. By late May, Commander Rochefort and his group knew as much about the Japanese plans for Midway as Yamamoto himself.

So did Admiral Chester W. Nimitz, now serving as CINC-PAC, and Nimitz sensed that the time was right to finally strike a major blow at the Japanese. By refusing to bite on the bait of the Aleutian invasion and rushing his three remaining carriers and the rest of the Pacific Fleet to Midway instead, Nimitz would have one hell of a surprise waiting for the Japs.

Midway itself was manned by a thousand Marines and had 114 aircraft based on it, ranging from brand-new Grumman TBF Avenger torpedo bombers to obsolete F2A Buffalo fighters. By 2 June 1942, the *Yorktown, Enterprise,* and *Hornet* had rendezvoused northeast of the atoll at a spot designated "Point Luck," along with the eight cruisers and numerous smaller vessels that made up Task Force 16 and Task Force 17. Hardly an armada, especially considering that they would be facing a Japanese fleet that numbered nearly two hundred ships, but it would have to do.

The sun wasn't up yet on 4 June 1942 as Phil and Jerry climbed into the Dauntless's cockpit, but the eastern sky was tinged with red. The gassing crew and the ordnance mates were finished with their work. The Dauntless was fully fueled and armed, ready to take off.

Phil checked the radio and found it working perfectly. Everything on board the *Yorktown* had been repaired and refurbished during a two-week layover at Pearl Harbor before the orders had come to steam northwest toward Midway. Phil and Jerry weren't privy to all the plans the brass had made, but they had learned enough from the pre-dawn briefing in the *Yorktown*'s ready room to make some good guesses. Phil had an idea the Japs wouldn't be expecting them.

The day before, a flight of B-17 Flying Fortresses based on Midway had spotted several Japanese troop transports on their way to the area. The B-17s had bombed the transports but missed with their loads. Also on 3 June, Jap forces had struck at Dutch Harbor in the Aleutians. As far as Phil knew, there wasn't going to be much of a response to that attack. The two task forces had steamed instead into the waters north of Midway, hoping to intercept the Japanese fleet.

Only scout planes were taking off now. Airedales shepherded the Dauntlesses forward, and a few minutes later Phil and Jerry were airborne, heading west by southwest toward the area where the Japanese fleet was located.

After flying for nearly an hour without seeing anything important, a report came over the radio that Jap bombers and fighters had been spotted on their way to Midway. "They think they've drawn us off," Jerry said. "They've got another think coming."

With only a crackle of static, the news came that the Japanese bombers were striking at the atoll. "Heavy damage on Sand Island," the *Yorktown*'s radioman reported.

"Those poor leathernecks," Jerry muttered without keying his microphone, so only Phil heard him.

"We'll try to even the score," Phil said. He looked out at the horizon where the sea met the sky, hoping to see some sign of the enemy fleet.

Before he or Jerry could spot anything, the order came to return to the *Yorktown*. Phil clenched a fist and thumped the instrument panel in frustration. He wanted to be in on the attack.

But orders were orders. He banked the Dauntless and headed for the carrier.

By following the chatter on the radio, he kept up with what was going on. The *Enterprise* and *Hornet* launched their flights of bombers as the sun came up, and some of the planes based on Midway were in the air, too. Less than an hour later, as Phil was making his approach to the *Yorktown,* Avengers and B-26s from Midway struck the first blow against the Japanese fleet, arrowing in on one of the flattops. Losses among the American planes were heavy, and Phil bit his lip as he made his landing on the *Yorktown*'s flight deck. He should have been out there helping those Marine fliers from Midway, he thought.

So agitated that he forgot for the moment how he had broken his ankle, he climbed out of the cockpit and jumped to the deck. He remembered when his boots hit hard against the thick planks. The ankle held up just fine, however.

He and Jerry walked over to the hatch leading into the island and stood there watching as the airedales wrestled their Dauntless and the other scout planes off the deck and began replacing them with fighters. Phil knew what that meant. They would go up again soon and head for the Japanese fleet, but the Wildcats had to be in the air first, then the Dauntlesses, followed finally by the Devastators.

When they took off again, it wouldn't be on a reconnaissance mission. It would be an attack.

Jerry took off his helmet and ran his fingers through his sweaty brown hair. "Man, I wish I could have a smoke," he said. "A Camel would taste mighty good right now. How 'bout you?"

"I wish I had a chance to write another letter," Phil said.

"To that pretty nurse?" Jerry asked with a grin. "I thought you wrote to her last night."

"I did, but I'm not sure I said everything I wanted to."

Jerry laughed and put a hand on his shoulder. "When you're head over heels in love like you are, buddy, there's never enough time to say everything you want to."

"Since when did you get to be such a fountain of wisdom?"

"You forget, I'm older than you."

"Yeah, by six months, o wise one."

"You can learn a hell of a lot in six months . . . but probably not where women are concerned, I'll grant you that one."

The bantering went on while they waited for their turn to come again, but it didn't distract Phil completely from his thoughts of Missy. He had written to her nearly every day since leaving the *Solace,* and he had gotten as many or more letters back from her. She knew he loved her; he was convinced of that. But he wished he had been able to tell her just how much he cared for her. It was difficult to put the depth of his feeling into words.

He would show her the next time he saw her, he told himself. There *would* be a next time.

It was almost mid-morning before the full-deck strike from the *Yorktown* took off. Phil's impatience and frustration had grown during the wait, and he was glad to be back in the air. They'd had no official word, but the scuttlebutt was that the planes from the *Enterprise* and *Hornet* had hit the Japanese fleet with little success and heavy losses. With the Americans badly outnumbered to start with, the situation was growing more desperate by the minute for them.

It was easy keeping the other Dauntlesses in sight, but the Wildcats far above and the Devastators far below soon vanished into the clouds. "Damn it, Phil," Jerry said, "where'd everybody go?"

"They're around," Phil said, hoping that he was right.

A short time later, more Dauntlesses appeared. They had to be from one of the other carriers, either the *Hornet* or the *Enterprise*. Maybe they had gotten separated from the rest of their flight, too, Phil thought. Together now, four squadrons of dive bombers flew on toward the west.

Phil heard an excited voice over the radio that he recognized as that of Lt. Cmdr. Lance Massey, the leader of the *Yorktown*'s Torpedo 6 squadron of Devastators. "There's one of the Jap flattops!" Massey said. "Keep an eye on us while we go in, Jimmy."

Phil knew Massey was talking to Jimmy Thach, leader of the Wildcats that were supposed to protect the bombers from Jap fighters. A few moments later, Thach reported in his usual laconic tones, "Got our hands full up here with Zeros."

Massey said he and the other torpedo bombers were going in anyway. Phil could visualize the scene even though he couldn't see it. The Devastators would be roaring toward the Japanese carrier, not far above the water, no doubt harassed by fighters and anti-aircraft fire. Phil heard Massey calmly reporting the range to the target; then suddenly his voice ended with a squawk of static. Phil's jaw tightened. Massey's transmission being cut off that way couldn't mean anything good. In all likelihood, the lieutenant commander's plane had been hit.

Within minutes, the radio brought more bad news. All but two of Torpedo 6's Devastators had gone into the drink. They, along with the surviving two bombers, had launched their torpedoes, but the Japanese carrier had swerved to avoid them. No hits recorded. Phil's hand tightened on the stick. It seemed that no matter what the Americans did, the Japanese were invincible on this day.

The Americans were running out of planes and time. If the Japs took Midway, Phil thought, it was only a matter of time until they would go after Hawaii. They *had* to be turned back, here and now.

The clouds thinned and broke away, and the large flight of Dauntlesses emerged into the blue sky. In the distance to the west, Phil saw dots of black smoke and realized they were the deadly puffballs of anti-aircraft fire, being dispersed now by the wind. That could mean only one thing: The Jap carriers were over there, waiting for the next wave of bombers after having repelled the Devastators.

But the Jap flattops didn't have radar, or so Phil had been told, so they had to rely on visual observation to know when they were being attacked. They'd had their hands full with the torpedo bombers for the past few minutes, so it was likely they weren't paying as close attention to the sky in the east as they might have been otherwise.

Anticipation made Phil lean forward against the harness that held him in his seat. "Hang on, Jerry," he called to his friend in the cockpit's rear seat. "Here we go!"

FIFTY-FOUR

As the flight of Dauntlesses roared closer to the Japanese carriers, Phil saw to his amazement that the four flattops were clustered together in a box-like formation with no more than 1300 yards between them. Carriers going into battle usually scattered out in a haphazard fashion with gaps of a mile or more between them, so that it would be difficult to attack more than one at a time. The Japs seemed to be playing right into American hands.

So far, however, that lack of strategic dispersal didn't seem to have hurt them. The carriers were unhit. They began putting up a tremendous screen of anti-aircraft fire as the dive bombers approached. Phil tilted his head back and searched the sky above them. He didn't see any Zeros. Jimmy Thach's Wildcats were keeping the Jap fighters occupied.

"They're big bastards, aren't they?" Jerry said.

"That just makes them bigger targets," Phil said.

"I like the way you think, partner."

The Dauntlesses split into several groups as they approached the carriers. Some of the planes from the *Enterprise* went after the carrier on the rear left-hand corner of the box formation. Phil saw the first couple of bombs miss, going into the water with huge splashes near the flattop, but then, one after another, there were four explosions on the flight deck. Flames shot high into the air, reaching as high as the ship's bridge.

Another group of planes targeted the front left-hand carrier. Several bombs slammed into the vessel, but though the damage was heavy, it didn't stop the carrier's gunners from filling the sky with anti-aircraft bursts.

From the cockpit of his Dauntless, Phil watched his fellow pilots trying to climb up out of that fiery hell after they dropped their bombs. Some of them made it, but several of the planes disintegrated as anti-aircraft bursts struck them. Others burst into flame and, trailing black smoke, spiraled into the water. Phil and Jerry were both grimly silent as their plane zoomed over the devastation.

They wouldn't be above it for long. Phil had his eyes fastened on the leader of his squadron, and when Lt. Cmdr. Max Leslie peeled off and dropped toward the Japanese carrier on the right rear of the formation, Phil and the other remaining pilots followed. They plummeted toward the carrier, wind howling around the cockpit and through the dive brakes. The pilots began releasing their bombs, and Phil saw one of them land right on the Japanese rising sun emblem painted on the flight deck. That symbol of naked aggression was obliterated in the explosion.

A cold calm gripped Phil as the Dauntless dove toward the carrier. This wasn't like the Battle of the Coral Sea, where emotion had taken over and led him to dive to such a low level before releasing his bombs. He was a veteran now, and he knew what to do. He held the dive until he was just low enough to feel confident that the bombs would have a good chance of hitting their target. Then he thumbed the release button on the top of the stick and hauled back an instant later. With a sickening lurch and a roaring engine, the Dauntless changed directions, climbing toward the open sky as its bombs, freed of their clamps, fell toward the Japanese carrier.

A couple of heartbeats later, Jerry whooped in excitement. "We got her! We got her! Right on the flight deck, old buddy! I'll bet we blew up at least half a dozen planes parked there."

Phil was glad to hear it. He banked away from a burst of anti-aircraft fire and turned his head to look down at the sea. Three of the four flattops were ablaze. The fourth one, which hadn't been attacked, was steaming away to the northeast, obviously bound on getting the hell away from there. More bombs fell on the smaller vessels that had been attending the carriers, and as Phil watched, a devastated Jap cruiser broke in half and sank.

"We've done all we can do," Phil said. "Time to go home." He banked again, turning east.

Suddenly, something slammed into the Dauntless with the sound of the worst hailstorm in history. Phil felt the airplane shake under the hammering it was receiving. From the rear cockpit, Jerry yelled, "Zero!" and opened up with the machine gun.

The Japanese fighter whipped past them. When Phil got a look at it, he saw smoke trailing from its fuselage. Jimmy Thach's Wildcats had been engaged in a ferocious dogfight with the Zeros far above the battle going on at the surface. This Jap must have suffered some damage in that fight and limped away from it. The Zero's pilot hadn't been able to resist the temptation presented by the Dauntless, however.

"You okay?" Phil called to Jerry as the firing of the machine gun died away. When he didn't get an answer, he shouted into the microphone, "Jerry!"

"Yeah, yeah, I'm all right," Jerry said. His voice sounded tinny and weak through the headphones. "I'm hit, but it's not too bad. I can still shoot if that son of a bitch comes back."

"He's coming back, all right. Watch out! He's pulling up!"

The Japanese pilot put his fighter into a loop that carried it up and over the Dauntless. Where the hell were the Wildcats? Phil wondered. He and Jerry were sitting ducks for this Jap.

The rear machine gun began chattering again. Phil waited for the hammer blows of bullets from the Zero, but they didn't come. "I hit him!" Jerry yelled, sounding stronger now. "I hit the bastard!"

Again the faster Zero tore past the Dauntless. More smoke was pouring from the Japanese fighter now. Phil watched it, hoping that it would explode or fall into the ocean. The Japanese pilot must have been stubborn, though. Even though the Zero was shuddering and bouncing, it stayed aloft, as if the pilot was holding it up through determination alone.

The Zero banked sharply but didn't climb or roll. Instead, its nose came around until it was pointed at the Dauntless. "Shit!" Phil said. "He's coming straight at us."

His thumb went to the firing button of the front-mounted machine gun and pressed it. Flame licked from the muzzle of the weapon. Phil saw the orange flash of the Zero's guns firing. Now he felt the shivering impact of slugs against the metal skin of the Dauntless; now he heard the pounding of the giant hammer. The Plexiglas of the cockpit canopy starred, then shattered. Phil felt the sting of shards against his cheeks. A huge fist punched him on the left shoulder. He cried out in pain.

The Zero was close now, looming up right in front of him. He shoved the stick forward and dropped the nose of the Dauntless. The Japanese fighter roared over him, so close it seemed as if he could have reached up and touched it as it went by. Smoke coiled around Phil's face, thick and choking. He didn't know if it came from his plane or the Jap's.

Then a huge explosion buffeted the Dauntless, knocking it into a spin. The stick jerked itself out of Phil's hand as if it was alive. He tried to grab for it with both hands, but his left arm wouldn't work. Flailing with his right, he managed to get his fingers wrapped around the stick and held on as tightly as he could as it snapped back and forth like a snake. Gradually, he brought the stick under control, but the plane was still spinning and falling. The world was tilted crazily outside the cockpit. Phil fought the instinct that told him to haul back on the stick as hard as he could. He knew if he did, he might throw the plane's engine into a stall. Instead he eased the stick forward, going with the spin.

Suddenly the stick seemed more responsive. He was regaining control of the plane. When he finally eased it out of the spin after seconds that seemed like hours, he saw that the Dauntless was no more than two hundred feet above the water. Debris littered the ocean below him. He knew what had happened. The fire that had been burning in the Zero had finally reached the fighter's fuel tank, causing an explosion that had blown the Japanese plane into a million pieces.

Something was dripping into Phil's eyes. He wished he could lift his left hand and wipe away whatever it was, but his left arm was numb from the shoulder down. He looked at that shoulder and saw the huge rip in the flight jacket, the blood that formed a shimmery coating all the way down his arm. One of the Zero's bullets had nicked him there. He didn't know if the slug had shattered his shoulder or just caused his arm to go numb. Either way, he had to get back to the *Yorktown* before he bled to death.

And that might be a problem, because the Dauntless's engine was still smoking. Phil looked at the instrument panel. The needles on the oil pressure and temperature gauges were in the red. Not only that, but the needle on the fuel gauge was dropping a lot faster than it should have been. Either the tank had been holed or the fuel line had busted. He and Jerry were lucky the whole plane hadn't blown up, like the Zero—

Jerry.

Phil realized he hadn't heard anything from his partner in several minutes. Not knowing if the radio still worked or not, he shouted, "Jerry! Do you read me? Jerry!"

There was no response. Phil twisted in his seat but couldn't turn around far enough. And he didn't have a free hand to unbuckle the harness. Cursing, he took his right hand off the stick long enough to fumble the buckle loose, then turned.

Jerry was slumped forward over the rear-mounted machine gun. There was a black, gaping hole in the back of his leather flight helmet. Blood had welled from the hole and covered the back of his neck.

"Jerry!"

Forgetting all about the stick and the need to control the plane, Phil twisted more and reached back to grab Jerry's collar. He tugged his friend toward him. Jerry flopped backward, his head lolling on his neck with a looseness that could mean only one thing.

Phil blinked his eyes against tears and whatever it was that was still dripping, hot and sticky, from his forehead. "Jerry," he whispered.

Then the plane lurched, drawing Phil's attention from his dead friend and back to the problem at hand. The Dauntless would never make it back to the *Yorktown,* not shot up like it was. Phil was going to have to ditch it in the ocean. There was a small survival raft in the rear cockpit. He'd have to get the plane down, clamber over Jerry's body into the back before the Dauntless sank, get the raft out of its compartment, and inflate it. Theoretically, it could be done.

But could it be done by a guy with a bullet through his left shoulder and his eyes filled with blood? Phil didn't know about that.

Still, he was going to try. Jerry's death filled him with a worse pain than the bullet wound, but Phil didn't want to die himself. He had to live, to fight on against the Japs, to see Missy again and hold her and tell her that he loved her, would always love her as long as he lived . . .

Which might not be too much longer. The Dauntless had lost more altitude. It was almost skimming the tops of the waves now. Phil fought the stick as it bucked in his hand. To have a chance, he had to keep the plane level. If one of the wings hit the water first, that would tip it over and it would smash to pieces, taking him along with it. He had to get the belly of the Dauntless down first . . .

The plane smacked the water, leaped into the air, came down again. The impact almost threw Phil out of his seat. He let go of the stick and grabbed a better hold on the seat. There was nothing else he could do now except ride it out and pray.

Twice more the Dauntless slammed into the water and bounced back up, but the wings remained level and finally the plane stayed down. Phil had been thrown back and forth so violently in the crash landing that he was disoriented for a moment and couldn't remember what he was supposed to do. Then instinct and training took over. He turned, climbed awkwardly onto the seat with his left arm hanging, and half-crawled, half-fell into the rear cockpit.

The plane was already starting to settle in the water. It wouldn't be afloat for long. Phil pushed Jerry's body aside, trying not to look at the destroyed face as he did so. For however much time he had left, he wanted to remember Jerry the way he had usually been, smiling and laughing.

Hanging almost upside down in the cockpit, Phil found the compartment where the life raft was stored. It was full of holes. It had been chewed to pieces by bullets, probably during the Zero's first pass.

Useless.

He still had the Mae West life preserver under his flight jacket. He pushed himself up, crawling out onto the fuselage behind the cockpit. The nose of the Dauntless was already under-water. Despite his resolve, Phil glanced back at Jerry and saw the huge bloodstain on the middle of Jerry's uniform. He'd been hit worse than he let on, Phil realized. But he had kept on fighting anyway.

"So long, pal," Phil said.

A wave of dizziness struck him as he slipped from the plane into the water. He had lost too much blood. Consciousness was slipping away from him. If he passed out before he inflated the Mae West, he would die. It was as simple as that. He fumbled for the cord to pull but couldn't find it.

There was another danger, too. When the plane sank, its backwash might pull him down with it. He had to get away from it. He started kicking, but he couldn't stay up. He went under, flailed with his one good arm as he kicked hard, and came back up again. He couldn't tread water, couldn't inflate the life jacket, couldn't do anything but give up and die . . .

Missy. Missy wouldn't want him to give up.

But he was so tired, and he couldn't see anymore. His head went under and he swallowed water. He kicked and came up into the air. Where the hell was that cord?

The water closed over him again, and with the last of his strength he came to the surface a final time. His fingers closed around something, but he couldn't tell if it was the Mae West cord or not. Somehow he found the breath to cry out, *"Missy!"*

Then he slipped under the waves, and the depths came up to claim him.

FIFTY-FIVE

Around noon on 4 June 1942, as the surviving planes were returning to the *Yorktown* and *Enterprise,* a flight of Vals and Zeros came roaring out of the sky as well. Only one of the Japanese carriers had made it unscathed through the rain of death from the American dive bombers, but that one was striking back.

A dozen Wildcats were already in the air on patrol above the Navy vessels, but although they closed in on the Japs and exacted a heavy toll on them, half a dozen of the bombers made it through and bore down on the *Yorktown.* Her skipper, Captain Elliott Buckmaster, swung the carrier back and forth in an attempt to avoid the bombs as the Val pilots released them. Three of the bombs splashed harmlessly into the ocean.

The other three were direct hits on the *Yorktown.*

One blew up on the flight deck, while the other two penetrated the deck and exploded below. Her boilers blown out by the blasts, the ship shuddered to a dead stop in the water. Fires blazed furiously, filling the carrier with smoke and forcing Admiral Frank Jack Fletcher to move his flag command to the nearby cruiser *Astoria.*

The *Yorktown*'s valiant firefighters brought the blaze under control, and by early afternoon the ship had steam up again and was ready to resume flight operations. The deck was cluttered with Wildcats being refueled and rearmed.

Before the fighters could get airborne, radar picked up another flight of Japanese planes approaching. These proved to be Kate torpedo bombers, escorted by Zeros. Anti-aircraft fire from the *Yorktown* herself, as well as from the cruisers and destroyers accompanying the American flattop, knocked down half the Japanese flight. But again, several of the bombers made it through to launch their torpedoes. More course changes by Captain Buckmaster avoided several of the torpedoes, just as he had done earlier with the bombs falling from the Vals, but two of the metal fish crashed into the port side of the carrier and exploded. Again the engines died as water flooded the interior of the ship. The *Yorktown* began to list heavily to port. This time, it seemed sure there would be no saving her.

Captain Buckmaster gave the order to abandon ship.

The *Yorktown* was down and out, but the *Enterprise* was still fighting. A flight of Dauntlesses took off from her flight deck and backtracked the course of the Japanese bombers to the lone remaining Jap carrier. Taking the defenses on the carrier by surprise, the American dive bombers attacked out of the late afternoon sun and sent their bombs smashing down onto the flight deck. The explosions destroyed the planes parked on the deck and set off fires that soon raced all through the ship.

By the next morning, all four Japanese aircraft carriers had burned and gone down, along with a Japanese cruiser. The loss of life was tremendous, as was the loss of aircraft. The remaining ships of the Imperial Navy fleet turned tail and ran away from Midway as fast as they could. Admiral Yamamoto's glorious plan was a failure, an utter disaster for the Japanese.

This crushing defeat had come at a high price. Outnumbered to start with, the United States Navy, Marines, and Army Air Corps had lost men and planes at a staggering rate. Some of the torpedo bomber and dive bomber groups suffered one hundred percent casualties, and the losses in many other units were nearly that bad. The American forces had been shaved whisker-thin . . .

But they had won.

The final casualty was the gallant old *Yorktown*. For a while on 5 June, the day after the battle, it appeared that the carrier could be salvaged. The fires had burned out. She refused to sink, so she was taken in tow by a minesweeper. The next day, 6 June, water was pumped into the ship to stabilize it even more, and the *Yorktown* slowly came back level. The destroyer *Hammann* came up beside her to put a salvage crew aboard.

Then a Japanese submarine that had slipped undetected into the area fired a torpedo into the *Hammann,* breaking it in half and sinking it with a loss of eighty men, and two more torpedoes hit the *Yorktown.* The carrier could not recover from this damage.

Early the next morning, it rolled over and went to the bottom.

At least they had plenty to keep them busy. That helped a little, Catherine thought as she stood with Missy, Billie, Alice, and several other nurses on the dock next to the seaplane ramp. A row of ambulances was parked on the dock. The *Solace* lay at anchor nearby, waiting for the next load of patients to be delivered by PBY from Midway.

The battle that had taken place a few days earlier had resulted in such heavy casualties that the hospital at Pearl Harbor was overloaded. Some of the patients were being brought here to Tonga, where they would be cared for on the *Solace.* Others were sent back to the States.

Missy's face was pale and drawn. Catherine felt a rush of sympathy when she looked at her friend. Missy hadn't been able to find out what had happened to Phil during the battle, didn't even know whether he was alive or dead. She wasn't a relative, so she hadn't gotten any sort of official notification. Dr. Johnston had been willing to put out a few back-channel feelers in an attempt to get any information that was available concerning Lt. Phillip Lange, but so far those hadn't yielded any results.

So all Missy could do was wait, and all her friends could do was wait with her.

Catherine heard the drone of the flying boat's engines before she was able to pick it out, high among the clouds. The PBY dropped lower and lower, finally landing in the harbor with a great spray of water from each of its pontoons. It taxied over to the ramp and came to a stop.

The door opened and a medical corpsman hopped out to secure the plane. Then he and several other corpsmen began unloading the patients. Some of them were ambulatory and were able to walk across the gangplank that was laid from the dock to the door of the plane. Others had to be carried off on stretchers.

Catherine took charge of the files that accompanied each patient. She had a thick stack of them in her hands when she heard Missy suddenly cry out.

Catherine turned and saw Missy standing beside one of the stretcher cases that had been carried onto the dock. As Catherine watched, Missy dropped to her knees and threw her arms around the man on the stretcher.

"Jeez, lady, at least let us put him down," one of the corpsmen carrying the stretcher said.

Catherine's heart thumped with excitement as she hurried over to Missy's side. Missy was crying and hugging the man on the stretcher as the corpsmen lowered it to the dock. Phil Lange, his face pale and haggard, lay on the stretcher and managed to smile as Missy draped herself over him. He had a large bandage on his forehead, and his left shoulder was wrapped and splinted.

"Be careful, nurse; you got a wounded man there," the corpsman said to Missy, who ignored him and started kissing Phil.

"What happened to him?" Catherine asked the corpsmen.

One of them took the chart from the stretcher and handed it to her. "This flyboy's one lucky son of a gun, that's what happened. The way I heard the story, he had to ditch in the ocean on the way back from the battle. The guy with him was killed, and the lieutenant here got shot up pretty bad. But one of our cruisers happened to be close by and saw his plane go down. They sent a rescue boat over and pulled him out of the water before the sharks got there." The corpsman grinned. "He was out cold when they got to him. They say his fist was clenched so tight on the handle of his Mae West that they thought they were going to have to break his fingers to get it loose. This guy *really* wanted to live."

"Yes," Catherine said. "He has good reason to."

Phil had come through this battle, Catherine thought, but there would be more battles. And Adam, if he was not already on the way back to the South Pacific, soon would be. The fighting—and the dying—were far from over.

Finally, Missy let the corpsmen pick up the stretcher and put Phil into one of the ambulances, but she took his hand and didn't let go of it as they were loading him in. She climbed in with him, still holding his hand, and held it all the way back to the ship.

ABOUT THE AUTHOR

James Reasoner has been a professional writer for the past twenty years, writing dozens of novels in a variety of genres, including several Wagons West historical novels (as Dana Fuller Ross) and nearly a hundred short stories. He lives in Texas with his wife, award-winning mystery novelist L. J. Washburn.